A PERILOUS COMPANION

Sarah's attention returned to Davinoff. She had never met a man who knew so much about the land, and about what had happened here. They made their way back into the tavern in silence. There, Davinoff went to pay their shot.

The landlord was busy smoothing a paper over the bar, a copy of the crude line drawing the strange witness to the murders in London had made. He came out from behind the bar and pushed the sheet upon a nail next to the hearth, the lettering on the parchment proclaiming that the man in the sketch was wanted. There was a reward of a thousand guineas. Sarah shuddered. From the instant she'd first seen it, the drawing reminded her of Davinoff.

He clinked coins on the table behind her. He, too, was examining the portrait. "You are right," his deep voice rumbled almost in her ear. "It could be anyone. Even me." She turned, and he raised one eyebrow in a gesture she was coming to know too well. His eyes were dark, darker than any she'd ever seen. "Shall we get on the road?" he asked.

Sarah's heart throbbed against her chest. He was right. The drawing could be anyone. But was it? She couldn't put her question into words, but he must have seen it in her face.

"I thought you hated to spoil mysteries," he chided, and strode out to the curricle.

Other books by Susan Squires:

NO MORE LIES
THE ONLY ONE (Anthology)
DANELAW
BODY ELECTRIC
DANEGELD

SACRAMENT

SUSAN SQUIRES

LOVE SPELL

NEW YORK CITY

To Harry, who first read a Georgette Heyer novel to me, who pushed me into writing, who believed in this story from the start, and who was my critique partner throughout its gestation. This book is as much yours as it is mine.

LOVE SPELL®

April 2007

Published by

Dorchester Publishing Co., Inc.
200 Madison Avenue
New York, NY 10016

ISBN-10: 0-505-52472-4
ISBN-13: 978-0-505-52472-0

Printed in the United States of America.

SACRAMENT

Chapter One

To Sarah Ashton, Lady Clevancy, chaos seemed to swirl in the damp night like leaves in the wind. The last place she wanted to be this evening was locked in a carriage with George and his mother. Huddling into the musty squabs of red velvet as the Beldons' lumbering barouche inched through the crush of carriages converging on Carlton House, she shivered. It might have been because of the chill in the spitting October air. It might have been because her life was unraveling.

"I don't care what you say, Sarah," Lady Beldon remonstrated for the hundredth time, pulling her lap rug more securely over her knees. "These dreadful murders strike fear into one's heart." The many ostrich feathers on her massive aubergine turban shivered in dread.

Sarah didn't care about the murders. She had come to London to see Mr. Lestrom, her solicitor. She would have seen him today, but the coach had lost a wheel on their way into London from Bath. The letter from Lestrom's son, its crumpled pages now carefully refolded inside her reticule, *must* be a mistake. How could there be a challenge to her ownership of Clershing? She had just paid off the debt her father left when he died, finally almost escaped her genteel penury. If she lost Clershing, what would she do? The house in Laura Place would go as well with nothing to support it. Amelia, the servants Addie and Jasco, they depended on her. What would become of them? And of Sarah, herself? Would she become a governess, a housekeeper? She could never take orders from some haughty, thoughtless creature; she'd be sacked within a week.

"George, how can you take your own mother into a metropolis where I am like to be killed at any moment?" Lady Beldon poked her second son's knee with one plump finger.

George Upcott did not even turn from looking out the window. How could he be calm, Sarah wondered, when she thought she might scream at any moment? "If you like," he said, "I shall order John Coachman to turn around."

"But I cannot miss the prince's ball," the dowager almost wailed. "He's opening Carlton House for the first time since the Nash renovations. People are begging for cards. If one were not to go . . . well, I hardly think one would be considered fashionable at all."

George shrugged. "As you choose." He was a well-made man of medium height, his hair a sandy blond, his eyes translucent gray blue. He was a handsome specimen; everyone told Sarah so. His lips were thin and straight like his nose, his complexion rather wan since he spent most of his waking hours in a laboratory. He was serious and single-minded, a promising man of medicine. All Bath had expected him and Sarah to make a match these three years and more. It should be natural to confide her dilemma to him. It wasn't. He had never approved of her managing her affairs herself with only the aid of dear Mr. Lestrom. If she lost Clershing, George would claim it was her own fault. And if her penury was not even genteel? What would George say then?

"I wouldn't miss being in London now for the world," he remarked, unmindful of his mother's nerves. "I can't for the life of me see how the blood is entirely drained from the victims' bodies. Once the heart stops beating, the blood ceases to flow."

"How can such crimes be committed in the most civilized city in the world eighteen years into the nineteenth century?" Lady Beldon complained.

The coach lurched to a stop. Horses snorted and stamped around them. Coachmen shouted. A young woman shrieked with laughter. Sarah heard the noise only dimly.

What kind of challenge to her ownership was there? Her solicitor's letter gave few details. She had never heard of this dreadful Julien Davinoff who laid claim to her land. Her thoughts stole to her grandfather's disastrous propensity for gambling. Had he lost Clershing gaming? Surely a note of hand so old could not be brought to a court of law. Well, she would never relinquish Clershing without a fight.

Sarah had no desire to go to the prince's ball. She had tried to stay home tonight, pleading that her head ached, but Lady Beldon had insisted. Since Sarah needed the woman's chaperonage to stay in London while she conducted her business, and Lady Beldon required an entourage at every social occasion, Sarah was going to Carlton House, whether she would or no.

She didn't even have the satisfaction of knowing she looked well. She wore the only dress she owned fit for a ball. The tiny puff sleeves and high waists that were the height of fashion were not always kind to women with voluptuous figures. The dress was rich looking, to be sure, but the cream-colored lace would have been better stark white for Sarah's dark hair, green eyes and pale, almost translucent skin. The cream color pulled the freshness from the lavender satin and muddied it somehow. George had helped her choose it, had insisted on the fabric. The lace tucked modestly into the neck and cascading over the hem was his suggestion, too. The deep rose silk he had so disparaged rose to mind, with a daring Austrian neckline and a black beaded fringe. He was probably right. It would have seemed fast.

"We'll never get there at this rate," Lady Beldon complained.

George finally looked exasperated. He leaned out the window and called for the driver to take an alternate route. The carriage swung into a side street and the going got better. But shortly before Hyde Park Corner the barouche pulled up again amidst the noise of a crowd.

George thrust his head out the window again. "Why are we stopping, John?"

"The way is blocked by a mob, sir," came the answering call.

"Well, push through," George ordered and sank back inside. "What could induce a crowd to gather? Everyone is either locked indoors in terror or on their way to the ball."

"I don't know and I don't care," Lady Beldon declared. "Tell him to hurry, George."

There was nothing to be done, however. The carriage crept into the gathering. Those in the crowd craned their necks to look ahead. The streets were wet and black. Bare branches clicked in the wind. What could all these people be looking at?

As they came to the center of the throng, Sarah began to dread what she might see. Two very official-looking men stood in a pool of light cast by one of the new gas lamps. One held a notebook in which he was writing. The other questioned a beautiful woman, wrapped only in a shawl of Norwich silk over a diaphanous gown, in spite of the chill night. She was red-haired, with wide lips and blue eyes. Sarah was struck by a sly quality in her expression. One would never forget that face. A few feet away a woman lay supine on the cobblestones.

Was this a murder? The body on the cobblestones was very still. Instinctively Sarah put her hand to her mouth. "George," she whispered. He must have come to the same conclusion, for he leapt out of the carriage without a word to his companions and elbowed his way through the crowd, shouting, "I am a doctor, let me through."

"George, don't leave us," Lady Beldon cried. When she saw that she was having no effect on him, she rapped her cane on the inside of the roof and ordered the driver to pull ahead.

Sarah leaned out the window as the barouche pulled up to the barricade. All thoughts of her own predicament seemed instantly insignificant. She didn't want to know what had happened here, yet she could not turn away. Lady Beldon sank back into the cushions with a low moan. George pushed his way through the barricades into the circle of light.

One of the constables, the younger and stockier of the two, blocked George's path to the corpse with a broad shoulder. "This 'ere investigation is official." Sarah strained to hear.

George pulled at his cravat. "Of course. But you must require a physician's opinion."

"We know what we got 'ere. Same as the other twelve."

George was being dismissed. Sarah realized with a shock that this was one of the murders they called the "vampire killings."

"Are you a fool, man?" George protested. "I'm a specialist in blood transfusion."

"What's that you say?" the stocky one asked, suspicious.

George mastered his impatience enough to snap his reply without actually shouting. "Draining blood out of healthy people into sick ones."

"Then," the thinner constable interrupted in more cultured tones, "we could use your perspective, doctor." He held up a hand against his cohort's protests. "My name is Chaldon, sir, and this is Barnett." He gestured an invitation toward the body. "What do you make of it?"

George pushed past and knelt over the body. Sarah could see a dark stain on the walk. The too-pale countenance had already begun to sink in upon itself without the support of filled capillaries, so the body had a shrunken look. Even Sarah knew that its blood had been drained. Her mouth went dry. She couldn't look away from the dead woman's staring eyes. George didn't seem perturbed at all. He turned her chin. She wasn't stiff.

"Well, what do you think?" the constable named Chaldon asked. His voice almost trembled.

"I see no possibility that these two small puncture wounds could account for this woman's death," George pronounced, wiping his hands as he rose to his feet. "So much blood could not be drained, even using my new invention. I call it a syringe," he added.

The two policeman exchanged disappointed glances.

"Is this how the other bodies were found?" George asked.

"Aye," Barnett answered. " 'Cept one where the throat was just ripped open, like by an animal, maybe. He bled to death more natural-like." Sarah was shocked; this fellow thought bleeding to death was natural.

"Can you think of no way someone could drain the blood?" Chaldon pressed.

"Well"—George rubbed his chin—"perhaps if there were some sort of pump connected to the syringe to create a greater suction . . ."

"You sound as if you have the beginnings of a theory, Doctor,"

Chaldon encouraged. "May we prevail upon you to come down to the magistrate's office in Bow Street tomorrow? We are quite anxious to learn how these murders were accomplished." He paused and looked down at the corpse. "If we know how it was done, we are one step closer to catching this madman."

George gave a gratified smile. "I shall place myself at the magistrate's disposal."

"May I go?" The red-haired woman the constables had been questioning broke in upon their contemplation of the body. Sarah had almost forgotten her. Now all eyes turned her way. Her ruby lips were fascinating. Her flaming hair gleamed.

"Well, miss, since you have seen his face and can identify our murderer, it might be best for your own safety if you came with us." To Sarah's surprise, the girl chuckled.

"I am enough safe. There are never two deaths in one night, yes?" She had an accent. Continental. Germanic?

"Never been a witness before," Barnett rejoined.

"You saw the murder?" George asked. His gaze was rapt upon her. "How was it done?"

"I cannot say," the woman replied as the fingers of the chill evening breeze caressed her hair. "I saw the man's face. I heard the girl scream. But while the deed was done his back was turned. His cape covered all. Me, I hid myself in the shadows. But I have told all this."

This woman should be frightened, Sarah thought. Death had barely passed her by tonight. And you should want to take her hand and soothe her, Sarah told herself, reassure her. Instead she shuddered when those cold blue eyes scanned the crowd.

"Even drew us a pi'ture." Barnett waved a page of his notebook. The drawing was a few lines merely, but evocative. "Tall, well made, dark 'air, dark eyes, 'igh cheekbones, dressed in an evening cape," Barnett recited.

"With your kind description, we will set the Runners out to comb the city and beyond. He cannot escape." Chaldon apparently felt he needed to reassure the cold-eyed woman with lies. She hardly seemed to need it. And they *were* lies. Hundreds fit the description she'd given.

Barnett looked up from his notebook. "You sure that's all, are you?"

"Really, gentlemen, no more. I will go home now."

And they let her, in spite of the danger, in spite of their questions. Sarah couldn't believe it. They all looked into her eyes as though they had been turned to stone and watched the only witness in a string of grisly murders walk off alone.

Sarah put her hand to her forehead. The whole scene was like a play revealed by the garish glow of the street lamps, the emotions stirred yet drifting in the wet air. George, the officers, and the beautiful woman were actors on a stage at the denouement. The climax done, they played out their parts by rote, flattened by the light. The people who pushed and shoved for a better view of the tragedy were a dim chorus, a surge of humanity in the darkness between the lamps.

George came to himself. "I say, I hope you know where to find her."

"Course we do." Barnett shook his head. "Bristol Court, off Dean Street." He flipped through his notebook to read the address.

Chaldon snatched the notebook from him. "Did you say Bristol Court?" The two constables looked at each other for a long moment, surprise and then dismay crossing their faces in turn.

"What is it?" George asked.

Chaldon snapped the notebook shut and tossed it to Barnett in disgust. "There is no such address off Dean Street."

George returned to the carriage. Looking smug, he swung into the seat next to his mother and patted her hand. As the coach inched away Sarah sat forward and craned to see the constables still standing over the body. She couldn't relinquish her awful fascination.

A countenance in the gloom at the edge of the crowd jerked Sarah back. The man was tall, well made, with dark eyes, arched brows and high cheekbones, with sensuous, curving lips and wild black hair against pale skin. A cape swirled about him. The evocative lines of the red-haired witness's drawing flashed into Sarah's brain. Could this be the man who had murdered here tonight? His eyes burned as he surveyed the scene. They were hard, unforgiving. He had seen everything, forgotten nothing, and he was obviously angry. The crowd shrank back from him. He seemed to float in his own space. Sarah strained to see, leaning over to press her breasts against the door of the coach. He was beautiful, she thought, but like the forces of disorder, he lurked at the edge of the tenuous circles of light. This man could kill; she was sure of it. She shuddered. *Be sensible. Your mood is coloring your thoughts.* But she could not look away from that face. Was it fear that wound its way into her heart, or fascination? Before she could decide, his cape swirled and the man disappeared into the darkness.

Sarah stared after him, wondering if he had ever been there at all. *Foolish girl.* There was nothing to connect this strange man to the victim lying in the circle of light. The drawing could have been anyone. Behind her George apologized for having left them. His mother revived and began to scold. It didn't matter. What mattered was one face in the dark, barely discerned. The face of anarchy, perhaps the face of evil, infinitely repellent, infinitely attractive.

Sarah trailed behind George and his mother as Lady Beldon remarked on each new wonder of Carlton House, finding fault with each. The noblewoman scanned the Dutch and Flemish paintings for *The Shipbuilder and His Wife* by Rembrandt, as she was pushed through the Blue Salon by the crush of people. "Rumor has it the regent paid five thousand guineas for it," she yelled into Sarah's ear. It would have been a whisper, but the cacophony made that impossible.

"There it is." Sarah pointed. Souls gleamed out through Rembrandt's daubs of paint.

Lady Beldon examined the small, dark portrait. "Disappointing, really," she pouted. "It doesn't look worth so much. They aren't even handsome subjects."

Sarah gritted her teeth. This was worse than she had imagined.

The crowd spilled through the public rooms and downstairs into the prince's private apartments. The Beldon party surged with it. The long Gothic Conservatory was a fairyland. Chinese lanterns hung below the stained-glass ceiling that fanned out in a spider tracery above its supporting columns. Here the regent would serve his intimates late supper at a table 200 feet long.

It was said that the stream running down the center of the table held real fish.

The money spent upon Carlton House over the protestations of Parliament was a symbol of the regent's power. With his father locked up at Windsor, he was king in all but name. The nation was grateful there was no danger of the old king regaining his senses to rule again; Carlton House was the regent's reward.

The crowds pressed in around them. Sarah felt elbows and knees prodding her. Why was she here? Just as she was ready to turn tail, she heard a familiar tinkling laugh above the hubbub. It could only be Corina, her lifelong, sometimes best, friend. She craned to see, but she was too short. Instead she started through the crowd into the mirrored dining hall said to be modeled after Versailles. Of course Corina would be drawn to mirrors. Sarah would find her at the center of a dozen young men. Her beautiful friend was a magnet for them. It was some minutes of concerted pushing and many muttered apologies before Corina's golden hair appeared.

"Corina, I thought I would never find you in this crush," she called over the din of conversation. Her friend wore white satin with topaz dripping from her ears, trembling upon her breast, around her wrist, from combs in her hair. She was draped on the arm of Sir Rodney Kelston, of blond mustaches and broad shoulders, who hung on her every word. And there were several other young men that Sarah knew. John Kerseymere was here, eldest of the Kerseymere brothers—about to give up the handsome regimentals he wore tonight and muster out—and the young Viscount Alvaney. They looked uncomfortable in their collars, so high they could not truly turn their heads. Each had dressed in his finest. Fobs and seals and diamond rings, gold and silver snuff boxes, and patterned waistcoats in a rainbow of colors were everywhere.

"Sarah, what are you doing here?" Corina challenged, frowning. "I thought you were a stick-at-home in Bath when you wouldn't come with me."

Ten pairs of male eyes focused on Sarah. She cleared her throat. "I came up to see my solicitors at the last moment. George and his mother were good enough to bring me."

"And no time to order a new dress, I see, though I have always liked that lavender."

Sarah felt herself flush. It wouldn't have mattered what she was wearing, she told herself. She always felt dowdy around Corina.

"You're looking very drawn tonight. You must let me suggest strawberries, just under the eyes here." Corina touched Sarah's face with one elegant finger, then leaned in. "How fortunate we are to have escorts who can procure us their mothers' invitation cards," she whispered. Sarah recognized the signal that she was forgiven, and thought it might have to do with her dress. What woman wouldn't want a friend who set her off to advantage?

"Oh, I had a card of my own," Sarah replied. Corina frowned, then consciously relaxed her brow and turned dismissively back to her admirers.

Lady Beldon puffed up to the group with George behind her. "I refuse to stay another night in a town where murders occur on every street corner," she breathed. "I am going home tomorrow, whether you come or not, George."

"So soon? But I told you I must see my solicitor." This was awful news for Sarah.

"And meet your death, no doubt. No, no, no, no." Lady Beldon shook her head. "You had best come home with me."

"I can't." Worse, Sarah could not stay at Beldon House alone with George.

"Stay with me, dear Sarah," Corina offered. "I do not return, to languish in Bath, for a week."

"Thank you." Sarah sighed. She felt an elbow in her back. "I wonder why we came," she said to George. "No one can even dance."

"Everyone who is anyone is here," Corina snapped. "Perhaps even your disreputable Mr. Davinoff, Kerseymere. Why, Sarah, whatever is the matter?"

"Did you say Davinoff?" Sarah managed. Her throat had unaccountably closed.

"Upcott, take her arm, I think she is about to faint," Corina ordered. "I hardly thought to bring on a spell by the mere mention of rakes. Kerseymere here was just telling me that Mrs. Hertford may have given him a card, even with all the stories."

"What stories?" Lady Beldon asked.

"Word has it he was the root of the Marquise Barone's suicide in Paris last year," Kerseymere disclosed. "Her husband called him out. Dashed cool customer had a tailor present at the duel. Fellow got two orders for coats, with fabric and cut, while Davinoff paced his fifteen. After he killed the husband, he left the marquise flat. She was a suicide the next morning."

Could the man be here? Sarah might bump into him at any second.

"Shall I take you for some air, Sarah?" George asked. "After seeing that dreadful murder tonight, any lady of sensibility would be distraught."

Lady Beldon turned to greet a dowager whose turban had even more feathers than her own.

"I am quite fine." Sarah glanced around wildly. Her heart was skipping beats.

"I say, what murder is this?" Sir Kelston pounced upon George's revelation. "One of those where the body is drained of blood?" The crowd in their circle of conversation grew.

"The very same. I go to Bow Street tomorrow as a consultant." George smiled with satisfaction. "My new device may have a bearing on the case." A hue and cry of questions began from several of Corina's young men.

"Who could be committing these murders?" Corina interrupted.

"The magistrates believe a madman is involved," George announced, with a harrumph.

"Could draining blood be sane?" Sarah murmured, scanning the crowd. What would he look like, her persecutor?

"I shall experiment to see if a pump might have pulled the blood from the body." This drew clamors for information on George's role in the investigation. He held forth.

Corina began to tap her foot impatiently. Sarah knew her expression. George was monopolizing attention Corina felt rightfully belonged to her. She turned to her escort. "Let us go and see the murder scene, Sir Kelston."

"Dash it, no, madam!" Kelston was shocked. "What man would take a lady into such danger?"

"I'll wager Kerseymere and his friends will go there yet tonight." Corina answered with a pretty pout, then glanced at the crowd. "Won't you, you rogues?"

Several pairs of eyes gleamed with excitement.

"I would not take your wager, madam," Kelston said after glancing around. "But that does not mean *I* will take you there!"

Corina looked into one of the gigantic mirrors to catch her reflection, then yelped and spun back toward the room. Sarah followed her eyes to a dark form at the edge of the crowd, like a black bird of prey among gaudy peacocks. He was so tall that even Sarah could see him. She trembled. Classic profile, high cheekbones, long straight nose. His black coat was cut by the best of tailors, not English, though. The soft curls at his neck and the comma of black hair that strayed over his forehead gave him a boyish look. Sensual lips promised secret knowledge. He was the personification of anarchy from the murder scene.

"Sir Kelston, whoever is that man in black?" Corina caught at her escort's arm.

Kelston looked dismayed. "Davinoff has procured an invitation after all."

Sarah's knees went weak. She grabbed George's elbow for support. Of course! The chaos of murder in London and the chaos likely to engulf her life if Clershing was lost seemed to merge into a single pinprick of light illuminating a man called Julien Davinoff. The face of iniquity on the streets of London and the force of evil that threatened her future were one and the same. She raised a hand to her forehead, feeling alternately faint and flushed.

"Of course that would be him," she whispered. George drifted away to tell more responsive guests about his new device. Sarah had eyes only for the harbinger of doom.

"What a quiz he is"—Corina laughed—"all in black. How have I never encountered him?"

"I expect he doesn't run in your circles, Mrs. Nandalay." Kerseymere laughed.

Sarah let her eyes follow Davinoff as he moved closer and spoke to a fellow in the group surrounding George. They were discussing the murders, no doubt. Others were pushed and jostled by the crowd, but not he. The crowd swirled around him.

He seemed distracted, scanning the room for something or someone. Sarah felt his gaze brush her, and it burned.

"You must introduce me to our rake, Sir Kelston," Corina murmured, behind her. Sarah glanced over to see that she was fascinated, too. Her friend had no time for her admirers now.

"But no, madam—it is not an introduction you would enjoy. He is an evil man!"

"You have already denied me one opportunity for excitement tonight," Corina pouted. She and Sarah both watched as Davinoff made his way toward a ravishing woman wearing an oriental-collared brocade, lavishly embroidered. He bent and whispered into her ear. Her eyes searched his in shock. She grasped his arms, frantic, shaking her head. The dark man was implacable. Suddenly the woman drooped. She almost fell before Davinoff grasped her elbow. Sarah could not help but wonder what he had said.

"Come, you are surely not afraid of this man, Sir Kelston?" Corina asked, rapt. Sarah turned back to her. What game was her friend playing?

"I should think not," Kelston replied indignantly, then stopped. Corina had him.

"What can happen in a room full of people?" Sarah's friend placed her lace-gloved hand on Kelston's arm and looked up, expectant.

The man sighed. "I hope you have no male relative present, Mrs. Nandalay, who would take me to task for the deed I am about to perform."

"None whatever, Sir Kelston. I am my own mistress."

Corina and her escort maneuvered through the crowd toward the man in black, leaving Sarah and the others to stare after them. Corina was on the hunt. And her target tonight was Sarah's persecutor. Sarah gathered her courage. Her target must be Davinoff, too. Perhaps she could find out some detail of the brute's claim against her land. She pushed after Corina.

"Mr. Davinoff, allow me to introduce Madam Corina Nandalay," she heard Kelston say as she approached. Davinoff at close range was a frightening man. His eyes were black pools of dreadful knowledge, his form a study in languid power. Sarah tore her eyes away with difficulty. They came to rest on his beautiful companion. She heard Kelston stutter, "Countess Vadim . . ."

Corina curtsied just in front of Sarah, her eyes never leaving the face of Davinoff's companion. The soul-engulfing need still emanating from that woman was evident. Corina would be drawn by that need. It would make her want the object of it all the more.

"His Lordship provides his introduction at my request," Corina said lightly.

Davinoff's eyes flicked over her. "Perhaps you do not know my reputation." His voice was a deep rumble, utterly masculine, used to command. Sarah shuddered.

"No, Sir Kelston was careful in his duties on that point." Kelston reddened beside Corina, but her quarry did not even glance in his direction.

"Yes? Then you are, perhaps, an unusual female." At Davinoff's words, the woman at his side came to life, her eyes sparking.

"I have been told as much," Corina agreed. She glowed with a dangerous radiance.

Sarah stepped up beside Corina and saw her friend frown at the unwelcome intrusion. She did not like to be disturbed at the hunt. Sarah didn't care.

"May I present Sarah Ashton, Lady Clevancy?" Kelston murmured, throwing to the wind all reservations about introducing young women to the notorious rake.

"Ah, the owner of Clershing." Davinoff eyed her gown with an almost imperceptible flicker of distaste. Sarah's color heightened. She raised her chin half an inch.

"Who are you?" Sarah asked. Perhaps not a propitious means of introducing her topic.

"Your neighbor," Davinoff said, then nodded, a contemptuous smile just visible at the corner of his lips. Still, some curiosity lurked behind his eyes. "I look forward to the time when Clershing runs again with Thornbury Abbey."

"No one owns Thornbury Abbey," Sarah sputtered.

"I am desolate to disagree with you," Davinoff observed.

"I don't know what you think you can get away with, but I have no intention of letting Clershing run with the abbey." Sarah trembled with emotion.

"How final. But there is always a way to get what one wants." The brute seemed amused.

"Not always," Sarah said between clenched teeth. "You may be mistaken."

"That would certainly be surprising." Davinoff bowed. He seemed taken aback by Sarah's vehemence. How could he be so maddeningly sure of himself? "Who knows what time will bring?"

"How true." Corina inserted herself into the conversation. "But one thing time brings is never a surprise. 'Time always brings death." She cast about for a way to interest him. "I saw you conversing, sir, with Mr. Upcott's circle. You have no doubt heard there was another murder."

"I heard."

"Mr. Davinoff is not unfamiliar with these murders," Sarah said in a low voice, watching him. "You were present at the scene of the murder tonight, were you not?"

He looked down to search her face. "One hates to admit a fascination with the macabre. You have caught me out, Lady Clevancy."

"I don't hate to admit it at all," Corina said, glaring at Sarah as though to announce a prior claim to her quarry. "I have only now been pressing Kelston here to take me to the scene."

"It seems we have much in common then. It is unfortunate that we will not have an opportunity to pursue our acquaintance." He swept his eyes over Corina, Sarah and even the Countess Vadim. "I leave London tomorrow."

The countess's bleak expression said that this was the whispered confidence. He was leaving her. She touched her throat, covered so strangely with that oriental collar.

"Where are you bound, Mr. Davinoff?" Corina boldly ignored both the countess and Sarah.

"My plans are not set." His horrible, wonderful eyes swept the crowd.

"If you own land near Bath, perhaps that should be your destination. My own estate, Chambroke, is near Bath. How is it we have not seen you in those parts?"

"Bath . . ." He seemed to consider. "How common a name compared to Aquae Sulis." He came to himself. "I have not lived there for many years."

"But you must remember how beautiful the country is this time of year," Corina rushed on. "As for society, my own estates attract a small but select guest list. The hunting is tolerable, if you are hunt-mad."

"Perhaps I cannot avoid Bath," he drawled, then glanced to Sarah. She thought she might melt. Unaccountably, she did not want to watch Corina at the hunt anymore.

"Then I shall expect to see you," the blonde said, a tiny note of triumph in her voice.

"Perhaps." He committed nothing. "Excuse me. I have business yet tonight."

And he was gone, cutting once more through furtive glances and murmurs toward the great double doors, leaving the countess to drift after him, her handkerchief to her mouth.

"Well, I must say, you were very bold," Sir Kelston reproached Corina.

"I hope so," she answered in a murmur, gazing toward the giant doors. "For the course I have set requires boldness." She spun on Sarah. "What's this about Clershing?"

"He contests my ownership." Sarah gazed after Davinoff, her stomach churning.

"Well, you were certainly rude," her friend admonished. Then she turned her smile on her escort. "Sir Kelston, I am afraid I have quite a headache. I find I must retire immediately."

"But, but the evening has hardly begun. I thought . . ." Sir Kelston trailed off.

Corina glanced at the doorway. "I can see you want to stay. I shall call for the carriage."

Kelston applied to Sarah. "Tell Mrs. Nandalay that her plan is out of the question."

Sarah roused herself. "I never tell Mrs. Nandalay anything is out of the question."

"I could not allow you to go home alone," Kelston announced stiffly.

"I shan't be alone," Corina confided. With that she whirled and hurried through the crowd, Kelston sputtering behind her. Somehow she would get Davinoff to take her home; Sarah knew it.

Chapter Two

Julien gazed out the window of his carriage at the waxing moon, brooding. What had made him take up the Nandalay woman, tonight of all nights? He should have simply compelled another to take her home. He glanced over at the blonde woman huddled in the squabs of the upholstery, obviously frightened. Well, she'd got what she wanted tonight, a ride with the devil. Let her stew in her fear. She reminded him of Charlemagne's cousin. What was her name? Both were beautiful, surely.

"Why do you leave London?" she finally asked, her voice trembling only slightly.

Reluctantly, he dragged his gaze from the moon. "My business will be finished tonight."

"Business at night is dangerous in a city where there have been twelve murders," she claimed, making conversation he didn't want. "With the one tonight, I suppose that makes thirteen."

"Yes, thirteen," he agreed, his lips pressed into a thin line. The silence stretched between them, filled with the clatter of coaches outside, the halloa of the grooms on the Pall Mall. He dreaded his business with Magda tonight. His thoughts strayed to a time when she had seemed vibrant, fascinating, different from the others. He had been a fool. Examining Mrs. Nandalay in the dim light of the moon he remarked, "You appear to have recovered from your headache."

"I never had one," she said, staring into the darkness in his corner with a bold look.

He couldn't keep his lips from curving. "Are you always so honest?"

"No," she admitted. "Only when it serves my purpose. Do you care?"

"Not at all. Do you usually get what you want?" She didn't know the stakes of the game she played. They never did.

"Always." Her own small smile held the confidence of those with limited experience.

As they broke through into Haymarket Street, Julien took his cane and rapped on the wall of the coach to attract the driver's attention. "Where do you live?" he asked his guest.

"Berkeley Square." The vehicle slowed. Julien put his head out the window of the coach.

"Germain," he called to the driver. "Brewer Street. Then take the lady to Berkeley Square."

"Do you not escort me home?" Mrs. Nandalay cried.

He shook his head. "My obligation tonight is elsewhere." She wedged herself in the corner of the coach, unable to gather enough courage to ask about his business. Just as well.

They were clipping along at quite a pace, up through Great Windmill Street, its name the only remnant of the great "moulin" or windmill patterned after the Moulin Rouge of Paris and signal to an equally tawdry area. In the alleyways, shadowy wretches lolled on the stoops exchanging mugs of Blue Ruin. Julien opened the door and stepped out even before the carriage stopped. He strode to the opposite corner. "Thank you," he heard her call, but he did not answer. He just melted into the shadows of Brewer Street.

Silently, he made his way into the rooming house. The carpet on the stairs was worn, the banister greasy. This was not like Magda Ravel. She always stayed at the best hotels. He approached the door at number ten, trying to suppress his anger. He had thought he was long past such feeling, but he was angry at himself more than at her. The sconces in the halls flickered. He touched the doorknob almost delicately. How quaint. She had bothered to lock it. Didn't she know he would be coming for her after this evening's carelessness? Tearing metal screeched in the doorknob, followed by a snap as the lock broke. Magda called, "Come in, Julien."

He pushed the door open, his cape swirling around him. The redheaded beauty sat on the dingy bed inside, her diaphanous shawl still clinging about her shoulders. Her eyes were sly. She thought she could handle him. Julien glanced to the other occupant of the room, whose narrow face and prominent eyes reminded Julien of a rat—the kind that frequented crypts. The rat was afraid; Julien could see it. Blood stained his fingertips.

"I am not thrilled to see you, Julien," Magda remarked. "You intend to be boring."

"These deaths are yours, Magda?" he asked softly. Her answer didn't matter.

"I should say, ours." She gestured toward Keely, quivering against the window.

She, too, had made a partner in her image. His own crime made hers possible. He flicked his gaze over Keely. "You do not know how to behave in the world at large, Magda."

She laughed. "You have been no better. Life is easy here."

"Too easy," he mourned. His eyes flicked again to Keely. "You shared the Companion. You know that is the one forbidden act."

"From you I hear this?" she taunted. "You who made me what I am? Don't think I am not grateful, love. The blood is life. You gave me eternity, and I mean to make use of it."

Julien said nothing for a moment, mastering his guilt. She had only followed his example. Her own small nature had picked an even more unfortunate recipient of the gift. "That is regrettable." The words twisted from his mouth. The silence in the shabby room stretched to the breaking point. "I have no choice but to foist you and your new creation upon Rubius at Tirgu Korva, where you cannot continue your indiscretions. The Elders will help you see your way."

"You expect me to take the Vow?" she cried, incensed. "I will not lock myself away at Mirso Monastery. I would be mad in a week. And why should I? You are responsible, not I."

"That is the point." He lifted his chin. "But the Vow is voluntary. You need not take it. We only require you to take time for reflection."

"You sacrifice me to salve your conscience," Magda shrieked, pacing the dingy room.

"My conscience is not salved."

The woman spun to face him. "Fate is not with you, Julien. I told them *you* had done these murders. If you are not gone by morning, they will be upon you like a pack of dogs."

"You know better than that, Magda."

Keely slowly stood, shaking, beside his mistress. "Get out! You are not wanted here."

"Our kind is never wanted, apprentice. You will learn that." Julien fixed his gaze upon the man. Keely wobbled, then gasped for breath, clutching both hands to his throat as though his body as well as his mind were being squeezed. Let him see the full power of what he faced.

"Enough!" Magda barked.

Julien considered, then turned away. Let Rubius deal with this. When the man took on the leadership of their kind, dealing with the likes of Keely became part and parcel of the job. Keely gasped in pain and sat suddenly down. "I thought you had better taste, Magda."

"I do," Magda sneered. "I left you." She set her jaw. "I won't go, Julien."

He brought a leather pouch from his coat pocket and tossed it onto the bed. "These will more than pay for your journey. Sell them to Jameson in Bond Street. He knows Roman coins. Tell him I sent you. You should reach Tirgu Korva within the fortnight."

"Remember Lisbon?" Magda softened her voice. "Come back with me to Lisbon."

"That was too long ago, Magda."

"I was a babe. Now I am wiser." The woman had always known her smile was seductive. She used it now. "Besides, I think, who else is a fitting consort for you, if not one of your own kind?"

"And what about me?" Keely raged from the corner.

"What about you?" Magda asked, never taking her eyes from Julien.

He shook his head. "You are too late, my dear. I am past the need for company."

Magda examined him closely. "Then you truly *are* the living dead." She took a breath and fought to maintain her composure. "You know you will not hurt me, Julien. I don't want to go to Tirgu Korva. And you have no other recourse." She sat deliberately in a chair, sipped wine and looked at him over her glass.

He fixed his gaze on her in the firelight. With a single, fluid move he raised one white-gloved hand and held it out. Magda stood and smiled. She had no choice, though she didn't know it yet. Her wine made a bloodred stain across her pale blue satin dress as the glass fell and shattered. She didn't notice but took a step forward, and another, until her hand touched his. He drew her to him, her breasts just touching the fabric of his white waistcoat. She turned her face upward. He brushed her forehead with his lips. "You are wrong on both counts, my love," he whispered.

He saw her realize too late that it was not desire emanating from his eyes. She could not rip her gaze away. He would not allow it. So she fixed him with her own clear blue stare. For a moment, they were locked there, like two lovers in the firelight. Then her lip began to tremble. Her hand on his chest shook. Her forehead beaded with moisture at her effort.

Julien smiled without humor. He raised his hand and touched her hair, but his eyes never left hers. "Did you think you were a match for me?" he whispered. His hand stole to her white throat, his long fingers caressing her. "You are a murderer, with no sense of discretion for yourself or for your race." Julien tightened his fingers. Fear bubbled up into her gaze. Even when she began to choke and gurgle, she could muster no resistance. He could have rent her limb from limb.

"Keely," she sputtered, a guttural, animal sound. The rat must have realized that he needed Magda to survive in his strange new world of night and blood. He dove for Julien with a growl.

Julien did not remove his eyes from Magda's face. He tossed the smaller man against the far wall like the rodent he resembled. Keely shrieked as his head hit the windowsill. There was a sigh, as of air escaping from a sealed room, as the man collapsed.

Davinoff lifted Magda with his hand around her throat and with one stride placed her in the room's only chair. There he released his grip. "I think that clears things up, my love."

The woman collapsed, choking and coughing. The marks on her neck were red now, but would course through purple and blue in a few minutes. "You beast," she gasped as sense returned.

"How ironic that it is you who say so." He waited for her choking to subside, until she stared resentfully up at him, her hands rubbing her throat. "I can find you anywhere, Magda. And next time there will be no second chance." He made his voice inexorable.

She slumped in her chair. "I cannot live at Mirso Monastery."

"We all end there," he said shortly. "Sooner or later we all take the Vow."

"How can I deserve such a fate?" she cried, still railing against his will.

Julien drained his wine and set the glass on the sideboard. "You dictated your course. Now you live with the consequences, as I do." She closed her eyes, shoulders sagging. He glanced at the still figure in the corner. The man's neck was broken. It would take some hours to heal. "Take that one with you." He drew the darkness and leaked out of the room.

The morning after the prince's ball, Sarah lay curled in bed at the Beldons'. Her sleep had been racked by nightmares, half remembered and unsettling. An image flickered at the edge of her mind of Corina, of sun-drenched Sienna, and of forbidden feelings she thought at twenty-six she had outgrown. Yet now the hot languor of Italy contained a black stain upon it: the image of Davinoff. She sat up abruptly and pushed those thoughts away, as she always did.

How could the man she had glimpsed at the scene of a murder, a man who might be capable of murder himself, be the very one who coveted her land? Things were far worse than she had imagined. Then there was Corina. Sarah had seen her friend's intense infatuations before. Corina was on the hunt, and she always got what she wanted. But what was she hunting this time?

Sarah groaned and put her chin in her hands. Corina would land on her feet. Her darker nature was surely a match for Davinoff. The puzzling part was why she had suddenly fixed upon someone at least as strong as she; usually, the blonde preferred the upper hand. The rumors cycling periodically in Bath about the poor boys she entertained at Chambroke—boys who would do anything for money—were more than just rumors. Sarah knew that, though she'd never confronted her friend about her habits, not since Sienna. But Corina's wildness had a shadowy side that would shock Sir Kelston and his compatriots. Sarah didn't think it would shock Davinoff.

She could not deny that he was fascinating. Those kinds of men always were. Sarah shook her head to clear it. She must find a way to defend the life she had made for herself, at such cost. A maid knocked, then came in with hot chocolate and a slice of bread and butter. Sarah shocked the girl by leaping out of bed, but she had to see Mr. Lestrom immediately.

She dressed hastily in a bottle-green wool merino walking dress with a plain round collar, and asked the maid to pack her trunk. Next she scribbled Corina's direction on a scrap of paper to have her trunks sent round and raced down the stairs, past the breakfast room where she might encounter George. Then she dismayed the Beldons' butler by ordering a hackney and refusing a footman to accompany her. Any servants of George's would certainly gossip.

As the hack transported her the city of London reeled past Sarah, a hum of activity in the daylight. She stared out the window, unseeing, wholly occupied with her predicament. Old Mr. Lestrom had never failed her. It was he who had helped sell the properties so grossly encumbered after her father's death, all except Clershing. After all her father's drifting neglect, the solicitor seemed to welcome Sarah's decisiveness. He had hardly raised a bushy brow when she took the reins of her own affairs. When she'd told him she wanted to grow potatoes instead of barley, he had not raved about tradition at all; he'd only asked if she had researched the market. She had. It was her potatoes that paid the mortgages and saved the land at Clershing. She had even begun to dream of rebuilding the house. This Davinoff was like to dash those dreams.

The coach turned off Fleet Street and into Falcon Court. The building she sought looked stolid and impassive, not at all like the shabby yet comfortable offices Lestrom kept in Bath. Over the provision shop on Monmouth Street, Sarah had learned to associate her business affairs with the smell of sausages. She hoped the Lestroms would not abandon the offices in Bath altogether.

It was Mr. Lestrom's son, Rutherford, who rose to greet her in an expansive office on the second floor. He was fashionably dressed in yellow pantaloons and a very high starched collar. His eyes were light, his hair was light, and he had a decidedly weak chin.

"Lady Clevancy," he greeted her. "I take it you had my note. Most distressing."

Sarah sat in one of the leather chairs. She did not have to move a pile of papers or ledgers, as she did when she visited his father. "Distressing doesn't begin to describe the situation. What is this ridiculous claim?"

"His claim is not ridiculous, Lady Clevancy; of that I can assure you."

"Does he have a more recent deed?" She tried to keep the panic from her voice.

"Actually, his claim is older." Mr. Lestrom, Jr., did not meet her eyes, but rearranged some papers already stacked neatly on the desk.

"Older? Then of course my deed supersedes it!" Sarah exclaimed.

Lestrom cleared his throat. "I am afraid, Lady Clevancy, that we do not have your deed."

"How can that be?" Sarah remembered Davinoff's smug sureness last night.

"I hardly know what to tell you." Lestrom the Younger spread his carefully manicured hands. "We have torn the offices in Bath apart. I have been thinking"—he examined his nails—"could it have been in the house at Clershing when it burned?"

Sarah stifled a gasp. She shook her head silently, but it was perfectly possible. She and her father had lost so much in that fire: a home, a heritage, a wife, a mother, everything but the land itself and the Dower House. If she could not produce the deed, what would she do? "Where is your father?" she asked instinctively. "I need to talk to your father."

The young man before her leaned forward. "And so you shall. But you mustn't be disappointed if he doesn't seem as sharp as he once was. It is difficult for him to know when to retire from the lists. But have no qualms; I have taken a personal interest in your affairs."

Sarah drew her brows together. She had seen Lestrom the Elder less than a month ago. He didn't seem to have lost a whit of his edge. Indeed, they had begun arguing about how to use next year's returns. "What can be done?" she asked.

"Perhaps very little. I have written to your agent, Josiah Wells. Perhaps he knows something about the deed. He and his father before him have been paid by Davinoff's family to keep an eye on Thornbury Abbey."

Sarah grimaced. "Mr. Wells acts for this . . . this interloper? I never heard that anyone owned that old ruin. How do we know he owns it?"

"My father reviewed the deed. It clearly includes what is now Clershing."

Sarah shuddered. To be at the mercy of a man such as Davinoff! What could be worse? "We need my deed," she murmured, chewing her lip in thought. "Is there nowhere else to look?" He shook his head. She rose and began to pace the office. The house in Laura Place? She didn't think so. Her father's desk was her own, and Sarah knew its every nook and cranny. There was no need for a locked cupboard with the offices of Lestrom & Son so close, and the house itself was Georgian, long past the time of priests' holes. Lord, she was beginning to sound like a Gothic novel! They had never kept important papers at the Dower House. Still, she could leave no place unsearched. "When can he take the land?" She needed time.

"When he likes, I suppose."

"Can I challenge his rights to delay him at least?"

Lestrom looked startled. "Fighting the claim would be costly. I should not like to see your affairs dragged before the magistrate in a public court." The young man looked for her agreement.

"If you think to throw yourself on his good graces, I would refrain. He is a formidable man."

"I have seen him." The prospect of a humiliating courtroom announcement of her destitution was daunting. She would lose the house in Laura Place without Clershing to support it. What then? Go for a governess? And what would happen to those who depended upon her?

"The Bath magistrate sits in five days. We should settle the matter before that."

She had five days. Lestrom stood. She picked up her reticule with a trembling hand.

"Don't worry, Lady Clevancy. If there is anything to be done, we will do it." Lestrom the Younger smiled. He had perfect teeth.

At that moment, Mr. Lestrom, Sr., chugged through the door still huffing from the stairs. He glanced up in surprise as he peered about the room and found it occupied. "You here early for once, Rutherford?" he asked. He was as thin as ever, his hair almost transparent, his spectacles still perched upon his nose at the wrong angle. His eyes squinted a bit more, perhaps, and his skin seemed looser somehow. But she could not say he looked addled.

"Sir, I was just discussing with Lady Clevancy the most unfortunate development at Clershing," his son said hastily, motioning to Sarah.

The elder Mr. Lestrom turned as if seeing her for the first time and took both her hands in his. His eyes were mournful. "I am so sorry, my dear," he said and kissed her cheek. "I cannot think how we do not have the deed. We seem to have everything else."

Don't be resigned, Sarah pleaded silently. I shall not be able to bear it if you are resigned. She fumbled in her reticule for a handkerchief she did not yet need while she mustered her courage. "You have seen his deed. Is it legitimate?"

"Quite genuine." The old man sighed. "I saw it Tuesday last in Bath. Henry the Eighth, royal seal, witnessed by the king's remembrancer. Henry was selling off the abbeys, you know."

"I can't believe that no one has lost a deed before." Sarah twisted her handkerchief. "These old piles are always burning down. There must be some record of the grant by the Crown."

Rutherford Lestrom waved a hand. "No one can find anything in the public records. They have been kept so badly over the years that most are rotting away. And the ones that remain could be anywhere—the Tower, Westminster Abbey, the Rolls Chapel. Why, they are planning to move some to the stables behind Carlton House, I believe."

The man's father shook his head. "The House of Commons appointed a committee to find out where everything is, my dear. But they are having the devil of a time doing it. And they have been at it for almost twenty years."

Sarah put her hand to her eyes. It wasn't fair that this dreadful Davinoff could just destroy her life. She raised her head. "Well, I am not the kind to wait for the ax to fall, sirs," she announced. "If the records of the Crown are my best hope, then I shall comb London for them. If I have five days, I shall use them."

"It is a fool's errand," Mr. Lestrom, Jr., said, coming out from behind the huge desk.

His father raised his eyes from where they rested upon the neat pile of papers on the desk. "Lady Clevancy is right, of course," he said, with rather more resolution. "I shall go with you."

"No, Mr. Lestrom," Sarah announced. "We must split the territory. Who is in charge of these public records?" she asked, the task unfolding before her in her mind.

"The Master of the Rolls," old Lestrom answered. "The public records are all strung together upon parchment rolls affixed with the king's seal. If there is any knowing, he does. But we must apply to see him. It will take time."

"All right, Mr. Lestrom," Sarah said. "Do you apply to see him. I have another idea." With that, she strode out the door, leaving two generations of Lestroms staring after her.

She ordered a hackney to Finsbury Circle and the new library of the London Institute. If Parliament was looking into public records, there must be a report from the committee. She couldn't begin to search everywhere in only five days. Perhaps the report would give her direction.

She braved hostile male stares in the library to accost an unwilling clerk. It was not long before he handed her several handsome volumes, cornered in calf with marble boards. She sat at the tall table, sifting through the indices until her feet were both asleep. Thomas Ashton had been granted Clershing as reward for services rendered upon the Restoration. That focused her search. But grants of land were buried in with grants of every other sort: medals, honors, titles. Sarah began to bite her nails. Finally she found it. Grants of deeds from Charles II through the present were located in the Rolls Chapel. Now she had the trail. She would stop in Berkeley Square to make sure her trunk had arrived; then she was off to the Rolls Chapel.

When Corina's butler, Reece, opened the door in Berkeley Square and let her inside, Sarah could hear her yelling even from the hall. A footman scurried up the stairs with an empty trunk while the housemaid stumbled down them in hysterics, resulting in a near collision. The housekeeper shouted to the groom for the mistress's carriage. Reece did his best to seem unfazed by this maelstrom, but even he replied with some abstraction when Sarah asked if Corina was at home.

"For the moment." He frowned.

"Oh dear! She invited me to stay." Sarah felt like an intruder.

"Your trunk came this morning, Your Ladyship." Reece made no suggestions.

She had to see Corina. "If you don't mind, I will show myself up to Mrs. Nandalay's room."

"Of course, Your Ladyship." Reece stepped aside. Sarah passed the harried housekeeper, who looked on helplessly as Corina's two Yorkshire terriers completed the pandemonium by tumbling down the stairs. They skidded on the polished floors as they raced after the housemaid.

Sarah stepped over the yapping balls of fur and made her way up the stairs with a feeling of impending disaster. When she reached Corina's boudoir, her friend was pacing up and down while Lansing, Corina's dresser, and the second housemaid hastily put clothes and hats, brushes and face creams, feathers and wraps into four huge trunks, which crowded the room.

Corina still wore a yellow striped satin wrapper. "Is it so hard to comprehend that I would like my servants to make a little *haste?*" she asked the chandelier with upraised arms. Then,

"Sarah!" she cried, spying her friend. "What have I forgotten? The carriage is called for. I sent the second groom ahead to Chambroke. I cried off from Lady Hertford's rout. Whatever is left?"

Sarah wondered if Corina remembered her promise. She sighed. "Why all this haste?"

"What I want will appear in Bath very shortly, and I want to be there when he does," Corina snapped. She stalked over to the wardrobe and began pulling hats off the top shelf.

Sarah sat on a footstool. She was in a real dilemma. "Corina, come and sit with me a moment. They will do better without you, you know." Anger flashed in her friend's blue eyes. Then she laughed and sat in the chair beside Sarah.

"You are probably right. One cannot find servants who move at more than a snail's pace."

Sarah saw Lansing's dark look behind Corina's back. "Have you forgotten that I was to go home with you?" she asked, smiling ruefully at her friend.

"Of course I did not! You are welcome to come with me."

"But I need to stay in London for a few days," Sarah reminded her. "That was why I could not go with Lady Beldon this morning. I suppose all this haste is related to Davinoff."

"As Julien thinks upon our time together, he will make haste for Bath," Corina confided.

"Did you make a definite engagement when he drove you home?" Sarah pressed.

"Men are never very definite." The young woman waved a hand.

"Corina, you may be disappointed." Her friend's fixation seemed curious . . . unless one had seen Davinoff in person.

"He will come." She smiled slowly with the glowing confidence of the truly beautiful.

Sarah paced the room. It was no use asking Corina to stay. "I cannot leave yet."

"Stay at the Clarendon, then hire a chaise and four whenever you like," Corina returned, moving to supervise her servants once more. She didn't offer to keep the house open.

"And outriders too, I am sure," Sarah snapped back, but it

was lost. Her friend did not seem to care how she solved her dilemma.

"You're crushing that dress, Lansing."

Sarah's mind raced. A hotel? What could she afford? As for her way home, it would be the Mail coach, with all the difficulties traveling alone would bring. So be it. "I will see you in Bath," she said, as she left. Corina did not even see her go.

Sarah borrowed *A Picture of London, 1806*, a well-thumbed guidebook from the library at Berkeley Square, on her way out, to get the exact location of the Rolls Chapel. She gave the hackney driver the address and told him to wait, since the coach now held her trunk. She resolved to stay at the Two-Headed Swan, the inn from which the Mail started for the west country. In the coach she carefully counted out the money she had left in her reticule. The hire of hackneys had depleted her resources. Enough for two days, not more, what with lodging and food and the ticket to Bath. She had better find the record of her deed at the Rolls Chapel.

The guidebook said the place had begun in 1232 as a church for converted Jews built by Henry III. One certainly couldn't tell that now. It had been rebuilt so many times it was rather a hodgepodge of styles. Inside, the stone floor of the nave was bathed in the dim blue light of stained-glass windows. Sarah couldn't see anything like rolls. The aisle held nothing but monuments. She peered at the nearest and saw that it was for one John Yonge, a Master of the Rolls in the sixteenth century. Well, that was a good omen. Peeking about between the dark wood of the carved choir screens, she saw several stacks of rolls and sighed in relief. This wasn't so bad. If need be, she would look through every roll herself. Still, it would be better if she could find a keeper. She pushed through a short wooden door that rose beside the choir.

The sight that greeted her stopped Sarah as though felled by a blow. Gone was the dim stained-glass light. The ceiling of this huge stone room was supported by buttresses, ornately carved. Its windows streamed sunlight onto tables, shelves and piles, all stacked with paper rolls. They were everywhere, tied with red ribbons and closed with official-looking seals. Some, near the door, appeared new and bright; most were cracked and moldering. The smell of damp pervaded all, contradicting the bright sunlight.

Between the stacks ran a maze of narrow walkways, half overcome in several places with rolls that had tumbled from their piles. An old man scurried about, dressed in a dusty coat twenty years out of style, mumbling to himself and loaded down with an armload of fat, flaking parchment cylinders. At several points about the room narrow places were cleared on the tables. Clerks had unrolled bolts of the crumbling paper and were transcribing furiously.

Sarah felt her stomach churning. Each roll appeared to be thirty or forty feet long, once unfurled. And there must be thousands of rolls here. She hovered uncertainly. "Excuse me, sir," she said as the old man tottered down the nearest path. "Are you the Master of the Rolls?"

He peered up at her, distracted. "Oh dear me, no. No, no, no, no. I am just the head indexer, ordering up this mess. No, I am definitely not the Master of the Rolls."

Sarah pounced upon his implied knowledge, hope rising again. "If you are making the index, you are just the one I want to talk to, sir." He peered at her again, over his spectacles.

"To me? What business could a young lady have with me?"

"I need to find the record of a deed. The *Report of the Committee on the Public Record* said that memorials of deeds were in the Rolls Chapel."

The old man looked around. "We have all sorts of things here. We just don't know where."

"Are they sorted into any order at all?" Sarah asked, clutching at straws.

"We've made some progress," the head indexer acknowledged.

"The deed was granted by Charles the Second in 1664." Then, as the old man looked ever less certain, she pleaded, "I do need to find the record ever so badly. It means everything."

"Well"—the old man seemed to regret that he couldn't help—"I just don't know. . . . Wait!" He stopped suddenly and turned to face her again. "Did you say Charles the Second?"

She nodded eagerly.

"We had those rolls out. Was it last week? Someone else asked about deeds from that period."

"What?" Sarah asked, wary. "Someone asked you to find deeds from Charles the Second?" Was this coincidental or the forces of chaos at work? "Who was it?"

The indexer waved his hand. "I don't remember faces, you know, just documents. But Geoffrey was able to help whoever it was." He led the way to a sallow young man bent over a roll. "Geoffrey, this young lady wants a land grant by Charles the Second. You had those out last week."

The younger man nodded and pointed. "Over by the window."

"Who came to look at them, can you recall?" Sarah asked, torn between the desire to rush to the window and a strange sense of foreboding.

"Can't say. I just pointed him to the pile over there, same as you," the scribe said, then turned dismissively back to his roll and his cramped lines of indexing.

Sarah went to the stacks by the window, hope fluttering her heart, as the head indexer drifted back to his former task. "Careful not to damage them," he called over his shoulder.

The stack of parchment was nearly as high as Sarah was. She lifted one from the top. It was surprisingly heavy, and inscribed with *Charles II, Rex, xxiii* for the twenty-third year of his reign. That meant her deed would be numbered iv. What could protect her from Davinoff was right here somewhere! She pulled down others: xvii, ix, v, iii. All years except the fourth. Her stomach clenched. Number ii, then i. She began to run into rolls labeled with *Charles I* and bearing his seal.

"Geoffrey," she called to the young scribe who'd pointed her here. Her voice was not quite steady. "There is a gap here."

"Cromwell didn't keep rolls," the man replied absently. "Dismantled the whole system."

"No," she managed. "I mean you are missing the fourth year of the reign of Charles the Second."

"Nonsense," he said impatiently. "That was a complete set." He flipped through his closely lettered sheets. "I indexed the whole sequence. You must have missed it."

"Come look," she called in a flat voice.

He rose from his stool and strode to the window. Searching her pile, he next began taking down others in growing frustration as he looked for the missing year.

Sarah stood like a statue during his flurry of activity. When he finally stood and put his hands on his hips to survey the disorder, she asked, "Could someone have taken it?"

"Of course not. What would anyone want with one of these moldering ruins?"

"You can't remember who came to inquire after these particular records?"

The clerk looked at her in growing consternation. "I can't say I paid much attention."

Someone was taking a great deal of trouble to make sure Sarah could not locate any record of her deed. Circumstance seemed to be building an impenetrable wall around her. Davinoff was the cause. She was sure of it.

Chapter Three

Sarah came back to the waiting hack in the yard outside the church, her thoughts awhirl. The driver whipped up his horse to take her to the Two-Headed Swan, but Sarah hardly noticed. She needed either the deed, or the Crown record of the grant. She had neither.

What to do? She racked her brain. Could Davinoff have taken the deed from the Lestroms' offices? Her heart contracted. If he had the deed, he had destroyed it. He would not leave a record of his perfidy intact. Damn him! It wasn't fair! She brushed angrily at her cheeks. If he had destroyed all trace of her deed, there was nothing she could do. Yet she could not slink home to Bath to let Davinoff have Clershing whenever he liked. She lifted her head. After all, she did not yet know that her own deed was irretrievably lost. She only knew that the Lestroms couldn't find it.

Sarah sat bolt upright in the carriage. Lestrom, Jr., had written to Josiah Wells. That man might know. He had been her steward and her father's for more than thirty years. And she had another score to settle with Mr. Wells. He was acting for Davinoff. How could he betray her thus? Yes, she would see Mr. Wells, but first she must go back to Bath and gather her resources. She might have to sell her mother's pearl earrings. They were all that was left except for the ruby set her father had given her mother when they married. Sarah had resolved never to sell them. Unless, of course, it came to putting food on the table. Which was entirely possible at this point.

That evening, Sarah squeezed herself into the Mail coach between a taciturn clerk and a stout woman with a child sitting on her lap who smelled of garlic. The other passengers were a cleric and a middle-aged man with luxuriant black whiskers and a decided paunch tightening his unfortunate mustard-colored waistcoat. She noted with some distaste that his coat was spotted and his cravat not what one could call fresh. His broad smile did not reassure her.

On the open road between stops, the drafty, creaking coach jolted over potholes and lurched around corners. It seemed to Sarah to creep along at a snail's pace. It stopped often, but only long enough to check the passengers' tickets, heave off luggage and the mail, and hoist on the new cargo. There was no time to eat or even warm oneself with a cup of coffee. Passengers came and went. Only Sarah and the man in the mustard waistcoat always remained.

As her thoughts went round and round her predicament, something began to nag at her. No one remembered who had asked to see the records of Charles II at the Rolls Chapel. Surely anyone who had seen Davinoff would remember him. An unimportant point, but one she could not explain. Soon, she could no longer think clearly at all, dulled by the rattling coach. She dozed fretfully through several stops. Just before dawn she found herself sitting next to the man in the mustard-colored waistcoat.

"Good morrow," he said, smiling down at her. At close range his whiskers were greasy. A pungent smell emanated from his person.

Sarah wiped her eyes and straightened. "Good morning," she responded, then pointedly turned her head to watch the sky lighten. She tucked her cold hands under her arms to warm them as the coach lurched, and the man in the mustard waistcoat leaned against her. She pushed herself as far as she could into the corner of her seat. "Please, sir," she protested.

The man slowly righted himself. Too slowly, to Sarah's mind. "Pardon, Miss." He grinned. "Jes' part of riding the Mail. I'd guess you ain't familiar with the Mail. Me, now, I rides coaches very frequent. Me lay makes me most familiar with coaches."

Sarah ignored the opportunity to inquire about his "lay," but she could not cut off his attempts at conversation. "Not as familiar as Jemmy 'Icks, o' course," he guffawed. " 'E was so familiar with the Mail, 'e swung fer it. Why, when me an' Gin Lane Jane was lookin' fer that servant girl what loped with them pearls, we was all the way to Manchester on the Mail." Sarah was sure his "lay" was on the shady side of the street.

At dawn, she took the opportunity provided by a change of horses to walk about the inn yard. The chief purpose of this stratagem was to change her place in the coach. But her persecutor contrived yet again to sit next to her by offering his seat in the corner to an elderly lady. As the coach moved off he steadied himself with a hand on her knee.

"You will kindly keep your hands to yourself, sir," she ordered in no uncertain terms.

Her adversary only chuckled. "Coaches just cain't be trusted, now, can they, m' sweet?"

Sarah had no desire to make a scene by asking the driver for help, and she wasn't even sure he would care. The day seemed to stretch forward interminably. They would be lucky to reach Bath by dark at this pace.

It was ten o'clock when next they stopped. Sarah was driven to distraction between her disagreeable seatmate, a crying child, and a prim woman who eyed Sarah's clothes and spoke loudly of the free ways of the servant class these days. Sarah escaped from the coach like a shot, and breathed in the crisp air of late October like a tonic.

The yard was a buzz of activity, ostlers, horses and carriages crisscrossing in the mud. It smelled of wet earth and horses and frying ham from the inn. Sarah looked around her in a daze. She wandered toward the inn door, following the scent of ham, almost into the path of a team of horses trotting briskly toward the gate with their tilbury. She leaped back, but not in time to prevent her pelisse from being muddied as the carriage splashed through a great puddle.

"Look about you, girl!" the annoyed driver called over his shoulder. As she backed toward the safety of a stationary coach just in front of the taproom door, Sarah ran smack into the dreadful man in the mustard waistcoat.

"Oh, ho, missy," he cried and pretended to drag her to safety. "You got to watch yerself in these yards." He had her pinned against the coach. She was overwhelmed by the bulk, the stench of him. "Now you jes' let Ned 'ere take care o' you, and you'll be right as a trivet."

Sarah pushed at him, trying to catch her breath. "You have no manners, sir, to persecute me thus!" She turned from his breath. Would anyone even notice her plight in a busy coachyard?

"Perhaps you would care to have me school him, Lady Clevancy?" a deep voice rumbled. The handle of a driving whip poked into Mr. Mustard Waistcoat's shoulder, forcing him back.

Both Sarah and her oppressor looked up to see Julien Davinoff, his many-caped driving coat splashed with mud, but looking otherwise immaculate, staring down at them. Sarah gasped and glanced with frightened eyes between her two adversaries. The man in the mustard waistcoat gave way in the face of Davinoff's burning gaze. There was an intensity, a commitment in that stare that said the dark man observed no limitations he did not make himself.

"Beg pardon, sir," Sarah's tormentor stuttered.

"Be off with you," Davinoff almost whispered. "Or you will beg for more than pardon."

With that, Mr. Mustard Waistcoat's eyes grew wide. His mouth opened and closed once, as though searching for a reply. Then, without further ceremony, he turned and hurried back to clamber into the mail coach. Sarah watched him go in relief.

She turned to Davinoff, flushing to her ears. She seemed destined to keep meeting the man. Here she was in crumpled and stained traveling raiment, her hair no doubt awry, and looking haggard. He had found her in the lowest situation, being accosted by a churlish rogue who had seen better days. And she was coming off a common mail coach, a fact that clearly advertised her straightened circumstances. She had no deed, no record of her land grant, and no protector as she faced the man who would strip her of everything she owned. Frightened, she was angry, too, that he should look down upon her, as indeed he must. She pressed her lips together and took two breaths. There was no one to rely on but herself.

"Thank you, sir." She made it a dismissal. But as her eyes met Davinoff's, she was riveted.

They still stood in the center of the yard. The carriage behind Sarah moved on. The Mail driver came out of the taproom with his sack of letters. Activity swirled around Davinoff, but could not touch him. He was a black smear on the bright afternoon, the dark post of a sundial whose shadow picked out a single moment while all the celestial bodies turned around him. No carriage would run her over, no ostler jostle her, as long as she stayed in that shadow. For an instant, she found the prospect tempting. Her body stirred in a way she'd never wanted to feel again.

He gazed down at her, his intensity searing. The man had taken in her situation in its entirety; he thought he knew all about her. The driver called out for passengers to get aboard. Mustering her strength, Sarah turned away. She had a few surprises yet for Mr. Davinoff. The moment broke. The noise of the yard pressed in on her again.

A strong hand gripped her elbow. Her gaze jerked up. He looked grim and absolutely purposeful. "You will finish your journey with me, Lady Clevancy." It was an order.

She struggled in what she hoped was an unobtrusive manner to take her arm back. "You cannot force women into your curricle." A tiny tendril of fear circled around her spine.

"I should hope I would not have to do so." The grip on her elbow did not slacken. His vehicle gleamed black in the sun that shone through fast-moving clouds. "The Mail is impossible at this juncture and hardly the place for you in any case." He released her. "I assure you, your virtue is in no danger," he observed, looking her over. "Do you see any alternatives to hand?"

What a maddening person! She would rather he had forced her. Now she would have to humiliate herself to follow him, or race with unbecoming speed to the Mail Coach, where the driver was at this moment climbing into his seat. She hesitated. She could not bear another moment seated next to that horrible Mr. Mustard Waistcoat. But the last thing she wanted was to spend the afternoon alone in a curricle with a man who was capable of anything. Capable, but *not* willing. The way he had looked at her when he said her virtue was not in danger! As she flung about for alternatives she grew angrier and angrier. She did not even have enough money to stay at the inn and purchase a ticket for the next mail.

When her gaze returned to Davinoff, he was watching her calmly. "Put off the lady's trunks in Bath," he called to the driver of the mail and tossed him a coin that gleamed gold in the sun. Then he turned his back and strode off to his equipage.

"What right have you?" she gasped after him.

But Davinoff's attention was apparently fixed on an ostler who was fussing with the straps on a huge leather trunk at the back of his curricle. "You there," he boomed. "Leave that trunk alone." The ostler jumped back from the trunk with raised hands.

Sarah was outraged. As though the trunk contained priceless objects! The ostler had only tried to help. Davinoff seemed to order everyone about and think it his right to do so. Right, indeed! Oh, dear Lord. Indeed. *Her* deed. Her deed might be in that very trunk! If he had kept either the roll or the deed in order to alter them, would they not be in his trunk? No wonder he did not want anyone to touch it.

The Mail Coach door slammed behind her, but she had already made her choice. When Davinoff turned before getting into his curricle, and raised an eyebrow of inquiry, she stalked over and allowed him to hand her up into the seat without a word. She resolved to spend the afternoon with the devil, and find a way to search that trunk.

Davinoff climbed up beside her, took up reins and whip, and backed expertly into a position in the crowded yard where he could wheel and turn the carriage. Then he coolly whipped up the horses and tooled through the gates at a smart clip. He cleared a barouche just entering the yard with inches to spare and feathered the turn into the road to a nicety.

Sarah could not help but admire his skill. She pulled her mind back to devising a plan to get at his trunk. If only they would lose a wheel as the Beldon barouche had done. That would force a stop. It was hardly like to happen, of course. She clutched at her plain beaver hat, pulling against its ribband as it was taken by the brisk wind rising from the northwest, that wind pinking her cheeks. She stole a glance at Davinoff. Why had he taken her up? The look on his face as he guided her to the curricle made clear his reluctance. Anger filled her again. To make her practically grovel was the outside of enough! Then, she had a dreadful thought. No doubt he intended to badger her to cede him the property out of court. What a dreadful afternoon she had set herself!

For the moment he was silent as he negotiated the busy thoroughfare. The curricle seemed to fly in comparison to the Mail Coach. They met many vehicles and passed not a few, but no one passed them from behind. Her hat became more annoying as it lifted in the wind. She had no desire to sit holding it on with one hand, so she untied her ribbands and put the hat in her lap. Because her hair would be soon escaping from its knot in this breeze, without another thought for propriety she twisted the knot free and shook out her heavy dark locks. He might dismiss her as a mere nothing, but he no doubt didn't care a jot about whether her hair was properly tied up.

The silence dragged on. There were two coats between them, but still she thought she could feel the warmth of his shoulder as it brushed hers. A thought of begging him to abandon his plan to take Clershing flickered across her mind. She banished it with a mental shudder. The man who sat next to her so sternly would only think her more contemptible if she was stupid enough to throw herself upon a mercy he didn't have. Was he not anarchy incarnate?

As the roadway cleared a bit, he looked down at her and made as if to speak.

"If you are about to press me on the Clershing issue," she interposed, "please do not. You must talk to Mr. Lestrom. A gentleman would not take advantage of this situation."

Davinoff raised his brows, then turned to mind his horses without a word.

She should find the silence comforting. At least he wasn't questioning her about her deed. But with no conversation to distract her, Sarah could not but be conscious of the strong thighs that swelled beneath his breeches next to her or the broad shoulders under the man's driving cloak. She glimpsed the line of his jaw and the soft lobe of his ear beneath the curls of dark hair before she turned her eyes resolutely back to the road. That way lay madness. That way she could not be trusted, as she had been shown in Sienna. A flash of shame rushed over her before she turned her thoughts to her immediate problem. How could she divert Davinoff's attention from his trunk?

It was Davinoff himself who presented an opportunity. As they came out of Marborough, he looked down at her with what seemed like disgust and broke the silence. "You will allow me to ask if you have eaten at any time in the near past?"

Sarah realized she was famished. She struggled for a moment with wanting to snub him, but her stomach and the sudden flash of a plan won out. "Actually, I have not," she said stiffly.

"I will find a place to stop. The White Rose will do in West Overton."

No, Sarah thought. The White Rose wouldn't do. It was a large inn, bustling with carriages. Davinoff's curricle would be given over to the ostlers and hauled round to a busy stable for safekeeping. No chance for her search there. She needed somewhere quiet, out of the way. She would excuse herself during luncheon . . . Her mind raced ahead.

"Isn't the White Rose near to Beckhampton?" she asked.

"Some three miles."

Sarah took the bit between her teeth. "Then do let's go on to the village of Avebury," she said with a brightness she did not feel. "There is an inn there, not so well-to-do as the White Rose, but there are the stones, you know. My father and I were used to stop there and see them." Memory washed over her, all her fondness for her father, all the tristesse for those simpler times when she had been protected and loved and innocent. She felt her own brittle smile soften. "You could take a hamper out from the yard and directly down into the circle on warm days," she added with a sigh. "They are much older than Stonehenge, you know." She looked off toward Hackpin Hill and the Marborough Downs. "I have thought sometimes that you could feel the past welling up out of those stones, soaking the air with centuries." She caught herself and cursed her lack of self-control. Blathering on about picnics with her father. How stupid could she be? She looked up at Davinoff to find him examining her, then began to twist the ribbons of her hat.

"Actually, the stone circle at Avebury is one of my favorite places," he said, urging his grand bays to pass a slower phaeton.

Sarah was surprised. "It is?"

"Less elegant than Stonehenge, but more elemental, I have always thought."

"Exactly so." She resolved to make conversation about the stones, no matter how difficult. He must agree to stop there. "And one doesn't sacrifice a jot of the mystery," she said, casting about. "Who made them? How did they come to that farmer's field?"

"It wasn't a farmer's field back then." She thought she saw a smile flicker across his lips.

"Of course not," she replied, rushing on. "But the stones are from the downs. I have always wondered how men got them there."

"The way they moved the stones cut for the pyramids in Egypt," he said. "They rolled them on logs, back when most of this area was forested."

"I have heard that said." She imagined it for a moment, her interest caught in spite of herself. "And it doesn't spoil the mystery at all."

"Is mystery so important?" he asked, his eyes sweeping the road ahead.

"Sometimes . . ." She trailed off. Why couldn't she be bold and dashing like Corina? Then she would be able to get him to do whatever she wanted.

He met her eyes, and she saw speculation there. "Well, there is one mystery about the stones that now will never be solved," he said as they turned into the road to Avebury.

"What is that?"

"The secret of why they were built. No one knows anymore, or at least no one who cares to tell the world."

"Oh, but that is the one thing which is not a secret at all,"

Sarah exclaimed, not quite understanding what he meant, yet determined to continue making conversation. "They were built as a connection to the unknown. We don't have to know exactly how. Perhaps they are a calendar to signal the years or the solstice. They could be a monument to some god or a place for ceremony. But in any case, they were built to serve the human need to discover order, to explain and connect. I think that is at the root of almost everything we do, mathematics and language, every religion, every science." She paused, then said suddenly, "George Upcott is a specialist in explaining." She could not think why George had come to mind precisely then.

"And who is George Upcott?" he asked.

"A friend." She hesitated. "And a proponent of the sciences. He experiments with blood transfusion at the hospital in Bath."

"Has he studied with Blundell?" Davinoff asked, his voice sharp.

"Why, yes, I believe so. That is the London doctor?"

Davinoff seemed interested indeed. "Yes. He has been doing some fascinating work. I must meet Dr. Upcott."

The tiny inn at Avebury had been built of stones broken where they stood in the circle, their pieces carted up the hill. The villagers did not break the stones now that they knew that people would come to see them, but it always seemed to Sarah a sad comment on the process of history that the glory of one civilization should be reduced to rubble to build another. She said as much to Davinoff as they dismounted. There was a single boy to walk the horses up and down, and he looked none too bright. Excellent! Davinoff ordered him to water the gorgeous beasts, and he and Sarah made their way into the coffee room for a late nuncheon.

When should she excuse herself and sneak out the back to the curricle? If Davinoff was as ravenous as she, the middle of the meal would be best. She had a moment of embarrassment when she took off her muddied pelisse and looked down at her plain brown crumpled dress, worse for two days of travel. "I look as though I spent all night on a mail coach."

"Exactly so," Davinoff returned with a remarkable lack of courtesy.

"Well, you needn't think I enjoy looking this way," she exclaimed. "You may as well know that I *intended* to look like a governess, to avoid attracting attention," she continued, stung into what her father would certainly have called an unbecoming retort.

"In short, a disguise?" Davinoff queried with a single lifted brow.

Sarah could not help the smile that rose to her lips. "Oh, you must find me ridiculous. I know I do." She sighed as they sat down.

"Not at all," Davinoff said with much more politesse. "And, may I ask why you were not returning with your friends to Bath?"

Sarah twitched uncomfortably. She took some fruit from the bowl on their table. "I thought I had arranged matters. I needed to be in London. Since Lady Beldon was returning home, I arranged to stay with Mrs. Nandalay." Here Sarah realized that her explanation might become tangled. "But that ended being inconvenient for her. I found myself upon the Mail."

"I see." Davinoff did not mention the economic straits that led one to the Mail instead of a post chaise. Now he would know she had no money for a prolonged fight over Clershing.

The landlord brought heaping trays of food as Sarah tried to stifle her growing apprehension. How could she slip away? She could say she needed to tidy herself, but not in the middle of a meal. Who would believe that? Perhaps if he was very intent on eating . . . But he picked lazily at the dishes presented, and seemed more intent on watching her. Not a good sign. After the meal, she told herself. She put off her coming crime with food. She made her way through a slab of steak pie, a piece of bread with butter, and part of a cold pigeon, not to mention the fruit and the sweetmeats. She could scarcely believe she was going to do something so rash or so unbecoming to a lady of quality as to search a man's trunk.

Davinoff ended his meal with an apple, which he consumed slowly as he watched her eat. When at last she pushed her plate away, he quizzed her. "Finished?"

"Veni, vidi, vici," she announced. The time drew near.

"You did conquer the landlord's repast," Davinoff agreed. "Are you a lady scholar?"

"A bluestocking?" Sarah frowned. "How unkind! My Great Aunt Cecily worried that my father was turning me into a dreadful bluestocking."

"Did he succeed?"

Sarah was taken aback. "No. I am not a scholar. Curious, perhaps. I have a smattering of facts about a variety of subjects and am learned in none." She gave a nervous laugh. It was clearly now or never. She hoped she did not look as frightened as she felt. It was a stupid gesture to search the trunk. He had destroyed the deed and the record of it, too. Her heart clenched in desperation. She must leave no stone unturned. And she would never forgive herself if she didn't take advantage of this God-given opportunity to make certain that he didn't have it with him. She rose so quickly she almost overset the chair. "If you will excuse me, I will refresh myself."

She hurried past the surprised landlord, murmuring that she had left something in the carriage, and out into the rear yard. The dull fellow who held the horses received a perfunctory excuse that she had need of something in her trunk. What if it was locked? She went around to the back of the curricle. There was no lock, only the heavy leather straps that buckled it to the luggage rack. What need did a man like Davinoff have for locks? Who would be mad enough to molest aught that belonged to him? Mad enough or desperate enough, she told herself as her shaking fingers fumbled with the stiff leather. It seemed to take forever to unlash the trunk. She looked over her shoulder a dozen times expecting to see him at the inn door. The boy at the horses' heads clucked quietly to them. She threw the latch and heaved up the lid of the finely tooled and studded leather case. Inside, black coats were carefully folded along with the evening cape she had seen him wear at the scene of the murder. A murderer? Her heart thudded in her breast. She fumbled down through fine linen shirts and perfectly starched cravats, stockings, and smalls. She could feel nothing like a paper. But what was this? She felt a leather pouch and heard a clinking sound. Did Davinoff keep his purse in his trunk? How odd. She opened the pouch, and tilted its contents into her hand.

The sun struck the oddly shaped silver disks and made them gleam. They were coins, she realized with a start, but like none she had ever seen. She peered at them. They had pictures of a boat on one side and writing she could not decipher on the other. The boat looked like pictures she had seen of a Viking ship. What was Davinoff doing with coins like these? There was no time to wonder. He might appear at any moment. She fumbled the coins back into their pouch and stuffed it back under Davinoff's clothes. Strange coins were not her object here.

Thinking quickly, she searched the lid for secret openings in the lining, feeling for the rustle of paper. He would come out to look for her if she tarried. In one corner, she felt a cool, smooth tube. Yes! She drew it out. But it was only a longish bottle, sloshing with some clear solution more viscous than water. Inside, dozens of tiny dark cups tinkled against the glass. What were these? They looked like nothing she knew. She peered at them. Dimpled circles of smoked glass? Not what she needed. Her hand rose to stifle a small sound of despair. But then the thought that he might find her there jerked her back to action. She pressed his clothes back into the trunk, and tucked the glass bottle with its mysterious contents under them. The fine fabric was soft on her hands. Startled by the intimacy of touching his things, she jerked away and pulled the lid down, threaded the buckles with the straps, then pulled them tight with all her strength. When she turned toward the inn, the doorway was still empty. She rushed away, calling her thanks to the oblivious boy.

When Sarah reached the taproom, Davinoff stood in silhouette in the front doorway of the inn, gazing out over the field of stones. Had he seen her? He turned as she approached.

"We cannot leave without taking a turn through the stones," he said, his voice brusque. If he knew what she had been at, he gave no sign.

Out of breath, she felt more disheveled than ever. She didn't want to walk with Davinoff. She wanted to race away to talk to Mr. Wells. Maybe he would know where else to look. But she couldn't let Davinoff see her desperation. She took a single deep breath as she felt his eyes upon her, questioning, and nodded her assent. Down the hill they walked, through the moat created when the mound of earth ringing the stones was built.

As she walked into the circle, her breathing calmed with the enormity of the place. The wind-tossed clouds, the blue of a sky that could break one's heart, arched over the straw stubble in the field and the huge irregular stones in their gigantic circle. The frantic need to find the deed receded with that strange peace that the earth could lend you. There had been probably two thousand such Octobers here, maybe more, breaking over these stones. Sarah walked to one of the large lozenge-shaped rocks that alternated with the slimmer pillars, drawn to touch its cold, rough surface. She felt Davinoff behind her.

"How long have you been coming here?" he asked after a moment.

"Years," she said. "Since I was a child. And you?"

There was a pause. "A long time." She turned and put her back to the stone. The wind took her hair. She looked out over the hills to the south, and he turned to look with her.

"There is a Roman road that crosses that hill," he said, pointing.

"Ridge Way?" she asked.

"No, that runs north and south here. It is a small branch of Fosse Road. It was used to connect Cirencester with a Roman town just south of Reading."

"I never heard of a Roman town at Reading." She was floating away on the October wind.

Davinoff pointed again. "The road follows the line of that ridge. Later, just to the other side, the Celts built the Wansdyke to defend against the Saxons. Terrific battles took place there, with much loss of life on both sides." He seemed lost in thought. "The Celts were doomed, of course. They retreated across the Wye and the Saxons took all of this country. But for a while, the Wansdyke held them south of here."

Sarah's attention wandered back to Davinoff. She had never met a man who knew so much about the land, about what had happened here. But he did not go on. They made their way back to the tavern in silence. As they approached the yard, a rider was leaving in haste, a heavy man on a large horse. Davinoff approached the landlord, busy smoothing a paper over the bar, to pay their shot. It was a copy of the crude line drawing the strange witness to the murders had made. The landlord came out from behind the bar and pushed the paper upon a nail next to the hearth. The lettering under the picture proclaimed that the man in the drawing was wanted in connection with the murders in London. There was a reward of a thousand guineas. She shuddered. From the instant she saw it, the drawing had reminded her of Davinoff.

Davinoff clinked coins on the table behind her. He was examining the portrait too. "You are right." His deep voice rumbled almost in her ear. "It could be anyone. Even me." She turned and he raised one eyebrow at her in a gesture she was coming to know too well. His eyes were dark, darker than any she had ever seen. "Shall we get on the road?" he asked.

Sarah's heart throbbed in her chest. He was right. It could be anyone. Was it? She could not put her question into words, but he must have seen it in her eyes.

"I thought you hated to spoil mysteries," he chided and strode out to the curricle.

Sarah hesitated a moment. This man was anarchy incarnate, a force of disorder disrupting her existence, even if he wasn't an actual murderer. Then she thought of Corina, leaving the ball to chase after this man. Corina would not have hesitated. She was not as bold as Corina. But Corina was not here. Instead of making her cautious, that thought gave her a tiny thrill of satisfaction, brief and guilty. She looked out after Davinoff, giving instructions to the stable boy to stand away from the horses' heads upon command, and smiled. She must keep an eye on her adversary, she told herself. Besides, he was her only way home. She went out the door and allowed Anarchy to hand her into his curricle.

The rest of the trip home was a jumble of emotions for Sarah. The ache of not finding the deed left her wondering where else it might be but, in spite of herself, her interest shifted to her conversation with Davinoff. They talked of many things: the influence of the Danes upon the language, the probability that Arthur and Guinevere were historical figures, the legend of the Holy Grail and its journey to England with Joseph of Arimathea. She wanted to ask him about the coins in his trunk, whether he was a collector, whether they were Danish. She caught herself forgetting that he was her adversary and that he was likely a murderer into the bargain. The devil had no doubt charmed his victims in this manner many times before, she admonished herself.

"You are well versed in history," Davinoff remarked. "You had it from your father?"

"He enjoyed the past for what it could tell us about ourselves," Sarah remembered. "We were especially fascinated with the Romans. There is a ruined villa on the land at Clershing, you know." Immediately she cursed her wayward tongue.

"I know."

There was silence for a long moment. The sun set in a dramatic gesture of black clouds and red sky. Finally Davinoff said, "Josiah Wells said that you had plans to excavate it."

"I . . . I have always dreamed of reconstructing the ruin, and using it to show how Romans really lived." She wanted to justify the project to him somehow, to show him that she was a worthy owner of the property. If he understood why Clershing meant everything to her . . . It wouldn't matter to a man like Davinoff. But she pressed ahead. "I want it to be different than those horrid reconstructions of the King's Bath. They didn't care at all what the originals looked like. I want to display the finest Roman pieces in the settings where they were made and used. I want people to understand who the Romans were and what they left us." She trailed off, feeling his silence before she even allowed to occur. Of course he disapproved.

It was some time before he said, "An admirable ambition. Is it more than a dream?"

Sarah took a sharp breath. How could he even ask that question? If he took her land from her, her dream would turn to ashes. "There are one or two obstacles," she replied. "But I expect to start the excavations this year, now that the mortgages are cleared." Too late, she realized that her urge to set him down had confirmed that her financial situation was precarious. He must know her words were idle threats since he held her deeds.

"I see," her foe said, and she was most afraid he did.

From that moment on, the journey was just as strained as when he first took her up. Sarah wondered that he did not press her, that he did not gloat. She would have expected that. But she was bone-weary. Her mood sank lower as she contemplated the prospect that she was riding home with the future owner of Clershing.

It was near to seven o'clock when they reached the house in Laura Place. Its cheerful lights and the wafting aromas of Addie's cooking seemed like a haven from bad dreams filled with stuffy coaches and mustard waistcoats and anarchy. She did not thank him or pause to say good-bye. She wanted dinner and her bed. She would deal with deeds and Davinoff tomorrow.

But her ordeal was not yet ended. It was true that she sighed in relief as she walked through the door. The dark of the night outside could not touch the sunny marbleized paper of the entry hall. Its light, sand-scrubbed floors and the intricately carved white crown moldings all seemed indescribably dear to her, now that they might be lost. Jasco was there to take her wrap. Treasured Jasco. He had gotten jowls of late. She would give him references of course, though he was too old to get a place of the first order. Sarah wished he could do the same for her.

"Mrs. Williams asked most especially to see you when you arrived," Jasco intoned as he relieved her of her gloves. He cleared his throat, a sure sign that he was about to cross the line from servant to advisor, admonisher, or friend. Servants who had served your father while you were in frilly skirts thought they had every right in the world to advise and direct you. "It was perhaps not wise to leave the draft of your note to your solicitors on the desk."

"Oh dear. Is she upset?" Sarah had forgotten all about that half-written missive, abandoned when she decided to go to London herself.

"Very upset." Jasco handed her an envelope bearing Corina's flamboyant hand.

Sarah took a deep breath. She would not have chosen to tell Aunt Amelia about their bleak prospects just yet. Was she strong enough to bear a note from Corina? She ripped it open.

Sarah—

The moment you return, make haste to Chambroke. I shall expect you.

—Corina

Sarah heard a sob, and looked up to see a woman come drifting down the stairs, clinging to the white spindle banister and holding a handkerchief—no doubt soaked in camphor—to her lips. Amelia Williams was a plump woman some forty years Sarah's senior, bearing a connection to the family so tangled Sarah could never quite recall just how they were related. Sarah had searched out Amelia in Harrowgate, when she needed a chaperone in order to continue in Bath on her own after her father's death. There was never any question of who looked after whom.

Amelia's hair escaped in distraught wisps and her red-rimmed eyes and trembling lower lip told of recent hysterics. "Cruel child," she gasped. "How could you stay away? Are we ruined?"

Sarah prepared herself. "Come into the study, Aunt. You are needlessly concerned."

"You know the study reminds me of your father," Amelia fussed. But she followed Sarah.

Jasco had made sure a fire crackled in the marble fireplace. Normally the calm taupe walls and the heavy walnut bookcases soothed Sarah. Her eyes traced the pattern of the taupe and beige and blue Aubusson carpet, familiar now for so many years. They moved over the niches in the far wall and the bookshelves, mostly empty. So much had been sold to buy off the mortgages at Clershing. Perhaps the rugs would bring something. She shook herself. Her job was to calm her volatile aunt, no matter that weary anguish churned in her own breast. She sat in one of the two massive leather wing chairs in front of the fire and gestured invitingly to her aunt to take the other.

"I cannot imagine who could be challenging your right to Clershing." Amelia sniffed into her handkerchief. "You realize we are ruined if Clershing goes."

Sarah tried hard to remember that Amelia felt she had left behind forever the genteel poverty that the size of her competence forced upon her. Indeed, one of the most telling arguments for living with Sarah was that she should have no expense for her own upkeep. Still, her use of the word *we* was the tiniest bit annoying. After all, Amelia at least had her competence.

"If only you were safely married," Amelia wailed. "I cannot

understand *how* you never accepted one of the offers you had during your London season. And one a viscount, too!"

"None of them attracted me."

"You never tried," the woman accused. "True, you don't have the looks that are in fashion, like Mrs. Nandalay," she mourned. "But if you would make a push to show yourself in your best light, we might yet bring off a match with George Upcott. You cannot be waiting for a love match at your age, and so I have told you these many times."

"Many times." Sarah tried to smile. "So I absolve you of your duty to repeat them." She rose and tugged at the bell pull. "A glass of ratafia might be the thing. You will ply your needle while I play. We will put away worries until tomorrow." Sarah thought that was unlikely in her own case.

Chapter Four

She drove out from Bath the next day in a hired gig with Jasco up beside her and her valise in the back to obey Corina's summons. Her mind was still full of her ride with Davinoff. He seemed a mass of contradictions. He was anarchy, the evil force about to strip her of her land, and yet she had found so much in common with him. The mystery fascinated her in spite of all.

But now she was for Josiah Wells. Even with the delay she would encounter at Chambroke, they could make the twenty miles to Clershing by midafternoon. She should refuse Corina's periodic demands, but she somehow never did. Her role was attendant nymph to the goddess and she knew it. Fascination with the goddess made nymphs agree to be attendant. It was raining hard as she swung up the graveled drive toward the east front of the great house. The park was green and wet. Its acres of grasslands and the huge, ancient trees rolling down toward the lake were set in a design that only seemed natural, created by Capability Brown himself.

The house was seventeenth century, a gift to the dukes of Bimerton from Queen Anne for services unspecified. A taste for dice had finished the Bimerton fortune in three generations and

Corina's nabob father bought Chambroke outright. Sarah studied its symmetrical pediments and towers rising before her in the rain. She loved the park as if it were her own, but she could not love the house. It was built to be great, but it was without sympathy. Its columned porticos and huge dimensions, its cupolas and crenellations were simply overwhelming.

Jasco took the gig around to the stables as Sarah stepped up to the grand portico. Inside, she shook the droplets from her hair. Corina's emaciated butler, Reece, handed her gloves and pelisse to a footman. The marble columns supporting every door lost themselves in echoes above her. A coat of arms carved on the entrance to the great hall just ahead was forty feet above the floor. Reece murmured that Corina was in the gold drawing room. Sarah followed him as he drifted through the maze of rooms. She hoped to be away in half an hour.

When Sarah reached the gold drawing room, Corina was just sitting down to a late breakfast in front of the huge French doors that looked out over the terrace and the formal gardens. Reece announced her and melted away. Corina was more radiant than Sarah had ever seen her. Her eyes snapped and her countenance glowed. That was a dangerous sign. The green sarsanet morning dress she wore reminded Sarah of a tart apple. As Sarah approached, Corina's countenance darkened. She motioned Sarah to the table. Corina continued with the last bite of her chilled salmon in champagne cream sauce. She pushed her plate away and glowered at her friend.

"How dare you conceal the fact that Julien Davinoff drove you home to Bath!"

"I . . . I did not conceal it," Sarah sputtered. "I haven't had a chance to mention it." How had Corina discovered her?

"In answer to your unspoken question, Kelston saw you together on his way to Jackson's. Davinoff played most of the night, then ordered his curricle and left town again," Corina accused.

Sarah chewed her lip. She would not willingly have told her friend about her drive with Davinoff, given Corina's strange preoccupation.

"You little traitor!" the blonde raged, misinterpreting Sarah's regretful look. "You contrived to captivate him for an entire afternoon, before he could ever see me again!"

"Corina, you mistake," Sarah soothed. "I did not want to go with him. But the stage was horrid. Arguing with Davinoff about Clershing all the way to Bath was simply less horrid."

"You argued with him?"

"When we weren't freezing each other with silence."

"Is Clershing all you talked about?" Corina was still suspicious.

"We talked about the stones at Avebury and Roman roads." Sarah braced for her friend's anger, but Corina snorted a laugh.

"Only you would bore on about such nonsense with a man like Davinoff." She smiled in satisfaction. "Hardly auspicious, Sarah. Here is a man finally worth having, and you don't even make a push to acquire him." Corina mused, "I wonder why."

"Corina, you don't own men, as you do horses."

"Oh, but you do, Sarah." Corina smirked. "You talk about history with a man who is physical, capable of passion beyond the ordinary. Couldn't you see that? In an instant, I knew."

"I am not like you," Sarah almost whispered. She both wished it true and dreaded that it was.

Corina leaned forward. "But you are," she breathed. "Somewhere down inside you. You can't hide from me. Can you forget that I was *there* in Sienna? You just won't admit it."

Sarah stood, her napkin pressed to her mouth, and watched the gray billows of rain flap over the garden. "I do not speak of that time, Corina."

"All right, Sarah." She could hear the smile in her friend's voice. "It is safe to sit down. I believe that meeting Davinoff was accidental."

Sarah turned, memories threatening to flood over her. She pushed against the door in her mind to shut it tight against the streaming, glowing, remembered light of Tuscany.

"Sit down," Corina repeated.

Sarah sat and took the slices of Seville orange Corina served her. The fruit was tart, each section perfect and glistening with juice. The door closed at last. Sarah sighed.

"Now, let us talk about what to do with my Mr. Davinoff," Corina was saying. "He will be back. When he comes, we must entertain him, mustn't we? I will meet him at the Assembly Rooms, of course. And one could expect to see him in the Pump Room. But we need something more exciting." Corina got up to pace. "He must hunt. I look well on horseback."

"Will he come?" Sarah frowned in doubt. "Bath society seems cramped for such a man."

"Silly girl! He can find me only here. He will come."

Sarah swallowed her dismay at this single-mindedness and tried to focus on her own mission. "Corina, I must go. I am on my way up to Clershing to speak with my agent."

"To Clershing?" Corina asked sharply. "Next to the property Davinoff owns?"

Sarah nodded. Did all roads lead to talk of Davinoff? But Corina had sniffed a new scent.

"That is why he isn't beating down my door," she mused. "I'll wager he has gone up to finish his business there!" The blond woman rose and threw her napkin to the floor. "I'm coming with you."

"What?" Sarah asked, stunned. "But, Corina, you aren't packed and I need to start now."

"Nonsense, I can pack in a moment." Corina dismissed her objections out of hand. "Reece, tell Pembly to bring round the landaulet immediately."

But the packing took time. Corina's trunk had to be brought down and clothing chosen. It was half past one by the time the carriage crunched off through the gravel of the front drive, with Pembly in the driving seat.

Corina chattered like a schoolgirl during the first part of the journey, but she could not sustain her manic mood. After a while, she lapsed into the fidgets and finally into silence, which was just as well since Sarah found her restless energy tiring.

Left to herself, however, Sarah could find no thoughts that brought her peace. The prospect of penury saturated her mind. She held to the slender thread of hope offered by her impending visit with Mr. Wells. When she tried to move her mind away from that unhappy subject, the memories of her continental tour with Corina threatened to leap up and overwhelm her.

Sienna. She had been eighteen. She forced her mind to skitter over that time to the aftermath. Her father never knew why she'd come home early with a hired chaperone instead of with Corina and Corina's Aunt Letty. Sarah spent that time after the trip feeling small and frightened, sure that her lifelong friendship with Corina was over, unsure who she was.

She didn't see Corina for quite some time. She heard that her friend's mother had finally left her father. There were rumors of his strange proclivities, not unlike those that swirled around his daughter even now. Only Sarah knew how true these rumors were. Apparently, the man's taste for England paled. He left for the Far East, leaving his wealthy daughter in the charge of Aunt Letty, who was certainly no match for her. Corina toured again in the spring and came home to marry her lieutenant, Charles Nandalay. Sarah was not invited to the wedding.

Corina wore black for her simple, beautiful husband for less than three months after she got word that he had been killed at Salamanca. She had probably begun regretting her marriage as soon as she had captured her pretty pride of the regiment. Being a widow was so much more convenient, as Corina explained later. She could do anything, everything, with no need of chaperones. She did do everything, according to some.

So Corina was a widow and Sarah almost upon the shelf, except perhaps for George's expectations, when they'd met again by accident as guests at a dinner party. Sarah smiled when she saw her onetime friend. Corina was holding court, as always, and the scene was so familiar. Perhaps there was nostalgia in that smile. Corina glanced up as she transferred attention from one admirer to another and saw Sarah standing there, smiling. Corina smiled, too.

Sarah knew why Corina forgave her. The most brilliant stone still needs a setting. Sarah was always very clear about who was the setting and who the jewel. Why she had a need to forgive Corina was more difficult. These days, Corina's usual demeanor toward Sarah was one of amused deference. And Corina never spoke of Sienna. Why now? Sarah had some confused idea that it had to do with Davinoff. She imagined his dark hair and fair skin bathed in Tuscan sunlight. Was that how Corina saw him? She must never suspect Sarah of feeling the shock of his touch. Davinoff made them both think of Sienna. Sarah resolved not to feel the shock again.

When they arrived in Littledon-on-Severn, a mile or two from Clershing, it was growing dark. Corina was shocked that Sarah intended to stay at the Tongs and Hammer. Sarah explained that everything was in dust covers at the Dower House. She should not need to remind Corina that she kept no servants on call, but Corina purposely forgot facts she found inconvenient. Anyway, Corina was preoccupied just now with other things. Other things named Davinoff.

The next morning, Sarah rose early to go see Mr. Wells. She contemplated the meeting with some trepidation. The knowledge that the man had been acting for her nemesis ruined her trust. Still, he might be able to tell her something about the deed, or about Davinoff and his hideous plans. Sarah was surprised to see Corina making a hearty breakfast in their parlor.

"Sarah, my love!" Corina greeted her with excitement blazing from her blue eyes as she dove into a plate of eggs and grilled mushrooms. "Do sit down and eat. I have been thinking of all sorts of ways that we might wangle an invitation to Thornbury Abbey."

Sarah sat on Corina's left and reached for the coffee. "What are you talking about?"

"You turn your ankle, just near to Thornbury Abbey, and I go up and get assistance, quite heroically, by the way, and then we all sit down to nuncheon!"

Sarah sighed. "I hate to spoil your fiction, but Thornbury Abbey is not a great house with butlers and footmen and maids. It is a ruin, plain and simple. No one lives there."

"What?" Corina was too startled to pout. "But it belongs to Davinoff, doesn't it?"

"Apparently," Sarah said, buttering toast. "But he must be staying at an inn hereabouts."

Corina's face fell. She shoved away her plate. "I can't go searching every inn to see where he is staying," she protested.

"Do as you like. I am going over this morning to see my agent, Mr. Wells."

Corina jumped up and began to pace the room. "Why didn't you tell me this before, Sarah? It could take days to find where he is staying. While I kick my heels here, I may miss him in

Bath." She whirled decisively on her friend. "I shall go back to Bath immediately. There is no use in staying here if I have to scour the countryside."

Sarah put down her coffee cup in alarm. "But I must see Mr. Wells this morning at least."

"Rubbish," Corina snorted. "Davinoff is probably already in Bath. We start immediately."

"Wait," Sarah protested, thinking quickly. She did not want to be stranded by Corina twice in one week. "Mr. Wells has been acting for Davinoff. He will know where he is staying."

Corina was halfway out the door when she turned.

"It is certainly worth finding out," Sarah said, enticing.

"We'll see this Wells person," Corina announced. Then she was out the door to order Pembly to bring around the carriage, leaving Sarah to gulp her coffee in haste.

The Wellses' house sat down a long lane that ran between hedgerows covering the slate fences that divided the Clershing fields. The two-storied cottage was whitewashed, its thatch neatly tied and chrysanthemums blooming in the dooryard. Sarah worried about how to be private with Josiah. She did not want her friend to know about her difficulties, and she could hardly expect confidences from Mr. Wells with Corina champing at the bit to question him.

Sarah's knock at the iron-strapped door of the cottage was answered by Mrs. Wells, an ample, ruddy woman who wiped her hands on her apron. "Well, well, Your Ladyships, this is a surprise. Come in, come in," she clucked as she ushered them into the tidy sitting room. "Josiah," she called, "you have visitors." Then to Sarah and Corina, "Let me get you ladies some cider."

Sarah thanked Mrs. Wells, and glared at Corina when she rolled her eyes. "You wanted to come, Corina. Now you can be polite," she admonished in a whisper.

"Cider? Please." Corina threw herself into a rocking chair and held her hand to a brow.

Mr. Wells strode into the room. "Yer Ladyship, what brings you here?" He was a tall man with a graying beard and piercing eyes. He looked the way a steward should look, Sarah thought, sharp and lean. Excellent, if he was with her, formidable if he had aligned himself with Davinoff.

"Mr. Josiah Wells, let me present my friend, Mrs. Nandalay." Corina glared at Sarah impatiently as Mr. Wells nodded his head in greeting. "I wanted to review the detail of the crop disposition with you. Do you have the time?" Sarah could practically hear Corina groaning.

"I always have time for yer affairs, Yer Ladyship. Were ye wantin' me to get out the ledgers?" He looked so serious that Corina eloped hastily to the kitchen for cider.

"My missus baked some apple tarts just fresh too, miss," Mr. Wells called after her. "The smell has been tormentin' me." He turned back to Sarah. "Was there somethin' ye missed the *last* time ye went over the ledgers with a tooth comb, Yer Ladyship?" he asked. Only a gleam in his eye indicated that he had divined her ruse, and acted as accomplice to obtaining some privacy.

"Of course not, Mr. Wells." Sarah smiled ruefully. Her agent sat in the rocker vacated by Corina, folded his hands calmly in his lap, and waited for her to tell him her purpose. She took a breath and decided to be blunt. "Mr. Wells, I wondered if you had heard that my neighbor is contesting my ownership of Clershing?" She wanted to judge his reaction. She was on the alert for nervous gestures and eyes that could not meet hers.

His eyes widened in shock, then narrowed, but they never left her face. "Never say that Davinoff is challenging the split."

He knew, at least, about the history of the place. "So Mr. Lestrom's son tells me."

"Aye," Wells murmured softly. "I never woulda thought . . ."

"Neither would I, Mr. Wells. Apparently, however, it is quite true."

"Show the deed and there's an end to it, Yer Ladyship," Wells told her resolutely.

"Ah, but there is the problem. The deed cannot be found." At her words, the man's eyes widened again, almost imperceptibly. She saw him purse his lips, considering.

"Well, that's a hard thing, certain," he said after a minute. "Were ye thinking that it might be at the Dower House, or burned in the fire?"

"We never stored anything of value in the Dower House, unless you know something I don't," Sarah said. "What do you think, Mr. Wells?"

He pressed his lips together. "Can't say as I like to tell you this, Yer Ladyship," he said, in his deliberate way. "But it seems mighty peculiar that Lestrom don't have the deed and he ain't noticed it all these years if it was burned in the fire."

Sarah drew her brows together. "I think Davinoff took it."

"Mayhaps. Don't Lestrom usually keep valuable papers locked up? Shouldn't think he'd be able to get at it without help."

"But I have known Mr. Lestrom all my life!" Sarah protested the unspoken accusation.

Wells's eyes were watchful. "I knowed him all my life, too, mind you. But Silas didn't get to be the sharpest solicitor west of London by not knowin' where his client's deeds were."

Was he accusing Mr. Lestrom or not? "He seemed very old when I saw him in London," she mentioned. "What exactly are you saying?"

Wells did not answer directly. "I expect ye'll be wantin' company when you go to straighten this out with Lestrom or with Davinoff. I'll tell my rib to pack my bags."

Sarah was truly touched by his concern. "Thank you for your kind offer of help, Mr. Wells. But I can manage. There's nowhere else the deed could be, is there?"

He stroked his beard. "Not that I can see."

Sarah sighed. There was one more question. "How is it that you act for Davinoff?"

"As to that, my father was his agent before me," Wells responded, with gruff embarrassment. "Or his father's agent, at any rate. I been gettin' a draft on banks from right around the world every quarter day, just to keep an eye on the place, keep people from hauling off the stones, see it ain't used by the gentlemen. Then he appears, suddenlike, a few weeks ago. I must say, if I'd a seen him, I woulda refused them drafts. He's a hard man. I never knew he meant to challenge your right to Clershing," Wells ended with brows raised in apology.

Sarah could not help but believe him. "I wonder what brings him here now."

"He asked me to take charge o' payin' the workers he's bringing in from some furrin' country to dig up the abbey. I told him you were thinking of doing the same down at those ruins on the corner of Clershing. He looks startledlike for a minute; then those eyes of his go dead black. He says that he can't allow that, and he stalks off."

"He was most interested in my plans for excavating the villa the one time we spoke of it," Sarah thought aloud. "What is he doing up at the abbey?"

"Reinforcin' the structure, I would guess, since they been haulin' timbers for a week."

"He can't hope to make it habitable," she puzzled. "It is long past that."

Wells pursed his lips and stroked his beard. "Can't ask the workers; they don't none of 'em speak English. Should I refuse to act for him?"

"No," Sarah answered after a moment. "It will be as well that someone I trust is close to him and can inform me of his intentions." She glanced up at Mr. Wells, a question in her eyes.

"Oh, aye, I'll keep an eye on him fer ye, Yer Ladyship. Though I'll lay odds as he's a man used to gettin' his way, an' what you or I say be damned."

"I may not be able to stop him from doing as he pleases, but knowing you are on the watch will comfort me." She smiled. "Is he staying hereabouts? He left Bath last night."

"No." Wells shook his head. "The last letter I had from him said he won't return until next week. When he comes back, I'll find out what he's up to with Clershing."

Corina came out of the kitchen. "I say, Wells," she began. But Sarah took her arm.

"It's time to go, Corina," she said smoothly. "I have all the information there is to have."

"Really, Sarah," Corina sputtered. "I . . ."

Sarah was already drawing her out the door. "Thank you, Mr. Wells, for all your help."

"You remember, Yer Ladyship, that I'd be right glad to come to Bath at a minute's notice to help you finish your business." Wells followed them out into the dooryard.

At the gate, Corina took her arm back forcibly and glared at

Sarah. But her attention was diverted by something behind her friend. "Whatever is that?" she asked slowly.

Sarah turned and saw the remains of Thornbury Abbey on its cliff overlooking the Severn, outlined against a blue October sky strung with fast-moving clouds. "That is Thornbury Abbey," she murmured. Corina seemed frozen, staring up at the imposing ruin. Sarah took her arm again and turned her resolutely toward the carriage where Pembly waited to hand her in.

"Good-bye, Mr. Wells," Sarah called back. "And thank your wife for her hospitality."

As the carriage moved off, the spell that held Corina broke and she came to life. "Well, where is he staying? You must have some news, Sarah, since you would not let me say a word."

"He told Wells he would be in London."

"Wells was lying to you," Corina sputtered. "He is about here somewhere, I know it."

"I am ready to go back to Bath if you are." Wells had started Sarah thinking in new lines. Who could have helped Davinoff do the deed? And what could Davinoff be doing at the abbey?

"I'm not going back to Bath just yet," Corina declared. She turned to gaze back at the dilapidated abbey. "I suggest we make an expedition. I would most like to explore some ruins."

Sarah's brows creased. "You can't go touring private property." At least not Davinoff's.

"He doesn't live there. Besides, he is in London according to you."

"I just don't think it is right to go snooping around other people's land, Corina."

"Sarah." Her friend stared at her. "Can you sit here and tell me you are not curious?"

Sarah sighed. "Curiosity is not the point."

"I knew it," Corina crowed. "You are much too honest."

Sarah nibbled her lip. Corina was right. She wanted to know what Davinoff was doing up there. "Very well, Corina. We can arrange for a couple of hacks from the landlord. The road to the abbey has been impassable to carriages for years."

Chapter Five

As they began the steep climb toward the abbey, Sarah had to admit that the day was beautiful. The air was crisp but not punishing, and the sky between the clouds was that shade of vibrant blue peculiar to autumn. It was the kind of day that quickened one's blood with promised hardships and made one want to store up nuts for winter like a squirrel. Sarah felt her pulse race. Corina, too, seemed tense with suppressed excitement.

A rise concealed the abbey, so it seemed to burst upon them when they reached the top of the rutted track. It rose against the sky, its towers streaming clouds across the flat green expanse of the promontory. Up close the devastation was much clearer. The entire east section, away from the cliff edge, consisted merely of walls in various states of disrepair, with grass growing like an unkempt lawn within. The part that faced the mouth of the Severn was in slightly better condition, with one tower at least intact. In the brisk morning air the place seemed melancholy, as ruins will when they have seen the centuries pass them by. A large stack of fat timbers, smelling of new wood, lay to the side of the track. Sarah and Corina wandered over the grassy expanse that must once have been feasting halls and prayer rooms. The tallest standing walls had huge empty Gothic arches that looked to the west. In several places winding stone staircases spiraled up to empty air. It was a place of promises broken. What could Davinoff be doing here? Sarah wondered. A ruse, no doubt, to explain his presence and cover his sinister plot to seize her lands. She could feel his presence. Her own brand of ghost, she thought, shuddering. She looked about to find Corina skipping away, laughing and twirling like a leaf in the wind.

"Sarah, come with me!" she called. "Don't stand there like a pillar of salt!"

Thus prodded, Sarah strode after her companion. She found her friend standing in the doorway of the tower that occupied a corner of the abbey. Now it had two stories only, with jagged walls and one room made dark by the broken timbered floor of the second story. Corina stood staring into the gloom. Sarah came and peered over her shoulder. In the center of the dirt floor, a huge stone, round and flat, had been lifted aside to reveal a stone staircase, winding down into the black bowels of the earth.

"Oh dear," was all Sarah could say.

"I wonder what is down there," Corina whispered.

"Don't you dare wonder that, Corina Nandalay!" Sarah knew exactly what was coming.

"How can we not?" Corina asked.

"I am not one bit tempted to go down that hole." Sarah put all her will into refusal.

Corina began her assault. "You should feel ashamed to let me have adventures all alone."

"I don't want you to go either," Sarah returned. "I am sure it's very dangerous."

"Nonsense, don't you think that every picnicker for miles around has gone down these very same steps a hundred times?" The blond girl put her hands on her hips. "Just for the thrill?"

"What if that stone were recently opened? What if no one has been down there since the 1500s?" Of course, if it was recently opened, who lifted the stone aside? Davinoff's foreign workers? Not without a block and tackle. She looked around in vain for some such apparatus.

"Don't be silly. Who could move that stone?" Corina huffed. "It's much too heavy. Depend upon it, this stone has been laid here since the monks abandoned this abbey three centuries ago and fled with all their treasures." As she uttered the word *treasure*, Corina's eyes grew brighter. "Who knows, some might still be there."

"Corina." Sarah made a last stand. "What is likely down there are moldering crypts." Such a horrifying image *must* discourage her intrepid companion. It certainly discouraged Sarah. Her desire to find out what Davinoff was doing here evaporated if the answer were in those crypts.

Corina was not discouraged. "Delicious." Sarah could see her shiver. "That settles it!" The blonde gathered her skirts and placed one russet kid boot upon the top stair.

"It's dark," Sarah cried after her disappearing form. "You won't be able to see anything."

"Then I shall stand and see nothing. Are you coming?" The girl's voice was only an echo.

"Corina, why do I let you persuade me?" Sarah asked, talking to herself rather than to her friend as she peered into the abyss. "I am past this kind of foolishness." She started down. The stairs were wet with moisture and the walls clammy to the touch. She thought briefly about rats and wished she hadn't. Into the darkness she circled. "Corina?" she called, her voice small.

"Down here," came the echoing reply.

"What can you see?" Sarah asked. The light above her dimmed as the stairs curved. Though her eyes began to acclimate to the darkness, she almost bumped into Corina. The stairs came abruptly to a halt. Her friend stood stock-still. In the faint light from the stairwell, Sarah got a sense of immensity. The stone floor stretched away into darkness. The round arches and columns with ornate capitals said clearly that this was the Romanesque crypt of the original abbey, burned above ground three centuries before. It smelled of damp and mold and other smells she could not name. "Corina?" she whispered. Corina did not answer. Sarah looked past her friend to see what had frozen her. Far away across the crypt, a torch burned in a holder.

"My goodness, someone *has* been down here!" Sarah gasped.

"Or is here still," Corina whispered in return.

Sarah shuddered. Was it the workers? "Do let us go, then."

Corina turned to look at her. "Why would we do that?"

"Because we have no idea who might be here or why, and that is a dangerous situation for two women alone," Sarah declared. Perhaps it wasn't the workmen who had left the torch. Perhaps it was someone or something worse. "Let us get back up these stairs."

But the other young woman was already moving off toward the flickering light that seemed so distant.

"Corina!" Sarah whispered fiercely, knowing she would receive no response except her friend's echoing footsteps on the stone floor. They sounded unnaturally loud. Corina was alerting anyone who might be near to their presence. Sarah glanced back at the comforting light cascading down the stairway, but she could not leave Corina alone here. She hurried off after her friend, a shadow among shadows in the echoing darkness.

"I knew you would come," her friend whispered as Sarah scurried up beside her. At least she was whispering, Sarah thought. Even Corina dared not hear the echo of her voice.

They walked on between the huge round arches. As they approached the torch, Sarah realized it must be set upon a column close to the far wall, for it illumined the ancient stone biers and caskets that lined the crypt, stretching away into the dimness. Ornately carved and inlaid, they looked small, as ancient coffins always did. Yet their stone made them vessels to defend against eternity, even if now they were dust-covered and musty. Spiders had practiced their art through the centuries. The wrecks of their webs still drifted from corners and carvings.

Sarah clung to Corina's arm and Corina clung back for all her bravado. Sarah's shocked senses finally rested on one casket, slightly to their left, whose lid was definitely pushed askew.

"You were right, Sarah," Corina whispered. "Moldering crypts."

"Why a torch?" Sarah asked in a tiny voice. There was no sign of workmen.

"I was thinking the same thing." Corina turned and reached for it. She held the torch, flickering, above her head. To Sarah's horror, she moved purposefully toward the casket with the opened lid. Sarah did not follow, but put her hand to her throat as the circle of light descended upon the stone coffin.

Corina stood beside the sarcophagus, and after a moment, peered inside. Sarah could not breathe or move. To her shock, her friend reached into the coffin's dark recesses, and pulled out a greenish, iridescent chalice, perfectly formed. For a long moment, Corina and Sarah locked their eyes. Then Sarah darted forward as she recognized the glass.

"What is this?" she cried, echoes forgotten. Corina handed her the chalice and reached in to produce several coins. They gleamed in the light of the torch as they fell through Corina's fingers to the floor. Sarah put down her precious goblet gently and bent to take a coin between thumb and forefinger and hold it to the light. The figure of a man adorned one side, with a prominent nose and a laurel wreath around his head. The coin looked shiny new. Sarah leaned over the gaping stone, and felt in the coffin for more treasures. She pulled out a long hairpin, set with rubies or perhaps garnets. Corina snatched up a large aquamarine stone, laughing.

"Sarah, we *have* found the buried treasure!" she exulted.

"Actually," came a rumbling voice behind them, "those are my personal souvenirs."

In unison, the two women shrieked and turned, their booty slipping from nerveless hands.

He walked out of the shadows, into the sputtering light of the torch, his ebony cape swirling around him. His eyes were impossibly black, his face pale. Just as it had under a street lamp in London, time seemed to stop as Sarah was raked with those eyes. He had cast aside the intriguing conversationalism she had experienced at Avebury. All that was left was the devil incarnate, angry and powerful.

Sarah took a wrenching breath and realized that Corina, too, was speechless beside her. They clutched each other as they would life preservers on a sinking ship. Some part of her wondered that one or both of them had not fainted away to meet such a man in such a place. Just as she felt Corina's knees go weak beside her, the torch slipped from her friend's limp fingers. Sarah put her arm around Corina's waist to support her. The abbey's owner just stood there, looking at them, waiting.

Was he real? Her nemesis confronted her once again, and now he held all the cards. She had to say something. Something that would get them out of here.

"We are sorry to disturb you, Mr. Davinoff," she finally managed. "You gave us a start."

To her surprise, he smiled. "I expect so." The voice crashed over her. "Let me escort you out." He reached forward and scooped the torch from the floor where it lay sputtering and motioned toward the staircase, so dim and far away. Sarah pushed Corina forward and hurried across the echoing floor. Fear sped down her spine when she heard the footsteps in their wake. By the time they reached the stairway, panic had set in and she was practically running. She pulled Corina up the stairs into the tower, half expecting the apparition behind them to melt away once they were safely out of the catacombs.

She and Corina reached the top, panting, and collapsed against the wall of the abbey tower. As Sarah looked back toward the stairway, she shuddered to see the dark man winding up after them. Fear clutched at her as he came to stand over them in the gloom. Not even the dusty motes of sunshine leaking into the tower through the ruined window embrasures touched the black of his cape, his boots, or those eyes.

"What are you doing here, if I may ask?" His face was impassive.

Sarah found her voice. "We came on a walk and saw the stairway. We didn't mean to trespass." But that was exactly what they had meant to do.

"I seem to find my belongings ransacked whenever you are in the vicinity," he said. If he had been amused by their fear, he was not amused now. His voice had taken on a positively threatening tone. "Would you like to confess to any other trespasses?" He had found evidence of his rifled belongings in the trunk; she could see it in his eyes. She was so confused by fear and shame and outrage, she hardly knew how to react.

"There is a treasure down there," Corina interrupted as her senses returned.

"Only some old things that came down to me from other years. Now, I would appreciate it if you would remove yourself from my property," he finished with contempt.

"As you wish, Mr. Davinoff. But those *are* treasures." What was he doing with such priceless objects? Sarah's rush of curiosity surprised even herself. She remembered the Viking coins in his trunk. "I have never seen a finer example of first-century Roman glass."

He examined her. "Yes. You would know, wouldn't you?"

Sarah looked up into this impossible man's face and felt her fear mingle with something else. Curiosity, perhaps, about what kind of man kept Roman treasures in stone coffins. Beside her, Corina staggered to her feet. Who knew what the woman might say if she remembered her preoccupation! "I am very sorry we have disturbed you, Mr. Davinoff. Corina!" She almost shook her friend. "We must go now."

"Yes," Davinoff agreed. "I commend you for not fainting. I suspect I surprised you."

"I should think you did." Sarah glanced up at him and her anger flared. "I expect you quite enjoyed it, too. Never fear, we are leaving immediately." Corina shook her head.

Davinoff nodded, his eyes hooded. "Discretion is the better part of valor. But don't think you shall escape me. I come to Bath directly. I believe you said I should deal with your solicitors." His eyes bored into her, a smile touching his lips. "You will end by seeing things my way in a day or two."

Just before the magistrate would sit. He was counting on her to give in. And that was just what she would have to do, damn him. Sarah found her courage revived by his obvious contempt for her. "Perhaps I shall let the magistrate settle the matter after all," she threatened, wanting more than anything to wipe away that small smile.

His expression grew puzzled. "The magistrate has nothing to say to the price agreed for land. It is painful to let go, I know, but soon it will be over, and you will be the better for it."

That was the outside of enough. "I will be the better for being left destitute?" she whispered fiercely. To her satisfaction, his eyes narrowed.

Finally he murmured, "I offered fair value for your land, Lady Clevancy."

Sarah practically laughed, she was so angry. "You can't dissemble with me, Davinoff. If taking my land by force and leaving me with nothing is what you call 'fair value,' then you live in a different world than I."

"Sarah!" Corina protested.

Davinoff's eyes grew distant. His thoughts seemed far away.

"You threaten me," Sarah went on, riding her emotions, "because you think a woman alone can be no match for you, and you would use any base means to deprive me of my heritage and my livelihood and all my dreams. Well, I tell you, Mr. Davinoff, that I will excavate my Roman villa, and one day I will rebuild Clershing Manor, too." Empty vows, all. Davinoff observed her outburst with an expression of interest she found insupportable. She could only draw Corina away. They hurried toward the horses munching serenely on the grass of the promontory. Sarah refused to look back as they mounted, though she felt his eyes upon her.

On the ride back to the Tongs and Hammer, Corina came to life. "Sarah, did you see him? He was there," she said breathlessly.

"Of course I saw him, Corina," Sarah snapped. "How could I not when he popped out so disagreeably down in those crypts? I almost began to believe in ghosts."

"Ghosts should all look like that," Corina announced.

"He wanted to frighten us." Sarah dwelt upon her anger rather than her fear.

"I wasn't frightened," her friend declared.

Sarah raised her brows. "Of course you weren't. You just have a history of weak knees."

"Don't be difficult. You cannot tell me you don't think he was quite amazing."

"I think . . ." Sarah paused, reliving the last few minutes in her mind. "I think that I would rather we were not caught trespassing. It was quite our own fault we were surprised." She did not want Corina to know how frightened she had been.

But Corina was not to be distracted. "Let us go back, Sarah. I didn't get a proper chance to speak to him." She pulled her horse's head around. "And you! You were so rude!"

"Corina, leave it be." Sarah put on her most damping tone. "He did not take kindly to our presence on his property. I shouldn't wonder if he was engaged in smuggling antiquities."

Corina only smiled. "Perhaps he is. . . ." Sarah could see her turning over the romantic possibilities of being in love with an outlaw.

"Besides, you heard him," Sarah tried again. "He is coming to Bath directly. You had best meet him there, where you can shine. Perhaps he will have forgotten by then that not only did you trespass, but you fainted at the sight of him."

Corina considered this and seemed to waver. "I did not appear in the best light, perhaps."

"Don't feel alone." Sarah sighed. Corina allowed her horse to mope along beside Sarah's while Sarah gazed at the October trees, unseeing. Davinoff would push her off Clershing. If he had felt kindly disposed to her at Avebury, that feeling was burned away by the impression that she was searching all his properties. Which was exactly what she was doing. Unsuccessfully, she had to add. In spite of her outburst, she was hardly a worthy adversary for a man like Davinoff. Sarah felt herself sliding downhill, toward what she did not know.

Her depressing reverie evaporated when Corina cried with animation, "I shall captivate him at Chambroke. A select party of the best people. You'll help me choose. Hunting, and gaming, and everything capped by a masquerade ball. What do you think, Sarah?"

Sarah shook her head in disbelief. "I think you are losing touch with reality, Corina. He did not look as though he were coming to Bath for entertainment."

Corina only smirked. "That is what he wanted you to think, silly Sarah."

"He looked fairly serious to me." Grimly serious, Sarah thought.

"Oh," Corina said airily. "He is most serious in his pursuit of me." She dug her heels into her horse's side and clattered off down the hill, leaving Sarah to frown after her.

The ride home for Sarah was frustrating at the least. Corina chattered on about her plans for Davinoff, her assessment of his interest in her seeming to grow wilder with each mile. No matter what Sarah said, her friend's belief that she had captured his attention—indeed, even his heart—was not shaken. As if a man like that had a heart. Sarah's only defense was to subside into silence.

Once home, she had to contend with Amelia's predictions of doom. There was a note from Rutherford Lestrom asking her to come round to the office in Bath at her earliest convenience. She crumpled it and threw it in the study fire. It was only when she was locked safely in her room that she could try to calm her thoughts.

She began to review the facts newly come to light. Was Davinoff stealing antiquities and storing them in the crypt of the abbey? She was willing to bet he wanted Clershing to excavate the Roman villa. But it didn't matter why. To stop him, she needed a deed. Davinoff was behind that missing article somehow. But how? Josiah Wells didn't believe that trustworthy old Mr. Lestrom had helped Davinoff to it any more than she did.

She was determined to review the facts one piece at a time. But, as Sarah stood in her nightdress and looked out over the chill street below through the bare branches of the plane trees, the truth washed over her. Young Rutherford Lestrom and Davinoff were in the plot together. Of course! That was why the scholars at the Rolls Chapel had not remembered the most remarkable man she had ever seen. It was young Lestrom who went to the Rolls Chapel and removed the Crown grant. What could be more forgettable than his light eyes and weak chin? And who better positioned than Rutherford Lestrom to make her original deed disappear?

She began to pace the room in excitement. It was all so clear! Davinoff must be paying dearly for the services of that traitor. To have betrayed one of his father's oldest clients!

Her pacing slowed. All this deduction changed nothing. The fact that young Lestrom was in it with Davinoff only made matters worse. It meant that Davinoff knew her straitened circumstances. It meant that a record of her deed would never be found. What proof could she present of her fine theories? Any accusations she could make were empty threats.

Sarah went back to the window and leaned against it. The cold of the glass pane seared through her nightdress. She held back the tears. There were only three days left until the magistrate sat. She had three days to give up her land, or . . . or what? What was there to do?

Sarah tried to find solace in her regular visit to the Bath hospital early the next morning with her friend Madame Gessande. She was assigned to help Dr. Parry apply his new theory of inducing withdrawal in drug addicts. The man believed that by giving them the drug, always less, over time he could reduce the effect of breaking the addiction. It was difficult to watch the anguished wretches begging, from where they were tied to their cots, to be given access to their demon. Dr. Parry's way might be better then the old method of locking them up until they died or were cured, but Sarah wasn't sure.

On the way home in Madame's giant barouche, the weak sun pushed through the rain and silvered the wet landscape with radiant light. Madame's friendship was a gift George had made unknowingly when he had encouraged Sarah to volunteer at the hospital. The woman had fled the Revolution in France years ago. Her speech retained only a flavor of the Continent and a penchant for French endearments, and while she was old, she had managed never to lose the gleam in her gray eyes or her ready laugh. The two women had begun at the hospital by rolling bandages and patting hands, but as the nurses had little more training than they, Sarah and Madame had quickly graduated to real usefulness. It was a difficult place, but it gave them a joint purpose. Now Sarah found the whole story of her suspicions spilling out to her friend.

"Sarah, I cannot let this happen. I will testify myself," Madame sputtered.

"Testify to what?" Sarah asked. "That you believe me? I have no proof."

"But you have friends, Sarah!" the woman protested. "And those friends are not without influence. If we told everyone what was happening, those two devils could not get away with it."

"You will not tell a soul, Madame!" Sarah exclaimed. "Can you imagine that I want my impending poverty bandied about? Do you think that would make the magistrate's decision any different in the end?" She got control of herself with difficulty. "No, if there is nothing to be done, I want to go away quietly, to some place where no one knows enough to pity me."

Madame grasped her hand and squeezed it. "We will think of something, *cherie*, I swear. This man Davinoff is a devil. And Corina, all she can talk about is how he is in her thrall. She has spread the word everywhere that he is coming to Bath to woo her. Is it true?"

"You know how she is. She sees what she wants and can't imagine not getting it." Sarah pulled at her side curls. Corina had no discretion. The whole town must have heard the story.

"You are in distress, *ma petite*," Madame announced. "Therefore, you will come to dinner." She raised her voice as Sarah began to protest. "*And* we will discuss how to prove this deed exists, even if we cannot find it. Besides," she added, "you need company tonight."

Sarah sighed. With that, she could not disagree. The stress and isolation of the past days had left her nerves raw. At least with Madame she did not have to dissemble.

It was a delicious dinner. But though they racked their brains until the candles sputtered, their endless round of schemes all came to nothing. Sarah trudged up the stairs to the house in Laura Place feeling more hopeless than ever.

Dressing for bed, Sarah realized that Rutherford Lestrom and Davinoff were about to get just what they wanted. She climbed into bed and blew out the candle, knowing she would not sleep. Dear Madame, offering to testify on her behalf. The testimony was useless, of course. Sarah sat up in bed with a jolt. But there was one whose testimony would be most valuable. Possibilities tumbled over each other and began to take a tangible form. Her plan was dangerous. But it might be her only hope. She had to try.

The next morning, she was about early. She wanted to be waiting for Rutherford Lestrom when he arrived at his office. She rehearsed her part as she strode over the wet leaves and slippery paving stones on her way to Monmouth Street. Her breathing was shallow with dread as she thought about what might happen here today. She considered going to Rutherford's father and rejected the idea. How could she go to a man she considered her friend and accuse his son? Especially with no proof. The son must give her proof. She had decided to push him into being her ally instead of Davinoff's. It involved an untruth, but desperate times and rogues required desperate, roguish measures. There were a dozen points where her scheme could break down. But what else was left to her?

With the smell of sausages wafting about, she asked for Lestrom, Jr. She took a long breath and exhaled slowly to relax her mind. The clerk showed her in to the office. She smiled what she hoped was her best as Lestrom the Younger bade her sit.

The knave seated himself on the great chair behind the desk as though it were a throne and looked at her with those light blue eyes. "Well, Lady Clevancy," he began unctuously, "I take it you found no record of the Crown grant?"

"No," Sarah replied in clipped tones. "You knew I would be unsuccessful, did you?"

"I suspected," he agreed smugly. "Have you thought about the need to settle this?"

Sarah let her voice sharpen. "You mean, just give Davinoff Clershing?"

Lestrom's smile was edgy. "In return for some small settlement, you sign an agreement not to contest the ownership."

"I don't think so, Mr. Lestrom. I believe I shall let it go to the courts."

"But you can't!" he blurted. His tone became cajoling. "This way, you might expect to get a little something for the future."

"I could never face myself if I did not do everything I could to keep what is mine by right," she said. "You see, there *was* a record of my deed at the Rolls Chapel." She saw him grow wary. "Oh, don't worry. The roll itself was gone." He blinked once and his smile relaxed a notch. "I thought Davinoff had taken it, so I questioned the scholars most particularly. They couldn't remember who had been there looking for Patent Rolls of Charles the Second. Unlikely that they wouldn't remember Davinoff. Then I described you. They remembered you, Mr. Lestrom, quite clearly. They would say so to the magistrate."

He began to sputter denials. "Please refrain," she pressed. "Your only salvation is in testimony to Davinoff's crime. Save my land, and I will not prosecute you." She lifted her brows.

Lestrom's eyes were hard, but he began to fidget with his

pen. "The brute would surely do me physical harm if I bear witness against him."

"But if you fail to testify, you are proven guilty yourself. Gaols are very unpleasant, I hear." She let the threat hang in the air. "It is you who have little choice, Mr. Lestrom."

The rogue stared at her from narrowed eyes, then confessed. "I need this money. Half will go to a cent-percenter in London for my most pressing obligations. But I have others. My case is desperate. How else would I dare to become embroiled with a man like that?" Rutherford Lestrom ran his hands through his hair and pushed his chair back, standing. "I have hatched a thousand schemes to make my fortune, each more certain than the last. Yet, every time, something went wrong." He leaned over the back of the chair toward her, his face lit with intensity. Sarah began to be frightened. "It is not fair, I tell you! I wanted to show him that being an agent for other people's money was nothing, nothing." He laughed, and the laugh turned into a keening sound that sucked at her courage until he raised his wrist to his mouth to stifle it. "He has money, you know. He stacked it up inch by inch as he slaved his life away. That is not for me."

His father. The man meant his father. Sarah blurted, "If your father has money, go to him. He will pay your debts. Then you testify for me, and you are right with the world."

"I can't do that." The younger Lestrom glared about. "He can't know." As his voice crescendoed, he opened the desk drawer and pulled out an unwieldy pistol. He pointed the tiny black O of its mouth at Sarah, who froze in astonishment. "You stupid girl, this is all your fault!"

Good Lord, Sarah thought, *I have sorely misjudged the situation*. The muzzle of Lestrom's gun swung around the room. The man was so desperate anything might happen. "What do you expect to do with that, Mr. Lestrom?" she asked, her voice quaking only a little. "You must be sensible. Put it down. We are in a busy street, during a very busy morning in Bath." She strove to sound prosaic.

"You should not have come here threatening me," he almost shouted.

The door opened. Lestrom, Sr., stood there. His dour face

was the sweetest sight Sarah had ever seen. The man looked from her to his son; then his gaze fell to the gun. There was a moment when all was still. Then his expression changed from his usual distracted frown to surprise and pain. His son quieted. The gun dropped to his side as though it weighed a great deal. Lestrom, Jr.'s, light, ugly eyes turned opaque.

"Father," he said. The word carried such a weight of supplication and despair that Sarah was suddenly unsure she knew these two men at all.

"Put the gun on the desk, boy."

Sarah was shocked to see the son obey, all spark of savagery tamed.

"What did you expect to gain from this, Rutherford? Did you expect to shoot her here in my offices this morning?"

"I don't know. I only wanted to frighten her, I suppose." The son's voice was colorless.

"I am sure you were a blinding success in that." His bitterness spoke of other disappointments. Sarah wondered if the old man who was so kind to her was as forgiving of his son. The young man seemed to shrink before her eyes. There was an aching silence.

"Well, at least I know what happened to the deed," the old man said at last. Sarah swallowed. Lestrom's tired eyes moved from his son to her face. "Why did you not come to me?"

"I had no proof, not really." Lestrom, Jr., raised his head in dull surprise. "I wanted to force a confession from him," Sarah replied, anguished. "Then I would have come to you."

The father smiled, sad. "It is my fault it has come to this. I have known about the weakness in my son's character for a long time." The old man's brows raised and he pressed his lips together. He squared his shoulders. "Now to devise a way out of this mire. Rutherford can testify to the existence of the deed, and his perfidy. That should put Davinoff off."

"I . . . I can't testify against Davinoff!" the younger man stuttered. His father just stared at him. Finally Rutherford muttered, "He wasn't in on it. He offered fair value."

"What?" Sarah cried. "He never plotted to steal my land at all?"

Rutherford shook his head. Heedless of his son, Lestrom, Sr., came to stand in front of her and take her hand. "If you still trust me to handle your affairs, my dear, let me try to settle the matter with Davinoff. I shall send a note round to you as soon as I connect with him."

Sarah's eyes filled with tears. The excitement was over, and she had hurt Mr. Lestrom. Helpless in the face of his mourning for his son, she nodded and kissed him on the cheek.

"Now do go home, Lady Clevancy. And leave my son to me."

Sarah squeezed his hand and went to the door. As she opened it, she turned to see the two men staring at each other.

She closed the door quietly after her and crept down the creaky stairs.

All that afternoon, no word came from Lestrom. Sarah stayed at home fidgeting about the house, lighting upon no activity that could claim her attention for more than a few moments. Davinoff still had a valid claim if he cared to use it. She had no deed to prove him wrong. Could Rutherford Lestrom's testimony really save her land?

She received a card from the Countess Delmont inviting her to dinner on Monday evening. She always looked forward to the countess's dinners. But now, all she could think of was Clershing. She suffered all night without knowing the outcome of Lestrom's dealings with Davinoff. Early the next morning, a note arrived in her solicitor's spidery hand.

My dearest Lady Clevancy,

I saw Davinoff too late last Night to send Word. He seems to conduct his Business in the Evening Hours. However, I can report a successful Conclusion. He knows you do not have Proof of ownership. (I regret that Rutherford burned the deed and the Patent Roll.) However, he has agreed not to contest your Right to Clershing. His very generous Offer to buy the Property stands. The Price would leave you a rich Woman. I can never redeem my son's Actions or my own Blindness, but I shall spend my Life in the attempt.

Lestrom

P.S.: Rutherford left this morning for Calais. We decided

he may do rather better when he is out from under my thumb.

Tears of relief rolled down Sarah's cheeks. She rushed to share the news with Amelia. Clershing was free of Davinoff's shadow! Chaos had been held at bay! Sarah and her aunt celebrated by sharing a glass of ratafia before their nuncheon, while Sarah listened with great goodwill to Amelia's assertion that she had known they would win through all along.

When she went to see Lestrom, Sarah found that Davinoff had indeed renewed his offer, but would not force her hand. Sarah had never expected the dark man to practice restraint upon his desires. Why didn't he press his advantage? She would never give up Clershing! Too much of her, of her father, of her mother's death, was tied up there. When Mr. Lestrom promised to convey her sentiments to Davinoff, Sarah went disquietedly back to her life.

Over the next few days, she heard Corina was much in evidence in Bath. Sarah's friend was seen at the Assembly Rooms—dancing with Davinoff, according to Madame Gessande. Thornbury Abbey's owner had apparently procured the coveted voucher in a single day from Countess Delmont, one of the patronesses of the rooms. Sarah did not want to think how. She wondered if she should go to the countess's dinner, since there was no telling if her adversary would be there.

Sarah met Lady Varington in Milsom Street on Monday and had to endure a dithering recital of Corina's electric encounter with Davinoff at the Theater Royal on Friday. Corina had worn a dress cut at a V of scandalous depths. According to Lady Varington, Davinoff had come to Corina's box during the interval and, there, in full view of everyone, he had taken a white rose bud from a passing flower girl, carefully stripped it of all its thorns, and kissed it once, brushing it past his lips. He'd then placed it between Corina's breasts. Several women fainted.

To Sarah, it was just Corina on the hunt: pushing the boundaries, being outrageous, knowing her outrageousness would capture her prey. But Bath had never had a close look at the young woman in full flight. There had been rumors, Sarah knew; but never anything so public as this. Bath was too small for Corina. What would happen when she finally went too far? Of course, nothing would matter to Corina if she captured Davinoff—and Sarah had no doubt that her friend could do it. Corina was invincible, larger than life. She was probably just the woman for Davinoff. And he was just the man for her.

Which meant Davinoff would likely never go to a dinner hosted by Countess Delmont; those dinners were known for delightful conversation rather than magnetic young heiresses. Sarah decided she would go.

Chapter Six

When Sarah arrived by sedan chair at the Royal Crescent, she was fashionably late. She had first been to the countess's handsome house at number seventeen the Royal Crescent two summers ago when the countess included young people in her party to capture the interest of Percy Shelley. He'd been staying with William Godwin and his daughter Mary down in the abbey churchyard at the house of William Meyler. It was a perfect residence for Mr. Godwin, since Mr. Meyler ran a circulating library from his house. From that circumstance Sarah had seen them often. Mr. Shelley was proofreading *Childe Harold* and introduced Sarah to the works of Lord Byron.

The countess lived almost at the center of the graceful Crescent. The doors to each house were spaced equally between the Georgian columns of the grand facade to provide the symmetry John Wood the Younger had intended. But, inside the doors, the houses were of vastly different sizes. The countess had one of the grander residences. As Sarah entered the drawing room the owner descended and collected her into the room.

"So glad you've come, Lady Clevancy. When Upcott arrived alone I almost gave you up."

"I am surprised you have torn him away from his work, Countess."

"Confidentially, I invited Dr. Parry so they might talk about their experiments and leave you free, my dear." The countess was a ripe woman of forty-five, still handsome, a gardenia just curling at the edges. Word of the beauty regimens she used to preserve her natural endowments routinely sent everyone in search of cucumbers to lay over their eyes, or strawberries soaked in milk for their complexion. Tonight she wore off-white satin, cut very low across her creamy swelling bosom and adorned with ropes of pearls in varying lengths. An ethereal scarf was tied about her neck, trailing to the back. Charming, but not in the countess's usual decorous style.

She ushered Sarah into a room already full. Sarah saw immediately that she had misjudged Davinoff's taste in company. There he was, an elegant black blot upon the room, a glass of wine held negligently in one hand. He stood talking to George and Dr. Parry in the far corner, looking amused. Sarah caught her breath and looked away. Numbly she noted perhaps a dozen other people. There was Reverend Jay, whose sermons were so stirring, and Mr. Wilberforce, whose career as a politician was sacrificed to his fight against the slave trade. Mrs. Piozzi, Madame d'Arblay, and of course, Madame Gessande. She knew Mayor Palmer by sight, though she had never met him. The countess concocted her guest lists for their conversational possibilities, not for the social standing of the participants.

Would Davinoff have second thoughts about Clershing? Best to avoid him. But before Sarah could attach herself to Madame Gessande, George waved to her. She could not pretend she hadn't seen him. Dr. Parry and Davinoff both turned to look in her direction. After a moment's hesitation, she made her way to George's side.

"Sarah," he greeted her. "I was just explaining to Parry here and Davinoff about my new syringe. Tell them that even you were able to draw blood from that young fellow's arm with it last week," he commanded. Sarah felt Davinoff on her left like a magnet.

"Even I," Sarah agreed, smiling crookedly at Dr. Parry. "I plunged the needle into that poor man's vein and proved that even an idiot could use Dr. Upcott's invention."

"Nonsense, my dear, don't say it like that," Dr. Parry sputtered. He was a man in his late fifties, his gray hair receding over a shiny crown. He had a lucrative practice among invalids drawn to take Bath's waters and performed research on the side. He was George's principal rival for academic honors in the city. "You have a great deal of courage, more than most any other woman I know. Why, just look at what you have done with Clershing."

"That is not courage, but necessity," Sarah replied. She resolved to keep the conversation as far away from Clershing as she might. "I must admit I did not relish using that syringe."

"We can take blood without incisions," George said, his lips pursed around a self-satisfied smile. "I can inject blood or drugs at will, even if the patient is unconscious."

"One might use it to inject a nutrient solution to give failing patients strength," Dr. Parry mused. "I have been working on the formula for just such a solution."

"You have?" George asked, his lips tightening. "You must tell me about it."

Davinoff interrupted what was likely to be a protracted discourse. "Lady Clevancy, will you have champagne?" He gestured to a footman bearing a tray with two bottles and several glasses he was about to set upon the sideboard.

"Yes, yes, of course, my dear, you must have some champagne," Dr. Parry chimed in. "Whatever were we thinking?" Davinoff poured the wine into a fluted crystal glass as the doctor continued, "What I want to know, Lady Clevancy, is whether you could feel the pulse as the tube filled, even though it was a vein." Parry had published a monograph called *The Nature, Cause and Varieties of the Arterial Pulse* that put George out of sorts for a week.

"Yes, the pulse was quite pronounced. It pushed the plunger back out as the tube filled." She could feel Davinoff's eyes upon her.

"You could not use an artery. The injection site would leak," George hypothesized.

"And have you resolved the inconsistency in your results, Upcott?" Parry queried.

"Not precisely." This subject was obviously less satisfactory. George frowned.

Davinoff, to Sarah's surprise, now entered the conversation. "Ah, some patients get better and some die," he observed in a most languid manner. "And you cannot predict the difference."

"You seem to be familiar with the problem," Parry said, examining Davinoff.

"A sidelight only to my own interests." Which the dark man dismissed without elaborating. "I suggest you examine the blood you are inserting under a microscope."

"I am not an idiot, Davinoff. The blood is not contaminated," George declared.

"I believe you will find it is a matter of matching," Davinoff elaborated as he finished his wine and gestured to a servant for another glass.

"Matching?" George asked, incredulous. "Matching what?"

"Types of blood, of course." With a small smile, he took his full glass and Sarah's arm. Sarah could see George's brain working furiously. Davinoff turned and led her away.

"I say, what is it you mean?" Dr. Parry called.

"I'm sure Upcott can tell you," Davinoff threw over his shoulder. "That ought to hold them for a while," he said, leaning toward Sarah.

Behind her, the voices of the two medical men rose in earnest conversation. She did not look forward to a tête-à-tête with Davinoff but, though she meant not to encourage him, curiosity got the better of her. "How do you know so much about Dr. Upcott's researches?"

"Blood is a special interest of mine, though perhaps in a different way than for our fine physician friends." He guided her to a sideboard set with a huge epergne. "Your Mr. Upcott understands much, but not yet everything." Sarah looked at Davinoff in astonishment, but he gave her no time to remark. "We have a matter to clear between us," he began. Seeing Sarah's face, he added, "I do wish you would contrive not to grimace at me. I saw young Lestrom. My intent was to determine his role in my proposed transaction. As you must know, I discovered the worst. I expected to have to take a hand in removing him from the scene." Here Davinoff paused. Sarah looked at her hands, her head bowed with the weight of his gaze. "But I found you were before me." He cleared his throat. "I want to assure you, Lady Clevancy, that I had no intention of driving you off your land without recompense. Though why I should feel obliged to tell you so, I cannot, at the moment, divine."

Sarah pressed her lips together and shook her head without looking up. Yet the point that bothered her bubbled to the surface in spite of her best intentions. "You did brandish your deed as a threat. Silas Lestrom went on Tuesday before last to verify it. Was that not in support of Rutherford's efforts to strip me of all proof of ownership?"

After a moment, he said, "You make me out to be a dupe in this affair, a role I do not relish. If you must know, young Lestrom asked for proof of the boundary lines, in order to draw up the terms of the sale. I produced the deed and showed it to his father, at his request."

There was an awkward silence. Sarah searched his eyes as she wondered whether to believe him. The hard eyes and sharp planes of his face gave her no clue. He looked only put out.

"I hear from Silas Lestrom that you have refused my price."

Now it would come, she thought. Would he bring up the fact that she still did not have a deed? "Yes. It was most generous. But Clershing means too much to me."

"A fact brought home to me," he acknowledged. "I am not used to being refused."

She might as well get it out in the open. She mustered her courage. "You can still use your deed. I have no proof against it, thanks to Rutherford Lestrom."

"I have considered it." Sarah quailed. What had she done? "But I think not," he continued. "Apparently, I am still capable of surprising myself."

"But how do *I* know that?" Sarah cried, then lowered her voice as she saw heads turn in the drawing room. Madame Gessande and Mrs. Piozzi looked as though they were about to stage a rescue. "I cannot live all my life wondering when you will think better of your resolution."

"You are much less trusting than you look, Lady Clevancy," he observed. "Have you not heard the expression, a man's word is his bond?"

Sarah eyed him warily. This man's word?

"I see I have not yet reconciled you to my devotion to honor." He sipped his wine and seemed to cast about. "Perhaps I have not yet reconciled myself. What will suffice you? I swear by the Goddess Minerva, patroness of Aquae Sulis." He lifted a brow. "No?" Another sip of wine. His voice was low and serious this time. "Very well. I swear on the stones at Avebury by the gods of those who made them, that for a time not less than they have been standing, I will not use my deed against you or your heirs."

She looked up, shaken, directly into his impossible dark eyes. Anarchy promised to restore order to her life, and she believed. "Accepted," she murmured.

"Now that we have that settled," Anarchy pursued, in a lighter tone, "When do you plan to start excavating the Roman villa on your land?"

Normally this was a subject upon which she could hold forth eagerly. But with Davinoff, she was cautious. "I hope to begin digging shortly, now that my affairs have been settled." What she needed was the income from this year's crop of potatoes, but he need not know that.

"Oh, has the site already been catalogued?" Davinoff asked. "I had not realized you were so far along. Who did the mapping and all that tedious recording of features?"

Sarah was taken aback. "Why, no one. Do I need to go through all that?"

"One really can't just dig up the place," Davinoff apologized. "That is, if one is interested in authenticity and leaving a record for posterity."

Sarah fumed. To have him lecture her was more than she could bear, especially since his knowledge of antiquities was got by smuggling, no doubt.

"Lord Elgin could put you on to one of those archeologist fellows, I am sure. He is always digging up antiquities or cutting up friezes," Davinoff suggested.

More delay, thought Sarah, disappointed and angry at the man for being right. "Thank you for the advice," she returned in a voice as precise as she could muster. How soon could she get started on the cataloguing? First the money from the crops. Hire a scholar. She wanted nothing more, suddenly, than to show Davinoff she could excavate her villa and do it right.

Countess Delmont and Madame d'Arblay interrupted her train of thought. "How dare you monopolize our guest, Lady Clevancy?" the countess began. She turned coquettishly to add, "Mr. Davinoff, may I introduce one of our most illustrious citizens, Madame d'Arblay? You may know her best as the authoress of *Evelina*, Fanny Burney."

Madame d'Arblay was perhaps sixty and still a beauty. She had fine, sensitive eyes that saw right through one. She was said to keep a diary that laid open Bath society as efficiently as one of George's scalpels.

Davinoff bent over the author's hand. "I am charmed to meet so beautiful and so talented a woman."

Her bright eyes drank him up. "Nonsense. Do you always flatter old women?"

"Let us say I look through age," Davinoff replied.

"Nonsense yourself, Madame." Sarah laughed. "Mr. Davinoff is right. That portrait you have hanging over your mantel still shines out through every pore."

"Any portrait painted by one's brother is not objective," Madame d'Arblay said dismissively with a wave of her hand. "I like you, Davinoff. Get me some champagne." He allowed himself to be led away with surprising good grace.

"Well, what do you think, Sarah?" The countess watched Madame d'Arblay carry off her prize. There was a look of peculiar longing in her eyes.

"Of Davinoff? I am hardly the person to ask, Your Grace. I am afraid I wrangle with him within five minutes of saying 'how do you do.' "

"You did seem to be at cross-purposes," the Countess observed.

"It seems I can hardly be civil to him, or he to me. Oh," Sarah pleaded, "let us talk of anything but him. You know, I have wanted to compliment you upon your scarf."

The countess seemed to come to herself. "Is it too noticeable?" She fingered the item. "I was driven to distraction over how to hide these horrible insect bites." Pulling the scarf down on the left side, she revealed two red and swollen perforations.

Sarah was shocked. "Have you seen a doctor?"

"No, no. I do not want to see one." The woman pushed the scarf back into place.

"But they look inflamed," Sarah persisted.

The countess paused. "I may have a fever from them. I have had strange dreams."

"Nightmares?" Sarah asked.

"No. I wouldn't call them nightmares." The woman seemed remote. "Not nightmares."

"Promise me you will let Dr. Parry look at them."

The countess gathered herself and chuckled. "I am sure that is unnecessary. Now let us get this crowd into the dining room. Dinner, ladies and gentlemen," she called.

Davinoff surprised Sarah by appearing out of nowhere to take her arm. Other guests trailed after them. Sarah could hear whispers behind her linking Davinoff's name and her own. Why did he distinguish her? If she were not careful, she would cause as much talk as Corina.

The countess was famous for her dining room. It had a round table just for the purpose of easing conversation. The woman took her seat, glaring as Davinoff seated Sarah. Courses began appearing from the kitchen: veal shanks and poached salmon, buttered lobsters and pigeons with rosemary, potatoes of every kind. Just as Sarah felt exhausted by variety, trays streamed in again with stewed lamb and mussels, sweet yams and buttered peas, then syllabubs and trifles, fruits and cheese.

Through all coursed the conversation. What roles best fit Edmund Kean on the stage? Who the author of *Frankenstein* might be. Was it a social tract or a Gothic novel? They talked about the repeal of the suspension of Habeas Corpus, the death of Princess Charlotte, the prospects of the regent actually ascending to the throne. Madame d'Arblay had attended one of Mr. Coleridge's lectures. Mr. Wilberforce was scandalized that an act abolishing the practice of sending climbing boys up to clean chimneys had been defeated. Each subject blossomed and entwined with others until the evening's conversation grew into a living plant, pruned and shaped by the particular interests of these particular people on one particular night in early November.

Sarah stole surreptitious looks at Davinoff. She hardly knew what to think of him, since he had forsworn his role as persecutor. Once she believed he was a murderer. Now that belief seemed the product of a mind overwrought with stress. If he was not a criminal when it came to the matter of the deed, what was left of her other conjectures?

He said quite little, but his remarks were pithy, often a difficult question posed simply or a sarcastic remark that defined the problem of the argument. The countess was clearly entranced. So was Mrs. Piozzi. Men, too, were drawn to seek his approbation, hardly won.

After dinner, the men were given leave to retire for smoking and brandy for half an hour only. When they returned to the drawing room, Countess Delmont read selected verses from Byron's *Childe Harold*. She seated herself by the large window that looked out into the Crescent with her book. The others lounged about the room with glasses of brandy or coffee, and listened to the words roll from their hostess's fulsome lips.

She had chosen passages about Byron's type of hero, who so fascinated readers that the author had grown famous overnight. The hero was a wandering man with terrible secrets that isolated him from his fellows, a soul capable of ecstasy and keen suffering but with a strength and pride that gave him a strange power in spite of his fate.

> I stood among them, but not of them, in a shroud
> Of thoughts which were not their thoughts.

The countess's eyes stole from the page to look at Davinoff. She cared not for the reaction of the rest of her audience. Davinoff seemed lost in his wineglass, not even listening.

> What is the worst of woes that wait on age?
> What stamps the wrinkle deeper on the brow?
> To view each loved one blotted from life's page,
> And be alone on earth, as I am now.

"Bravo," Mr. Wilberforce cried when the countess was done, and had sunk her chin upon her breast in dramatic self-deprecation.

When the clamor subsided, the countess turned to Davinoff. "What do you think, sir?"

"Ask Lady Clevancy," Davinoff replied in clipped tones. "Young ladies are the most enthusiastic experts on Byron." He made "young lady" sound interchangeable with "criminal."

To Sarah's dismay, everyone in the room turned toward her. "His verse does have a certain clarity of conception." She hesitated. "He uses simple abstract language to sweep you along and make you see the panoramas and the large actions just as he felt them, with a peculiar kind of vehemence." How dare Davinoff corner her like this?

"But surely," Reverend Jay said, distaste obvious in the curve of his thin lips, "he does not have the intensity in his language of Mr. Wordsworth or Mr. Southey." Reverend Jay was well regarded for his good works, but Sarah had always found him narrow.

"That is part of his success," she returned. "And he is in good company, since Chaucer and Homer were much the same."

"But what did you think of the *subject*?" pleaded the countess.

"I would like to know the man," Mrs. Piozzi remarked, "if I were thirty years younger."

"I think he is an example of the declining morals of our youth," insisted the reverend.

"What do you say, Mr. Davinoff?" The countess turned limpid eyes on him.

"I think the pup does not know whereof he speaks," Davinoff said with such low intensity that everyone was startled into silence.

"He is much the same as that Shelley fellow." Reverend Jay continued his thought.

"You cannot say Shelley has no density of language," Sarah protested.

"I am speaking of morals. Why, Shelley was practically living with that Mary Godwin at Myler's last summer, in spite of her father being in the house with them. And he a married man."

"I expect you were relieved when he posted up to London to make her Mary Shelley," Madame Gessande said.

"Two weeks after his first wife drowned in the Serpentine?" Mayor Palmer objected.

"You cannot hold poets to the same standards of conduct as we mere mortals," the countess weighed in.

"Mr. Shelley seemed so idealistic with all his talk of pantisocracies and perfecting society," Sarah mused. "Mary told me he married his first wife because his ideas had shaken her faith in religion and he felt obligated to do so. That seems very moral. I believe that when he found himself in love with Mary, Mr. Shelley thought it would be dastardly to deny it."

"Come, Reverend," Madame Gessande asked. "Could a poet deny love?"

"Actually, Mayor Palmer, Mr. Shelley had quite a bit in common with you," Sarah said, smiling at the reaction she knew she would elicit. She was not disappointed.

"What, what is that?" The old man harrumphed in astonishment.

"With Mr. Wilberforce, too," Sarah added. "He believed men could shed their imperfections if one could find the perfect form for society. He planned a society based upon simplicity, living off the land and off of poetry."

"That kind of balderdash has nothing to do with me," the Mayor returned.

"I see what Lady Clevancy means, Palmer," Mr. Wilberforce interjected. "We are reformers, you and I. You improve society with your system of mail coaches just as I do with my fight against the slave trade. We, too, believe man can form a more perfect society."

"The way to improve mankind is to improve his knowledge," George stated. "When man knows for certain his place in the universe, his finer nature can emerge."

"Hear, hear," Dr. Parry agreed.

"Man knows his place through God." Reverend Jay's faith brooked no contradiction.

"Why are you looking so bemused, Davinoff?" the countess asked.

"I don't happen to think man can be improved." Davinoff sipped his brandy.

"You must believe man is redeemed in Christ," Reverend Jay exclaimed.

"I do not. And scientific knowledge only makes us more efficient. It will not change our moral deficiencies. We learn to make better guns, not to prevent war. We progress, then regress. Empires rise, empires fall in endless cycles. Misery and miserable acts remain constant."

"I agree with Davinoff," Madame Gessande chimed in.

"Madame?" Sarah queried in surprise.

"You forget, *petite*, I lived through the Revolution. I saw the hope of a new society rot from within because it was built upon Madame Guillotine's foundation. Then Napoleon's megalomania was followed by a return to monarchy. Davinoff's cycle exactly."

"But our philosophy has been refined over the ages . . ." George began.

" 'There is nothing so ridiculous but some philosopher has said it,' " Davinoff quoted. "As I am sure you recall, that was said in Rome before the birth of Christ. It was already true then."

"If you are going to quote Cicero," Mayor Palmer retorted, "you should acknowledge that his opinions were considered so dangerous to society that he was assassinated shortly thereafter."

"The cycle of progress and suppression. You prove my point," Davinoff agreed.

Sarah felt the need for a satisfying argument with Davinoff. He was maddening. But Madame d'Arblay cut off debate. "Well, our Mr. Davinoff is a cynic. And there is nothing to say to a cynic. So I will take my old bones home."

With that, the party broke up. Sarah was left with her retorts spinning unsaid. There was a bustle in the hall as carriages were called. Davinoff took his hat and cape, his cane and gloves, and was the first to swirl out the doors into the Crescent. A carriage already waited there. The bustle quieted. The guests, as one, peered past Davinoff. There could be no mistake. It was Corina's yellow landaulet. The butler was about to shut the door when the countess put her hand out and stopped its progress. No one noticed the frosty November air sweeping into the house.

Davinoff stepped calmly out from under the pediment as Corina opened the door and leaned out of the carriage. "I have come to rescue you from a deadly dull evening, Davinoff," she announced, smiling. She wore her ermine-trimmed blue pelisse that matched her eyes, and an enormous ermine muff rested in her lap. Her sparkle was perilous.

Davinoff stopped midway down the steps to the walk. He leaned on his cane and perused Corina with head cocked under his high-crowned beaver. "Do you always arrive at parties to which you were not invited?" he asked amiably.

"The party to which I want to be invited is just beginning," she said, staring up at him with provocative lips pursed in a pout.

"It seems you are the one doing the inviting," Davinoff observed.

"You are right." The intensity of Corina's will burned through that smile and shone in her eyes. "Are you going to stand in the street all night?"

Breaths were held inside the foyer behind them.

Davinoff put his cane under his arm and stepped into the yellow carriage. Corina pulled the door shut behind him, her eyes never leaving him. She did not acknowledge that there was an audience to her little drama. Indeed she seemed to be aware of no one but Davinoff. Her hair gleamed golden in the darkness as the carriage clattered off into the night.

Inside number seventeen, the stunned silence lasted for a moment more. Then Sarah began pulling on her gloves, hoping no one could see the tremor in her hands. Mr. Wilberforce took jovial leave of the countess, who stood immobile at the doorway, staring after the carriage.

Mrs. Piozzi took the countess's arm. "Come away from the door, Mary."

Sarah buttoned her pelisse. She had herself well in hand now. She only hoped Madame had not seen her shaking hands. "Soon it will be too cold for anything but a cape and a muff."

Madame examined her. "You are quite right, my dear."

"Come, Sarah. I shall drop you off home," George said as he took her arm. Sarah kissed Madame on her old cheek and promised to be faithful to the nuncheon engagement they had made the day before. Then she allowed George to guide her to his carriage.

Chapter Seven

Sarah went to Chambroke the next week for Corina's house party with a sense of foreboding she could not shake off. She could not look forward to Corina and Davinoff performing their magnetic dance. The rumors about town were conflicting. Some said Davinoff had not spent twenty minutes in Corina's carriage after she picked him up at number seventeen the Royal Crescent. Others said he was more enthralled than she was. Some said he demurred at attending Corina's masquerade. All Sarah knew was that, if he came, something would be set off. The scent of gunpowder and the smoke of the flare that would ignite it hung in the air. She knew she would not like the result. Still, she could not stay away.

She had written to Lord Elgin and received a reply directly from a Mr. Thorpe, archeologist by trade, who promised to meet her at Clershing and view the dig site the following week. That left her time to dance attendance on Corina.

She arrived on Friday morning before the other guests to help her friend with last minute preparations. She found Corina in the Green Salon, lists strewn over the floor. Corina stood in front of a huge mirror, dressed in a deep rose wrapper, and stared at her reflection. She started when she saw Sarah. "Sarah, darling," she turned and tiptoed over to kiss her cheek. "I am at my wits' end. I cannot bear all these dreadful details alone."

"Would it help if I speak to Mrs. Derwent and go over her plans?"

"Yes. But I really needed you yesterday." Corina pouted. She glanced back toward the great mirror. "You know," she continued, Sarah already dismissed from her thoughts, "getting Davinoff to Chambroke will win him to devotion. He needs to see Chambroke to truly know me. It has grandeur. It has beauty. It is of my scale."

Sarah compared Corina's scale to her own, which seemed to run to keeping the household functional. The comparison made her angry, whether at Corina or herself she could not say. "Perhaps you are right, Corina." Her voice was only just controlled. "Perhaps he should attend one of the little parties that take place when only Reece and Lansing are about. The kind with guests from the stables instead of from the pages of Debretts. Does Davinoff know about those?" Sarah stopped herself, aghast that she had brought up a subject she had resolved to ignore.

Corina only laughed. "Not yet, Sarah. Not yet. But who knows to what his tastes will run?" She gazed at Sarah with smug assurance. "My father loved those kind of little parties."

Sarah felt her insides contract. She rose, slowly. "I am for Mrs. Derwent."

When Corina came down to where Sarah and Mrs. Derwent were directing the staff, she was dangerously radiant. Her gown was sea green lustring with gold braid trim. Its half-skirt, trimmed in gold fringe, was the latest Paris style. Sarah would never have chosen it, but she had to admit it made Corina look as fresh as a new-minted coin. Corina was just ahead of the arrival of the first guests, and she set out to greet them and play the hostess.

The grand carriages pulled up the circular drive and deposited their passengers. Though the affair was to last only three days, several trunks were needed for each fashionable guest to accommodate morning wear, dinner attire, a costume or a domino for the masquerade on Saturday, sporting gear for the men, and riding habits for the women. Each brought a dresser for the women, a valet for the men, and, of course, their grooms. Chambroke would house them all and the stables would find room for the carriage horses and the personal hacks and hunters, too.

Inside the house, guests were shown to one of Chambroke's innumerable bedrooms to freshen themselves after their journey. Everyone from the vicinity who was remotely titled was there. Corina had even invited the Countess Delmont. No doubt she wanted an audience for her triumph. And they all had come to see the truth of the rumors about Davinoff and Corina.

Madame Gessande was on the guest list, so at least Sarah would have someone to talk to while Corina held court. Madame was distantly related to the French throne, a circumstance most uncomfortable during the Revolution. "Who is going to take Celine du Fond in hand and give her some taste?" the older woman whispered to Sarah as she held her skirts to mount the stairs. "Mink and blue? I can hardly hold my tongue."

Sarah gurgled her laughter. "Madame, you are a shocking gossip!"

"And what other recreation are we likely to have for the next three days?"

Davinoff did not appear. As the afternoon waned, Corina grew petulant. Sarah was relieved. She did not want to see Corina at the chase. Perhaps she did not care to have Davinoff see Corina in scale with Chambroke. Others whispered, afraid the main entertainment was lost. A storm blew up outside. The men began to wonder whether the hunt tomorrow would go forward.

Dinner was awful. Corina's chef had extended himself tonight to the point of embarrassment, but his mistress was in an ugly mood. Her mouth turned down unhappily and her tone was angry. Sarah was glad to be relegated to the foot of the table. John Kerseymere and Sir Kelston sat across from her, describing their horses' innumerable fine qualities. She listened for as long as she could, but she could not help glancing toward Corina. Those around her friend carried on a stuttering conversation, confronted as they were by a hostess who looked likely to explode.

Finally, she did. Pretty young Lady Varington apparently laid the last straw.

"I could care less for watercolors," Corina fairly shouted. "Or Italian or the pianoforte, either. If you think these are the accomplishments that attract a man, I'm sure you will get just the one you deserve." She half stood, leaning on the table, unsure, Sarah thought, whether to continue her tirade or rush from the room. Lady Varington, who had apparently been extolling the virtues of a classical ladies' education, looked as if she had witnessed a murder. Her round brown eyes filled with tears. The table went silent, everyone fixed on their hostess in fascinated horror.

The door under the imposing marble columns behind Corina opened. "Mr. Davinoff." Reece's voice revealed no excitement, no expectation.

All eyes turned toward the new arrival. His black coat molded to his form, exuding elegance. His waistcoat was white satin with just a hint of woven pattern. A gold signet was his only piece of jewelry, gleaming in the warm glow of the chandeliers. Suddenly, all the men who had worn brown or blue or dark green coats and vibrantly colored waistcoats, watches, fobs, seals, and rings, seemed tawdry. Their clothes shouted rather than sang. Davinoff swept the huge assemblage with a glance, and his eyes came to rest on Corina. "To each his own, don't you think?" he asked.

The room turned back to Corina. She had been transformed from a sullen child into a luminous creature whose radiance put a glow into the room the chandeliers could not account for. "My dear Davinoff," she cooed, straightening. "Wherever have you been hiding yourself?"

He raised an eyebrow. "Hiding? I?" He moved with languid grace into the room.

Corina forgave him instantly. "Well, never mind, you are here now. Will you eat?"

Davinoff shook his head and waved the thought away.

"Then let us retire to the drawing room," Corina commanded. The party rose in a confused rustle of chairs and shuffled in clots into the white drawing room through the twenty-foot carved and gilded double doors.

It began. Corina vivacious, Corina coquettish, Corina moving beyond all limits. Sarah faded into the background purposefully. She did not want to make a fool of herself as the countess was doing, her eyes constantly upon Davinoff and Corina, her mouth turned down in disapproval as she moved from one knot of people to the next, gossiping her way about the room. The countess wore no scarf. Her insect bites had faded until they were merely red circles.

Sarah sought out Madame Gessande and talked intensely about everything, anything but Davinoff. When Madame sat to piquet, Sarah hinted to John Kerseymere that he should counsel Lady Varington upon the selection of a horse, and saw with satisfaction that young lady turn her doelike eyes up to her newfound benefactor most irresistibly. If John Kerseymere did not find the reality of a young admirer more alluring than chasing after Corina the Unattainable, Sarah would give him up. But even matchmaking could not hold her concentration. Corina badgered Celine du Fond into sitting at the pianoforte. Corina would request a waltz, Sarah was sure, and Sarah knew just with whom the girl would dance. She melted away to her bed before that could begin.

The next morning, Sarah stayed abed. The weather had turned fine for the hunt. Sir Francis Burdett supplied the hounds. Everyone would rise early for a light breakfast and be up and out to the fields. They were to lunch at Burdett Hall and return in time to prepare for the masquerade.

Sarah despised hunting, though it was certainly exhilarating to leap over hedges on a fine horse in the brisk morning air. She could not forget the horror of her first hunt, as the dogs found the fox and did what dogs will do, what we have all forgotten dogs were born for. She waited to come down until the breakfast room was quiet. She savored toast and jam and tea, undisturbed, over the latest copy of the *London Magazine*.

After breakfast, Sarah put on her own plain navy riding habit and walked down to the stable. She hoped that Pembly had not lent Maggie to one of the guests for the hunt. Maggie was one of the joys of coming to Chambroke whenever Sarah was summoned to relieve Corina's boredom. In the stable yard, she found Madame Gessande in serious conversation with the head groom, Pembly.

"Now, don't you give me a slug, mind you," Madame was saying. "Nor one of those nervous creatures that Corina creates."

"No, Madame," Pembly said, "I'll wager I have just the horse for you. Workmanlike, but pluck to the backbone." He motioned to a young groom and said, "Bring out Sultan." Then seeing Sarah he added, "And saddle up Maggie."

Sarah grinned. "Thank you, Pembly. I was afraid you might have lent her out."

"And who else would she allow to ride her, now?" the man shot back. "You've ruined her for anyone with heavy hands, Lady Clevancy."

She smiled in thanks. "Are you up for a ride, Madame? The park will be beautiful."

"I'll give you a lead wherever you need one, *cherie*," the woman returned with a gleam in her eyes. She went to choose her saddle, not trusting Pembly.

When Davinoff led his huge black horse out of the barn, saddle on his arm, Sarah was surprised. Corina would be so angry that he had not chosen to hunt! She drifted closer, drawn by his horse, a great creature, well over seventeen hands if he was an inch, shining black. His neck had the thick arch of a stallion, but he had an ineffable grace about him. He minced at the end of his lead, impatient as the saddle was thrown over his back.

Sarah stopped three feet or so behind Davinoff, so as not to startle either him or his mount, but he must have known she was there for he said, "Good morning," without turning, as he pulled on the girth straps.

"He is wonderful." Sarah could think of nothing else to say.

"What, don't you ask how I manage him? Most women do."

"It is too early in the morning for insults, Davinoff," Sarah replied. Then her attention was drawn back to the smooth muscles beneath the beast's shining coat, the fine dark eye that examined her. "What is his name?" she asked. *Please let it not be Jerry or Welly after Wellington,* a name so popular after the war.

"Quixote," Davinoff said.

"Quixote?" Sarah exclaimed, delighted. "Now let me think why you have named him Quixote. 'I can see with half an eye' as Cervantes would say." She paused. "It is because he is steadfast and will run all day and all night if you give him the office to do so, just as our friend from La Mancha was steadfast in his quest."

Davinoff snapped a stirrup to the end of its leather. "And . . . ?"

Sarah approached and held out a hand to steady the horse. He snorted softly into her palm. "And, and, and because he will jump anything you set him at, even if you overmatch him. It may be impossible, yet he will try." Sarah looked up at Davinoff's profile. "I would not have guessed you for a devotee of Cervantes. Quite out of keeping with your reputation as a cynic."

"We are talking, I believe, about my horse." Davinoff went round to the other side of Quixote, and she heard the snap of the other stirrup leather.

A young groom led up a saddled bay mare. Sarah always had to smile when she saw Maggie. She was fifteen hands and two, a dark bay built upon petite lines, with a delicate head and expressive eyes. There was no mistaking her for anything but a mare. That was not to say she was not strong. She was, and a good jumper besides. Her quarters were well muscled and her legs clean, with small, well-formed hooves. Sarah was always careful not to overmatch her. Like Quixote, she would have tried things she could not reasonably do.

The groom grinned. "Ye'll have a ride on your hands today, m'lady." He bent over and cupped his hands together. Sarah placed a boot carefully in his hands and he tossed her up. She turned, just the degree required, and landed in the sidesaddle. Then she lifted her right leg over the horn and arranged her habit. Madame emerged from the stable on her solid gray, Sultan.

"Will you ride with us, Davinoff?" Madame called. "I warn you, we will not be neck or nothing this morning, with the footing as bad as it is like to be after last night's storm."

Sarah busied herself shortening her stirrups.

"Then I must politely decline," Davinoff said, in a manner

Sarah thought hardly polite. He swung into the saddle and urged Quixote on. "My horse needs a run."

"Come on, Madame," Sarah said tightly, disappointed, and disappointed in herself for being so. It was just that she would have liked to see Quixote jump, she told herself. Then she grew a little angry. Davinoff thought she rode like a slug.

In any event, they had a lovely ride. They cantered about the park and through the woods. Maggie took logs and hedges, everything in stride. As they came round to the meadow and turned toward home, Davinoff and Quixote appeared, trotting along the crest of a hill. She could see him looking down at them and imagined his disdain. She had already decided that she and Maggie would take the stile to the left of the large, white-paneled gate leading to the south pasture. But now she changed her mind. Don't be petty, she told herself. But it was too late and she knew it.

"Madame, there is a stile to the left of the gate," she called and gestured toward the easier route. She patted Maggie's neck. "Well, my dear?" Most horses didn't like the stark-white panels of the gate and it was four feet high. But she knew Maggie was a match for it, even this late in the ride. She brought the mare up to an easy canter with her haunches up under her for power and curved right to approach the gate. She did not even look up to the ridge.

Slow, slow, she thought to Maggie, as the gate loomed. Don't rush. She sat back on Maggie to shorten her stride with that instinct that came from many jumps for how many strides were left to the fence. Maggie rose under her as Sarah looked up across the field. She just touched Maggie's shoulder with her short crop. Maggie responded with extra effort and tucked her forelegs neatly up to clear that gate with room to spare. Sarah laughed, as she brought the horse down to a trot and stroked her neck. "You are very generous," she praised. Maggie snorted and pranced, proud of herself.

Sarah applauded Sultan as he cleared the stile. Then she could not master the urge to look up toward Davinoff. He stood under an oak, too far away to see his expression. Perhaps he was just giving Quixote a breather. She turned Maggie toward the stable and refused to look back.

* * *

The afternoon was deepening to dusk and the wind was blowing as Sarah burst into the house in search of Madame Gessande. She found her ensconced in Corina's library. Sarah could just see her reach for her tea from a comfortable wing chair at the far end of the grand room. "She is very independent." Was there someone in the other wing chair? Sarah's steps slowed.

"Stubborn, some might say." Sarah stopped in her tracks at the all too familiar voice.

"And curious, and courageous. I find her many things. Not just in the ordinary style."

"Ah." Sarah saw Davinoff's hand wave. "I expect you knew her as a child, perhaps think of her as your own. It colors your opinion." Sarah wondered if she could escape unseen.

"I *think* of her as a good person and friend," Madame returned. "One is never objective about the people one truly values." What was Davinoff doing closeted with Madame, talking about her?

Madame glanced up. "What is it, *ma petite?*" she asked calmly.

"Minton was quite helpful in the matter of pruning." Sarah cleared her throat, pushing some strands of escaping hair behind her ears as she approached. "My peach trees, you know . . ."

"Ah. And did you have a reason for seeking me out?" the woman asked.

"Well . . ." Sarah shifted her weight to her other foot. Davinoff had Plato's *Dialogues* spread open over his crossed knee. "I thought you might like to play some whist."

"I'd love to," her friend said, setting down her tea and copy of *Frankenstein*.

"If you find a bearable fourth, I'll join you." Davinoff peered round his chair.

Sarah could not believe her ears. "I am sure you would be bored stiff unless the stakes were high enough to ruin someone." Madame glanced up. Well, how could one help but be rude to the man?

He turned to Madame Gessande. "I shall strive to stay awake," he drawled. "But only if you give me leave to veto the choice of a fourth."

* * *

Sarah was interrupted in the midst of a gurgle of laughter as Corina flashed into the library, still in her hunt clothes, red and military, with black braid and a high-crown beaver with red feathers at the brim. Corina had dressed to kill this morning in more ways than one. Madame and General Wentworth had just won a closely contested hand from Sarah and Davinoff. The general could only be said to be crowing. Madame exclaimed over his skill. Davinoff tossed his cards negligently on the table. But his mouth held a ghostly smile.

Sarah could see Corina take in the scene at a glance. Her eyes darkened. "Well, there you all are, wasting the afternoon with cards." She stripped her gloves off.

"How was your hunt?" Madame inquired. Sarah looked up, anxious.

"Fine, except there was no fox." Corina stalked up to the table. "He got away."

Sarah smiled to herself and gathered the cards.

"I thought you were scheduled to hunt, Davinoff," Corina challenged.

"I rarely adhere to schedules," he answered and pushed back from the table.

"Are you squeamish, like Sarah here?"

Davinoff looked up, considering. "I hardly think you could call me squeamish," he remarked, and rose. "You will excuse me," he murmured then and nodded to the table. In a moment, he was gone.

"Sarah, come help me put off this habit," Corina commanded. Sarah recognized a summons. She shrugged her apologies to Madame and the general, and followed.

"I can't believe he spent an entire boring afternoon at cards when he could have been hunting with me," Corina said. Sarah seated herself on a small divan, as Corina paced her dressing room. Now she would accuse Sarah of monopolizing Davinoff.

"We did not play for long," Sarah excused.

"Then what in heaven's name did he do all day?" she cried.

"I believe he rode in the morning," Sarah said, as if she didn't know for certain. "And he was talking to Madame Gessande and reading in the library when I came in from the greenhouses."

"Reading?" Corina fairly shouted. "When he could have been hunting with me?" She calmed and sat abruptly at the dressing table. "Last night, he was mine," she muttered. "Today, he plays me the fool. What is his game?"

"He doesn't hunt." Sarah was grateful Corina did not blame her for Davinoff's defection.

"Beside the point." Corina dismissed Sarah with a wave of her hand and sat gazing into the mirror. "He is fascinated, I can feel it," she mused. "But he cannot commit to the consequence."

"What do you want of him?" Sarah asked, her voice so low that she wasn't sure her friend would hear her. "A man like that is not used to committing."

"I want him devoted." Corina rose from where she had been slumped against the dressing table and danced slowly around the room, her voice airy. "I want him to think of me, be where I am, do what I want to do. I want him to shower me with gifts and treat me like a cherished, treasured jewel." She turned to Sarah, and her voice turned also to reveal its edge. "I know what they are saying. They want to know whose heart will break, his or mine. Are they betting yet?"

"You can't listen to idle gossip, Corina. I should think you would be the last to care."

"I don't care if they all think I am outrageous. But they will never, *ever* feel sorry for me," Corina whispered. "And they will never laugh."

"Then you have your wish, Corina. Everyone in Bath thinks that you are outrageous."

Corina was not listening. "He just needs a push to make his declaration public. Once he has shown the world he loves me, it will be different. He is only skittish of going through the gate."

"Corina, whatever are you thinking?" All Sarah's feeling of foreboding assaulted her.

Corina stood, tapping her foot, her finger to her lips in thought. There was a long moment of silence before she began to laugh, low at first, then shouting and gasping for breath, gusts of mirth shaking her body.

"What is it, Corina? Don't do this. You are frightening me."

The woman controlled herself with difficulty, cupped a hand over her mouth. "Never mind, my sweet," she gurgled. "You run along now." She lifted Sarah and pulled her toward the door. "But watch what happens tonight at the masquerade."

Sarah stayed in her room until long after she could hear guests stirring in the corridors. She put on her domino, one of those clever satin capes that concealed one's clothes, and together with a mask constituted a perfectly acceptable masquerade costume. Dominoes were safe. In choosing an actual costume, one ran the danger of being too precious, or again too outrageous. George first encouraged her to wear a domino. She had got one from the lending library, which allowed borrowers to check out costumes or reticules designed for parties. Finally she had purchased her own red one, thinking it a very good value. A single domino might last one all one's life, she thought, unaccountably depressed. Madame planned to come as Marie Antoinette. One could count on the usual assortment of medieval ladies popularized by Mr. Scott, pirates and devils and monks. Corina had refused to reveal her costume plans. Sarah wondered what Davinoff would wear.

At a quarter to nine, she could put off the inevitable no longer. She descended the stairs and allowed Reece to show her into the first-floor ballroom in the central wing of the house.

Orange trees potted in silver tubs from Corina's hothouses sat around the edges of the room, exuding their heavy scent. Sconces and Venetian chandeliers glowed with a thousand refractions of light. The oak floor gleamed, whispering, as evening slippers shushed across it, that dancing was the order of the evening. Portraits and dim landscapes looked down from between the pilasters upon the guests below. Surrounding the perimeter several small tables had been set, along with chairs and divans. Across the back, a champagne fountain glittered and bottles rose in pyramids of what Sarah knew would be an excellent claret, brought up from the cellars of the Dukes of Bimerton. Corina's cook had produced tiny succulent bits of finger food to tide the revelers over until the late supper.

Sarah gazed out across the sea of costumes feeling rather lost. There was nothing for it but to wade into the crowd and try to locate someone to talk to, a difficult business when no one looked like who they were. Before she could get into the room at all she was asked to dance by a naval commander who turned out to be Edgar Kerseymere, John's younger brother. Then the general, dressed as a magician in conical cap and a black domino scattered with stars, begged for a waltz.

As she turned to sit, she bumped straight into Davinoff. "You have no costume, Mr. Davinoff," she exclaimed. His black satin coat with its black-figured waistcoat was impeccable, but his only concession to costume was a baleful ruby, winking redly from the folds of his cravat.

He raised one brow. "I do. I come as the devil."

Of course she could not imagine him deigning to dress up. "Perhaps you insinuate that your normal appearance is but a disguise," she observed, half taunting.

He examined her closely as the crowd whirled around them. She became positively dizzy, held by his eyes. "Perhaps," he murmured.

"Have you seen a Marie Antoinette?" she stuttered. "I am looking for Madame Gessande."

"Let me escort you." He offered his arm. She could feel his strength through his coat sleeve. The knowledge of his flesh beneath the fabric unnerved her, just as it had in the coaching inn yard, how long ago? She thought she would be immune to Davinoff after a week of watching him with Corina. But she could not say exactly how she arrived, breathless, to sit beside Madame Gessande, or as near as she could, since Madame's panniered skirt took up the whole divan and Sarah was forced into a nearby chair. When she looked up, Davinoff had already disappeared into the throng.

Corina made sure her appearance was the last of the evening. The musicians played a fanfare and the doors to the ballroom at the top of three stairs opened to reveal Corina as Juno, queen of the gods. Long curls threaded with tiny gold chains coiled over a bare shoulder. She wore a toga fastened at the other shoulder by a golden brooch and girdled at the waist by a net of gold and pearls. The fabric was the sheerest silk, which left little to the imagination. But the imagination was not deterred. Her bare arm bore a single golden bracelet above the elbow. On her feet, golden sandals, and most scandalous of all, her toenails were painted with gold paint.

The crowd hushed; then one of the gentlemen began to clap his hands, and soon the applause rippled across the hall. Corina nodded, most imperial, and descended into the room.

Sarah sighed. The feeling of her hand on Davinoff's arm receded. She felt acutely all the differences between her life and Corina's. Would she have felt better if George had deigned to come? Corina danced with Davinoff once, but she paid most of her attention to the bluff Sir Kelston, one of many monks tonight. Poor thing, he was not up to Corina's tricks. She simpered, she cajoled, she plied him with wine. She granted him dance after dance and he held her much too close for propriety at every chance.

Sarah was puzzled. "It is not like Sir Kelston to become foxed. What is Corina doing?"

"He is a trifle well to live," Madame agreed. "Likely he will end having shot the cat."

"Madame!" Her worldly friend's language could still make Sarah gasp.

"Don't pretend you don't know what I mean, Sarah Ashton," Madame replied tartly.

After midnight the guests indulged themselves at the great buffet table in the first floor dining room. Many witnessed Corina begging Sir Kelston to take her outside, saying that she desperately needed air. That young man hastily put down his plate, causing several glasses on the table to overturn, called to a servant to fetch her wrap, and led her away to the balcony.

"Only Davinoff seems oblivious to Corina," Madame observed. That man lounged toward the table holding the wine.

"A bad sign," Sarah said, her brows creased in worry. "She has some plan tonight to attach him to her. I thought if he was terribly attentive . . . but his indifference will urge her on."

Suddenly the door to the first-floor balcony burst open, and Corina struggled in, her hair disheveled, clutching the torn shoulder of her toga. A wail escaped her. The bustle of the room ceased. All eyes turned toward her. "Help me," she sobbed and threw herself past several other men, onto Davinoff's shoulder as he stood holding a glass of wine.

Sir Kelston appeared at the French doors, looking dazed. "Corina, pet, what are you doing?" he asked. His absurd mustachios and his fair skin made him look younger than his twenty-five years.

"Oh, Davinoff, this man has, has soiled my honor in my own house," Corina cried.

"Has he?" Davinoff set down his glass and disentangled her grip from his coat.

"But, Corina," Sir Kelston expostulated. "I didn't." Then more uncertainly, "Did I?"

"My honor demands satisfaction," Corina practically shouted, turning to the room. "Davinoff, you must be my champion. You must give me satisfaction."

"Are you talking about pistols at dawn, my dear?" Davinoff inquired.

"I am talking about honor," the girl sobbed. Sarah had never seen Corina cry.

Sir Kelston turned white as a sheet as he saw how matters lay. He steadied himself, and drew himself up to his full height. "I agree, Mrs. Nandalay," he said in a formal tone with only a slight slur to his words. "Honor needs satisfaction. My honor has been impugned with these accusations. I will meet you where you will, Davinoff. We shall let the bullets determine the right of it."

"I'll act as second, Kelston," John Kerseymere called.

"Fools," Davinoff whispered. Corina lifted her handkerchief to her mouth, as though to stop her sobbing. But Sarah could see the gleam of satisfaction in her eyes. Here was public proof of Davinoff's devotion. He would fight a duel in her honor. What could be better? The room held its breath. No doubt many were remembering the rumors of Davinoff's other duels.

"I pick up pistols only when I choose the cause," he said shortly.

Corina looked up at him with eyes brimming. "But my honor!" she gasped. The shoulder of her toga dropped to reveal the curve of her breast. Sarah wondered if she had practiced that.

"I'll fight for your honor." Edgar Kerseymere fought his way through the crowd.

No one heeded. Davinoff stared down at Corina. "You do not have honor enough for anyone to fight for," he said, his voice a deep rumble all the room could hear. Corina gazed up at him, her fists clenched, rage beginning to suffuse her. But she was held, apparently, by the power of Davinoff's eyes alone. "You will stop this charade. There will be no duel." With that, his eyes ceased to hold her, and she slumped to a chair. He turned the power of his gaze on the room, sweeping the faces, frozen in shock or in anticipation. "There will be no duel," he said again.

With that, he whirled and strode away. There was a moment of stunned silence, then an embarrassed shuffling toward the exit. A wail escaped Corina, to be followed by real sobs.

"Corina," Sir Kelston asked, "what was all this about?"

The whispers were already starting. Sarah could hear Countess Delmont's voice, first among many. Soon they would realize that Sir Kelston was too much the bluff innocent to have ravished Corina. They would suspect that she had staged the entire incident. Would they feel sorry for her, or would they laugh? Corina had managed to achieve her worst nightmare. Sarah put a hand on her friend's shoulder, only to be shaken violently off as Corina rose and ran from the room.

The party broke up the next day without the presence of its hostess. She refused Sarah entrance to her suite of rooms. There was nothing to be done but to slink home with the others.

Chapter Eight

Sarah's every venture into Bath was a disaster. By Wednesday she wanted to hear no more gossip, be asked no more questions about Corina. And while she was about it, she wanted no more speculation on what would happen next between the young woman and Davinoff. As she trudged up the steps to her own house, Jasco opened the door. Sighing, she gave him her gloves and her pelisse and looked at the several cards lying on the deal table in the hall. "More visitors," she remarked, taking off her hat. "Being a friend of Mrs. Nandalay is trying."

"Mr. Upcott called, and Her Grace of Delmont," Jasco intoned. "And one or two others."

"Please tell anyone who calls that I am not at home, Jasco. I cannot bear any more today."

"Of course, Your Ladyship. Shall I have Mrs. Addison bring some tea to the library?"

"That would be nice, Jasco, thank you." She sighed again, and made her way to one of the overstuffed chairs in front of the crackling fire in the study.

Corina hadn't been seen since the masquerade. She was probably in need of comfort from a friend. But Sarah couldn't go to her. She could not overcome her disgust that Corina would have let Sir Kelston go to his death at Davinoff's hands. No one could think him a match for Davinoff with pistols. All for a display to the world that she owned Davinoff's affections?

No one would ever own that man's affections. Sarah leaned back and examined the crown molding. She was trapped in the muddle, too. Part of her wanted to wash her hands of Corina forever. Part of her knew that in Bath just now, she was the only friend the girl had.

Sarah gritted her teeth and rose. She could not abandon Corina, foolish and cruel as she was. Sooner or later she would have to confront her, no matter how she felt about Corina's deeds. She might as well start now. "Jasco," she called. "Call for a gig from the livery. I have just enough time to drive out to Chambroke. I shall be back in time for supper."

What she found there disturbed her greatly. Corina was still in her sitting room, in her wrapper. Her hair had not been dressed. It hung about her face, lank. Her blue eyes were ringed with dark circles and her complexion was wan. She lay on a chaise, a down comforter covered in blue satin clutched about her.

"Corina, are you well?" Sarah asked as she entered. "Lansing said you were not yourself."

"Curse her," Corina mumbled. "I am simply bored to tears."

"Well, I can understand that, when you are not out of your wrapper yet at three o'clock. Why don't we give your horses a run?"

"Horses? What do I care for riding at a time like this?" Corina raged suddenly to life. "Enemies on every side, my reputation in ruins, my pride—my pride in shreds—and you think of horses!" She subsided into the chaise and her comforter. "You are worse than stupid, Sarah!"

"Perhaps." Sarah tried hard to remember how Corina must feel. "But it is just your pride."

"Just my pride," Corina echoed, staring out the windows to the park. The wind was tugging at the trees. "He has destroyed me."

Corina didn't need sympathy. She needed to be jerked out of the self-pity that paralyzed her. Sarah had never seen her like this. She found it disturbing. "Corina," Sarah said firmly, "you brought this upon yourself. I suppose you have not thought very much about what would have happened to Sir Kelston had you succeeded."

"He is not important." Corina waved a languid hand.

"He might have been killed!"

"What are you saying, Sarah? It is me who is ruined. And Davinoff who has done this to me." The blonde turned her face into the chaise and drew a corner of the comforter up under her chin.

Sarah realized she would never bring Corina to a realization of her almost crime. She sighed. Corina didn't have it in her. "Why not go to London for a while?"

"Don't you think the word has spread there too?" Corina's voice was small and hopeless.

"You cannot stay shut up here. Come to the assembly tomorrow night. You had better face them early than late. At any rate, the event will be less dire than the anticipation."

"No one will dance with me," Corina whispered.

Sarah tried to smile. "If you can stand his treading on your toes, I can assure you a dance with George. You know that when your retinue of admirers sees you looking ravishing but vulnerable, they will rush to your side in fits of knight errantry." Corina looked up, half convinced. Sarah was half convinced herself. Young men could forgive Corina anything. Sarah raised her brows in entreaty.

Corina put her hand to her mouth and shook her head, her eyes filling. Sarah came and sat on the end of the chaise. "You must go out sometime, you know," she said gently.

"Davinoff will be there," Corina whispered. "I cannot bear to have the devil snub me, or see him hanging on that aged Delmont fright. They will all take his lead. No one will even speak to me." Her voice rose. "I can't do it, Sarah."

Sarah fingered the satin of the coverlet. There was a solution to this, if she could get him to do it. She pictured herself asking in several different ways, and the scenes all came out badly. But Corina's misery was most real, to her. Sarah sighed, and knew she would try.

"If Davinoff does not snub you, the whole may be brought

off creditably." She patted Corina's foot under the coverlet. "I have a plan. Expect a note from me tomorrow, and be ready."

All the way home, Sarah cursed herself for being drawn into Corina's dance with Davinoff. But her heart had been touched against her will by Corina's obvious pain. Now she would be the instrument of their reconciliation, if she could manage it. She pushed away her very mixed feelings without examination. She was about to ask Anarchy for a favor.

There were few people in Henrietta Park the next afternoon as she waited anxiously on a bench. The wind had died down, but the sky was that dull pewter gray which signaled rain. The park smelled like wet growing things, and the faint rot of decaying leaves. Would he come? How dared she expect the devil to do a good deed?

Precisely at two, Davinoff strolled around the corner of the yew hedge and down the path that led to her bench. As he approached, he doffed his high-crowned beaver. "Lady Clevancy, I received your note," he said. Cool inquiry filled his voice.

"Obviously," she replied, more tartly than she wished. "Unless it is your habit to stroll in the park when the weather is coming on to rain."

"Hardly." He waited, looming above her.

"I cannot speak comfortably, if you are going to tower over me like that. Do sit down." Sarah did not look forward to this at all.

Davinoff nodded and sat in his casual way upon the bench. He looked in question at her.

Sarah suddenly became most confused. How to begin? How to ask?

"Let me guess," he began. She wondered if he would help her broach the subject. "You wish assistance in choosing someone to begin charting your villa."

"No, no. Lord Elgin has found me someone most suitable. I start next week." She saw a shadow pass across Davinoff's face. "That is not what I wished to ask you," she exclaimed, poised upon the brink but unable to throw herself over.

"Then . . ." Davinoff waited, enjoying her discomfiture, she thought.

"It's about Corina," she finally blurted.

Davinoff's countenance darkened, and his eyes narrowed.

"She is miserable over all of this," Sarah rushed on. "I think she is going into a decline."

"That is the last woman likely to go into a decline," Davinoff said.

"You haven't seen her." Sarah saw his doubt in his eyes. "Oh, I know she feigns emotions. The other night was all an act. But this is not. She is afraid to come out of her house." Sarah took a breath. "I am afraid the episode may have unbalanced her."

"She should have thought of that before she created a scene that might well have ended in bloodshed if she had got another victim besides me." The man was implacable.

"And do you think that you are blameless here?" Sarah burst out. "Do you think you did not drive her to extremities with your . . . your variable attentions?"

"She bestows variable attentions herself. I thought she liked the game of hide and seek."

"Au contraire, Mr. Davinoff. Corina is used to getting exactly what she wants. I know that does not excuse her," Sarah added. "But you must see that she was not prepared for your on-again, off-again observance. Now she is humiliated. And I think that is very good for her. But she shouldn't be beaten down so far she does not get an opportunity to learn from her situation."

Davinoff's expression was wary. "And you wish me to do what?"

"I want you to ride out to Chambroke." She saw his brow lift. "I know it is asking too much, but I saw Corina yesterday, and I knew I must ask. You could say that you just happened in on your way from the abbey, so it would not look like you made a special trip."

Davinoff looked ever more dubious. "But you *do* want a special trip," he pointed out.

"Yes, well, I know that." Sarah mustered her courage. "But all you need do is act as though you expect to see her at the Assembly Rooms tonight, and let her see that you won't snub her, and she will be drawn out of her house to face the town. Once she has done that, she will be better. And if you could bring yourself to dance with her at the assembly, why then it would lead the way for others to acknowledge her." Sarah looked up at him, pleading.

"I hardly think . . ." he began.

But Sarah could see him softening at the edges like the bank of a stream in rushing water. "She really is suffering, you know. And she would never have succumbed to such foolishness if you hadn't dallied with her affections most shamefully," she reminded.

"I suppose if she regrets her action . . ." Davinoff trailed off, still reluctant.

Sarah tried not to reflect on the fact that she had carefully neglected to say that Corina was sorry. "Eight miles. You will be there in half an hour with Quixote or your marvelous pair."

Davinoff looked disgusted with himself. He rose and put on his hat. "How did you grow to be so persuasive?" His voice was bitter. "I expect your father sold patent medicines on the side."

"Thank you." Sarah laughed. "You will not be sorry."

"I am sorry already," he said shortly, and strode off the way he came.

Julien rode Quixote through the gates of Chambroke in the afternoon. He had to make his way through a stream of servants, departing. They laughed and exclaimed at some unexpected holiday. That was odd, he thought. He handed Quixote over to a groom who himself looked anxious to depart, and turned toward the huge front doors. How had he let Sarah Ashton talk him into this? He had hardly lifted the knocker when the doors were opened by Corina's stone-faced butler.

"Mr. Davinoff," he intoned, taking Julien's cape and hat. "Mrs. Nandalay is in the white drawing room." He led Julien to the back of the house. It was unnaturally quiet, without the subtle bustle of servants that underscored life in a country house. Julien's eyes swept the white drawing room. It must take its name from the ceiling, where a single garland in gold leaf was picked out of ornately carved white plaster. Corina sat on a divan of chocolate-colored fabric, floating on ornate rugs of chocolate, maroon, and white. She smoothed the lace bodice of her white dress, looking charged with energy, not the despondent wreck Sarah Ashton described.

"Mrs. Nandalay, I see you are well."

"As ever. Would you like coffee or tea?" Her eyes sparked under her lowered lashes.

"I cannot stay more than a moment," he demurred.

"It will take but a moment. Reece," she called to the departing butler. "Bring coffee."

Julien saw Reece's eyes meet hers for a moment as he bowed and closed the door behind him. "To what do I owe the pleasure of this visit?" she asked, and gestured to a chair. Julien disposed his long form into its gilt frame.

"I wanted to see how you did."

A wave of emotion rolled over Corina's face and was gone. "I do as I always do."

"Lady Clevancy wanted to reassure herself upon that point." Julien wanted to make sure Corina knew that coming here was not his own idea.

"Ah. Dear Sarah. I had her note, mentioning that you might be wending our way. Is she the reason you have come?" Corina pretended to nonchalance.

"One of the reasons."

Reece returned with a silver coffee service. He set it on the sideboard and began to pour.

"And what are the others?" Corina asked. She eyed Reece and the tea service, eyes snapping.

Julien glanced toward the butler. What was amiss here? He cleared his throat. "I wondered if you planned to attend the assembly ball."

Reece set before them the cups of delicate maroon Haviland ornately worked in gold.

"I am thinking about it." Her eyes never left Julien as he lifted the cup to his lips and sipped. He examined her face. She was acting very oddly. Perhaps Lady Clevancy had been right.

Corina began to chatter on. "After last week at the masquerade, I am not sure I am up to public appearances." Julien held the delicate cup and drank again. "I suppose I will go eventually. One can't stay bottled up at Chambroke, after all." She stared at his cup and sipped her own coffee. "I cannot think what induced my father to buy a property so remote."

And on and on. He did not bother to hide his boredom. Her smile was forced as she waded on through the conversation. Actually, her expression was anxious. She peered at him intently. Why? Since his expression did not dissuade her, he resolved to interrupt and make his escape, no matter how rude. She came to the assembly or she did not, he had done his part. He cursed Sarah Ashton for her solicitous nature. This woman was beyond his reach. She didn't seem sorry at all.

Before he could insert his intention into the conversation, he noticed that his cup was chattering against its saucer. He glanced down, surprised. He tried to steady it, but it heaved and clattered all the more. He glanced about the room, which was busy bulging and contracting, too. Where was he? Was this the salon of Marie Therese of Austria? His gaze brushed Corina. Her blue eyes shone, and her teeth showed in a grin that stretched into a grimace. His breath quickened. This wasn't Marie's salon. He tried to set the empty cup and saucer on the table, but they clattered to the floor, shattering against each other. He staggered up. Drugs! They had drugged him. Drugged his Companion, too. The little blond toad laughed in triumph.

Julien stumbled up and reeled toward her. He wasn't done yet! They wouldn't have given him enough to incapacitate one such as he. He would make her pay for her betrayal.

"Reece," the toad screamed as Julien grabbed her arm and pulled her up.

The doors to the drawing room burst open. Reece raised a heavy dueling pistol and cocked it. A woman hurried up behind him. "Let her go, Davinoff." The butler's voice cracked with strain.

Julien turned his gaze on Corina, as the room wavered around him. He held her more surely than by his grip on her arm, as he had held her that night at the masquerade, her will seeping out, until she could not move, could not think.

He could not sustain it. His eyes lost focus on her. He turned toward Reece and staggered toward the door. He must flee. They had given him enough and more.

The gun roared in Reece's shaking hands. Julien jerked back. The searing pain of a bullet pierced his shoulder. But he did not stop. He had to get out of here. Putting a hand to his shoulder, he lunged for Reece. He got him by the throat. Corina screamed. Julien cast the butler aside and staggered toward the double doors. A crash sounded behind him as Reece slid across the room.

"He is escaping," Corina shrieked.

Julien grasped the doorway for support. Slowly, as his legs no longer did his bidding, he sank to his knees. He panted there a moment longer, unwilling to give up the struggle, but he thudded to the floor. He could still see Corina, panting too, above him. Reece pulled himself up, clutching his throat. The woman servant, one eye on him, comforted her mistress.

Corina's fright turned to fury. "Lansing, he *dared* to lay a hand on me! He knew what he did at the masquerade. He planned it all. I could see it in his eyes!" She strode forward to stand over him. He could hate her, but he could not move. "He pays his shot today," she shrieked.

"He deserves what he gets," Reece croaked, standing. "He was almost the death of me."

"Handsome bonuses for you both," Corina promised. "Now, let's get him downstairs."

She came to stand over Julien. "You need a lesson," her voice echoed as blackness closed in.

For the fiftieth time that evening Sarah turned to the great double doors leading into the Upper Assembly Rooms. It was nearly eleven o'clock, and neither Corina nor Davinoff had made their appearance. Amelia fussed to Lady Beldon about the Corina scandal over near the punch fountain. Beside her, George was telling Sarah about his latest round of experiments.

"That Davinoff fellow put me on to it," he said. "Inadvertently, I am sure. But something he said jogged my thinking into a new track. And now I have discovered slight differences in the blood of different patients. When you match the types . . . Sarah, are you listening?"

"I am sorry," she apologized. "I have been so worried about Corina."

"Did you expect to see her here?" George was annoyed. "After what I have heard about her party last week, I should think she would be ashamed to show her face tonight."

"She was," Sarah fretted. "That is why I sent Mr. Davinoff to get her."

"You what?" George balanced between astonishment and outrage.

"I asked Mr. Davinoff to drive to Chambroke, and just hint to her that he would not snub her if she came to the Assembly Rooms tonight. I thought if he acknowledged her, everyone else would, too." Sarah realized too late that George might not appreciate her enterprising effort.

"Sarah Ashton, you astonish me. I cannot say whether I think it more foolish to interfere in affairs that are not your own, or to involve the likes of Davinoff in your schemes." He frowned down at her as she glanced for the fifty-first time toward the doors.

"Corina was in distress, George," she pleaded, turning back to him. "I wonder what it can mean that she didn't come. I know he went to Chambroke. He would not break his word."

"You are an innocent, Sarah. If Davinoff did go to Chambroke, I know a reason they do not appear in the Assembly Rooms."

Sarah felt her color rise. Her thoughts were exactly on those lines but she would not tell him that. "I should not like to spread such speculations about, George, and neither should you."

When the rooms closed at eleven, Sarah allowed George to walk her back to Laura Place, since the night was clear, but her thoughts were elsewhere. For all her resolve not to watch Corina at the hunt, in the end she had been the one to help her to her prey. And Davinoff pretended to be reluctant to drive out to Chambroke when all the while he was champing at the bit to go, no doubt! Who was foolish in the end? Not Corina. She had just what she wanted, and society be damned. Not Davinoff. Sarah was sure he had just what he craved as well. George was right. She was laughably innocent.

Chapter Nine

Reece and Corina came down the stairs into the cellar cautiously, the butler holding a torch. Julien stilled himself, so his clanking chains would not serve notice that he was conscious. There would be no blinking out to escape his chains. The knockout drops had worn off, but he could still feel the effects of the laudanum. That must be what it was. He was groggy and heavy-eyed. They had accidentally found the only way to subdue his Companion and neutralize his power. His shoulder thudded with pain through the drug. Someone had dug the bullet out. The hard stone was cold against his back. This was an old meat cellar from some former incarnation of the house. To his acute senses, it still smelled of death.

Corina examined him from a safe distance near the steps while Reece replenished the guttering sconces. She seemed surprised to find him conscious. He almost smiled. They had probably given him a dose enough to kill another man. He winced as Reece pulled his hands above his head with the long chains run through rings buried in the stone.

Only when she was sure he was restrained did Corina move closer. "How are you this morning, my pet?" she cooed, and knelt beside him. She unfastened the bandage tied about his shoulder and peered under the pad. "Reece, come look. This wound is not as bad as I thought. The bullet must have been spent."

Reece leaned close with his torch. "That wound looks half healed."

"Nonsense. There has been no time to heal a wound. I am just glad to save the bribe a doctor would require." She wrenched the bandages tight, ignoring Julien's flinch, and stood.

"What do you want?" he managed. His speech was slurred in his own ears.

"Oh, there will be plenty of time to talk about that." Corina sighed. "I think you are going to be very sorry you ever met me."

"Sorry I met Sarah Ashton, too," he growled.

"Sarah?" Corina asked, glowering.

"Your accomplice."

"My accomplice!" Corina tittered. "Of course. She sent you to me, did she not?" She put a finger to her lips. "Should I tell you my plan?" Julien said nothing. "Addiction must be horrifying for a man like you. A few weeks, ever-increasing doses of laudanum, and you have a lifelong friend. You are half a man, wasted in body and mind. Your foolish pride disappears. You will do anything for the drug." Corina watched for the effect of her words.

Julien glared up, his labored breath fueled with disgust. He tried not to let her see the horror he felt at the picture she painted. "You are a monster."

Corina's laugh, half rage, echoed through the stone room. "I, a monster? I? When you tried to destroy me in front of all of Bath? You are the evil one. You *will* beg forgiveness. You may swear you love me. It will not be enough. You will suffer, Davinoff, as you have made me do." She whirled and strode to the steps. "Reece, keep him plied with laudanum."

"He is strong," Reece said. "We should give him more soon."

"Will our guest drink willingly, do you think?" Corina asked, her head cocked.

"I can get the drug down his throat straight, now he's chained up," Reece replied grimly.

Julien raised his head and stared at the butler, serving notice of a fight. Corina saw it, too. "You had better come prepared, Reece," she lilted, lifting her skirts. She practically skipped up the stairs.

Reece appeared in the cellars in his shirtsleeves the next evening. At least Julien thought it was the next evening. It had been many hours at any rate. The man had come several times. The key twisted in the lock with a hollow clank and the door swung open. He had a metal tumbler in one hand and a stout cudgel under the arm that held his torch. Julien tried to focus on him from the shadows. He had grown to hate that tumbler and the cudgel. Corina forbade her minion to mark his face. He could still feel the bruises, the split lip from yesterday's first session, but since then, Reece had concentrated his attentions elsewhere. Now his shirt was torn and soiled with dirt and blood. Breathing was an effort. They were giving him ever more laudanum in an effort to keep him stuporous. Reece had grown fearful at how much of the drug it took. As he reached the bottom of the worn stone steps, the servant peered into the darkness beyond the circle of light from his torch.

"How long does she think she can keep me here?" Julien rasped.

"As long as she likes."

"What about the servants?" He could hardly think, but he had to turn this man against his mistress.

"The others, if they happen to discover that Mrs. Nandalay has another guest, would never guess he is not a willing participant being paid for his services," Reece observed sourly. He replenished the lanterns from a skin of oil in the corner.

"What about you?" Julien forced scorn through the drug. "You do it for money?"

"I do it because she asks me," Reece snapped.

So, that was it. Julien leaned his head against the stone. "She has many captives."

"You do not understand," Reece almost shouted. "I am her partner."

"You are her dog," Julien breathed. "Even if she grants you other favors."

The man ran a hand through thin hair. "I do not share her bed, if you mean that. She trusts me."

"But trust does not help you to her bed, does it?"

Reece picked up the cudgel and stalked over to him. "Damn you, there are other things besides bedding a woman."

"But not for you. You want her the way she wants me . . ." Julien might have said more, but Reece raised his stout staff and silenced him with a blow to the ribs.

"She wants you?" the man cried. "She wants you to suffer, that's what she wants." Julien doubled over, unable to protect himself. Reece's stick continued to rise and fall over his shoulders, against his ribs. The thudding pain made him retch and gasp for breath. "You want to drive us apart. Well, you won't do it," Reece hissed.

When his anger seeped away, the butler stood panting. Julien sagged against his manacles. He could not remember ever being defenseless. It was not a feeling he liked. Reece stalked over to where he had left the laudanum, and picked up the tin cup. "She wants you drugged," he wheezed, "and drugged you will be." He pulled Julien's head back and pried his jaw open. The drug poured out in a gleaming stream. Julien felt consciousness slipping away, but he managed to crunch down on Reece's fingers.

"Bloody hell," Reece shouted, snatching his hand away. Julien sputtered as the drug went down. But down it went. He sagged in his chains, defeated, his chest heaving. Blood trickled from the corner of his mouth, brought up by Reece's blows to his belly. Its taste was metallic.

"You won't be so much when we get through with you," Julien's torturer sneered, bent over and gasping with his own effort. "We'll see how long she keeps her interest once you are reduced to drooling addiction." Reece drew his hand across mouth and stood upright. "I'll see you again in the morning," he promised. Taking the cup, he staggered up the stairs.

The days following the assembly saw Sarah feeling low and small. Davinoff had disappeared entirely. All of Bath was talking about it. Amelia could speak of nothing else. Only Sarah knew where Davinoff had gone, and she refused to satisfy the speculation.

The last thing she wanted was a visit from Corina, but Sarah's friend swept into the drawing room at Laura Place on the second day after the assembly in a manic mode. She sported a fetching russet merino pelisse and matching boots, her hat a high poke buff bonnet trimmed with russet ribbons. "I appear, as you suggested," she announced, tossing her hat onto a side table.

Sarah was seated at her father's desk writing a thank-you letter to Lord Elgin. Amelia had taken a chair to Milsom Street to buy some lace. "I am quite successful in my machinations, am I not?" she asked, though she could not coax animation into her voice. Corina examined her closely.

"Yes, you are." The blonde's laugh was nervous. "What are they saying about Davinoff?"

Sarah glanced up. She'd never realized Corina cared what people said. "They don't know where he has gone." She closed her ink bottle with a savage twist of the cork.

"But *you* know." Corina began to toy with the ribbons of her hat. Then she launched into explanation: "Davinoff and I decided that part of our problem was the pressure of speculation. What I had in mind was carried out much better outside the glare of Bath society." She stopped and glanced at Sarah with some hesitation. "You won't tell where he is, will you?"

Sarah shook her head. "How long does he plan to stay?" she managed.

Corina's hesitation disappeared. "Who knows?" Now she fairly gleamed with self-satisfaction. Did Corina think that she approved of this behavior? Sarah wondered. "Now he is mine, I am sure I will find he is like all the others." Corina waved a hand.

Sarah could feel her mouth harden and turned her eyes to the window. There was a light snow, just flurries really. It was not sticking yet. "I have no doubt." Then, as though she didn't care, she said, "I myself am going up to Clershing to meet Mr. Thorpe. I don't know how long I shall be gone."

Corina gave a knowing smile. "I understand your desire to

leave town." She grabbed her hat and swaggered to the door. "Come to me when you return." Then she was gone.

Corina and Reece kept Julien plied with laudanum. He couldn't tell how many days passed. Time in the dark cellar wavered in and out with his consciousness. He had always been here, would always be here. He had rejected the food Lansing brought, a small gesture of rebellion. They didn't care enough to force it down his throat. He had grown weaker as the drug took an ever-stronger hold on him and his Companion. At least it kept the pain away. It occurred to him that they could kill him. That might be possible now that the Companion was powerless. He had wanted that many times in his long span of years. It had sometimes held a dark attraction, but not at the hands of a smug blond bitch. He breathed what was almost a chuckle. Change the hair color to flaming red, and you had Magda, part and parcel. They were both sick sexual predators who had lost their balance. Perhaps it was justice that he suffered at Corina's hands. He had let the world suffer with Magda's depraved desires.

As he had grown weaker, Corina grew more confident. She came in alone now. She held her nose as she reached the bottom stair. The cell smelled of sweat and blood, mildew and stale urine. She called to Lansing to empty the chamber pot.

As Lansing left, Corina knelt at Julien's side. She had brought her little golden knife, the kind used for paring ladies' nails. Julien had learned to hate it as much as the cudgel. It gleamed in the dim light from the sconce in spite of the crusty flaking brown on its tip.

"Davinoff," she whispered. He lifted his head. "Is today the day you say it?"

He waited. She would do what she would do.

Corina leaned close. "You know you want to say it," she said throatily. "If you do, maybe I will stop all this. Or maybe not. But shouldn't you try?" The light of need glowed in her eyes, like a lover who longed for a kiss. She ran her hand under his torn shirt, feeling the muscles over his ribs, his belly. She still held the little knife. He could feel the metal of the point barely scrape his skin.

He said nothing, but looked what defiance he could still muster, though he knew defiance excited her. She ran her fingers through his hair with her left hand, leaning close and whispered. "Just say you're sorry, Davinoff. Just beg me to forgive your sin."

He whispered his disgust.

"What, my love?" she breathed.

"Monster," he slurred, louder this time, though he knew what it would mean. He could see the anger shudder down her spine and the excitement rise into her eyes.

"I could kill you," she hissed.

"I think you could." He couldn't manage more than a small, hazy smile. "Do it."

Corina's rage bubbled up and disfigured her face. She was not used to commands.

"Are you afraid?" he pressed. What matter what she did to him? The drug had made him into the living dead, a last dreadful joke at his expense.

She calmed herself, brushed her lips against his ear. "No, are you?" Her right hand caressed his flesh. Her rage pressed the little knife into his side. He stiffened in spite of the laudanum. She pulled her hand away, sticky with his blood, then closed her eyes and breathed in the sensation.

He broke her pleasure with his voice. If she licked those fingers, she would be dead by morning. "No," he said as though she had not cut him, just to enrage her. *Lick your fingers.*

"Wrong answer." She smiled and drew the little knife along his thigh, just lightly, not yet breaking the skin. "Shall we try again?" She smeared his own blood over his chest. She wasn't going to taste it. Julien tried to keep his breathing steady as she cut him again and again. Finally she rocked back on her heels in frustration. "You *will* beg forgiveness, you know."

Julien just stared at her.

She made a sound in the back of her throat. "I won't kill you. You probably want to die." She took a breath. "As a matter of fact, I really came down to check your bullet wound. I want you to last until I can finish with you."

He watched her tear away his shirt. She surveyed his bare chest, his shoulder still wrapped with a bandage now dirty and bloody. She touched several cuts softly, including the bleeding gashes she just made. "Your ribs are broken, your collarbone," she whispered. "You've lost blood." Then she cut the bandage away with her tiny golden knife and pulled away the pad.

He watched the truth of what she was seeing seep into her. He did not have to look. There would be no wound in his shoulder, only a faint blushing mark where the bullet had struck him, hardly even a scar. The initial doses of laudanum had not been enough to entirely subdue the Companion, though it was thoroughly dampened now.

She stared at his body in amazement. Her breathing came shallow and fast as she raised her eyes to his. What man could heal like that? she was asking herself, and the horror of the only answers she would be able to propose crept across her countenance. He let the faintest smile touch his lips.

With an effort she wrenched herself away and leaned against the wall, panting. "Reece!" she screamed and pushed up the stairs to the door. He heard heavier footsteps above him. "Reece, his dose of laudanum requires adjustment."

Sarah arrived at Clershing with Amelia, in a hired gig. They set about opening up the Dower House and getting in provisions. Mr. Thorpe arrived on Thursday as predicted. He was a friendly, rotund little man. Not at all the way one pictured archeologists. As they surveyed the villa, Mr. Thorpe grew more exited with each shard he retrieved from the rubble.

"This is an excellent example of a first-century Roman house, Lady Clevancy. I am so glad Lord Elgin was kind enough to suggest me."

"Do you think we will find more underground?"

"Undoubtedly. The mosaic floors and the hypocausts probably begin perhaps twenty feet below the surface. We must remove the soil of centuries, but the effort will not be wasted."

Sarah could hardly contain her excitement. During the next three days, she assisted Mr. Thorpe in taking measurements of the site. Then he was off to London. He would be back in a fortnight with workers and supplies to begin in earnest. Sarah had done her finances carefully. With the winter rents, if she scraped, she could afford a dozen workers for a month. Her dream was on the verge of becoming real.

With Mr. Thorpe gone, Sarah had no reason to stay on at Clershing. Yet she had no desire to return to Bath. She consulted Mr. Wells about planting the fields, fallow now. It rained for three days, which forced her to books and needlework until she was thoroughly bored. When finally the gray, wet sky cracked and revealed a blustery blue day, she walked down to the villa feeling restless and sat on a great stone that jutted up just outside the walls that were no more.

But the tiles of her villa could not compete with the view of the abbey that loomed up behind them. The abbey reminded her why she did not go home. She had run away from Corina and Davinoff. There was no other word for it. Corina had added Davinoff to her endless trophies of conquest. And Sarah was not enough like her to fascinate such a man.

Then the fear that she was too much like Corina returned. Not the bold, magnetic side. Sarah knew she had none of that. But she also knew, when she allowed herself to know, that she shared some of Corina's darker, less savory attributes. She, too, could do anything, no matter how depraved. Why else did she keep coming back to Corina, in spite of what she knew?

As she sat in the shadow of Davinoff's abbey, tears overwhelmed her unexpectedly. She had run away from what Corina was, from what she herself might be, before. Sun-drenched Sienna, nestled in the Tuscan hills, threatened to overwhelm the blustery day and bring back all the fear, all the doubts about herself. No one knew, except Corina. No one would ever know. She tried to slam the door as she had so many times before. But this time the door would not be closed.

It had been on the Continent. Corina was sixteen, Sarah was eighteen, and they were free for the first time, making the Tour. It was a ritual more for young men than girls, and that made it all the more exciting. Corina's Aunt Letty was acting as chaperone and they had Reece, but Letty tired easily, and Reece might be protection, but he was in no position to deny them. Anything was possible that summer. They were young and Corina had money. As they wandered through the narrow, twisted streets of Sienna, looking for treasures in the crowded market stalls, they must have looked like ripened fruit or colorful flowers in their pastel muslins. Corina bargained aggressively with every vendor, not caring what she bought, while Sarah smiled on, glad she did not have to tell some merchant that his carefully handcrafted wares were worth so little.

"If you're not careful, Sarah," Corina taunted, piling Reece's arms with another package, "you'll come away empty-handed. A wasted trip to Italy." Her laugh was golden, then as now.

"You cannot buy the Coliseum," Sarah answered her. "I'll have my memories." Then, feeling defensive, she added, "And you bought me that little painting in Venice."

"Well," Corina temporized, excusing Sarah as she gathered up a native doll of somewhat doubtful origin, "it is certainly getting too hot to trudge around these dirty stalls much longer." She looked around for refuge from the sun and caught sight of a tavern's swinging sign at the end of the road. "Let's get something to drink. I am dry as bleached bones." Sarah and Reece were left to trail in her wake as she pushed her way through the jostling throngs toward the tavern.

Sarah caught up with her as the crowds thinned at the end of the street. Paint peeled on the tavern's shutters, but its thick stone walls promised coolness inside. Raucous laughter spilled from the windows. "This doesn't seem the place for women alone, Corina."

"Reece can guard the door. Besides, I'll wager there are many lonely women who come here." With an enigmatic smile, Corina ducked into the darkness. She was right, there were several women in the tavern. They looked like the type who would not be lonely long. The rotund, sweating proprietor pretended not to notice that they were Quality. He brought what seemed to Sarah a huge bottle of ruby wine, nestled in a basket. They ordered steaming plates of fish and pasta in the spicy local sauce, and Corina poured a glass of the wine for Sarah.

"At home, places like this are everywhere." Corina enjoyed playing the wise woman. "Don't make faces when you taste it, or everyone will know you drink only ratafia."

Sarah rolled her eyes and determined to prove she was at least as old and wise as Corina. She put on her best effort at sophistication and quaffed delicately from her glass. Sarah knew, even now, she had done a pretty good job of concealing the burning of her throat and the bitter taste of the tannic acid in that funny local wine. She smiled at Corina, and managed to murmur, "Hmm, that is quite good, isn't it?" Corina laughed outright and, after a moment, Sarah laughed too. There was quite a bit of laughter that afternoon in the tiny tavern, and quite a bit of wine.

Corina paid the tavern keeper much too much and they stumbled out the door still laughing, into the stabbing light of the Sienna sun. That afternoon was a fog for Sarah. Corina ordered Reece back to the hotel with the packages while the carriage took them to the riverside, through the park near the old stone bridge. Corina was delightful, magic, a perfect friend. Her golden skin gleamed in the sunlight. Her blue eyes danced just as the river danced with light.

It was the quality of the light that Sarah would always remember that afternoon. Corina made the driver stop in the park and she waltzed away, calling for Sarah to follow. Sarah would have followed her anywhere. They skipped after the vendor who sold soft, chewy taffy. It was a childhood thing to do, but the candies were cool yellow like Corina's hair, and palest pink like her dress, and blue like her eyes. The coach swept them up again.

"This is a magic day, no?" Corina affected the accent of the locals.

"Don't let it end, Corina." Sarah lay back in the squabs of the coach, letting the sun penetrate to the very center of her. "Let's think of something else to do."

"Let me surprise you," her friend whispered. They climbed down from the coach and paid the man for his trouble and went laughing up the steps to the hotel. It was not a large affair as she recalled. Small but elegant. The proprietor was impressed by Corina's wealth. Corina was never at any pains to hide that she was very rich, so they had the finest the house could give.

When they entered the lobby, Corina went to have a word with the landlord. Sarah wandered out onto the terrace in the small courtyard to seek again the warmth of the sunshine. The haze of the wine was still upon her as she slid into an iron chair perched on the flagstones. Multicolored blossoms wove designs along the walkways that crossed the garden to the French doors of the rooms beyond. The heavy scent of flowers she could not name hung in the air.

Sarah rubbed the smooth skin of her bare arms and felt the tiny, invisible hairs that covered her body, all bodies really. She found herself looking absently at the boy who tended the garden as she waited for Corina to reappear. He was quite handsome, not coarse at all. He had discarded his shirt in the heat. His limbs were well formed, bronzed, but not burnt black, his hair streaked lighter by long days of work in the open. He had a cut across his chest, a fight perhaps or a falling garden tool. The red streak accentuated the mortality, the animal of him. She watched the muscles move fluidly under his skin. He was sweating slightly, well oiled, a living machine.

Perhaps he felt her gaze on him. He looked up, his brown eyes unsure. Surprised at herself, she continued to stare, daring him to return it. He turned hastily back to his work, raking leaves he had removed from the immaculate beds. The light flowed over his body as muscles and tendons, blood and bone moved the rake back and forth. Sarah felt something stir within her, something unfamiliar and exciting.

Corina startled Sarah on the terrace with a brisk accusation of concealing herself. Sarah jumped. Corina's gaze dashed quickly to the boy. "Well, my adventurous friend, are you ready to retire? Or are you enjoying yourself too much to think of adjourning?"

"I was only waiting for you, Corina." Sarah lurched up, blushing.

On the way to their suite of adjoining rooms that shared a large bath, Corina whispered to Reece. He nodded, eyes hooded, and the two girls went arm in arm up the stairs. They stripped off their dresses and slid out of their sandals. A girl brought up buckets of hot water. The elation of the afternoon slipped away. When the girl had gone for the last time, Sarah stood in front of the mirror. Her breasts and hips were already full in contrast to Corina's slim lines. Corina was silhouetted behind the painted screen that hid the tub. How strange to know you would live in this body for the rest of your life. She shrugged on a wrapper and brushed her hair.

Corina stepped out of the bath. In the mirror, Sarah glimpsed a whorl of white lines across her buttocks before the wrapper Corina swirled about herself covered them. Were those scars? What could leave marks like that? Sarah's eyes widened.

Corina turned and looked up from arranging the neckline of her wrapper. She must have seen the shock in Sarah's eyes. She almost flinched in the realization of what her friend must have seen, then hardened herself. Her lips crooked. "My father," she said matter-of factly and tied her belt in a careful bow. "He promised he would never mark me, but he lost control once. I learned all about power from my father, and pleasure, and control." She picked up a brush without looking at Sarah. "He didn't care what I did in public. I was my own mistress. But at Chambroke, I did his bidding." Her voice cracked, and she turned away.

Sarah felt sick. Corina's father beat her? And what did Corina mean that she had learned pleasure from him, too? Sarah didn't want to think. What could she say?

When Corina glanced back at Sarah, she tried a laugh. "Now he's off to India. And I do anything, anywhere I choose. I understand power and pleasure. He taught me well."

A knock interrupted any expression of sympathy Sarah might have been rash enough to offer. Corina didn't want sympathy, but rushed to the door and took a tray from unseen hands.

"Tell Signor Brugelli to remember—half an hour." Then the door shut and Corina turned triumphantly to Sarah, bearing her tray. It held a bottle of wine in a terra-cotta cooler, two dainty glasses, a plate of nuts and dried fruit, and a tiny covered dish.

"Is this what all the fuss was about?" Sarah asked with some asperity. Corina only smiled and put the tray on the table in her room that overlooked the river and the city beyond.

"You don't know anything. Now sit down." Corina spoke as if to a child, but Sarah sat. Corina poured the rich, red-black French claret. "To adventure," she toasted. The clink of the hotel crystal was brittle. She removed the cover of the tiny plate with a flourish. On the green-and-white patterned china lay an array of pickled mushrooms.

Sarah was unimpressed. "What are these?"

Corina's eyes gleamed. "What do they look like? Mushrooms, silly thing. These come from South America. I have wanted to try them for ever so long." She offered Sarah the plate.

"From South America?" Sarah picked up a fork and speared the nearest twisted shape. "Do you think they're safe to eat?" Her specimen did not look appetizing.

"Safe?" Corina shook her head. "Crossing streets is dangerous, but there is so little fun in it, it is hardly worth the risk. Now, for one of these mushrooms, I would entertain a little risk."

"What is the attraction?" Sarah asked as she sniffed the fungi. "Are they like truffles?"

Corina smiled, pierced her own, and popped it in her mouth. "No, not like truffles at all."

Sarah pursed her lips, determined not to allow Corina more boldness in trying new things than she had. She bit at the mushroom warily. It was dried, then marinated. She could taste the olive oil and a mixture of spices, perhaps oregano and thyme. But no marinade could cover the bitter taste. She grimaced and swallowed the piece half chewed.

Corina lifted her chin and closed her eyes for a moment; then her gaze snapped back to Sarah's frown. "They taste better with each bite." Corina speared another for herself. After the second bite, Sarah began to agree with Corina. It was not exactly bad. Between the wine and the mushrooms, she began to feel . . . feel what? She couldn't quite tell. Different. She looked around her, seeing the room, a mirror of her own, for the first time. Dressing table, delicate and ivory, counterpane, wrinkled and puffed, Corina staring at her from the window . . .

The fading sun gleamed red in Corina's golden hair. The mellow light of the Mediterranean afternoon had turned to liquid fire. Corina's eyes knew everything, all the secrets Sarah could only guess she didn't know. Corina shone with her own internal radiance, a being apart, not needing anyone, aware only of her own desires. Oh, to be a magical creature like Corina, illuminating the stone and dull flesh of the world around you, casting showers of incandescence on everyone you touched, only to reveal how inadequate they were by comparison.

Corina stared strangely at her. Sarah felt lost in those blue eyes. Corina rose and loomed over her, then took Sarah's hands. Sarah felt the contact like a blow. Corina's eyes were those of a goddess or a sphinx, ancient and knowing. "Now, are those mushrooms worth the risk?"

"Corina . . ." Sarah felt suddenly that her body was not her own, her senses out of her control. She staggered up from the table. "What were they?" she asked, too late. Panic circled in her stomach like some beast that would devour her. What had Corina done?

"Relax, Sarah, enjoy. They only exaggerate what is inside you." Corina's crystal laugh broke over her like shards of light. "They reveal what you have hidden, even from yourself."

The colors of the silken flowers on Corina's wrapper ran together, swirling like a living thing that fondled her body. That didn't sound so bad. The mushrooms made you more . . . you. The beast inside her disappeared. Instead she looked down at her hands, turning them slowly, and saw blood pulsing through the veins, the texture of her palms, the net of lines, the fine hairs on her forearm. She sat abruptly on the bed. Animal. She was a young animal.

A knock sounded at the door. Sarah watched Corina whirl to answer it in her living wrapper. "Who could that be?" she heard herself say slowly. She reached with effort to her robe. The belt had come undone. She clutched the collar to close it over her breasts.

"More room service," Corina called back. She seemed in control. Had she not eaten mushrooms, too? Corina's voice in the hall was only a hum in Sarah's ears.

Corina led the boy from the courtyard into the room. His hair was damp from bathing, his shirt fresh, open. Sarah realized she was naked under her wrapper. "Corina," she murmured, "why is he here?"

"He's ours tonight. I've paid handsomely for him. Isn't that what you want?" Corina purred.

"Corina, you know I've never—"

"Isn't that what you want?" Corina repeated, refusing to be denied.

Sarah watched the boy, who might have been twenty, as he looked at the floor. She was mesmerized by the firm belly, the smooth skin of his chest. The red welt was like a cord laid across the flesh. Her own body pulsed now in rhythm to some unseen force. "Yes," she breathed. She did want it. Wanting was the only thing that mattered.

"Well, then." Corina drew the boy forward. "Let's see what we have. Strip," she whispered. With fumbling hands, the boy slipped out of his shirt and undid the thick leather belt at his waist. Sarah watched in uneasy silence, feeling her breasts rise and fall. She had never seen a naked man. His breeches pooled at his feet. Sarah's eyes followed them. Then she raised her gaze over the hard muscles of his calves, his corded thighs, to the nest of hair that framed his manhood. Sarah's fascination mixed with a vague disappointment. Was this all? Corina's palm moved over the boy's chest, her other hand on his buttocks. Sarah stared. He looked away, embarrassed, as Corina pinched his nipples. But embarrassed or not, his most male part began to swell. All Sarah's blood seemed to be pushing into her loins. Too much blood, throbbing, demanding something, until the walls of the room receded and Sarah saw only the boy. When Corina achieved what she desired, she drew him to the bed, displaying his erection for Sarah. All that hard staff went inside one? Where? Sarah shrank away, overwhelmed with the physicality of him. But the aching in her own body responded to his body's call, a call she knew, somewhere deep inside, she should ignore.

"You see, he is quite willing, Sarah," Corina said. "Money does wonders. We can do anything." The boy eyes glowed. "Don't look so appalled." Corina shook her head.

Corina was wrong. Sarah should have been appalled. But she was not. He was a gift from Corina, who had taken special pains to see that he pleased. Sarah stood. Her robe fell open. She reached out and ran her hands over the boy's shoulders. Then she was touching him all over, feeling his animal flesh. Corina guided her hands and whispered of desires and possibilities.

Sarah did not care what might be unleashed here. She did not mourn what she would lose. There was only smooth, hard flesh and her power to make the boy respond to her touch.

Corina wanted this for her. The mushrooms wanted it. She wanted it, too. Corina drew them to the bed. The boy was hesitant, but Corina directed his hands, his lips. She whispered every caress. Sarah was all languid desire, held by Corina's eyes. She rubbed the boy's shoulders as he kissed her, arched into him, so that her breasts touched his chest. When he bent to lick her nipples, Sarah thought she might explode. Wanting couldn't describe what boiled inside her. She groaned with need. "Am I dying?"

"You're learning how to live," Corina breathed. She opened Sarah's knees and pressed the boy's buttocks down. The gasp that broke from Sarah's lips was drowned by his hot kisses. If there was some pain, it was the debt she owed Corina. Soon she was lost again in the urgency of desire unfulfilled. Hypnotic whispers from Corina as the young peasant moved rhythmically within her pushed her along. He stopped to caress her most secret parts, a mystery even to herself. Her body cycled further and further from her control, until some dam inside her burst, and sensation flooded in. Her mind focused down to a pinhole, and all her soul was pushed through it into the light beyond. She gasped for breath and her body bucked against the boy. She opened her eyes to find her hands clutching at his arms. Sobs overwhelmed her in a fountain of feeling. Her body had always known this was possible, if she had not.

The boy stroked her arms, her hair while she caught her breath. Corina sat on the edge of the bed and whispered that everything was possible. Sarah murmured her assent. She was dazed, all senses sucked away by the drug and the boy and her own body. She felt him withdraw.

Corina pulled the counterpane up around her. "Was that what you wanted, Sarah?" She smiled a languid assent. "Now, my turn." The boy raised himself on one elbow. Corina's robe fell open. "You are not done yet, young goat," she whispered and pulled him up.

"Can I share what you shared with me?" Sarah's words slurred, careful as she was.

Corina shook her head absently, her eyes opaque blue. "You are not ready to share *my* pleasures, Sarah. When you grow up, perhaps . . ." She went to the dresser. When she turned, she waggled a jingling leather purse. The boy snatched at it as Corina's eyes went liquid with desire, and she tugged him through the bath into Sarah's room.

Disappointment struck Sarah like a shard of glass. She wanted to join Corina, whatever might come next. The door of experience had cracked open and revealed a world she had never known. What else had she missed? She was ready for anything. Didn't Corina realize that? Sarah could see Corina pull the boy's head down to hers through the half-open door.

Sarah dragged herself off the bed, wanting to see what pleasures Corina had denied her. The coverlet clutched around her, she crawled toward the door. Corina's nails dug into the boy's biceps as her kisses intensified. They left red welts, just like the welt across his chest. Sarah felt the throbbing rise in her again. They were young animals. Corina's robe dropped away. It fell into a pool of swirling colors at her feet. How had Sarah never noticed that Corina held the boy's belt? She couldn't concentrate, what with the covers dripping off the bed and the last of the sun washing them all with bloodred light. Corina's face twisted with desire and Sarah's loins trembled in response. She still felt full where the boy had entered her. The colors of the Turkish carpet under her rewove themselves, undulating serpents of red and blue. What was she seeing? Sarah tried to focus, roused by the boy's grunts of pain, Corina's cries of ecstasy, the slap of leather on flesh. Not right. This wasn't right. But Sarah made no move to stop it. Was it even real? A tiny thread of revulsion wound about her spine, but she did not look away. Each tableau of pleasure or pain melted into the next, as though she looked through a kaleidoscope. She throbbed in concert with the rhythm of the strap, the coupling that followed. Corina moaned as the boy thrust inside her. Oh, to be Corina, riding her desire into ecstasy. Sarah floated away, body aching, rocked by the mushroom in her blood.

Sarah woke the next morning slowly, confused and hazy. Her head ached. The pain pushed her out of sleep. Light flooded the room. It hurt her eyes. She was curled in a counterpane on the floor. Something ate at her, demanding attention. Abruptly, the merciful confusion rippled away. The bitter, twisted mushroom, the boy, Corina, what she—*they*—had done. She sat up. She had sacrificed her virginity without a moment's hesitation! What would her future husband say? Her hand crept to her mouth. The overwhelming desire she had felt—was that the mushroom, or something that had always been inside her? She hadn't been frightened by it last night, but she was frightened now. Who was she, that she could lose herself to passion like that? She threw back the quilt and lurched to her feet, stomach revolting. The door to her room, commandeered by Corina last night, still stood ajar. Sarah stared in horror at it as other memories came flooding back. Oh, God above, what had happened last night? She pushed at the door with a trembling hand.

Corina lay across Sarah's bed, sleeping in lithe disarray. The boy's leather belt, supple as a snake, curled at her fingertips. On the floor, the boy himself lay facedown. Welts crisscrossed his buttocks and back, purple and swollen. Sarah shook her head convulsively. Corina's signature, inherited from her father. Pain begot pain. Tears welled into Sarah's eyes. She herself had used this boy and thanked Corina for arranging it! She burned with shame to remember how she had cast aside all she knew was right without even a regret, all at the behest of a mushroom. And those tableaux of pain had turned out to be all too real. She had watched Corina hurt him without even raising her voice in opposition! What had she become? Or what had the mushroom revealed about her? She stifled a sob with the coverlet. She had *asked* to join Corina in her pleasures. Would she have hurt this boy and gotten pleasure from it if Corina had not forbidden her? She did not even have Corina's childhood as an excuse! Sarah clenched her eyes shut.

He might be dead. Should she look? She fluttered, immobile as she gathered her courage. In a rush, she knelt and touched his shoulder. Slowly, he turned his head. He was alive, at least. He stared blankly at her. Then she saw pain and fear rise into his expression. He shrank away from her. He had catered to Corina's sick desires for money, but he got more than he bargained for. And he assumed that she was just the same as her friend. Why would he not? Sarah jerked up and went to the wardrobe, dragging the coverlet, heaved all her dresses out, and hauled them into the next room. She swept them into one of

Corina's trunks, donned a random dress hastily, and left a note for Aunt Letty feigning an urgent return to Bath due to the illness of an imagined relative. The landlord could send the trunk. She checked her purse. She would hire a chaperone at the consulate.

Only then did she turn back to the boy. He eased himself up onto one hip, wincing. Sarah's heart stuttered. She thought she might faint from guilt and shame. What to do? She couldn't think. The last thing she wanted was to wake Corina. She would tell Signor Brugelli to fetch a doctor to the boy and face the landlord's scorn and anger. Then she would run for the dull respectability of Bath as fast as she could get there.

Sarah stared at her reflection in a muddy pool lapping at the walls of her villa, filled with loathing for herself. She had run from Corina, from all she knew and feared about herself. At first she hated Corina for drawing her into an "adventure" with such consequences. Guilt had haunted her for seven years, for what she had done, for what she might have done if Corina had given her a chance. If she married, her husband would likely despise her after their wedding night. Oh, she would pay. Perhaps that was why she had never really cared that George did not propose.

But in the end she couldn't hate Corina. Perhaps knowing how Corina got so twisted made her forgive. Maybe it was that her friend had saved her from even worse things lurking inside her by refusing Sarah's request to join her that night. Or maybe Sarah had a need to overlook Corina's faults. Blinded by the light, she suppressed all knowledge of the dark. She would never know whether she would have joined her, if Corina had allowed it. Sarah only knew she didn't share her incandescent radiance.

The reason memories of Sienna would not be banished now was clear. After all these years, she had not grown wiser, or better. The dark side in her wanted Davinoff, just the way she had wanted that boy. His hand on her arm, the way she felt sitting next to him in the carriage, all excited her unruly body, and revealed those traits she most deplored in herself. Sarah wiped her tears. How could she banish the danger that Davinoff embodied? The cold of the stone seeped into her, the freshening wind off the mouth of the Severn ruffled the hair away from her face as she choked on her sobs. Her eyes darted over the broken bricks and tiles of the villa as her shame seethed.

She sucked in air. The villa's tiles had seen more pain than she ever would, more terrible deeds than she had ever committed. Their sweep of time made little Sarah Ashton's concerns seem unimportant. She breathed out. One went on, after all. She raised her gaze to the abbey. Those stones, too, could tell tales. The world was bigger than Sarah and Corina and Davinoff.

Her body finally moved of its own volition because the stone was cold and she was stiff. She could not change Corina, or Davinoff. She could not change the past, she thought as she trudged back to the Dower House. It was even doubtful she could change herself. But she had to try. She would suppress ruthlessly all those thoughts that were not from her better self. She would embrace the pure, the virtuous, the clean in life and stop running from Corina's affair with Davinoff. Those feelings that made her blush were moot. He belonged to Corina. There had never been any other possible outcome. She would ignore him, should they ever chance to meet. Her resolve almost covered a feeling of despair. It was more than time to go back to Bath.

"I'm bored," Corina said as she leaned against the stone wall of the cellar, peering at the chocolate she held in one hand. Julien could hardly raise his head to look at her. The fog that enveloped his brain made her words vibrate. "What is the point? I'm not even sure you're suffering. I must have imagined you healing so quickly." She paused. "Still, you take more laudanum than I would have thought." She moved closer and peered at him. "And your condition is a problem."

Julien's head lolled against the stone behind him. The healing of his Companion was gone. It was as weak as he without blood. How long had it been? Corina's image wavered before him.

She stood and put one hand on her hip as she finished her chocolate, her face puckered into a frown. "Of course you *are* mine, body and soul." Tossing the sweets wrapper away she began to pace, complaining to herself as she did. "But what soul does an addict have? You never really submitted. You're so stubborn! It's your fault I've had to punish you." She stared down at her nails, perfectly pared. "Too bad there is nothing left but to let you die." She looked over at him. "You would probably welcome that. And now the drug prevents you from truly submitting to me." It was a pout.

Julien followed her voice with difficulty. "End it," he managed.

Corina seemed to agree, except for details. "Here at Chambroke? What would I do with you? Reece could take you somewhere—out to the downs, or to Black Heath south of Devizes. Even if someone found you, you'd either die or they would have to give you laudanum, in which case you remain a hopeless addict. No one will believe an addict. Still, it just doesn't satisfy, does it?"

Suddenly a thought struck her. "Wait! All is not yet finished. You may submit to me yet." She whirled and raced up the stairs, screaming for Reece.

The butler did not appear with his cup of laudanum at the appointed time. No one appeared at all. The fog in Julien's brain receded to reveal raw nerves that began to nag at him and then to scream. He sweated until he was soaked, while his throat grew parched and swollen. The pain of his wounds, suppressed so long, now was magnified a thousandfold until he longed for Reece's tin cup of surcease. He was in withdrawal. Still, if the drug was reduced enough his Companion might reawaken. He might be able to escape. If the Companion were not too much weakened by lack of blood. If he could focus enough with all his senses shrieking. If he didn't claw his own eyes out because they itched so. He tried to breathe. Sooner or later, someone must come. And that someone might have grown careless, sure he was still stupid and tractable. It was his only chance.

The clank of the door above thundered in his head. Reece came down the stairs, grinning.

Chapter Ten

Corina's hand shook as she reached for the handle of the storeroom door. They were but a few steps from the stairs to Davinoff's empty cell. The images of Reece, his neck obviously broken, his wrist slashed, his face white with loss of blood, and Davinoff's empty manacles, trembled in her mind. What had he done to Reece? She didn't know. All she knew was that Davinoff had escaped and she was the person he hated most in the world. She'd been a fool to torture him by denying him the drug for the past few days. They had combed the grounds, the house, the outbuildings. Now the only place he could be was here, close to his cell. Corina knew why he might have returned.

"Do not shoot unless our lives are threatened," she whispered to her search party, consisting of Pembly and several of the stable boys, brandishing their guns. She held up the bottle of laudanum. "He needs this, and he knows it." She gathered her courage and turned the knob.

The door creaked open upon darkness. One of the boys raised a lamp. Corina saw Davinoff standing in the dim corner of the storeroom and her stomach began to churn. Shaking, he leaned on some crates for support. Yes, she thought with satisfaction. She had him now. As the light hit him, her glee faded. His eyes were fierce and malevolent. She had forgotten how evil those eyes could be. For a moment her resolve faltered and she almost ordered Pembly to shoot him where he stood. But glancing round, she saw the stunned look on the faces of the stable boys and remembered the questions she did not want to answer. No, just get the laudanum down him and get him back to the cellar. Silence from Pembly and his boys would cost her dearly, but it was still the way.

"Keep calm," she said, feeling anything but. "Nobody moves." She held up the cup and the bottle where the fugitive could see them. "You cannot do without this." She saw his eyes flash and heard what might be a growl. She could feel his frustration, see him weighing his options. "You have no choice," she said softly. Unstopping the bottle and pouring the liquid into the cup, she then set her lamp on one of the crates without taking her eyes off him. She walked forward, the cup brimming. Its contents sloshed onto the storeroom floor. She set the cup down, almost within his reach, and backed away. "Steady, Pembly," she whispered.

Davinoff looked at the cup for a long moment. Finally, his eyes closed for an instant, in resignation it seemed, and he stretched a shaking hand toward it. *Yes, my pretty*, Corina thought. *Your addiction is the most important thing in your life. Take the cup.*

He lifted the vessel to trembling lips and downed it at a gulp. Corina was astounded. The whole cup? Had he been getting so much? Surely that would kill him outright. The fool! With the craving in his body, the drug's effect should be swift. "Watch out, Pembly," she whispered. "He will try to get past us as soon as the shaking stops."

Davinoff tossed the cup clattering to the floor. Then, as he calmed, he stood tall, eyes closed, his face raised to the ceiling. When his head came down, the eyes snapped open. They were red and terrible, glowing out of the gloom. Corina gasped and peered into the corner where he was, but there was only darkness melting at the edges into the dim vegetable cellar, indefinite, obscure. Pembly held his lamp higher but Davinoff was not illuminated. He carried his darkness as he had shouldered his cape, swirling around his form. Only his face seemed to glow out of the gloom, punctuated by those terrible red eyes. They were wild and venomous, searing her with menace. He had healed himself, and she had ignored that fact at her peril. He was not human. She might well die at his hands or fall prey to something even worse.

A stable boy at her back let off his fowling piece. It sounded like the world ending in the small space, but it went wide. Pembly seemed stunned. The darkness gathered. Was Davinoff even there? Suddenly, the blackness evaporated and their quarry became clearly visible. A cry escaped him, anguished, terrible, like a cornered animal. He lunged forward. Pembly was caught off-guard. He fired his weapon, but Davinoff pushed the muzzle aside. The other stableboy's fowling piece went off. Blood appeared on Davinoff's temple as the shot grazed him. He tossed Pembly aside. Corina backed to the door. The stable boy lunged in from the side. Davinoff pushed him away, and the boy crashed into the crates.

Now there was nothing between Corina and the man she had tortured and humiliated beyond endurance. She stood rooted to the spot, frozen in horror. Silently he stepped toward her. Another step, slower still. She was riveted by his animal eyes, red with fury.

On the third step, his knee buckled under him and he fell to the floor amid a crash of tumbling boxes and vegetables. Corina stood with her back braced against the doorway, helpless. It was Pembly who finally dragged himself up, panting. Lansing, belatedly, came clattering down the hall. Corina returned to herself with a start, her eyes still fixed on the horror that had lurked here. *What was he*? she shouted silently. She ignored Lansing's cries and stared at the creature who had very nearly taken her sanity a moment before.

There was no trace of darkness now. The figure heaped at her feet bore no resemblance to a monster. He was as he had been, shirt in rags, breeches dirty and torn, his feet bare. He still bore the marks of her punishment. Corina looked for evil in his handsome face, but there was none. It was peaceful now, remote. The drug had taken him to its bosom once again.

Had she imagined the whole thing? She looked up and saw

the stable boys standing, incredulous. Their eyes said they saw what she had seen. But what exactly was that? "Pembly, get them out of here." She couldn't think. Taking Davinoff to the downs was no longer an option. She could not live in a world where he lived and might take his revenge. But she dared not kill him at Chambroke. Could they kill such a monster at all? Only the drug seemed to keep him in check. Corina turned to Lansing, her vision blurring with tears. "Have Pembly get him back to the cellar," she whispered to the maid, "until I can think what to do." Then she hurried up the back stairs before everyone saw her tears.

Sarah got back to Bath during the second week in December. Preparations for Christmas were evident everywhere. Cards galore invited her and Amelia to parties and routs. There was a note from George explaining that he was excessively busy, but promising her a Christmas dinner to remember at his mother's house and reminding her about the ball Lady Beldon was giving on New Year's Eve. Sarah still remembered the last Christmas dinner with Lady Beldon, who had been suffering from gout at the time. Amelia fretted about which invitations to accept. Parties seemed unimportant to Sarah. As a matter of fact, everything did. Mr. Thorpe wrote to postpone mapping her villa. His sister was ill. She did not care.

She made herself go to the hospital with Madame Gessande, since that was surely an act of goodness. It occurred to her, however, that she went as much because she was curious about the methods used at the hospital and for her friends there, as because it was an act of charity. Even in tending the sick her motives were not pure.

In the coach on the way home, Madame was full of commentary on her rounds. Finally she fell silent. "What is wrong, dear?" she asked at last. "You do not seem yourself."

Sarah started from the window where she was watching the winter streets of Bath pass by. "And who else could I be?" She smiled, trying to deflect the question.

Madame looked at her in that penetrating way that made Madame an unusual person and a treasured friend. "Will you tell me about it?"

Sarah thought she could say anything to her, but she was wrong. "Nothing to tell."

Madame looked hurt. "I won't press you, *cherie*."

Sarah owed her friend more than obfuscation. But she did not know what she would say until she had said it. "I feel I don't belong anywhere." She paused, surprised that it was true.

There was silence for a moment as Madame Gessande digested this. "That would account for it," she finally agreed. "Amelia, Corina, George, Lady Beldon. They are all very different sorts of people than you are. I should say that you will get past it, that you are not the kind to go dead inside and force yourself to become someone who can belong. But that is the real danger. You have it in you, *petite*, to take all the pain and doubt, all the dreadful knowledge of the world you will accumulate, and turn them into something more."

"What more, Madame?" Sarah asked, unable to keep the pain from her voice.

"Ah, that I cannot say for certain. Not yet," Madame smiled. "I still wait to make that transformation for myself. We are all alchemists, my dear, trying to turn the iron of our lives into gold. I do know this," she continued. "You must never shut yourself off. You must remain open for the alchemy to work. You must always dare, as a child dares, to embrace new things."

Sarah reached out and took her friend's kid-gloved hand in her own. She said nothing, could say nothing. Madame did not know about Sienna, or what Sarah had almost become there. New things were too dangerous when you were Sarah Ashton.

"Now, let me distract you with the gossip that is roaring around Bath," Madame continued briskly. "A Bow Street Runner is making inquiries after Davinoff."

"After Davinoff?" Sarah was startled out of her doldrums.

"About those murders in London. Apparently they think he knows something of value. The Runner has been round to nearly everyone with a drawing." Madame looked over expectantly.

"Well, no one knows where he went," Sarah said, adjusting her muff. Inside, her mind raced. She knew that drawing. Was it really of Davinoff? She might be the only one who knew where he was. What was one's duty in such a case?

"I am sure you are right. And the runner is most disreputable.

I understand they often recruit fellows who know the criminal class firsthand. He is only received because he supposedly represents justice, though whether that be true, I cannot say. I expect he has already left town."

But Madame was wrong. Late that afternoon, Jasco announced with distaste that a person claiming to be from Bow Street wished to see her. If the butler saw her dismay, he gave no proof of it, and waited impassively for instructions.

"Where is my aunt?" Amelia would faint dead away if there were a runner in the house.

"She is resting in her room, I believe."

Sarah sighed in relief. "Show him in, Jasco." She would be forced to do her duty now. She pretended to be reading as her servant announced Mr. Ned Snelling. She glanced up to see a mustard-colored waistcoat glaring at her.

"You!" she exclaimed involuntarily, as she saw the dreaded face once more, now itself screwed up in surprise. "You cannot be a Bow Street Runner!"

"Yer servant, Yer Ladyship." Mr. Snelling nodded with a speculative look in his eye.

"The forces of justice are hiring riffraff these days, I see." She let her distaste show.

"The better to catch the riffraff of the world, ye might say," Mr. Snelling observed.

"I cannot possibly have anything to say to you."

"Ye can't know that until ye know my business. I am a dooly sworn minion of the law." He stood implacably in her study and waited.

"Well, what do you want?" How could she rid herself of him without arousing suspicion?

"Well, now that I see yerself in person, Lady Clevancy, I remembers me that it was none other than yerself were mighty friendly like with that Davinoff cove what I'm lookin' fer. That Delmont Countess says you was the one what talked to 'im most in town, aside from someone called"—here he pulled out a worn notebook and fumbled through its pages—"Nandalay."

"What do you want with Mr. Davinoff?" Sarah asked. Let him tell her his evidence.

"They's been murders, 'orrible murders, miss, in London.

They put the runners out with a pi'ture of the cove they thinks as done 'em." He pulled out of his coat the much-folded drawing that might have been anyone, but might be Davinoff, and waved it in front of her face. Sarah deigned to glance at it, keeping her expression neutral.

"That picture could be anyone," she said, trying to convey little interest.

Mr. Snelling folded the paper carefully and put it back in his coat pocket. "I was on me way to Plymouth on another case when I bumped into you an 'im. Didn't think nothin' of it till about two weeks later when I got back and seen the pi'ture." He watched Sarah with those shrewd little eyes of his. "Took me quite a to-do to go back to Marlborough and ask about 'im. Then I checked each little town on the way. Everybody who sees 'im remembers 'im."

"Well, you know that he was staying at the Christopher here in Bath then," Sarah said brusquely. "What do you want of me?"

"That's the rub. 'E ain't at the Christopher, and don't nobody know where 'e's gone."

Sarah hardly even had to decide. Whether Davinoff had done the deeds was one question, one she could not answer for certain. However, whether she would give him up to the man in the mustard-colored waistcoat was another matter altogether. Of that she was very sure.

"You cannot think I know where he may be," she said sharply.

"I does think jes' that, Yer Ladyship." Snelling's voice was coarse, his eyes knowing.

How she could get this man to take no for an answer? She looked up at him, noticing the wrinkled cravat and the dirt under his nails. She made her eyes go frightened for a moment. "I can see you are an implacable foe." She sighed. "I suppose it is no use to defend him." She took her lips between her teeth and appeared to be thinking. "He will get a fair trial?" she asked hesitantly.

"Fair as the magistrates can make it," Snelling said, his eyes filling with avarice. Sarah remembered the reward offered for knowledge of Davinoff's whereabouts.

"He posted off to Brighton several days ago, I believe." How easily the lie sprang to her lips.

"Go on, Yer Ladyship." Snelling took out a stubby pencil to scribble on the dirty paper.

"He said he had business with Prinny, so I expect you will find him somewhere about the Marine Pavilion." Sarah managed to look as though she might begin to cry. "Have I betrayed him?"

There was a gleam in Snelling's eyes. "Ye've been cooperatin' with the law, that's all."

"But what if he isn't guilty?" she asked, distress lacing her voice.

"Then 'e'll have nothin' to fear." Snelling displayed the leer Sarah remembered so well, then made his exit.

She watched from the front window as he mounted his horse and rode off toward Pultney Bridge. That should do it. The next portion of her resolution was less pleasant. Someone had to warn Davinoff. *What if he is guilty*? part of her cried as she dashed upstairs for her cape and gloves. But a man who wouldn't shed innocent blood in a duel couldn't commit such a grisly string of murders. She looked in the mirror as she put on her hat, and gazed into her own green eyes.

Was she fooling herself? He was a cynic. He believed the worst of people. But he had a self-awareness that did not match the madness that must lurk in one who could commit those murders. She was right. She could feel it. That would be enough for now. It was time to meet straight on what she had run away from. She would go to Chambroke to face Corina and warn Davinoff.

Chapter Eleven

Sarah was in a foul mood by the time she got to Chambroke. She imagined Davinoff lounging by the fire drinking brandy while Corina engaged him with vivacious tales. It was a distasteful prospect until she remembered that she no longer cared about him and his dalliance with her friend. Why had she come? A man like Davinoff probably wouldn't care that Bow Street was after him. She would look naive for the thousandth time.

When Lansing ushered her into Corina's boudoir, Sarah stopped short. She had never seen this Corina who paced the carpet like a caged animal. Her eyes were red-rimmed, her complexion blotchy, her hair in disarray. Even when she had been listless, her friend had never seemed so brittle. Sarah was shocked. This was not what she had expected at all.

Corina seemed not to notice the opening of the door. "What shall I do?" she whispered fiercely to herself. "What shall I do? How dare that dreadful woman quit without notice? And Pembly is insubordinate, the wretch."

"Lady Clevancy is here to see you," Lansing announced with surprising gentleness.

Corina turned with wild eyes. "Sarah? I can't see Sarah, not until I know what to do." She glanced furtively toward her bedroom as though she might dash for refuge.

"Well, perhaps we can discover what to do together," Sarah said with all the calm she could muster. She sat in one of the room's delicate mauve silk-covered chairs. *Davinoff has left her.* She was not proud of the tiny glimmer of satisfaction she felt.

"I don't want anyone to know," Corina said slowly, appearing to gather herself together. "Lansing, I told you not to bring her up."

"Well, you won't take my advice, Madame," Lansing observed. "And we have to do something. Maybe Her Ladyship can help."

Sarah had never trusted the maid. She looked at Corina's haggard face, and said, "Lansing, send to Mrs. Derwent for a cup of tea."

"Mrs. Derwent is gone." Lansing let herself out.

Corina looked wildly about, so Sarah drew another chair close. She patted it. "Come and sit, Corina. You make me nervous pacing about. Sit down and we will decide what to do." Perhaps using her friend's own words would penetrate her anxiety.

Corina looked doubtfully at Sarah, but she sat. "That's better," Sarah declared. "Now let's talk about what to do. I'll help, you know." She considered with some disgust that she was likely to be pulled into some new plot to win back Davinoff's attention.

Corina searched her face. "You will, won't you?" she asked in a small voice. Some of the wildness went out of her eyes. She fell silent as she struggled for control, until Sarah thought she had forgotten her presence altogether.

Finally, Corina gave her winningest smile. Warning bells pealed in Sarah's brain. "Well, you know, Sarah, it began that day when you sent the note that Davinoff was coming out here. I hardly expected him to press his suit so ardently after what had happened at the masquerade." A shadow crossed her face, and her mouth was mobile with emotion for a moment. She got control with a broken laugh and continued. "Of course, I should have known. He was mad about me, kneeling before me, begging me to return his regard." Hysteria kited just below the surface of her voice. The content of this speech did not comfort

Sarah. It was not the Davinoff she remembered in Henrietta Park.

"He got quite out of control," Corina continued, warming to her subject. "He pressed himself upon me, and handled me quite roughly. He was an animal, I vow. I screamed for Reece, of course, but Davinoff attacked him. He quite deserved what he received," she ended, her mouth a petulant frown.

"What happened?" As Sarah examined the blonde's glowing face, doubt assailed her.

Corina glanced at her out of the corners of her eyes. "Reece subdued him." There was a long pause, during which Sarah held her breath. "And we locked him in the cellar."

"You what?" Sarah blurted.

"We had to do it, Sarah," Corina declared. "We had no other choice. He was mad for me and violent. He pushed Reece down. Shooting him was self-defense, no more."

Sarah gasped. "You shot him?"

"Reece shot him," Corina corrected. "It wasn't bad. He's fine." She giggled, then looked horror-struck for a single fluid moment before she went on. "But there is a problem."

This whole story was a product of Corina's overactive imagination. It must be. They had fought, of course. That was inevitable. He'd left her and that had overbalanced her mind. That was it, Sarah told herself, panic welling into her throat. "What is the problem, Corina?" she managed.

"Well," Corina confided, "I don't know how to get rid of him."

Sarah breathed out, afraid she would faint. He was still down there, she thought numbly, weeks later. How could she be sitting in Corina's boudoir thinking that Corina had kidnapped a man and put him in her cellar? Her surroundings turned grotesque, with patterns that danced on the damask before her eyes and flowers wavering upon the carpet.

Corina was already racing on. "You see my problem, Sarah. What can I do with him? I can't just let him go. Reece would have helped me, but when the devil was trying to escape, he killed him." Sarah's gaze snapped to Corina's face; her hand rose to her mouth.

Corina got up and paced the floor. "Pembly won't help me.

He says Davinoff is too dangerous. He actually threatened to go to the beadles until I paid him an exorbitant sum."

Sarah's senses reeled. Corina actually appeared to believe that some fabricated advances on Davinoff's part could justify such crimes against him. And what of Davinoff? Had he killed Reece? She had to keep Corina talking. "What about Lansing?" she managed.

"She keeps him drugged," Corina admitted. "But she says she is not strong enough to get him out of the cellar. Mrs. Derwent is gone, but she was never any use with this sort of thing, and Pembly won't help," Corina repeated in outrage.

"Drugs, Corina," Sarah gasped. "You never drugged him!"

"How else was I to get him down to the cellar?" She sat up and ran her fingers through her disheveled hair. "Sarah, you aren't any help at all."

Why? Sarah wanted to scream. But that might push her friend over the edge. Corina's mind looked very fragile. Besides, she knew why. Because Corina hated Davinoff for humiliating her at the masquerade. And Sarah herself had delivered Davinoff into her hands.

Corina babbled on. "All the trouble that Lansing and I had dragging Reece out in the middle of the night to the hole Pembly dug behind the stables. My dress was ruined." Corina squeezed her eyes shut. "I shouldn't think about that."

Sarah came slowly out of her shock. Murder had been committed here, and kidnapping, and who knew what worse? She would have to report the crime, of course. Davinoff would end in prison for murder and Corina for kidnapping. There would be a dreadful scandal. These thoughts tumbled over one another inside her. And it was her fault! She knew Corina. Why had she never guessed what could happen if she thrust Davinoff out to Chambroke just when Corina seemed unbalanced? Sarah found she was twisting the strings of her reticule into hopeless knots.

Wait! She almost laughed. It probably wasn't even true. How like Corina to wish for revenge and then pretend she had taken it. "Show me where you keep him, Corina. Then I shall know what to do," she said.

"I can't go down there," the girl said with difficulty. She rose and strode to the fireplace, then spun to face Sarah. "I don't go down there anymore."

"Can Lansing show me?" Sarah pressed. Corina nodded slowly. "I'll just ring the bell."

"Lansing," Sarah whispered to the woman who appeared at the door. "Is it true?"

"It's true, all right," the maid returned grimly.

Sarah examined Lansing's sour face, then glanced to Corina, now sunk in a chair. True? "You must take me to him." Perhaps Corina needed only to dispose of the body. "Is he alive?"

"Well, he was this morning," Lansing said.

"Promise me you will help me, Sarah," Corina pleaded.

"I promise," Sarah replied with more assurance than she felt. Her help might well consist in calling the authorities.

Lansing led the way down to the ancient wooden door. Sarah crept behind her. She tried to suppress her dread of what she would find in Corina's cellars. Her heart was thrumming in her chest and her mouth was dry. When they got to the bottom, at first she could see nothing. Lansing lit a lamp and then another. Sarah picked out his form, slumped in the corner on the stone floor.

"My God, Lansing! What has she done to him?" She ran to kneel beside the man. Lansing kept her distance.

"Bring the lamp," Sarah ordered. She was afraid to touch him. The shreds of his shirt did not conceal his injuries. In the dim light, she saw crusted blood on the newer wounds, swollen infection in the older ones. Her eyes filled. Revulsion pressed up into her throat with bile. No doubt Corina had gotten pleasure from inflicting these wounds. Memories of Sienna flashed inside her, along with all her years of doubt, all her dread at what she might have done, had Corina allowed it. But as she was confronted with a man who had really been tortured, all her doubts receded. Looking inside, she found not a shred of titillation at his pain, only a shuddering disgust for Corina, pity for her victim, and a deep guilt that she had delivered him thus. She took a breath. As she exhaled, more was released than air from her lungs.

Pity was not enough. She owed for her role in his torture, inadvertent as it was. Action was what was required. Resolve seeped into her spine and she steadied herself. Slowly she lifted his head from his breast. He blinked sluggishly. He was alive at least. But the eyes that had been so full of power they had frightened her were now glazed and dead. Sarah bit her lip. "What did you give him?"

"Laudanum," Lansing replied uncomfortably.

Sarah wanted to scream at the old woman for what she had helped do to this man, but that would not help. She had to get him medical treatment. Though that was definitely not what Lansing and Corina had in mind. She thought quickly. "She wants to get him out of here without being able to trace him to Chambroke, doesn't she?"

"I knew you would help her, Your Ladyship. I knew she could trust you with the truth."

"And the story of him attacking her?" Lansing's look of surprise was all Sarah needed. She imagined weeks of vengeful torture and drugs. *I made it easy for her.* "I've an idea. I'll go explain it to Mrs. Nandalay," she said briskly, standing up. "You go get a gig—not the one I came in—and meet me here."

"I'll bring one of Pembly's driving capes to wrap him in. The servants will be in for dinner. No one will notice if we slip out the door into the yard, Your Ladyship."

"Hurry," Sarah commanded, and rushed up the stairs without looking back.

"All right," she said, returning to find Corina picking through a box of chocolates. She had refined her plan on the way up from the cellar. "You want him taken away, don't you?"

Corina nodded, anticipation gleaming in her eyes.

"You cannot dispose of him anywhere close. He should be taken to an asylum on the Continent, where no one can identify him. It will cost you, but you can buy their silence. I suspect you will not have to support him long."

"Excellent, Sarah," Corina exclaimed, her relief evident. "I was going to leave him on the downs. But no one inquires about inmates in asylums."

Sarah did not bother to tell Corina that leaving him on the downs in his current state would be murder; she would not care. "I will need one of Chambroke's gigs. Lansing can return the one I hired so no one comes looking for it. I also need a supply of laudanum, enough to last two weeks. Will that serve?" Sarah looked at her with new distaste.

The blonde came with arms extended to embrace Sarah, friend no longer, though she could not yet know it. "I knew I could count on you, in spite of all Lansing said."

Another lie, Sarah thought, as she untangled herself from Corina's embrace. She wanted only to escape, and to make good Davinoff's escape as well. She had to get him to a doctor.

"You will need money, Sarah," Corina remarked. "I will prepare the drafts."

Sarah resolved to tear up those drafts at the first opportunity. "Yes, Corina." She turned to Lansing, who had come to stand inside the door. "Where are his trunks?"

The maid looked uncomfortable. "I left his trunk at the Christopher with directions for the Crown and Cushion in Shepton Mallet when I paid his shot."

"Well enough. They would have kept it, expecting its owner to arrive. Have Pembly pick it up and deliver it to Jasco at Laura Place. His horses and his carriage?"

"Tattersall's," Lansing said shortly. They had sold his pair and Quixote! Sarah's stomach turned again. It was another symbol of his violation.

At the door, Sarah turned to see Corina open her gilded box and pause over the difficult process of selecting a chocolate. Her problem was solved, her distress forgotten. "Someday, Corina, your account will come due. I hope you have credit enough to pay it."

She looked up, puzzled, as Sarah shut the door firmly after herself.

The next events took place in a whirl of fear and haste that left no time for Sarah to think. She and Lansing again made their way down to the cellar, while Lansing warned her how dangerous Davinoff was. Sarah pressed her lips together against a reply. The creature she had seen hurt and drugged in the cellar was not a threat. These two were the dangerous ones.

Lansing produced a key and released the long chain from the ring in the wall. Sarah knelt beside him, in spite of the maid's warning. She raised his head and looked into those dead eyes.

"I am going to get you out of here," she whispered, "but you must help." She had no idea whether he understood or not. "Lansing, give me the key."

"Your Ladyship," Corina's servant admonished. "I can't say I'd go near him with his hands free."

Sarah sighed. She needed Lansing. "I must unlock his ankles. We are not strong enough to drag him bodily up the stairs."

Reluctantly, the maid proffered the key. Sarah bit her lip when she saw the open sores the iron bands revealed. No time for revulsion. Just get him up the stairs. She paused to look into Davinoff's face. Had he killed Reece? "No tricks," she whispered, whether he could understand or not, "or you will never get out of here." She took the cloak from Lansing and fastened it around his shoulders. Then she put the key into her reticule.

"Lansing, you have to help me," she commanded. When the woman hesitated, Sarah barked, "Can't you see he's stuporous with drugs? He cannot hurt you now."

Lansing moved reluctantly into Davinoff's range. "Get on your feet," Sarah ordered him. She took an arm and pulled the man up as he struggled to get his feet under him. His touch shocked her still, just as it had in an inn yard, at the masquerade, in his curricle. She might get no pleasure from his pain, yet she still could not trust herself; what had been in Sienna could arise again. Sarah pulled Davinoff's manacled hand across her shoulder resolutely and Lansing supported one arm as they struggled to the stairs. The stairs provided an unfortunate revelation: They weren't wide enough for three.

"Lansing, follow behind." Sarah was already panting. "Davinoff, you have to get up these steps if you want to see daylight," she urged. She put her free arm around his waist under the cloak and felt the warmth of his body against hers. She shuddered as they took the first step. It seemed as if there were hundreds. Somehow, they made it to the top. She let him sag against the wall. They gasped together with their effort.

Lansing took up his other arm and together they got him out a small side door into the deepening twilight. Pembly stood at the head of a horse harnessed to the gig. He made no move to help as they allowed Davinoff to fall into the back of the vehicle, manacles clanking. Sarah gathered up Davinoff's legs and folded him inside. Lansing hurried back into the house as Sarah threw a blanket over him. Sarah went round to the driver's seat and took the whip from Pembly.

"That one is a devil, Your Ladyship, and no mistake," the groom growled. Sarah drew her cloak around her against the freshening wind. Only eight miles back to Bath, but three-quarters of an hour at the least. It was dusk, four-thirty and drawing on to five.

Lansing appeared in the lighted doorway. She held a wooden box up to Sarah. "Laudanum," she murmured, as Sarah set the box beside her on the seat, "and money."

"How much does he get?" Sarah asked, suddenly realizing how important that piece of information might be. She would have to tell the doctors.

"He gets a cup," Lansing said. "A cup in the morning, a cup at night."

"No, no, I meant how much is in the cup?" Sarah demanded as she gathered up the reins.

"I told you," Lansing replied, her voice hard. "He gets a cup, night and morning."

Sarah turned to stare. "A third that dose would kill a man."

Lansing turned wary. "Well, that's as it may be. But that's how much he gets. He's strong, that one is, and dangerous." She closed her mouth as if determined to say no more.

Sarah sat, stunned for a moment. Then she turned fiercely to Pembly. "Stand away," she shouted, and cracked her whip. The horse broke from the house at a canter.

As she passed the gatehouse, Sarah was flooded with relief. They were out of that house of horrors and away from basements and chains and Corina's brittle laugh. She found the road that led through the village of Langridge and thence to the Bath road and looked back at Chambroke, all its lights blazing across the park as night drew on. Sarah's mind reeled. She had thought Davinoff evil once, anarchy incarnate. Perhaps he was. But evil seemed rampant in the world tonight. It glowed out of Chambroke's symmetrical windows. Glancing down at the still cargo in the rear of the gig, she then turned and urged the horse back into a canter. She prayed the clouds would not obscure the full moon that promised to light her way.

What to do? Now that they had escaped Corina, Sarah began to tremble. Should she knock up the magistrates at this hour to report the foul doings at Chambroke? No, first she must help Davinoff. She imagined a scene wherein she took him to George and begged his help in breaking the addiction. Would George do it? And then there was the dosage. Dr. Parry and George never took on those with severe addictions; they sent whoever who could afford it to asylums to receive their drug and the simple care they needed to finish their days in a vegetable state. The man she knew as Davinoff would never willingly accept that. But it was the only choice George or Dr. Parry would give him.

Sarah slowed the horse to a trot to save his strength, her mind boiling. Was there another choice? The authorities would just throw him in a cell and wait for him to die. She could not abandon Davinoff. She owed him that. But where did that leave her? Fear licked at her mind as she realized what the way ahead must be.

She had to try to save him herself. Perhaps if she used Dr. Parry's method of removing the laudanum slowly, she could rid him of his slavery to the drug in spite of the high dosage. Dr. Parry's method was meant to soften the blow of withdrawal to the system. Maybe it would save Davinoff's life. It was a chance at least. A chance the man would not get from anyone else. Did she know enough from her days at the hospital to do it? Her mind darted over the process, the things she would need. He might die anyway, she thought, and she faced that possibility. But not before she had done the best she could for him.

This meant that she could not report Corina's crime. If she did, Davinoff would be discovered. Then it would be the asylum or the cell. Corina deserved punishment, but Davinoff came first. If he died, she would have to explain a body to the magistrates. She smiled grimly. She would be in much the same dilemma as Corina. She could end in jail herself. But it didn't matter now. She was committed.

It was eight o'clock before she started to Clershing. It was the only place she knew where they could be private. She bundled Amelia off to a friend in Bristol for the holidays, and Jasco and

Addie to relatives. Jasco would close up the house in Laura Place tomorrow, after shipping the trunk Pembly brought round to the Dower House. She sent a note to Lady Beldon, crying off from Christmas dinner but promising to be back for the New Year's ball. Then she had braved the hospital, pretending to look for George. Would he miss the things she had stolen from his laboratory? She had now lied to Corina and stolen from George. And she didn't care.

The trip to Clershing was a nightmare: sixteen miles of bone-chilling wind and worry. The crowded streets of Bath delayed her. The landscape on the post road to Bristol had a ghastly quality, strange and unfamiliar. She had never been so far at night alone. She had entered a world where the sun never shone. There was only night, the snorting of the horse, the wind, and her living cargo—living how long she did not know. She stopped twice to check Davinoff. He was growing restless for his laudanum. Yet he had to wait until she got him to the Dower House. She skirted Bristol; the busy streets of a port city were no place for a woman unprotected.

All her doubts assailed her now. Why had she taken it upon herself to kill what was left of this poor man? She had feared and hated him when she thought he wanted Clershing. She had been disgusted by his infatuation with Corina. She had been attracted to him in the most dangerous way. But the man who treasured the stones at Avebury deserved more than what Corina had left him. Sarah had made her choice, and there was no turning back.

When finally the looming darkness of the Dower House rose up behind its wrought-iron gates, it was almost midnight. Sarah threw off her lap rug and allowed the tired horse to stand as she jumped down. She almost fell. Her feet were numb with cold. The gates creaked open. She led the horse through, then closed them behind her and climbed back into the driver's seat. In one way she was glad it was late. She could not let anyone know she and her charge were here.

The gardens of the Dower House were eerie in the moonlight. The trees that provided such lovely shade in summertime now towered, black skeletons, above the gig as she trotted up the drive. Then they were out of the shadows and into the silvery glow that brushed the unruly bushes with ghostly winter fire. She brought the gig up in front of the portico and leapt down to tie the horse to the hitching post almost buried in the shrubbery beside the doorway. He should be rubbed down, but he would have to wait until she got Davinoff inside.

She strode to the back of the gig and threw off the blankets covering Davinoff. He raised one hand, clanking with manacles, to the side of the gig and dragged himself into a half-sitting position. That was more life than she had yet seen.

"Where is this place?" he murmured.

"The Dower House at Clershing," Sarah replied, her nerves making her voice quake. "Not far from your precious abbey." Feeling in her reticule, fingers made clumsy by cold and her gloves, she finally produced the huge key. She held each of Davinoff's wrists in turn and opened his manacles. "Let's get inside before we freeze."

She grasped his hand, more icy than her own, and pulled his arm once more across her shoulder. His body seemed to engulf her as she moved her arm round his waist. Leaning on her heavily, he stumbled up the shallow steps to the front door. Sarah managed to produce her key and push the door open. They practically fell into the house. The wind gusted in around them and twirled the last damp leaves of autumn onto the wood floor of the entry hall. Sarah dragged Davinoff into the dark drawing room and allowed him to drop upon the shadow of a divan. She felt for the lamp she kept upon the table near the door, then fumbled for the flint striker. It took her several frustrating moments to produce the spark to light the wick, but finally a sturdy flame lit her way to other lamps about the room.

When she turned from the last lamp, Davinoff watched her with dull eyes. His chest heaved with the exertion of getting into the house. In the light of the drawing room, his condition was even more appalling. His cheeks were hollow. Dreadful black circles under his eyes made them appear sunken. Through his stained and tattered shirt she could see not only the cuts that had shocked her in the cellar, but horrid bruises in various colors over much of his upper body. His breeches were shredded, and similar violations on his hips and thighs peeked through. She would have to heal these wounds as well as challenge his addiction. Already he trembled with need. It all seemed overwhelming.

As she stood there, daunted, he raised his head from the back of the divan where he was sprawled. Was there hatred in his clouded eyes? "Why do you change my prison?" he whispered.

Sarah was shocked into silence. Of course he thought she was in league with Corina. She flushed to the roots of her hair. "You may think the worst," she said with difficulty. "But I did not know Corina's dreadful plans when I sent you to Chambroke. She thinks I took you to an asylum on the Continent tonight." She stopped. How to tell him of her plans to risk his life? What did *he* want? Was he capable of deciding in this condition? She took a deep breath and went to sit at the end of the divan. His flat gaze followed her. "I want to help you," she said. Her voice sounded small in her own ears. "No hospital will take you with your dose of laudanum. They would send you to an asylum, continue your addiction. That kind of life . . ."

"No," he croaked, shaking his head. Then with even greater effort he focused his eyes upon her. "If you want to help, kill me."

Sarah moved her hand to her throat, abruptly unable to breathe. "I . . . I could never kill you," she said. Was there a pleading in his eyes? He was definitely shaking now.

"Yes, you could," he whispered. "Easy now. A knife, a pistol . . ."

"But there is another choice," she said. "If you agree to try. I . . . I have seen Dr. Parry reduce the dose of laudanum slowly, over time. He has had some good results, not with anyone taking so much as you, of course," she rushed on, aware of how inadequate her plan sounded. "I could try the same with you. That is, if you agree." He watched her, his hands shaking with his need. She must tell him the whole truth. "You could still die."

She looked for acceptance, defiance, anything that indicated he understood. His eyes closed. Had he lost consciousness entirely? Then he did something surprising. She heard a low rumbling chuckle escape him.

"Cast the dice," he muttered. "I win either way." Then his eyes closed again.

That was all the absolution she would get from him. When nothing further was forthcoming, she rose reluctantly. "I will try," she whispered, the promise almost choking her.

She brushed down the horse while she mentally toted up the supplies left from her last week's visit. She would not starve, and neither would the horse. Four trips with the bucket for water, then it was back to the house with her lamp and the box of laudanum. She could not face bringing in her trunk and the bandbox from the hospital just now. As she crossed the midnight garden to the house, the wind pulled at her hair and her cloak. She began to think of Davinoff killing Reece with his bare hands. Would he be there, slumped upon the divan? Or would he be lying in wait somewhere in the darkened house to give her as good as he had given Reece? She went round to the front door, to enter into a lighted hall, rather than trek through the dark house from the back. She stalked up onto the porch, and felt her steps slow involuntarily. She mustn't stop. She must keep moving toward that door. If once she stopped, she might well turn and run. The handle of the door seemed to reach out and grasp her hand. She turned it with a force of will and pushed into the hall. But there he was, still sprawled where she had left him. When a sigh escaped her, she realized she had been holding her breath.

Well, enough of that. She must be overtired. Even so, it was time to get to work. Davinoff was trembling and needed the laudanum. She set down her lamp and opened the box. A cup? Could he really be taking that much? If he wasn't, she would kill him before they were fairly begun. Sitting beside him, she poured out slightly less than a cup into a vial she had stolen from George's laboratory, and touched Davinoff's arm. He rolled his head in her direction and opened his eyes. They fixed upon the vial.

"Lansing said you got a cup at night and one in the morning," Sarah said, taking a breath. "Is that true?" He only stared at the vial. "If it isn't, this will kill you. You may want that, but I don't want you to die," she whispered fiercely. "Tell me the truth!"

The eyes broke the fascinating hold of the vial with effort and brushed against her own. He only nodded and took it from her with shaking hands. He pressed it convulsively against his lips and upended it, eyes closing in relief. The first of many, Sarah thought. Before the drug had time to cloud his senses any further, she had to explain.

"There will be less and less each time, until you are free of it. When you begin to withdraw you could hurt yourself." *Or me*, she thought. She rushed on. "I have seen it at the asylum. I know you will not like this . . ." How could she say what she must? "When it begins, I will have to tie you up, and the only place I can do that is the cellar." The words sounded hollow. "It won't be like Corina, I promise you. But I cannot afford lights to be seen at night in the upper house. I can't let anyone know we're here." She chewed her lip and looked for his response. His eyes closed. A small smile touched his lips, as if from far away. She needed more. She needed to know he did not blame her. "Please tell me you agree. I cannot do it without your help, you know." The smile lingered. He nodded.

Sarah breathed a sigh of relief. "I will prepare the way." She took the lamp and began the scavenger hunt. Bedding, candles, and a large mixing bowl were her first finds. Then it was down to the cellar, smelling musty and damp. One end was crowded with items no longer used: a trunk, a huge mirrored wardrobe, a birdcage for a childhood friend long dead, crates of china, a scarred marquetry table. Sarah set down her lamp and began to rearrange the room. She pulled a large dusty wing chair out from the wall to reveal the metal rings so reminiscent of Corina's cellar. A shudder ran up her back. All houses had a place for hanging meat. It meant nothing.

When she had cleared a place for the bedding and arranged the chair and table, she left a candle burning, and went to get Davinoff. The trip down to her own cellar was at least as hazardous as the journey out of Corina's. Davinoff seemed to have doubled his weight. As they staggered down the steps, Sarah pictured them falling in a heap of broken bones to the flagstone floor below. Somehow she got him to the pallet she had formed from a featherbed folded in half and several blankets. He collapsed to the bedding, and she was left holding only his hand. Even in this light, she could see the nails were dirty. But that could not hide the elegance of his bones. With a start, she released his hand as though it burned her, and it dropped to where he lay on his side. She turned away quickly and retrieved the candle.

Davinoff watched her through half-closed eyes. "I will leave the candle," she said. "You must sleep now, and save your strength." He seemed already to be fading as she drew a blanket up around his shoulders. She would treat his wounds in the morning. She made her way upstairs to douse the lights in the drawing room and find her own bed. Tired though she was, it was a long time before she fell into a troubled sleep, dreading the task she had set herself and him.

Chapter Twelve

As Sarah shook off sleep the next morning, her thoughts buzzed lazily about until they came to Davinoff. She sat bolt upright. What hour was it? She leapt out of bed and threw back the heavy curtains. The sun said it must be nearly ten. She hurried into her clothes from yesterday, hastily dragged a brush through her hair, and twisted it up in the back. She left the short hair that framed her face a wild dark halo and ran down to the drawing room to retrieve her supplies. Her patient would suffer for her tardiness.

The light of day suffused the house, dispelling last night's fear. Still the rooms had taken on a foreign quality, oozing Davinoff's presence in the cellar. She saw them through a stranger's eyes as she rushed to the kitchen to collect her boxes and bottles. The house was a comfortable melange of furniture garnered from other houses and thrown together into cozy rooms of human proportions. Tudor, like the main house now so long gone, it was half-timbered with an overhanging first story. It was by no means grand, even graceful, but Sarah had always liked it.

She opened the door to the cellar, balancing the clinking bottle of laudanum, the cup, and a lamp. As she reached the last stair, lamplight suffused the basement room and she could see that Davinoff was awake, shivering under his blankets. Sarah cursed herself for oversleeping. She knelt over him. He was sick, but his eyes were clearer than they had been last night.

"I am so sorry," she said as she turned to her bottles and her measuring cup. "This is my fault." She poured out the required amount. Less. It would always be less. "You'll be better in a moment. Can you sit?" He pushed himself up against the wall with a grunt of effort and reached for the cup with shaking hands.

Sarah hesitated before she reached out to steady his hands with her own and helped him drink. The sting of hot flesh made her realize that he had a fever. She took the cup as he closed his eyes and sank back against the wall. She pulled the blanket up around him, and smoothed it across his thighs. She could feel the shaking subside as the drug took effect.

"Better?" She was rewarded by a small nod. Those islands of tranquillity provided by the drug would narrow as the dose decreased, flooded by the storms that would wrack his body.

She rose. "I . . . I must do something about your injuries." Escaping up the stairs, she began another scavenger hunt. She thought only about what she needed, not what she must do when she returned to the cellar. Soap . . . lots of soap and some of Addie's best sheets cut into strips. She laid a fire, put water on to boil, and smiled to herself to think that she was about to use both George's science and Addie's. It was Addie who kept the gardens stocked at the Dower House and Laura Place not only with tomatoes and carrots, but with burnet and chamomile, pennyroyal and valerian. Sarah wished Addie were here to advise her. She racked her brain to recall the uses of each. The garden was winter-empty, but the pantry would be well stocked with dried herbs.

She lit a candle and made her way into the small, windowless pantry. Peering at the shelves lined with glass jars, carefully labeled, she could see yarrow and bergamot. No burnet, but thyme would do if she remembered right. Later she would need chamomile, or there was a jar of dried catnip. She gathered the jars and balanced her candle. At the last moment she saw the cloves of garlic heaped next to the onions and potatoes and remembered the garlic poultice Addie had concocted for an infected cut when she was eight. She grabbed several heads.

Sarah set her treasure trove upon the long table in the kitchen. Davinoff's most immediate needs were for disinfectants; sedatives or nausea-suppressants would come later. As she worked, the smell of crushed herbs heavy in the air, her task ahead seemed ordinary: soaking each herb in water or vinegar to release their properties, making poultices. She was a volunteer, just as she was in the hospital, and he was a patient, not a man. There was a difference, she told herself sternly, a difference that would be strictly observed.

Thus prepared, she made her way back to the cellar. It took several trips to get the herbs, the hot water, the clean cloths and bandages all down the stairs. Davinoff lay in a drugged dream state once again. As she prepared, he watched her for a while, but soon lost interest and turned his face away. That was good, she thought. It was better.

She knelt and began by cutting away his shirt. She made her breathing slow and regular, remembering other patients, other tasks. He was strongly built, his chest lightly covered with curling black hairs. She dipped her cloth in the steaming bowl of water, soaped it, and began her task. He did not flinch when she soaped the sores on his wrists. She bathed him, scrubbed open the infected cuts until they bled, then rinsed and dried him, one part at a time. Soon the water in her basin grew rosy with his blood. Slowly she worked over his body. But she could not quite lose herself in the task at hand. The feel of his flesh under her fingers made her nether parts throb. She got no pleasure from his pain, but she still did not have full control of herself. Her darkest desires were still there, waiting to be unleashed. Sarah's breathing quickened in spite of her best intentions. She chastised herself, but her thoughts strayed wantonly to his muscled thighs. Had she been forever tainted by Sienna?

He is a *patient*, she cried to her disobedient body. Assess the situation. His ribs were likely cracked, based on the terrible bruising about his torso, but as long as they were not pushed in, they would probably heal by themselves. Breathing was surely a torment for him, though. She had seen such patients cry with every gasp. He showed little sign of the pain. His addiction probably protected him for now. She worked upon his ankles. They were easy.

At last she could put off no longer dealing with the lacerations on his thighs, visible through his torn breeches. She would have to put her embarrassment aside. As he became ill in withdrawal, she would have to do everything for him. Which did not allow for breeches. With less control than she pretended, she took up her sewing scissors and cut them away. She had seen men at the hospital, old and young, she told herself. But that was not what came to mind. Sienna threatened to overwhelm her. She refused to look at the curling hair at his groin, the part that made him man, so she washed him too vigorously, blood oozing over his thighs and hips. Would there was a way to avoid touching him, but again and again as her flesh met his, her fingertips were scorched. She felt the heat even through the cloth she used to scrub him.

"I must do this." She murmured the mantra to herself as she patted him dry. "Open the wounds, clean out the infection. I will wash him many times, you know. Many times."

Finally she rocked back on her heels and drew her sleeve across her brow. With sudden self-consciousness she glanced up to his face, but his head was still turned away. Thank God. Without giving herself time to think, she laid on the poultices of garlic she had made and bound them securely with her strips of sheets. When it was done, she drew up the coverlet gratefully. To her surprise, she found his heavy eyes staring out at her.

"Thank you," he murmured. Sarah felt the flush spreading over her face and neck. He knew all along what she was doing. Had he turned away to save her embarrassment? If so, she thought—furious at herself, furious at him—it hadn't worked.

"I will get you food," she said and retreated up the stairs.

A search of the kitchen was sobering. There was a beef in the icehouse left from last week that would have to be used shortly and a ham that would last longer. Potatoes and yams, carrots and onions were in abundant evidence. She found flour and dried oats, and there were apples and some dried fruit from the summer garden, a round of cheese from last week. There would not be much variety, but she could make do for two weeks if she was careful. That would be enough. She realized she had not eaten since yesterday's tea time and suddenly was famished. Standing, she ate some cheese and dried apricots while she fixed a bowl of oats cooked into gruel for Davinoff. She would add other food when she was sure he could keep it down.

Sarah was entirely herself by the time she returned to the cellar. She helped Davinoff sit and offered him the bowl. "I know you won't like it," she said, not looking at him, "but it will lie easy on your stomach. I expect you have not been eating very much."

"Not what I need," he murmured, as he took it.

Men always wanted beef, Sarah thought irritably, beef and wine. No matter what the circumstances or how bad it was for them. "Well, this is better for you than what you think you need, believe me," she replied and rose to watch him eat. He was a trifle unsteady, but she thought he would manage. Later, that would be impossible.

Sarah busied herself in the afternoon with closing up the draperies in all the rooms, so no light escaped. The Dower House was fairly isolated from the people who still lived and worked on the estate. Now that the main house was gone, all activity was down in the village or in the lane that ran through the cottages of her tenants. Unlike Corina, Sarah went to great pains to see that these cottages were kept well. She had put in new drainage only two years ago, and had each cottage painted and repaired. Most of the money from her first crops had gone to improving the estate. Only this year had there been enough to spare for retiring the last mortgage.

Just when she decided she was safe from prying eyes, she was startled by a rap upon the front door. Her stomach turned over. Who could know she was here? The sharp rapping came again and continued. What should she do? She might as well know the worst.

She opened the door a crack and peered out. There was a callused and bored-looking carter there with a huge trunk. She sighed in relief. Of course. Davinoff's trunk. She bade the man leave it in the hall and swept him out the door. Then she went to the window and watched him drive his cart away to be certain he was really gone.

Davinoff was feverish again when she went downstairs,

though there were still several hours until the next dose. *It begins*, she thought. She put down her tray and knelt beside him. He looked steadily at her, less dulled, perhaps. She pulled out the cups that held her herb pastes.

"Let me rub these into your wounds," she proposed. "They will help you heal." She could see the pain now in his face at each breath. He nodded tightly, and she steeled herself to touch him. The odor of the pastes was strong. Davinoff was sensitive and flinched under her touch. She almost flinched as well, in spite of her resolution. For him it was the beginning of the reaction.

"What is that concoction?" His question surprised her. He had been so quiet up to now.

"This one? It is garlic."

His head sank back against the stone wall and he smiled weakly.

"It's an old folk remedy," she explained.

"Not all the legends about garlic are true," he said.

"Well, this one is," she retorted and smoothed a fingerful of paste into his shallower cuts.

When she was done, she gave him food, which again he managed to eat. Then it was more of the drug, measured carefully now with the vial from George's laboratory calibrated in grains and drams. He got eighteen drams of laudanum. His eyes clouded visibly as the drug took effect. He fell almost immediately into an exhausted sleep.

Sarah decided that her own chamber was too far away. She would not hear him two floors away if he called. So she went upstairs, bathed, and changed, and brought down some books from the small library, several pitchers of water, and a plate of dried fruit with some fresh apples. There were candles; enough for weeks, she thought gloomily as she curled herself in the great, overstuffed chair and prepared to read herself to sleep.

She awoke abruptly in the small hours of the morning to find Davinoff vomiting uncontrollably on the floor beside his pallet. His body was wracked with heaves and he was spitting red. Not unexpected, though she was surprised it had happened so soon. Still, he had already shed fifteen drams from his daily dosage, more than most men ever received at all.

She held his head until the sickness passed. He gasped for breath and held his ribs as she laid him back on his makeshift bed. "I'll do something for that," she whispered, and hurried up the stairs to the kitchen.

She rushed down to the cellar with a pot of the tea she had brewed from dried bergamot, now cold. "This will help the nausea," she said as she held the cup to his lips. She wished she felt as sure as she sounded. He gulped with difficulty. But shortly thereafter the liquid was vomited up as another spasm shook him. Again she held him until the sickness passed and again poured out a cup of the tea. "Once more," she encouraged as she held his head up to the cup. "But slowly, little sips." When it was down, she laid his head back on the bedding. She cleaned the floor and took the soiled quilt away, replacing it with a fresh one from the stack by the door.

Davinoff lay back, exhausted, but when he turned toward her, she saw his eyes were clearer than she had seen them since that day in Henrietta Park. "Why do you do this?" he rasped.

She looked away. There was no answer she could say out loud. "Who else is there?"

She sat with him for the three hours remaining, watching his torture begin. He tossed and shook and gasped for breath. But he said nothing and did not ask for the drug. As the sun was surely rising, she measured out fifteen drams and he drank it gratefully. They both slept.

Sarah woke while Davinoff still dozed fretfully, and she slipped up the stairs for food. She supplied the horse with extra hay for his manger and filled his trough with water, enough for several days. She brought an entire tray of dried fruits, some beef, and the strong cheese from the Cheddar Gorge down to the cellar. She might not want to leave the room again for a while.

During the next four hours, Davinoff alternately shook and sweated with the fever. The nausea came and was banished again, but he was greatly weakened. She sat on the floor and watched his torment. He did not cry out, but sometimes low sounds escaped him. Sarah changed his poultices and examined his wounds. She gave him water when he would take it. When at last six o'clock drew near by the delicate watch on the chain round her neck, she measured out the diminishing drams and waited for the time. If she started cheating on the time, she might start cheating on the amount. She wouldn't let herself do that. She owed him more than that.

More, more what, more pain? Death? That seemed closer than ever. Could she just reduce the addiction to a tolerable amount? Sarah sighed. He would not want any addiction. Not the Davinoff she knew. Never once had he asked for the drug. Not like all those pleading faces, clutching hands, shrieking mouths at the hospital. She could not undo Corina's evil. But she could do her best to help this man find the way back to his former self. Sarah watched him writhing on his pallet. Corina's mad revenge had not yet run its course. *The worst is yet to come*, she thought. *We've still half the way to go*. She glanced at her watch and found that six had come and gone. Rising wearily, she went to him.

"It's time," she said and held his head to drink. His eyes seemed not to register who she was. But he drank as she pressed the cup to his lips. The drug would give him peace for only a few hours. It was time for something else as well. She went upstairs and took the shackles from the cart. Refusing to think, she returned and hooked them to the ring in the wall, using a length of chain that had bound a trunk. Not like Corina, she said softly to herself. Not the way Corina tied him up.

She leaned over him to grasp his right hand and lock him into the heavy metal bands. She felt him stiffen and looked down, startled, to see him staring at her intently. His eyes jerked from her neck to her face. She was so close she could feel his breath, hot and ragged. His scent wafted up about her, a sweet muskiness that intoxicated her, not like her father, not like the Tuscan boy, not like any man she knew. The need in his eyes held her as surely as she still held his wrist. She knew that look. She had once seen one like it in Sienna. She should break the hold his eyes had on her, but somehow she did not. Her breasts brushed against his chest as she sighed into him. *Yes*, she told him silently. Slowly he raised his head from the pallet. She lowered her mouth to his, her lips parted in anticipation of his kiss.

It was he who broke the spell. With a growl, he wrenched

away and snapped his head to the wall. "No!" His anguished cry echoed in the stone cellar. "I will not lose control."

Sarah started back, shaking with shame, and dropped his wrist as though it burned.

"You must not know," she heard him whisper.

She rose hastily and turned away, palms pressed to her hot cheeks. What had she been doing here? The man was ill, for pity's sake, and she had wanted him. Were her impulses so mean, so uncontrollable? Chains clanked against the wall. She turned to see Davinoff clamping the manacles awkwardly about his own wrists.

His head lolled against the stones. "I did not mean to frighten you." His eyes were closed. Only the rasping whisper indicated that he was conscious. But it too was fading. "I need you."

Sarah stood there, eyes closed tightly, and tried to will away her shame. It would not be banished. Lord, her baser nature asserted itself at every turn. Yet . . . had he not wanted her as well? She had felt it in his eyes, in that one moment before he turned away. A tiny ribbon of excitement wound itself about her shame. She shook her head violently. Withdrawing, ill, he was not himself. How many times had she seen patients fix their feeling on those who cared for them? It was a result of dependency, not a true regard. He said it himself. "I need you." Her excitement faded through disappointment to resignation.

The time dragged on. Sarah was lost in reminiscences of her father when Davinoff's eyes snapped open. She felt more than saw it, knew instantly that a change had come over him.

"Davinoff," she whispered. "Are you all right?" As she rose to go to him, he pulled himself up to a sitting position by his chains. The corner where he sat was lost in shadows. Sarah turned up the lamp. His body gleamed with sweat and his breathing was shallow and rapid. His face was pale, his eyes intense as she had never seen them. He looked, well . . . mad. And he looked strong again. Sarah stared at him, wishing this were over. She stood by her chair, wondering how long she would stand there, how long he would stare blankly, and what terrors he was fighting.

It was this thought that finally brought her back to herself.

Every nerve in his body was rebelling. He was in pain. He might be hallucinating. It was to be expected. "Davinoff," she called again. "What can I do for you?" She went toward him slowly, stood over him, and saw that he was trembling. She reached out a tentative hand.

Abruptly his gaze snapped up and she saw a vortex of pain and courage and old, secret knowledge. Even at the abbey, she had never seen his eyes like this. She caught her breath and stepped back. From clenched teeth a strange voice echoed. "Don't touch me." It boomed in her mind. She took another step back involuntarily. She, too, was breathing hard.

For a long moment she was impaled by those eyes, willed to move away. She stepped back again and again until the stone wall poked at her back. Slowly she slid to the floor and crouched there, unable to look away from the gaze that held her. Finally, the stare that transfixed her moved to penetrate some other unseen object, and the bond forged between them was ripped asunder.

Relief flooded her when the power of those eyes moved elsewhere. She couldn't cry out. She could hardly even breathe. She crouched where she was and hoped not to draw his attention again. There was something more than human in his voice, in the way she had felt impelled to move. Had he spoken at all? She had felt his words more than heard them. Who *was* this man?

Sometime in the night she began to wonder what would happen if she couldn't get near him to give him any more laudanum. More likely she would never have the courage to move. Perhaps he could kill her with the power she had felt. He did not move, but stared ahead.

Sarah forgot her stiffness when he spoke. She raised her head from her clasped knees, not sure what she heard. He was still locked in his terrible trance, but now he was mumbling, speaking, and listening in turns as if there were a partner in his one-sided conversation. The language was unfamiliar. Then his voice rose and the words took on the chanting cadence of an incantation. Over and over he repeated the same words with greater and greater intensity. Every fiber of his body shook in the struggle.

What was his struggle? Was he wrestling with pain, with the drug, or with something larger? He seemed to be casting spells, as did the ancient Cornish crones, believing they could control destiny with their rhymes. As he writhed and thundered the words she couldn't understand, he pushed himself up until he was standing. The words spiraled up into a shriek that was insane or inhuman. Sarah covered her ears and felt that she was shrieking too.

The shriek was replaced by a snarl. Davinoff stood, naked, before her and growled and snapped with bared teeth. He was an animal, the like of which she had never seen—cornered and deadly, no light of rationality in his eyes. He filled the shadowed room and threw himself against the manacles, howling as no human could. He must break the chains or loosen the mortar. Then he would be upon her, ripping her throat like a beast. She sobbed and gasped, sure he would twist free and descend upon her. The stairs were behind her. But thoughts would not translate themselves to movement. She sat frozen in her chair, unable to take her eyes from his.

His dark eyes flamed and glowed now. He had become a predator in darkness, a feaster on souls as well as bodies. The room grew dark around him. The lamp dimmed visibly. Suddenly, his reflection in the wardrobe mirror to his left winked out. Only the ring and the manacles were visible as Sarah stared in horror at the mirror. Darkness and terror eddied out from the mirror and swirled around her.

When she came to herself, she lay draped across the arm of the chair. Her hair brushed the floor. She could not see him. She heard no sound. For some time she resolved she would never move so she would not draw his attention, but she was uncomfortable and at last her body moved of its own volition. She heaved herself up and lay with her cheek on her hand, looking at the mirror. His reflection flickered there. He was no longer the terrible beast-thing she had watched in horror. He lay crumpled in the corner looking terribly human. She glanced at her watch. It was late afternoon somewhere, but down here it was always night.

The past terror nibbled at the edges of her mind. What had

she seen? She had expected frenzy in withdrawal. She had expected him to struggle in his chains. She had not expected . . .

What? She could not think if what she saw was real. A darkness? Was that simply her faint coming on? And the mirror? She put her hand to her forehead. Of course not. She shook her head slowly. Stupid girl. Was she hallucinating? She couldn't know. But she still must do something. Could she climb the stairs and ride the horse back to Bath? Could she leave him here? A tiny chuckle rose in her throat and turned into a stifled sob.

She was a prisoner here of her own making. She could not run away. She would not abandon her vow. She had placed the manacles about her own wrists as surely as Davinoff had. It could end in death, his or hers. She knew that now. It was a debt she owed. Because she had refused to look on darkness in others, in herself, so many times, she would stare it down here in her cellar. If she ran away again, she would die for certain, not in body perhaps, but in her soul. She owed a debt for who she was, what she knew about herself, beginning in Sienna. If peace waited somewhere beyond the darkness, well then, the debt was paid and she was free.

At last the watch said six. Mechanically she got up and measured out seven drams of laudanum. He was too weak to gulp it from the cup. She would inject it. She went to the bandbox and took out George's syringes and the needles. Back at the bottles, she pressed the plunger down to eject the air, pushed the needle into the laudanum. She drew the drug into the tube, just as she had done at the hospital. Of this much she was sure. She held the syringe upright as she crossed the room. To her surprise, he had drifted into consciousness again. He watched her. His eyes were not beast-mad any longer. They were glazed and dull.

"How much?"

"Seven. A third of your former dose." She knelt and pulled back the coverlet. Laying the needle carefully to one side, she tied a piece of rubber tubing tightly around his biceps, all concentration. She hardly noticed his flesh as she held his arm and waited for the vein to stand out, blue and mortal. She had done it before. She could do it now. Testing the angle, she placed the needle against his fragile flesh. He did not flinch as the needle went in. She pressed the plunger slowly home. When she looked up, he had lost consciousness.

Jerking the needle out, she moved away. She wondered whether by giving him the drug she was actually giving him strength. She wondered if that was good or bad. She was beyond deciding. She went on with the plan because it was easier and because she saw no alternative. The death struggle of this creature with the drug was her death struggle too, now.

In spite of all her explanations to herself, she was not surprised when the lamp beside the chair dimmed. It was his doing, of course. She turned her head slightly. She had not seen him stand, though in the darkness he was standing now. Those two red embers in the blackness were his eyes. They seemed to move closer, then recede. Sarah made no move. She was resigned. The terror was a part of her. The eyes grew larger and smaller, red and glowing, absolutely inhuman.

The light glowed dimly each time the embers receded and she was able to see him, large and luminescent black, a cape of darkness thrown over his shoulders. His lips parted slightly and his canines gleamed. Then the lamplight faded out altogether and there was only the darkness. It gathered in his corner and swirled with invisible currents around the vortex of his eyes. His power drew her, and she knew she must not go. He called her because he could not come to her. She must come to him. Must come.

But she did not. She would not cross that space to him. She would see this thing through, and to do that she would not set her foot on the floor. She must sit safely on the island of the chair. If she moved, she was lost.

Calmly she realized that she knew exactly what he was. He had no reflection in the mirror. His canines were elongated. He drew the darkness, was a master of the night. The composure with which she managed such clear thought hid fear that gnawed at her soul. She had always wondered where he came from. She had never been quite able to place his accent. Now she knew. The Carpathian Mountains struck dread among the superstitious: a country where dwelt things undead. It was the stuff of ghost stories, told late at night. Yet in her cellar was one of its sons. She remembered the two puncture wounds on the neck of the Countess Delmont. How had she not recognized them at the time? And she, poor fool, had thought he wanted her. His lust was not for kisses, but for blood. She was too exhausted to feel shame.

Sarah found she was moving off the chair, her eyes fixed on those glowing orbs. No, she mustn't go! She had lost her concentration, let his will seep into her and eat at the foundations of her resolve. With an effort, she pushed herself back into the chair, breathing hard. She must not lose her focus. It took her some minutes to rip her eyes from those two red circles in the darkness. She cried out with effort and covered her face with her hands. She sat there for an eternity, hands over her eyes. Then she felt stronger. Careful not to look anywhere near the corner where the creature was, she took her hands away. Her light flickered, then flickered again. It, too, seemed to be fighting against the darkness. Then the light came on.

Sarah chanced a glance to the mirror and saw his figure there, light dying in the eyes. The black shape shook its head violently and shed a layer of darkness. A gut-wrenching cry escaped from between the canines, one that stripped the soul of civilization. Sarah shivered from someplace beneath her spine. Then, standing with feet apart and hands still bound, he was suddenly enveloped in the darkness once again. He seemed to shimmer and become invisible for a moment. Then like the light, he flickered into view and collapsed upon the pallet. The light by the chair grew two shades brighter still.

Sarah sat, unable to move. It was just Davinoff in the corner now, not a vampire from the Carpathian Mountains. Sarah's senses reeled. But she knew now what she faced.

After a time, she got up. The watch said that it was almost dawn. She stared for a moment at Davinoff's reflection in the wardrobe mirror. The cellar seemed disheveled and ordinary. As if moving were itself enough accomplishment, she sat again on the floor at the foot of the chair.

The bruises and the poultices stood out against his pale flesh. How many days had it been? Three or four. He slumped against the wall. He might be dead. This was enough to move her. She ought to stay away. She tried to feel the terror she had felt but a little while ago, but she was numb. There was no sign of breath. So she crawled on her hands and knees to him and touched the hollow of his throat. A pulse fluttered, just barely there. She began to cry then for the first time, just tears, no sobs. What to do? Finally, she dragged him out upon the pallet, then staggered to the table and measured out five drams of laudanum. Such a tiny amount compared to what had gone before. The needle found his vein and her thumb pressed the drug home. It was early, but she didn't care anymore. She did the thing she knew to do.

He was close to death. The effort needed for the field of darkness had left him drained. She knew now what he had meant when he had promised he wouldn't lose control. He had refused to take her blood when she would have offered her neck willingly under the spell of his eyes. He might have been trying to spare her. She gained some strength from that.

Hadn't she seen other men become animals when deprived of the drug? How different was this man? More powerful, more strange, but no more violent, no more desperate than the others. One of the strangest things was that he had never once asked her for the drug. Of course, he had wanted it last night. The drug and something more. That was why he willed her to come to him. How had she been able to resist? She remembered the palpable force impelling her to move back from him. He must have grown weaker. She might not be alive if he had not.

That must mean that he was near the end. He would soon die. She squinted at him, sniffing. But life still coursed in his veins. He needed sustenance to give him strength. She had prepared for that, though the sustenance he needed might be different than she had anticipated. Rummaging through the bag, she drew out her supplies. She dragged a high chest near his pallet, then removed several large bottles from the bandbox. She would follow Dr. Parry's lead and put his food directly into his veins. She broke the seal on one bottle, inserted rubber tubing, and held up the opposite end. In this end, she fitted a syringe with a larger needle. The upended bottle she placed on the chest looming over Davinoff.

Making sure the valve was shut on the tubing, she took the syringe and knelt beside his still form. She exposed the vein in the crook of his elbow. With the heavier needle, she might well shove it clear through. The needle met the skin's resistance and slid into the vein. She strapped it flat to his arm with a strip of cloth. Earlier, the needle would have ripped from his arm at his first fevered thrashing. Now he would be still, perhaps unto death. The nutrient Dr. Parry invented would drip into his veins, giving him, perhaps, a little extra strength.

She watched him for some time. Finally, she got up and combed her hair using the wardrobe mirror. Dark circles hung under her eyes. With only a single glance at the still form in the corner, she left the room for the first time in two days. It was a gray and dreary morning elsewhere in the house. She fixed herself food and ate in the kitchen. The real world was comforting and ordinary. She went outside in a drenching, steady rain to feed the horse and fill his water trough. He nickered softly at her as she entered his stall.

"I have not been a steadfast friend," she said to him, startled at the sound of her own voice. "But I have been busy." She fed and brushed him, filled his trough. How she longed for a simpler time, before Corina, before Davinoff. She also longed for a bath.

It was almost two hours before she descended the stairs again, clean if not refreshed. She had steeped herself in steaming water. Her fear was gone. She knew the worst, after all. She opened the door to the cellar, not caring what she might see, and descended into the gloom. But Davinoff lay as before. The bottle floated above him, a slender link with Sarah now.

She sat beside him on the floor, her mind a pleasing blank. She checked his pulse from time to time. At what must be dusk, it seemed to weaken. She counted the beats. It *was* weaker. He was sinking toward death. She had done what she could. Roused from her lethargy, she bit her lip, rose, then knelt again to check his pulse. He couldn't die. Not after so much suffering for them both. It wasn't fair. She stood and paced the dusty cellar floor.

What to do for a creature so strange? This was beyond her. She ran her hands through her hair, distraught. She didn't know enough about him!

But she did. Every child knew what he was. He was a creature of fable become real. Some stories she knew to be true. Reflections and canines; these myths were only too real. The core of the vampire legends was that they drew their strength from human blood. If anything were true, would it not be this center of all the fear? Was that not what the Countess Delmont's scarf proclaimed?

Could she do this thing? But there was no reasoning about it. And she was beyond fear. She had come too far since that day at Chambroke to turn back. The decision was already made. She had done it to Davinoff. Could she do it to herself?

Kneeling at Davinoff's side, she clamped the tubing to stop the flow of nutrient into his bloodstream, then withdrew the needle. She emptied a bottle of the nutrient into the basin. Then, with the bottle and the tubing and syringe, she set about her task. The bottle she set on the floor by the chair where the light was better and tied a section of tubing around her left arm, tightening it between her teeth and her other hand. The blood pulsed in her vein.

This was just a matter of courage, of getting the needle in her arm. She would think no further than that. Her arm rested on a strip of cloth draped over the arm of the chair. She held the needle with its tube in her right hand. Could she do it from this angle? She positioned the syringe carefully and took two slow breaths. Then she forced the needle in. It was a simple sear of pain, no more. The tube darkened with her blood. She used the cloth strip to secure the needle.

Sarah breathed and loosed the tube about her arm, then removed the clamp. Her blood flowed down the tube with a life of its own, surging with the beat of her heart. She leaned back with that peculiar peaceful sense she had heard occurred with loss of blood. Perhaps it felt this way to die. George would have been proud of her technique.

When the bottle was full, she replaced the clamp. She withdrew the needle and pressed a bit of bandage into the crook of her arm. She rose slowly, feeling dizzy, and took the red bottle to the pallet. It was only four-thirty by her watch, but he might not last until six. So she injected three drams of laudanum into his arm. The red bottle sat beside her, along with the cup.

With the injection of the drug, small as the dose was, his

breathing deepened. She rubbed her hands over his forehead, down his neck, and over his chest. His flesh called to her. It felt human and mortal, no matter that she had seen him as an elemental being. "Davinoff," she whispered, "wake up." There was no response except for the labored breathing. "Wake up, Julien Davinoff, or you will never wake up. Do you hear me?" His flesh spoke to her. Her voice grew more urgent. She took his chin in her hand and shook his head. "Davinoff, damn you, wake up!"

The eyelids fluttered. She rubbed his chest, whispering to him, urging him to make another effort. The fringe of dark lashes finally raised. He looked up at her from far away. She poured the thick red liquid into the cup and lifted it to his lips. "Drink," she said softly. He did drink. His lips and mouth were stained with her blood, still warm. When the cup was empty, she poured the rest and he drank it, too. She watched a trickle run from the side of his mouth. His eyes were unreadable. Then they faded and closed. She lowered his head and wiped his mouth.

She was not ashamed or horrified at what she had done. She had done the most she could. She hooked him up to another bottle of the nutrient. Now she must sleep. There was no more laudanum to give. If he was alive when she woke, she would think what to do. She lay down on the floor next to the pallet and pillowed her head on her arm.

He *was* alive when she awoke. His breathing seemed a little stronger. She felt it even before she sat up, disheveled and stiff. She checked his pulse and felt its more rhythmic beat. It was almost midnight, six hours since the last of the drug had been given. She had promised herself to think what to do, but thinking still seemed beyond her. All she knew was that the blood had been good. There would have to be more.

Sarah sat in her chair with fresh materials around her. This time it wasn't quite so hard. But this would have to be the last. She wasn't sure how much blood she could give. This time the feeling of peace as the bottle filled was even more pronounced. She closed her eyes and managed to take more than she intended before she came to herself and clamped the tube shut.

She had to rest for some time before she could make her way

to where Davinoff lay. Her grasp was unsteady on the precious bottle. She hung her head as she knelt beside him to keep the room from fading and weaving. Finally, she sat heavily and leaned over him. This time he was easier to wake. She struggled to lift his head. He examined her face with eyes more puzzled than terrible. Again she poured the warm life into the cup and bade him drink.

This time she saved the second cup for later. She lowered his head and pulled the quilt up about his shoulders. "Sleep now." Then she closed his eyes with her fingertips and watched him sink into unconsciousness. Rising too quickly, she did a graceful pirouette as she grasped for the chair, failed to reach it, and fell to the floor.

Julien woke slowly to the dim room. He felt the air in his lungs and realized with a small sense of disappointment that he had come back from the brink, had almost seen his own death first-hand. He wondered briefly whether he was glad to be restored to the dilemma of living. He must be, else why had he made the tremendous effort required to fight the drug? Because he had been afraid he would continue and continue in that terrible stupor. That was not the same as embracing life.

He was weak but his will was his own. He felt the presence of his Companion, the one who shared his blood. Together they were Julien Davinoff. Together, they would be strong again, whether he would or no. With some effort he turned his head.

She lay on the floor, her blue dress floating on the stones. He remembered her face smiling above him, lifting the cup to his lips. Her outstretched arm was bruised from the needle. That meant the blood she had given him was her own. It was amazing that she knew the technique, more amazing yet that she used it to help such as she knew he was. She might be dead. He tried to move, but he could not raise his head. He sank back, sweating with exertion.

Why had she done this thing? He had known many women in his time. Many had loved him, some against their will. They bared their necks to him because he demanded it, and one way or another, they could not resist. But he had learned long ago that unless he sapped their will and replaced it with his own, fair, fine eyes shrank from him when the word *vampire* was whispered in the recesses of their souls. Fear and disgust, even hatred were the consequence of knowledge. He had not wanted Sarah Ashton to see what he was while he depended so completely upon her. He even managed to resist the call of her blood when he needed it badly.

But he had failed. She knew he was vampire. The cups of blood were certain proof. Yet she had given it freely. Her own. He did not understand how she had conquered fear, or why. He remembered a fugitive coil of dark hair brushing his chest, clear green eyes searching his face. Now he must go slowly. He still depended on her. He must not frighten her. Marshaling his small resource of strength, he made another effort and rolled onto his side. Then he saw her stir.

Sarah struggled to a sitting position, unsure of where she was. She was alive, at least. Turning she saw him, awake and clear-eyed, across the floor. A trace of fear tickled along her spine. There was no drug between them. And she knew what he was.

"Thank you," he whispered, "for your gift." His eyes were ringed with shadows.

Sarah parted her lips as if she would speak, but no words came.

He tried again. "I was not myself." He smiled, a touch of a smile. "I will not hurt you."

Sarah's eyes filled with tears at that prosaic statement. After all these nightmare days, it was very well for him to say he would not hurt her now. She wanted to shriek, in laughter or in anger. What could she say to such a creature? But he still looked sick. "There is one more cup . . ."

"Yes," he breathed. "The blood is the life."

She got unsteadily to her feet and came to sit beside him, hesitant. Everything had changed. She could see for the first time in a long time the force of personality behind his eyes. He was a man, but not a man. Some part of her gibbered that she did not know what he was.

She reached for the bottle, half full of the dark, red liquid. "I think it has clotted."

"It does not matter, if it is not spoiled." With effort, he struggled up to prop himself against the wall. Sarah moved to help him, drawn by his weakness in spite of her fear. She handed him the cup without looking at him. Had she not read that vampires could hypnotize their victims? It was true. She had felt his power. He reached for the cup of her blood, trembling.

Sarah's hand, too, shook. She tried to keep any judgment, any trace of fear or disgust from her expression, but he must have guessed what she was thinking, for he took the cup and gulped the thickened claret-colored liquid hastily. Then he set the bottle down with a sigh and wiped his mouth with the back of his hand.

He studied her as she removed the cup and the bottle to the table. "My race draws many of its most . . . peculiar qualities from a parasite in our bloodstream. It lives on red blood cells and it must be fed. It is difficult to resist the demands of our Companion when it calls for blood."

Sarah hazarded a glance in his direction. She had never considered that there might be a natural explanation for his bloodlust. The explanation, true or not, aroused her curiosity. Man or monster? But she had nearly fallen victim to his needs. Only the drug and his weakness prevented him from taking what he wanted. What would prevent him now?

She gathered her courage. "You are better. You will not need the nutrient again, I think."

"The One who shares my body helps me heal. The drug suppressed the healing, but now the addiction is gone, to your credit."

He was testing her, she thought, as she clipped the tube and removed the needle from his arm, testing her courage, her resolve. He still wore the manacles. Did she dare free him now that the drug was gone? She must have time to think. Taking the key from her pocket she studied it, uncertain. "Until we are sure that the effects of the drug are gone, I think it might be better to leave these locked." She said it without looking at him.

"Of course," he murmured. His gaze was much too penetrating.

She hurried up the stairs in confusion. Outside, she leaned against the door, her head sunk to her breast. Her hair fell forward, a comforting curtain to hide her tears. The last days had been unreal, an endless round of fear and nightmares. Now the nightmare should be over. She had done what she set out to do. But the nightmare wasn't over at all. She had not stopped to consider what would happen when the drug was gone. She had discharged her obligation. But she was left harboring a monster who drank blood, who would soon be incredibly strong and dangerous.

She went wearily up to her own bedroom and lay on the bed. It was morning once more. The rays of the sun leaked through the curtains, suffusing the room with motes of life, so different than the dim room in the cellar. After all, it was just Davinoff. She had dined with him, ridden in his carriage, talked with him about the stones at Avebury, argued with him about her land. Commonplace experiences. He had been a vampire then, too.

She had nearly come to grips with Davinoff as man, rather than as supernatural horror, when she remembered the murders in London. My God, she gasped. Drained blood. Thirteen bodies. Who else but a vampire could have done those murders? Who but Julien Davinoff? Even if he was not a monster, he was at least a murderer. The urge to run out of the house and straight to George was almost overwhelming. She clutched her knees convulsively.

"What to do?" she heard herself whispering. "What to do?"

It was that phrase, turning over and over in her mind, which brought her up short. She sounded exactly like Corina. Worse, she had chained what she did not understand to her cellar wall. She knew very well those shackles were no longer needed, except to comfort her. Would she now condemn him and begin to plan his death, as Corina had done? Would she turn away from darkness once again out of fear?

Well, Sarah, she said to herself as she sat up into a beam of the sunshine. *You committed yourself when you decided to stop running from Corina. The game is a bit rougher than you thought. But the rules have not changed at all.*

She took two deep breaths. He might be a murderer. She had decided once that the Davinoff she knew was too rational to have committed those murders. But the beast she had seen in the cellar was not rational at all. It was not possible to run away from that fact. She would look squarely at him. She would confront the vampire, the murderer accused. If she looked straight at him, she would know the truth. And it would change her, one way or another.

She rose deliberately, bathed, and put on her plain cherry-striped dress of lustring. She brushed her hair dry and drew it up into a knot. Then she went downstairs.

Chapter Thirteen

Inside the dim cellar, Julien wakened as he heard her pass above him. Her steps sounded resolute. He sighed in defeat. She had decided what to do with him. Would she go for help? Would she resort to drugs? He was still so cursed weak! He could not yet escape the manacles. He was not used to illness. He was not sure he could resist her if she chose drugs. Could he force her to do his bidding? Not even that was certain in his present state. If he tried, he would lose all possibility of her willing help. He had to admit he had hoped for that. She had given him her own blood, after all. Perhaps he just wanted the comfort of her understanding.

Damn it, he was weaker than he thought. *Where is your strength, Companion mine?* He thought. *Why do you forsake me now?* He heard her step upon the stair. *Grow strong, and quickly,* he commanded silently as she descended into view.

Sarah saw Davinoff lying on his pallet, eyes burning in his hollowed cheeks. She fingered the butcher knife she held concealed in the folds of her skirt and came to stand over him. The knife seemed small and silly. But it was all she had. "We must talk," she said.

He eyed her warily and nodded.

"You did those murders in London, the ones where the blood was drained," she said, almost without emotion. "Don't bother to lie to me." She wondered what she would do if he admitted it. Would she simply turn and run?

"I cannot remember that I have ever felt the need to explain myself." His tone was as urbane as it has always been, but his voice cracked with strain. "The murders were done by one of my kind, but not by me."

"I saw you at the murder scene," Sarah accused.

"That was the moment I knew it was Magda."

"I don't believe you," Sarah said, wondering how she ever expected anything but a denial, or how she would ever believe. "I don't know this Magda."

"But you have seen her," Davinoff said. "She is the redheaded woman who gave the constables my description. That was clever, really."

"It doesn't explain why you were there."

"I came to stop the murders. Such public killing attracts . . . attention." His gaze was steady. "Not something my kind tolerates."

"Killing is wrong!" Sarah cried. He *must* be a monster if he didn't know that.

"I did stop it," he noted. "I convinced Magda to reform her ways."

"How do I know it wasn't you?" Sarah asked in a small voice. "How can I know?"

"You want a proof you can test here?" Davinoff lifted an eyebrow. "You ask much."

Sarah clenched her eyes against the tears that welled up. What had she expected? A moment of silence scraped along her raw nerves.

"Wait," he said, his eyes casting about. "The murder before the one where you saw me happened the week previously, on the second of October, I believe. Did you read the list that was published so incessantly in the papers?"

"Yes. Yes, I remember that." Sarah searched her mind. "Yes, it was the second."

"And where was I on the second of October?"

"How should I know?" Sarah retorted. "Killing people in London, probably."

"I was in Bath. And you know that, because I was with your solicitor, Lestrom the Elder. He verified my deed. I don't suppose he mentioned that when he saw you in London."

Sarah stared at him, trying to remember. "You're right," she said slowly. "I saw him the day after the ball. That was the tenth. He said that he had verified your deed late in the afternoon of Tuesday last when he was in Bath. That would have been . . ."

"The second," Davinoff confirmed. "Not by the greatest stretch of the imagination could any man be in Bath at dusk, and murder in London that very evening."

"No, no, he couldn't." Sarah chewed her lip. "But that means only that there is one in that string of murders that you didn't do."

Davinoff sighed and leaned his head against the wall. "I can't prove my whereabouts for all the murders. Are there not some crimes, somewhere, of which I could be innocent?"

Sarah looked down at the stone floor and let the hand with the knife peek out from the folds of her dress. She stared at it pensively.

He glanced at the knife and raised his brows. "I see you came as executioner as well as judge and jury." It was said with some of his old sardonic tone.

"I came with scant protection against a murderer, or something worse," Sarah retorted.

"My apologies." He grew serious. "You have saved my life and something that I value more. You have nothing to fear from me, I swear."

"And what about the world at large? You must promise not to harm anyone!" she begged. Was it any use asking a vampire to promise that?

"We of Transylvania are haunted by myth because we are strange to you. We have our outlaws and our villains. But I no longer kill for sport or for blood. You have seen how I get what I need. The Countess Delmont showed you. She gave willingly and is none the worse for it. If you give me time to recover I will leave you in peace."

No longer! The words quivered in her brain. That meant he

had killed in times past. Then again, everyone in this room had a past. And Sarah wanted to believe him. She did not want to be locked up in the Dower House with a murderer. "You say you kill no one for blood anymore . . ." she murmured, trying to come to a conclusion. To her astonishment, a consternated look appeared on Davinoff's weary face.

"That is not quite true either," he admitted. "If I vow to tell the truth, I must tell all."

"Whom did you kill?" Sarah wasn't sure she wanted the honesty she required of him.

His eyes rose steadily to hers. "Corina's butler, Reece."

Sarah's eyes narrowed. Of course, Reece. She said nothing. She only waited.

"I had been locked in Corina's cellar for a long time." His eyes unfocused, remembering. "I needed blood. They had withdrawn the drug to punish me, which gave me back some strength. Reece was careless. I throttled him unconscious trying to escape. There he was, lying there with the one thing I needed running in his veins. I took more than I intended. Or maybe not. Maybe I wanted to kill him for his role in my . . . detention." He took a breath, coming to himself. "I was alive, but I could not escape. She had the other thing I needed. I stayed for the drug."

Sarah squeezed her eyes shut for a moment. What more could she ask him to say? He had admitted killing a man who tortured and abused him. That might be called self-defense. The other murders were at least in doubt. Now was the moment of epiphany she had told herself she wanted. She had looked at him squarely. Was anything clear? Yes. Surprised, she knew what she must do. It would be the hardest thing she had ever done.

She must unlock the darkness and set it free. Drawing the key from her pocket, she looked at it. Then she knelt beside him. He offered up his wrists. She pretended absorption in unlocking the manacles, brows knitted in concentration, but she could feel his breath, smell his scent. Man, yet not man. Musky, sweet. How had she never noticed that signature of strangeness? The manacles clattered against the stone as she rocked back on her heels.

"I should have done that earlier. I was afraid." She owed it to him to admit that.

"I know of no other woman who would have given her blood

to save a vampire's life." His voice rumbled in her ears. "I will always be indebted to your bravery and your sympathy."

He talked so naturally of vampires. She raised her eyes to find his eyes smiling at her. There was no evil in that expression. It was utterly human, only too self-aware. He was many things, things that were frightening and strange. But those murders were stupid for one who wanted to conceal his nature. And Davinoff was not stupid.

Sarah stood abruptly and went to get the plate of food, just ham and parsnips, and a pitcher of water. She came back and helped him sit without a word. There were so many things she wanted to ask; she asked none at all. He was still weak. It would be enough if he could eat. She sat beside him on the floor with her own plate and ate in silence. His food was not half finished when he leaned wearily against the wall.

"Rest," she said, taking the plate from him. "You should not forget that yesterday you were near to death." She pushed him down on the pallet.

His eyes closed as he murmured, "Yes. I will rest a moment. You must rest as well . . ."

Sarah stood staring at him. He looked like just a man. She had bathed and tended him. She had seen him sick and weak. He had tried to shield her from his nature. It was a bond between them that could not be broken just because the safety of the drug was gone. He had agreed to go away once he was stronger. For the time being, she would take him at his word.

She turned to go upstairs to bed. He was right. She was weak. But it was almost better to stay here where she could see him than to turn her back on the unknown. This house was isolated. No one knew she was here. She had not seen another face but his for days. In some way she had already given her life over to him. Some part of her was given with the blood.

She slept fitfully, red glowing eyes dogging her dreams, until the gray light of morning came peeping through the draperies. She was not rested, but sleep would not come again. She rose and pulled on a silk dressing gown that swirled gay-colored birds around her.

Opening the door to her nightmares, she saw only his sleeping form in the dim stone room. But as she turned to go, his eyes snapped open and darted in confusion about the cellar. She moved hesitantly to his side as he focused on her with something like fear. He struggled to sit, no recognition in his eyes. She thought suddenly that he, too, might have nightmares. With some chagrin he found himself still weak and sank into his pillows.

"I did not mean to wake you," she greeted him. "How are you feeling?" Recognition dawned. His eyes lost their unaccustomed uncertainty. The power focused in them.

He searched her face. "I am quite recovered, I think."

"You will pardon me if I disagree. But you do look much improved."

As if to prove his assertion, he pushed himself with obvious effort to a sitting position, propped against the wall. As the coverlets fell to his waist, Sarah noted with a start that the bruises and scrapes, even many of his cuts had disappeared. There were no scabs, not even any scars, nothing to say they had ever been. Sarah smiled nervously to conceal her amazement, but he saw it and looked down at his chest and belly to see what startled her.

"Now it is I who must talk to you," he said, before she could decide to retreat. "I must tell you what it means to be vampire, if I am to ask for your help." He motioned to the chair. With her heart in her mouth, she sat. Was it dangerous to know a vampire's secrets? "My kind are not true vampires since we do not feed on blood." His voice resounded in the darkened room. "The blood we drink is not digested. It is consumed by the parasite that shares our bodies." It all sounded so reasonable. "Our parasite Companion is the true vampire. It feeds on blood cells. Do you know what a parasite is?"

"Of course I do," she snapped. "You needn't talk down to me."

"My mistake." His tone was faintly amused, though his mouth was serious. "The parasite has two important proprieties. It regenerates cells. Thus it extends our life almost indefinitely. Regeneration also causes swift healing. Hence the legend that vampires are immortal or undead. I have never been dead and I can be killed by very ordinary means, but the damage inflicted must be great enough to kill before regeneration can begin." His voice was inexorable. "Stakes through the heart would do the job, as would decapitation, disembowelment."

Sarah winced at the violence in his words. He continued more gently. "I want you to know. It is important." She dared to cast a glance at him and nodded.

"The Companion uses energy for regeneration, but by focusing that energy, the host, too, can use the power. It is a kind of mental discipline, not something supernatural. A field of such force can be generated that light does not escape. Reflections in mirrors disappear. The field becomes so dense it collapses in on itself and the body disappears, pushed out of space. We have learned to control the reappearance with a fair amount of accuracy. The body may be transported a short distance before reassembling in another place."

Sarah looked at him incredulously. "You mean you can disappear?"

"In a sense, yes."

"And reappear in another place, perhaps from Bath to London?" she asked warily.

Davinoff sighed. "Don't let's go through that again. I am good for a mile or two, no more. You will have to take my word for that."

"Then how did you not disappear from Corina's cellar?" Sarah asked, puzzled.

"Ah, she found my Achilles' heel. Laudanum drugged my Companion as well as me. I could not disappear, or heal as the dose got bigger." The weary voice went on. "Vampires do not transform themselves into bats. I believe this tale was invented to explain swift and invisible relocation at night. They say, too, that sunlight kills us, that we only live at night. True in some sense. The ultraviolet component of sunlight is uncomfortable, like light that is too bright. I have used tinted lenses ground in Germany to my own specifications to circumvent this problem. They fit directly to my eyes. But I am most comfortable at dusk or at night."

Sarah remembered the little dimpled discs of smoky glass she had seen in his trunk.

He shrugged. "Most of the rest is pure fantasy. We are not harmed by symbols of religion. Plants or roots do not keep us away, least of all garlic, as you yourself must know."

Sarah glanced at the garlic poultices still bound to his body and thought back to all the stories she had heard. "What about your victims?" She blushed, realizing her blunder. "I mean the legend that people whose blood was sucked by vampires themselves become vampires?"

Davinoff chuckled and rubbed his eyes. "It *is* possible to become vampire. But the parasite would have to be ingested. The victim would have to drink the vampire's blood."

"How often do you need blood?" She was in some way accepting this fantastic story. But what was more fantastic than what she had seen in her own cellar with her own eyes?

He took a breath. "Not often. We can go as long as a month."

"Do you need more now?"

"Yes," he said simply. "Your gift saved my life. But I will need more soon."

"You will not take the blood by force. I cannot live knowing that I set free a force of evil." She deliberately set her will against his. Let him kill her now if he would.

"I swear the countess and all her predecessors gave most willingly," he answered dryly.

Sarah found herself uncomfortable with that fact, perhaps not for the right reasons. "I'm sure they did," she returned. "Enough now. I think you will be more comfortable upstairs in a real bed. Can you manage the stairs?"

He nodded.

She helped him rise, wrapped in his bedding. That was good. She didn't want to confront his nakedness, now that he was himself again. Heat suffused her face. She wouldn't think about that. Gingerly, she slid her arm around his waist to steady him. Weak as he was, she could feel the power radiating from his body. It struck her like a blow and wound around her spine and into her most female recesses. *Sarah Ashton,* she admonished herself, *stop this*. Resolutely, she moved him to the stairs. Let him break her neck, if he wished, as he had strangled Reece. The feeling around her spine shivered into fear. But nothing more dangerous occurred than the shock of holding him, knowing he was naked under the coverlet. They stopped to rest, then made their way up to the first floor. By the time she turned back his bed and laid him in it, he was exhausted. "I shall return in a few hours," she promised.

Sarah went down to the drawing room and pulled the heavy draperies back to let in the light. The sleet against the mullioned windows was turning to snow. How many days? She stared out at the front garden, bleak with winter. Five, or six. Wait! Tomorrow would be Christmas. She would spend the anniversary of the birth of the Son of God as man with a man who was very nearly the devil himself. Sarah chuckled and drew her hands across her eyes. She ought to think if she should be afraid. But she couldn't think anymore, so she went to care for the horse. She let the warmth of his hide under her hands heal her, his soft nicker soothe her mind. She sat in the straw and listened to the wind whistle around the stall. Her companion fixed his attention single-mindedly upon his oats. The rhythmic grinding of his great teeth was quite consoling.

Then it was back to the kitchen to make a meat pie for dinner. Fires were laid and candles lit as light faded in and snow began to fall. Finally she went to the front hall where Davinoff's portmanteau waited, and opened it, not for the first time. She rubbed her hands on her skirts and touched the fine white shirts, the crisply rolled cravats. She picked up the heavy black cape by the shoulders, almost reverently, and shook it out. In the gathering gloom, she looked for boots. Had he two pair? They were at the bottom of the trunk, wrapped in tissue to preserve their gleaming surface. She chose black breeches, a white shirt, a richly brocaded dressing jacket in black and red, and some soft slippers, then climbed the stairs.

Had her feelings changed since the first time she descended a darkening stair? A thrill of fear still hummed along her spine. The realization that she *liked* the fearful feeling struck her in midstep. How dull her life seemed before Davinoff! This was a thing she had in common with Corina. Corina was a thrill-seeker. Was Sarah not also enamored of risk? How else had she found the courage to face Davinoff in the cellar? She felt more alive than ever before. There was no joy in crossing streets, Corina had told her once. And Sarah, deep down, agreed. Dangerous to admit yet another way she was like Corina. Yet, in one way she was not like. She had taken no pleasure in Davinoff's pain. She continued up the stairs, easier in her mind. She didn't know if she would have participated in Corina's twisted sexual torture in Sienna. Who knew what the influence of the mushroom would have meant? But if the mushroom magnified what was in your soul, she could say for certain that it would not have found Corina's sick brand of titillation there.

Sarah had expected to tap on Davinoff's door, but it swung open and Julien ushered her into his room with the gracious gesture of a host. He had removed her poultices. There were no marks at all upon his body. Regenerating cells had made his flesh virgin once more, Corina's cruelty erased. He had bound a bath cloth about his waist. His manner had an animal ease and grace. She had seen him naked. She had tended to his every need. Yet she reddened in the face of his conscious undress. The heat in her loins told her she was still not to be trusted. The mushroom had revealed her other predilection most clearly.

"Good evening, Lady Clevancy." His rich voice had taken on new strength. "Let me take those from you." He gathered the clothing from her arms.

"I took the liberty of opening your portmanteau. I could not carry it upstairs," she said, excusing the second rifling of his trunk, still blushing, tingling. "I hope you will find these suitable."

He bent over the clothes now tumbled on the bed. The curls of his dark hair brushed the nape of his neck and contrasted starkly with the fine pallor of his skin. "Most welcome," he murmured. "My trunk from the Christopher?"

"I had it sent." She explained Corina's ploy for covering his disappearance in several convoluted sentences. All trace of the ease she had felt on the stairs had disappeared.

"Ingenious," Davinoff muttered.

Sarah did not like his tone and changed the subject. "Shall I bring your dinner here?"

"You have served me long enough." He nodded. "I shall be glad to go down."

Sarah watched the broad shoulders and muscled thighs disappear into the dressing room. She was alone with a man in the house, a very virile man. All the proprieties were offended. In such a case was it polite to wait or go downstairs? She waited, straightening the room, lighting a lamp, in case he needed something.

When the door opened, the alchemy was complete. He was the man she had seen in the crypt, the focus of the ball at Carlton House, Quixote's master. Outside, the snow was cold and quiet. Inside, she was aflame, lit by the intensity of his eyes upon her as he crossed silently to her and offered her his arm. Without even thinking, she placed her hand in the crook of his elbow.

"So there is a world aside from cellars and that bedroom," he marveled as they went downstairs. "I am afraid I scarcely noticed this morning."

"I regret to say it has been waiting all along," Sarah managed.

"I have been dead to it. What day is it?"

"As nearly as I can make out, tomorrow is Christmas." Sarah answered while leading him into the dining room. She could feel his eyes upon her as she lit the candelabra. "I am afraid we must fend for ourselves. I brought no servants under the circumstances," she apologized.

Davinoff followed her into the kitchen and offered to choose the wine. He emerged from the cellars many minutes later with a dusty bottle of claret and a gleam in his eye. " 'Ninety-eight, Lady Clevancy. That cellar is a treasure trove." He opened the bottle and left it to settle as he watched her move about the kitchen. He asked questions about how she had managed for the past week. She told him of the supplies left from her last trip.

"There is still a ham," she excused, "and potatoes and carrots in the root cellar, and flour and cheese. I'm afraid I will be able to produce only simple dishes." Sarah was acutely aware that well-bred young ladies barely knew the location of their own kitchens. But soon she found herself talking about her father's cook, Selby, and what a comforting retreat solid things like eggs and cream had been from mathematics and Italian in her childhood, as she cut the meat pie.

Davinoff did not even blink when she told him about the mathematics. That usually provoked surprise that any father would bother teaching such subjects to a girl. Instead, he volunteered to set the table.

"May I propose a toast?" he asked, as they sat to the long table in the dining room.

She nodded warily. What toast would a vampire make?

He lifted his glass, but his eyes held hers. "To new life," he proclaimed softly.

She searched his face. "To new life," she whispered in return. Her eyes retreated to her glass as they sipped in silence. She could still feel his gaze. Dinner might be very long. She could think of no topic that did not touch upon blood or murder or Corina's perfidy.

But Davinoff surprised her. He turned more voluble than she had ever heard him. He talked of his travels on the Continent. He spoke of Rossini's operas in Venice and seeing the work of a Spanish painter named Goya. Sarah had seen Goya's startling portrait of the Duke of Wellington and shared Davinoff's enthusiasm. She offered up her own enjoyment of the quality of light in a painting called "Frosty Morning" by an Englishman named Turner. The conversation stretched and turned. There was no need for glittering allusions and quotations designed to display one's education. Davinoff talked about what interested him. Sarah did likewise. Davinoff mentioned the death of Madame de Stael, Sarah the death in the same year of Miss Austen.

"I have never read her books," Davinoff remarked.

"I'd be glad to lend you one," Sarah offered. "You might not think her subjects grand enough to be great literature. Yet she has found favor, even with the prince regent."

"A recommendation beyond reproach," Davinoff remarked acidly.

Sarah was driven to defend her partiality. "She writes most tellingly of the human soul in its most common and uncommon manifestations. I find her reading of society very pungent."

"Upon *your* recommendation, I am agog to read her work," Davinoff demurred. Sarah had the feeling he was laughing at her behind his serious eyes.

"Well you might tease me, sir," she said, rising and taking their plates, "but I think we have little enough understanding of the human condition these days. Only look at the riots last year in Derbyshire." She moved into the kitchen with purpose and found Davinoff following her.

"Who was rioting this time?" he inquired. "Was it the weavers again?"

"You mean the Luddites? No, this was no protest against machines, but against wages that won't support a family. How can Mr. Wilberforce say we have banished slavery when people still live in such conditions?" Sarah scraped the dishes. Davinoff stacked them on the sideboard and waved her back to the dining room when she began to wipe them.

"Slavery has not been banished," he remarked, following her. "You have no slaves within the country, but your merchants still support the trade elsewhere."

Sarah found herself blushing. "That will be outlawed, too, one day." She collected their glasses. Davinoff took up the candelabra and the wine bottle.

"Perhaps," he said. "I expect that outlawing investment will take much longer than banishing the chains and whips themselves." They moved into the drawing room and sat by the fire Sarah had laid. She agreed, but Sarah was stung by his condescension.

"If you disapprove so, I am sure you will allow your voice to be heard."

He sat back in his chair and studied his glass. "The endless ingenuity of human cruelty holds only a mild interest for me. Did you know the Inquisition has been reinstated by the pope?"

"Excuse me?" Sarah was shocked. "A mild interest?"

"It is the repetition that numbs one, I expect. The insistent ignorance and intolerance, the bigotry . . ." He trailed off as though becoming bored already.

He was just as maddening as he had been at Countess Delmont's dinner party. But now she need not frustrate her desire to retort. "Do you mean we should do nothing to halt cruelty?" she snapped. "You may feel that way generally but certainly not in a particular sense."

His eyes flicked over her, their intensity masked by amusement. "I have forgotten myself, have I not? I should be grateful for your humanitarian impulses."

Her own boldness threw her into confusion. "You have no need for gratitude. I only did what any feeling person would have done in the same circumstance."

"I rather doubt that, but I shall let it pass," he said. Sarah hoped he would begin again their delightful conversation and restore the mood. But he brought up the one subject she least wanted to address. "I have been wondering, actually, how you and Mrs. Nandalay can possibly be friends." He reached to pour some winking ruby liquid into her glass and his.

There was a short silence. What could she say? "I have known her from a child," she said simply, then smiled and purposely lightened her tone. "You of all people know how magnetic she is. I am but a pale reflection. It always stung me that I was not more like her." Her smile evaporated. Why did she feel compelled to explain the final pain? "I knew what she was. I have known for years. I was also afraid I was too much like her. There are . . . things . . . we have in common. I could not criticize what I knew, somewhere deep down, she was becoming. That would have been too much like telling her I hated what she was." She chuckled bitterly and closed her eyes. "Let's not sidestep the issues. I would have been admitting I hated part of me as well." Her eyes snapped open. "Are we all tainted? I never believed in original sin. Yet you believe that humans are naturally cruel and violent. And there are other needs, needs that drive us . . ." Her voice trembled as she looked into his face for answers. "My only hope is that it takes an acknowledgment of evil to deplore it. I no longer know."

Davinoff did not speak, but watched her, his knuckles just touching the corner of his mouth as he leaned back in the wing chair, his elbow propped on its arm.

Sarah sat back in her chair. "I think she is mad. She has lost her balance."

"And you have not," he murmured.

"I have talked too much of me," Sarah said, wishing she could unsay all the things she had not meant to say. "Please speak of you."

"There is time for that later. There is always time." His words carried a weight of weariness that startled her. "Enlighten me on your method of wresting me from my captor."

"I did not have to wrest you at all," she waved a deprecating hand. "She wanted only to be rid of you." Sarah did not elaborate upon Corina's plans. She did not want to fuel the urge for revenge she felt lurking behind Davinoff's calm questioning. But he was before her.

"She had not yet worked herself up to the obvious choice, I take it?" he asked, his deep voice icy. "I thought it might be possible, with my Companion dampened as it was by the drug."

"You do not know she planned your death." Sarah sidestepped the question. "I offered to take you to an asylum on the Continent."

"Where she thought I would die in withdrawal, no doubt."

"I don't think she was thinking clearly at all. You must have frightened her." Sarah knew exactly how Davinoff might have frightened Corina.

"And why did you *not* take me to an asylum?"

"Have you ever seen one?" she asked. "I have. They are dreadful."

"A hospital then."

"They would not take so severe a case. Other men would have been dead on your dose."

"So you took my case upon yourself. Your father raised a fool," he observed.

"You're right." She sighed. "I certainly got more than I bargained for."

Again the dark eyes flicked over her face. "You did rather well, actually."

She stared at him only a moment before her gaze broke in confusion. "Look how late it is," she said suddenly. "You must be tired. You should retire." As he began to protest, she raised her voice. "I will brook no contradiction, sir, on matters of your health." She smiled. "Your courtesy would forbid argument in any case."

Davinoff looked at her from under his lashes and made a small bow. He rose and extended his arm. The impropriety of being alone with a strange man who was escorting her to her bedroom struck her forcibly. But after all that had gone before, propriety seemed a small concern. So she went up the stairs to her bedroom on the arm of a very polite vampire.

Chapter Fourteen

Sarah woke late the next morning after sleeping better than she had in some time. She hurried to dress, impatient to see if Davinoff was up. She regretted her instructions to Addie to pack only everyday clothes; the woman had followed directions too well. Sarah rejected out of hand her brown merino. Why did she keep such an old dress, whose color had never become her? She'd worn the cherry-striped lustring yesterday. Which left only the bottle-green walking dress.

She paced to the window and threw back the draperies. Weak sunshine glistened over four inches of new snow. The front gardens were transformed with icy loveliness, a consolation for the loss of their fine greenery to winter. It had snowed just for Christmas.

Brushing her hair vigorously, she tried not to feel wistful about it being Christmas Day. There would be no grand holiday dinner. Upon impulse, she refused to tie up her hair at all, but left it long and floating upon her shoulders. *As though I were a girl*, she told herself severely, and then dimpled at herself in the mirror. Never mind. Davinoff had seen her with her hair loose before, at Avebury. It certainly would not shock him, as it would have scandalized George. She smiled in anticipation as she opened the door to the hall.

The first sign that Davinoff was about somewhere was that his trunk had been removed from the hall. She checked the library where a fire snapped in the grate, and the drawing room, dim with drawn curtains. There was no sign of him. As she stood in the dining room and wondered if he was upstairs, she heard movement in the kitchen. She opened the door to find Davinoff in his shirtsleeves, pouring steaming coffee into a cup. A fire roared in the fireplace. Upon the sideboard lay a plate of dried fruit and slabs of cheese.

Sarah was astonished. "You seem quite at home, Mr. Davinoff," she stammered.

He glanced over at her and raised one eyebrow. "I have endured times of poverty and times of war both. They engender interest in how one is to eat. Will you join me?"

Sarah carried the tray and Davinoff the coffee. She laid out cups and plates from the great sideboard in the dining room.

"Did you know," Davinoff asked, "that a cook from Napoleon's army has actually preserved food in champagne bottles? The food may still be eaten months after it is corked."

"Truly? Just think of green vegetables in winter, and peaches all the year round, even if one is without a greenhouse." Sarah's mouth watered for green beans, or even spinach.

"It will free armies from stripping the local lands and starving the peasants."

"I'm sure you feel that war is inevitable. You need not even tell me so," Sarah observed, pouring out her coffee and selecting a lump of sugar.

"And you need not even tell me that you disagree."

Sarah smiled. "Well, that's settled. Can we avoid arguing, at least for the morning?"

"I should be the last to correct you in that case, Lady Clevancy. But I feel compelled to point out that it is afternoon."

"So late!" Sarah exclaimed. "I had not meant to sleep the day away."

"You must be feeling housebound. I should like to propose an expedition."

"I am," Sarah admitted. "But . . . but I have not liked to display the fact that I am staying here." She hesitated to point up the impropriety of their situation.

"Exactly so," Davinoff said. "But all the neighborhood will be at their Christmas wassail bowls and sitting down to goose and a plum pudding. Today of all days, a small expedition should be safe if we do not stray into the main thoroughfares."

Sarah pressed her lips together, torn, but she capitulated with a rueful smile in the face of Davinoff's raised brow of entreaty. "I expect we are both housebound, Mr. Davinoff."

Soon she found herself sitting up beside him in the gig, bundled in her muff and gloves and cape, he in Pembly's driving coat. The horse was snorting and anxious, and the snow on the road was fast melting in the wan sun. Sarah inhaled the brisk air deeply. It was good to be out.

"Where are we bound?" she asked as the horse trotted smartly out into the tiny lane. She looked up and could see the darkness of his eyes enhanced by the floating lenses over his pupils.

"Allow me to keep some secrets, Lady Clevancy."

It soon became apparent, however, that they were bound for Thornbury Abbey. As the horse slowed up the hill to the promontory, Sarah got up the courage to ask Davinoff what the workmen had been doing there.

"I am opening portions closed by falling earth." Davinoff looked down at her. "The repairs may be complete by now." He leapt to the ground and handed Sarah down. The wind off the Severn felt clean. The ancient ruined walls of the abbey were dusted with white, and snow nestled in small triangular heaps in the remaining corners. Leaving the horse to graze, Davinoff pressed into the abbey proper and made his way to the flat circle of stone now set flush into the ground once more. Sarah hung back as she realized that he proposed to take her into the crypts.

"Do you dare to come with me?" Davinoff smiled wryly. "You will have a vampire at your side to protect you from the ghosts."

Sarah laughed in spite of herself. "At least I won't be trespassing."

"I have something to answer for in that respect as well," he said as he lifted one end of the stone and rolled it smoothly away. Sarah gasped. It should take several men, or at least a lever, to lift that stone. Her hands gripped each other convulsively inside her muff where Davinoff could not see them. Was he that strong? She pressed her fear down lest it shine out through her eyes.

He lifted his hand. "Follow me." Then he stepped into the earth and began to disappear.

Sarah paused but a moment. A tour of the abbey crypt with its owner was a far different prospect than creeping down into the unknown with Corina, she told herself firmly. Or perhaps it was not different. Perhaps it was only that she had changed. At any rate, she started down into the dark after Davinoff, pressing her hand to the clammy stone walls to steady herself. When she got to the bottom, he was already working at the flint to light the torch laid there. Once again the musty scent of dust and subtle decay assaulted her. She stared into the darkness and wondered if even Davinoff were proof against what might lurk there.

Soon the torch smoked and flickered into life. He held it up and darkness fled around them. There were no signs of workmen, no lumber, no tools. Indeed, there were only marks in the dust of many feet to say that they had been there. "Where were the repairs made?" she whispered.

Davinoff did not deign to whisper as he said, "On a lower level. Are you up to a walk?"

"Of course," Sarah declared, swallowing. There was a level below even the crypts?

Davinoff led the way through the rounded Romanesque arches. Sarah took several deep breaths when the ornately carved stone coffins, tumbled and half open, emerged into the light. Every abbey and cathedral in England had crypts just like this, she told herself.

Her host marched on toward the corner of the crypt. There Sarah could see another yawning darkness, with another stairway winding down to what hellish place she could not think. Davinoff bent to light another torch laid at the stair, and handed it to her with a heartening smile.

"I expect you would like to have one of your own. Are you ready to explore?"

"Yes," Sarah whispered, incapable of reassurance or retort.

Davinoff held out his hand and took hers before he turned

to descend into the depths. He could snap the bones in her hand with a single squeeze, no doubt, but his clasp was gentle, his hand warm and dry. It had the usual tingling effect on her, signaling the dangerous attraction that he exerted on her, even here. They wound down into the earth for what seemed like forever. The stairs were cut into solid rock. Alongside the steps was a ramp. Ropes dangled from pulleys anchored into the stone walls. Sarah could not guess where they might be going.

At last, Davinoff seemed to rise in front of her. They had reached the bottom.

"Now, we shall see if my friend Razcocy has done his work." His words echoed eerily as he gestured toward a narrow tunnel in front of them. They had to walk single file. The torch lit up the blond wood of new lumber braces wedged in against stones and earth.

Sarah found her tongue in the face of this most ordinary evidence of human effort. "Do you think the tunnel might collapse?"

"Oh, I should think not. Razcocy has worked the mines most of his life. He knows how to keep a tunnel open." Davinoff's deep voice echoed off the stone.

They worked their way along the shaft for some distance. Sarah tried to imagine where they were in relation to the outside world. The weight of earth above them pressed on her. The narrow pool of their light moving slowly along the tunnel left a fearful darkness closing in constantly behind them. Sarah could not help but glance around. She hoped Davinoff could take care of whatever might come at them from behind.

An ancient wooden door blocked their path, braced with metal straps. Razcocy and his crew had buttressed the tunnel in front of the entrance. A huge metal lock secured the door to a frame cut into the stone. A sigh of relief escaped from Davinoff as she came up beside him.

"The door is still intact," he said. He produced a huge metal key from his waistcoat pocket and started forward. Abruptly he stopped and turned to Sarah. "Now you will see that it is I who have been trespassing, ever since Charles granted your ancestors the land at Clershing."

With that mysterious statement, he bent over the rusty lock

and inserted the key. He worked over it for some moments, and when it would not yield to his machinations, he reached out one white hand and grasped the lock in his fist. With a twisting wrench that provoked a groan of effort, Davinoff wrested the lock from its metal strap with a squeal of rending iron. Sarah bit a trembling lip as he tossed it, clanking, to the stone floor and pulled at the heavy door. A puff of dust smoked into the passage. Davinoff strode into the darkness beyond.

Sarah trailed after him. The first moment of wonder as the torch illuminated the marvelous room would stay with her forever. Its ceiling was lost in flickering darkness above them. Plaster crumbled from walls and pillars that disappeared into the gloom. The air was cool and dry with time. One corner, where a stairway wound upward, had collapsed, burying the upper steps in earth. Peeking through a layer of dust, tiny mosaic tiles in the floor peered up at her in patterns barely discernable, of grape leaves and geometric borders. In dim corners, statues of fine marble still bore traces of their original delicate paint. Sealed boxes and crates tumbled over each other. Paintings, shrouded and wrapped, were stacked against the walls. The foaming contents of one trunk had spilled onto the floor and gleamed gold under their dusty coats.

Sarah froze and scanned the room until her eyes returned to Davinoff. He was smiling at her. "Welcome to my home, Lady Clevancy." He looked around. "At least one room of it."

"Where is this?" Sarah asked in a choked whisper, though she knew already the answer.

"We are in a room of the villa you want so much to excavate."

"This is why you wanted my land?" she asked, brows drawn together.

Davinoff nodded. "I have been keeping some of my little souvenirs here for a long time, as well as certain other places. I was away when Charles split the parcel and deeded the portion with the villa to your family. But I had the abbey, so I built the tunnel down through the bluff and up into my cache. It still seemed as safe as any place. But the tunnel collapsed. I was in the midst of repairing it when I heard you meant to excavate. Thus my attempt to buy your property. You see, I have been trespassing for a very long time." Davinoff looked for her reaction.

"This was your *house?*" Sarah repeated, sounding idiotic, even to herself.

Davinoff nodded.

Sarah remembered his words in the darkened cellar at the Dower House. "*The parasite rebuilds endlessly rather than move on to a new host.*" She bit her lip and looked at his countenance flickering in the light of the torches. "How old are you?" she whispered fiercely.

He studied her. "I grew up in the Carpathians during the first years of the Roman Empire. For many years I considered myself a Roman."

Sarah's mind lurched from one thought to another. Two centuries before Christ or three? Twenty-one *hundred* years? "Why did you bring me here?" she blurted. Had he wanted to frighten her? If so, he had certainly succeeded. But his next words brought her back to earth.

"Isn't it Christmas Day?" he asked softly. "It is a poor guest who does not bring a gift." He placed his torch in a holder and moved to loom above her. Looking down, he touched her arm. "I wanted to show you things I know only you will appreciate. I wanted to show you your villa through my eyes, as my home."

He smiled as she searched his face in wonder. "First, let us see how my souvenirs have fared since my last visit." He took Sarah's torch from her and lighted several others in their holders around the room, until the contents leapt into flickering focus.

He started with the paintings leaning against the left wall. He threw back the shrouds to reveal dark oils in their gilded frames. Sarah looked over his shoulder. The red-haired nudes upon the riverbank in the first proclaimed a Titian. He placed it carefully aside. There was a Van Eyck that Sarah did not know, and a Botticelli, with his chubby pastel angels. Then he reached to the side and brought it up. It was small, its ornate gilt frame perhaps eighteen inches square and darkened at the edges with age. The young woman's face that glowed out of the center was ineffably sad with a knowledge and acceptance shining out of her eyes that made her sister with the mysterious smile seem shallow by comparison. Sarah found herself crying.

"He painted a companion piece?" she choked.

"He gave me my choice," Davinoff said, remembering. "I chose the melancholy version."

Sarah gazed upon the painting for several minutes, transfixed.

"I have something else here from Leonardo, somewhere," Davinoff said, looking around. Finally he moved to a crate in the center of the room, and plucked up a small wire model that looked very like a dragonfly. "His flying machine. He made it in the fourteen-nineties sometime, as I recall. I asked to have it as a keepsake."

Sarah touched the delicate wire wings. "Did he fly, then?"

"He could have done so. But he did not. It would have offended the Church," Davinoff called back. He was levering open a carefully sealed crate with a crowbar. He knelt and drew out several books. "This is a newer box," he said. "Ah." He pulled up one volume and held it to the light. "Milton. My prize for patronage was a first edition of *Paradise Lost*." Davinoff sat upon a crate and began thumbing through the volume. "Poor John. It galled him to accept support from one with morals such as mine." Davinoff looked up at Sarah. "He thought he made me a retort by modeling his villain after me. But I thought his Satan quite more interesting than God."

Sarah could not help smiling. "You were Satan?"

"Lady Clevancy, I have always been Satan," Davinoff observed.

Sarah looked around the room to see small jade statuettes and dusty piles of manuscripts. A fat wooden figure of a horse, perhaps three feet high and once enameled, a miracle of horseness, stood next to the overflowing golden trunk. She wandered over, and picked up a goblet, inlaid with winking stones, and a heavy gold chain, set with what looked like sapphires. "Where did you get this treasure? Were you a pirate?"

"That particular bit is Saracen gold from the first Crusade," Davinoff said, looking up from where he was opening another box. "Ah, this will interest you."

Sarah went to his side, kicking up small swirls of dust as she passed across the mosaic floor. He leaned over a box with books and scrolls that looked extremely old.

"*The Canterbury Tales*, one of my favorites," he said, opening the heavy leather cover to show the illuminated manuscript within.

"Chaucer?" Sarah asked, incredulous. "The illumination is beautiful."

"In here somewhere are the Lindesfarne Gospels. You will find their illumination much finer." He rummaged in the marvelous crate and passed a larger volume to her.

Sarah's wonder grew as she fondled copies of the *Kamandaki*, an Indian manual of government published in the year 750, and the *Kokinshu*, an official anthology of Japanese history from 905. The *Book of Fixed Stars* by the Arab Al Sufi was there, and the first results from Mr. Guttenberg's printing press. The treasures tumbling out of the crates made Sarah's head spin.

Davinoff showed her cabochon rubies from Roman women, and Celtic jewelry intricately wrought in silver, translucent white jade pieces meant to give luck to the Japanese ladies who wore them. He unfurled scrolls of Chinese landscape paintings by people with names like Yen Li Pen and Li Chao Tao and Wang Wei. The scenes were misty and evocative, alternating with incredibly precise detail. The afternoon was lost in times past and miracles of survival. Each new surprise brought a gasp from Sarah. A copy of the Magna Carta, the ring of Charlemagne, all these were things Davinoff called "souvenirs."

"And I thought you were a smuggler." She smiled. "It was the wildest thing I could imagine." Another thought occurred. "You do not sell these things, do you?"

"The world may someday need to have a copy of *The Canterbury Tales*, if all others have been burned or buried or destroyed. My needs are provided by my current holdings. But for something extraordinary, I indulge in selling the coins. He went to two chests by the wall and lifted their covers to reveal their gleaming contents. "Roman," he said, pointing to the one on the left. "And gold doubloons from the Spanish Main."

Sarah laughed and sat heavily upon a yet unopened crate. What wonders did it hold? "I am in heaven." She sighed. She looked at him curiously. "Why did you reveal this?"

"I wanted you to know why I coveted your land." His voice was an intimate murmur. "And why I tried to delay your excavation by insisting you have it mapped."

Sarah forgave him instantly. "And you talk of trespass!" she chided. "My family has trespassed all these years upon your home. Are you not afraid I will betray your secrets?"

"You have too much respect for the past." He waved her question aside. "What I wanted was to provide a Christmas gift for you, in return for the gift of life that you have given me." He gestured round the dusty room. "What will you have? Anything is yours."

Sarah almost shuddered. "I could not accept any of these things. They are too precious."

"Your gift was more valuable to me than any of these poor mementos."

Sarah shook her head. "I cannot take anything in this room from you."

"Do not insult my gesture, small as it is," Davinoff said, and laid his iron bar upon a crate. "I think you owe me the opportunity to thank you in my own way. Don't you agree?"

Sarah chewed her lip and knew she was lost. She looked around the room and tried to remember something she had seen that was less valuable. No jewels, that was certain. She cast about and her eyes came to rest upon the fat wooden horse, its enamel half gone, its gold caparisons gleaming dully in the light. It was carved so that it capered gaily, its tail braided and bound up between its chubby buttocks. It was a lovely rendition of a horse. But it was only wooden. It could not be so valuable. "Well," she said, "I do like that horse."

Davinoff glided over to the figure and raised it with both hands to the light of a torch. "An excellent choice. It is from the T'ang dynasty. The Chinese of that period had a feel for horses, just as you do. I knew it when I saw you ride that mare. It will look well mounted."

So he had seen her ride Maggie. "T'ang," she repeated. "When is that?"

"Roughly seven hundred to nine hundred."

Sarah gulped and raised her brows. "This horse is a thousand years old?"

"A mere babe." He smiled at her.

Sarah looked up at him and suddenly the magic of the afternoon melted away. A thousand years meant nothing to him.

How young she must seem, how childish to a man like this.

"Shall we assay all those stairs?" he was asking her.

She nodded dumbly as he extinguished the lights. Then with a last torch in one hand and her wooden horse tucked easily under the other arm, he led the way out to the nineteenth century.

It was four o'clock and dusk was falling when they came up into the brisk wind sweeping the promontory. The wan sun had turned to slate-gray clouds, and mist threatened to hurry the dark along. Davinoff collected the horse and hitched him to the gig.

The ride home was almost silent between the two explorers. Sarah's head was spinning with history and with Davinoff's impossible age. The warm lights of the small houses down in the village glowed merrily out of the deepening gloom as Christmas dinners were set on the table and families celebrated the possibility of salvation. "Life everlasting, amen" was a vague hope to cheat death for them. The body would die, but the soul did not. But what if the body did not die? What happened to the soul then?

By the time they got to the Dower House, it had come on to night. Davinoff took the horse round to stable while Sarah took her T'ang gift and went in to make up some fires against the cold. When Davinoff came in, his arms loaded with wood, the house was alight with the glow of candles and lamps. Fires burned in the kitchen and the drawing room.

They both busied themselves getting out what could be got of a Christmas dinner. At least they had the ham. Sarah felt constrained. She did not know what to say to him. What could she say that would interest one who had seen as much as he?

Davinoff began to talk of other times, of China before Marco Polo, of the beginning of the Renaissance in Italy, of the Danes conquering the Danelaw in England. Sarah was astounded, but also beguiled. As they set out their dishes in the dining room and Davinoff poured wine, she said, "You have seen the defining events of history firsthand, Mr. Davinoff. I cannot imagine the excitement that you must have experienced."

He seated her, then himself. "Excitement is a word no longer in my vocabulary."

Instantly Sarah saw all his experience in a new light. It was not a treasure to him but a burden. "Is that why I've never seen you laugh?"

"You provide quite enough laughter for us both," Davinoff replied, lightly.

"You hate excess, then?" Sarah followed his lead and lightened her tone.

"Oh, I have been quite excessive in my time. You hardly know the meaning of the word, I fear. But one grows bored with excess."

"Then boredom is your ruling passion? You sadden me, sir, that all of the wonders of the world are reduced to commonplaces for you."

He looked at her most strangely. "I used to think boredom was all that was left to me."

"You need to see the world through new eyes."

Davinoff cut her a slab of ham. "You are right. Perhaps I shall take your advice."

Sarah looked at him, cutting meat at her table, his face illuminated by the candelabra. She suddenly wanted things to stay just so. His flattering desire to attend to her, the wonder of his nature, the attraction she felt for him, all hung in the air, unrealized and yet undenied.

At the same moment, she knew change was inevitable. The moment was broken. He was asking her whether she had ever seen the Parthenon. She answered something. But her thoughts were consumed by the knowledge that this moment was stolen. Soon it would melt away, just as he would melt from her life. They could not stay immured in the Dower House forever. He would move on to other places where history was being made, far away from her little world of Bath. Her sense of loss was almost overwhelming. Her life, stretching into the future, short as it might be by Davinoff's standards, suddenly seemed barren and lonely.

Davinoff intruded upon her unpleasant revelations. "Did you hear me, Lady Clevancy?"

"I'm sorry," Sarah started. "What was it you were saying?"

As if to confirm her very thoughts, Davinoff looked up from his plate and said quietly, "I have imposed on your hospitality and your kindness long enough. Tomorrow, I return to Bath."

"Are you up to it?" she inquired with what she hoped was her lightest tone.

"It is exactly my physical condition that requires it. I am afraid I need more blood."

All Sarah's doubts about what she had set loose upon the world assailed her. She glanced quickly to his face, her fear no doubt writ plainly on her features. "You promised you would not hurt anyone," she stammered.

"I remember that quite clearly, Lady Clevancy. You need not remind me."

"I am sorry. It is only . . ."

"It is only that you are not sure yet whether I am a man who keeps his promises."

Sarah felt herself blushing.

"My only problem is the quantity of blood I need at this point," Davinoff mused, frowning. "I will have to be busy."

Sarah thought of him wooing a string of countesses. "I know where you may get blood. Dr. Upcott keeps a supply for his experiments. It is sealed in bottles, and kept on ice."

Davinoff murmured, with raised brows, "Your scruples do not extend to stealing?"

Sarah considered his question. "The blood is given every day by donors to help people. You need help. It isn't wrong to use the blood as it was intended."

"I could perhaps use the blood if it was taken within several hours, more and it is useless." He seemed skeptical.

"They donate on Thursdays," Sarah said in a small voice, "in the afternoon."

"Then tomorrow I am off to Bath. I may at least get a pint or two that way."

That was the end, Sarah thought. It was over, this dreamy interlude of fear and newfound courage and the wonder of a new vision of the world seen through the eyes of a vampire. Amputated at the root, it would never grow into anything more. "How will you go?" she asked.

"I shall walk into Littleton-on-Severn and procure a horse. That will cause less inconvenience to you, and be less conspicuous, I should think."

"You expect to rent a horse on Boxing Day? I hardly think the liveries will be open for business." Sarah rubbed her hands together. "I must be going back to Bath myself. I am promised to a ball on New Year's Eve. Why don't you drive me in the gig?"

"Does that seem discreet?" he asked, raising his glass to his lips.

"You drove me home from a stage stop in Marlborough and my reputation survived."

"Very well, my hostess," Davinoff said, raising his glass to her. "We shall to Bath."

They had not gone far the next morning when they met Mr. Josiah Wells trotting down the lane on his cob. The last person Sarah wanted to meet was someone she knew.

"Merry Christmas," Mr. Wells hailed them, as both he and Davinoff drew up.

"Are you still here, Lady Clevancy? If we'd a know'd you were planning to stay through the holidays, we woulda had you down to our dinner. Mrs. Wells fixed a right plump fowl."

"I wasn't aware you knew of my arrival," she said in confusion.

"Directed that fellow delivering your trunk about a week ago," Mr. Wells said.

Davinoff stepped into the breach. "Wells, can you send Razcocy to me at the abbey on Thursday next? I have some crates I want shipped. He is still at the Swan, I take it."

"We both been expectin' you for some time, sir." Mr. Wells touched his hat to acknowledge the order. "Didn't know you was up this way." Of a sudden, Mr. Wells's eyes leapt to Sarah's face and back again to Davinoff. "The landlord at the Rose over to Elburton said he hadn't seen hide nor hair of you."

"I found the Rose sadly deficient," Davinoff lied, his tone depressing further inquiry. "I was forced to stay at Morton." He snapped the reins over the horse's back.

"He knew," Sarah said in a small voice as they drove away. "I could see it."

"He is that type they call 'salt of the earth,' I believe," Davinoff reassured her. "He will not speak what he thinks, especially when he respects you so much."

"He thinks of me as a child," Sarah deprecated.

"He admires your management," Davinoff corrected. "He spoke of it when I asked about Clershing."

"The work is his, not mine."

"Ah, but you will admit you 'drug him into potatoes.' That is, I believe, how he put it."

Sarah laughed. "Oh yes, I did that."

"Wells thinks it was a brilliant move." Davinoff's eyes were on the muddy lane.

"Not brilliant, desperate," Sarah returned. "My father's estates were much encumbered. I sold what I could to preserve the rest, and found a better market for potatoes than for barley, though potatoes are *not* aristocratic. Clershing is all I have left now, but it is mine free and clear."

"Your father would be proud," Davinoff observed.

Sarah hesitated. "I am not sure. He never shared the state of his affairs with me before he died. It was a shock to see how things lay. I could have helped him, if he'd let me. I am much more practical than he was. But I am afraid he was disappointed that I was not a boy."

"You both loved antiquities. He allowed you to study mathematics. Not girlish pursuits."

"He let me follow my interests, but never trusted me enough to share his burdens." Sarah found this disclosure painful. "He wanted his little girl to be demure. Not my strong suit." At least he had never known what really brought her scampering home from Sienna.

"No, I shouldn't think so," Davinoff agreed. "Do you want to be demure?"

Sarah couldn't help but smile at this frontal assault. "I have never admired dependency. But I am sorry my father was disappointed."

"Then, I am sorry, too," Davinoff declared. "It was his loss. You will have to be content with being an educated, competent woman of affairs who has an intense interest in the world."

Sarah shook her head and laughed away the compliment. Davinoff didn't really know her.

The drive to Bath was long and cold. Sarah managed animation, but underneath she felt Bath approaching as though it stalked them as prey. What would happen when Corina found that Davinoff had not been taken to an asylum on the Continent? She would rage. She would storm. She would plan revenge of some kind, on Sarah perhaps, but definitely on Davinoff. Corina was not entirely sane. And what would a man like Davinoff do to a woman who had wronged him as Corina had? Sarah had felt the stirrings of his desire for revenge that first night, buried in casual conversation, but palpable nonetheless. It was imperative that he leave Bath immediately. Only then could their mutual desire for revenge be circumvented.

"What will you do now?" she asked. London was not far enough. He must go somewhere where he would never encounter Corina.

"I will repair to the Christopher. Do you know if my shot was paid?"

"She paid your shot." Sarah hesitated. "I do not know how your affairs stand, but I can provide for your immediate needs." Little enough, but he could not leave Bath without money.

Davinoff looked down at her. She could not read his expression. "Thank you for your concern. I believe I can provide for myself until my bankers respond to my inquiries."

"Do you plan to stay in Bath?" Sarah looked down at her hands and held her breath. She should want to hear him say he would go away at the first opportunity. She should want that.

"I have unfinished business here," he said.

Sarah was torn. Did he mean to take his revenge upon Corina? What could she do to stop him? "Mr. Davinoff—" she began, her heart almost audible, she was sure.

"Julien," he interrupted softly. "Surely after all we have been through, you might begin to call me Julien, Lady Clevancy?"

Sarah started, her purpose dissolving into confusion. "Julien," she almost whispered, feeling the sound in her mouth, strange and intimate.

"Yes, Sarah?" he answered.

"You must not revenge yourself upon Corina," she blurted. "I would have not bloodshed, no matter the provocation." She saw his countenance darken. "She deserves to pay," Sarah continued. "But if you wish revenge, let us go the magistrates. I will testify in your behalf." He looked startled. For a moment he said nothing, until she thought she would burst with anxiety.

"There will be no death," he said. "And no magistrates. A lengthy trial, the scandal of harboring an addict without even servants in the house, Corina's suspicions about my nature . . ." He trailed off. "The details of a trial would serve no one."

"Then you will go." Her victory was celebrated in bleak tones.

"In a few days," he answered pensively. "I must remove my souvenirs from your property to one of my other storehouses. You should not be burdened with their presence."

"Oh, I will not excavate your home," Sarah protested. "You need not move your treasures." If they were gone, he would never be back.

Davinoff only shook his head. "It is best," he said.

The outskirts of Bath rose up around them, damping further conversation. Sarah saw heads turn in their direction. So apparently did Davinoff.

"The story is that I have been at the abbey," he reminded her, "and have brought you back with me to town. I trust you can think of a reason we are using your horse instead of mine?"

"An accident, perhaps? It is I who am doing you a favor, since your cattle were injured."

"Of course." He bowed his head. "It is you who have done me a favor after all."

"Except that it is Corina's horse and gig." She saw Davinoff's brows raise. "I do not keep horses since my father's death." She did not say that she could not afford to keep horses.

"That is a shame. You of anyone should have horses."

"Perhaps someday." Once she could have looked forward to such a time.

"Do you chance to know what happened to Quixote and my pair?" Davinoff asked, as though it were a casual question.

Sarah knew better. "Lansing says they were sold at Tattersall's," she almost whispered. She was about to express her regret, but Davinoff's black look did not allow of sympathy.

In moments, they were through to Green Street. Then it was up to Stall Street, and over to Cheap Street, and so to the High and the Christopher Hotel, almost upon the abbey grounds. As

Davinoff leapt down, he looked up at Sarah, his dark eyes blazing, his ebony curls ruffled by the wind. "Adieu, my lady," he said simply.

"Adieu," she whispered, her heart aching for what would never be. She clucked to the horse and headed out of the yard toward Bridge Street and home.

Sarah found the house confining, but as yet she couldn't bear to go about her life again. She spent time in her sere and tiny winter garden, as clouds raced across the sky and the bare branches of the fruit trees clattered above her. Her thoughts were too tumultuous to be calmed. She could think only of Davinoff. Where was he? She might never know where he was again, would only know one place where he was not.

She did glean some news. She had a strange visit from George, berating her for being out of town without telling him. He regretted that he could not escort her to his mother's ball, since he was hosting, but assumed she would attend. He also hinted that he'd seen Davinoff at his laboratory, yet did not seem sure. There had been a theft. Some blood was missing. She could guess why George would not be sure, and her soul sang. Julien had his blood, and he had kept his promise. He had been seen at Jackson's gaming salon as well, engaging in deep play and winning most scandalously. She had that from Paulette Cantonfield when Sarah finally went out to the provisioner's shop. Davinoff seemed very adept at providing for his needs.

Jasco and Addie arrived on Wednesday and were duly picked up at the coaching inn. The butler informed her that Amelia would not be back until the third. Sarah was glad. She wanted to ease back into life slowly. But she was glad to see Jasco and Addie and tired of doing for herself.

On Thursday Jasco brought a message to the study where Sarah was writing a note to inform Mr. Thorpe she had changed her mind about excavating and wanted to cancel their engagement. "Leave it in the hall, Jasco." Sarah waved him away. "I shall look at it later."

"The boy has instructions to wait for a reply."

Sarah sat back in her chair. What could warrant so much urgency? She reached for the note and saw the ornate *D* pressed into the wax seal. Sarah felt herself flushing. She ripped open the heavy rag envelope, addressed in a decisive masculine hand.

> I apologize for the lateness of this invitation, Lady Clevancy. I should be grateful, however, if you would do me the honor of accompanying me to Lady Beldon's ball on Saturday. I shall call at eight.
> Julien

Sarah hesitated only for an instant before she snatched up her quill and a sheet of writing paper with her crest embossed on it and dashed off a single word in response. *Honored.* She signed it with her initials, *S.A*, then she folded and sealed it into an envelope. One last time, she thought. He offered her one night, and she would take it. She handed the envelope to Jasco.

Sarah called for Addie and rushed up the stairs. How had he gotten an invitation from Lady Beldon in so short a time? He got whatever he wanted. She knew that. What she wanted was one evening upon his arm, and the consequences be damned. She threw open one of the wardrobes. Addie appeared in the doorway.

"Miss Sarah, whatever are you about?" Addie asked.

"I am going to Lady Beldon's ball on Saturday," Sarah announced. She pulled the lavender dress out of the wardrobe.

"But of course you are, my lady."

Sarah turned to Addie, more friend than servant now, "I am going with Mr. Davinoff."

Addie gasped. "Never that man who dresses all in black!"

"The very one." Sarah examined the lavender dress with distaste. She tossed the dress upon the floor. "Even forgetting the fact that blond lace has never suited me, I cannot wear this rag again." She turned to Addie, speculation in her eyes.

"There is never enough time for a new dress, my lady." Addie's distress showed in her face. "Mademoiselle Courette is booked for weeks in advance."

"You are right." Sarah was thoughtful.

"We could change the blond lace," Addie offered.

Sarah brushed this suggestion aside without hesitation. "Blond lace is only the start of the problem. This is not a night for pastel colors." She paced to the window and back like a caged animal, not caring if Addie thought she had lost her mind. "I want electric blue, or royal purple, or red." She stopped, lost in thought.

"Those colors haven't been in fashion since your mother's day. Pomona green perhaps . . ."

Sarah turned on Addie. "You are a genius, Addie!" she crowed.

"But you don't own a Pomona green. There is no time . . ."

Sarah clapped Addie on the shoulder as she strode into the hall. "Not Pomona green. My mother's dresses!" She left Addie to trail after her as she climbed the stairs toward the attic.

Sarah's exuberant mood turned reminiscent as she trod across the dusty floor toward the trunks under the windows. Wintry light peeked among the crates and furniture, all that was left from Balacanell and Huntsford, sold after her father's death in order to save Clershing. Most of her mother's things had burned at that house. There was little left of her now.

She raised the lid of a trunk. The vibrant silks had not faded with age. Old gold, emerald green, midnight blue, and copper, they lay wrapped in silver paper just as they had been laid in the trunks so many years ago. The memory of her mother washed over Sarah, seen through a child's eyes. She had been diminutive, beautiful, red hair and green eyes. How Sarah had always wanted red hair. Her mother had been all her father had wanted Sarah to be, demure, a perfect hostess.

She took out the dresses one by one. They had been packed away as old even in her mother's time, else they would have been at destroyed at Clershing. Addie cooed and gasped at the fine fabrics as she related again the stories of Sarah's mother's triumphs. Sarah laid them each aside, calculating how to remove the panniers and which ones were best adapted to her figure.

In the second trunk she saw one that called to her immediately. It was soft red and black brocade, wrinkled now, but with the color singing of a time less discreet, bolder about its desires. The bosom was cut square, and tightly, decidedly décolleté. The sleeves were full, with long tight cuffs. The patterned fabric would hang in lustrous folds over a stiff satin underskirt of shining black, intricately embroidered and revealed by a wide slit in the front. Sarah held it up.

"I remember just the night your mother wore it," Addie reminisced. "It did not go with her red hair, so she went poudree, but it made her skin glow. She was eighteen, just married, and the talk of the town." Sarah shrugged off her dress and slipped it over her head. She stood in front of a dusty mirror as Addie fastened the endless row of covered buttons up the back.

The stiff whalebone pressed her breasts up. Delicate black braid was arranged in complicated fleur-de-lis up the cuffs and outlined the split skirt and the hem. It emphasized the tiny waist of the dress. How scandalous to show one's waist again! For a moment, Sarah had misgivings. She would be dressed audaciously, in a style not faintly like anyone else in the room. They would wear Empire waistlines, and pastel colors. The gossips of Bath would have a subject for weeks to come. But in her heart, she knew it was right for Davinoff, right for the way she felt.

Addie stood back and beamed at her. "Your mother never wore that dress as you do."

"Do you think we can get the skirt to fall naturally?"

"No sooner said than done," Addie declared.

As she walked downstairs on New Year's Eve dressed in her new old dress, she fingered her mother's rubies at her throat. This necklace was the one thing she had never sold; four square-cut stones with a pear-shaped drop hanging between her breasts. She would pay a high price tonight for seeing Davinoff once more before he left. Why not pay it boldly, in gold pieces, for all to see? She glanced in the mirror. Her dress told the world she paid the price gladly.

Addie waited at the foot of the stairs with her mother's heavy velvet cape. Addie, at least, had no doubts. "You are a vision," she said fondly. "No one will look like you tonight."

Sarah gave a wry smile. "I may be home early if no one will speak to me."

"Nonsense," Addie sniffed. "You'll not be lonely tonight, unless you have a hankering for female companionship. Whatever they might say, they'll all be at the dressmakers next week."

At that moment, Jasco opened the door to Davinoff. The apparition at the entry, all black and white strength and the swirling darkness of a cape, made Jasco step back involuntarily.

"Good evening. Lady Clevancy is expecting me." The deep drawling voice washed into the room. Jasco stood transfixed. The cape brushed him as the man moved smoothly past.

"A moment, Mr. Davinoff," Sarah called. She stepped forward, carrying her wrap. Busy with her reticule, she did not notice the effect she had on him. She looked up suddenly, fearing that he might not be enamored of her dress and the attention it would elicit tonight. He certainly looked stunned. "I am afraid I shall be sadly out of fashion . . ." she stammered.

"Fashion? Fashion is irrelevant, I believe." He stepped forward and took her wrap. "Allow me." He placed the velvet around her shoulders. She looked up with a trace of uncertainty. A smile brushed his lips. " 'You are the maker of manners,' Sarah," he quoted softly. It was Shakespeare, *Henry V*. "You will see that tonight." He offered his arm. As she placed her black-gloved hand on his, she found herself staring at the ruby winking in the snowy cravat. How had he known to wear a bloodred ruby? It was the only color to touch his elegant attire.

"We shall see," she said. But confidence straightened her back once more. They passed out of the door under Jasco's shocked stare and Addie's indulgent smile.

Sarah was surprised that Davinoff had procured a matched pair. She looked carefully at the magnificent beasts. She could have sworn they were the same pair that pulled his carriage from Marlborough to Bath that day so long ago. "Do I find your equipage and your horses familiar?" she asked as he handed her in. He stepped in after her and signaled to his driver.

"Yes." His deep voice cascaded over her in the dark. "I made a trip to Tattersall's—"

"Did you find who bought Quixote?" Sarah interrupted.

"I am quite resourceful," Davinoff disclosed. "The gentleman who had purchased him was quite eager to part with him, a fact I know not whether to lay at Quixote's door or my own."

Sarah raised her hand to her throat as tears of relief filled her eyes. "You have him back?"

"Yes. And Jupiter and Zeus as well, as you see." Davinoff

leaned back into the corner of the landaulet. "I met their new owner at White's while I was in London. He was not eager at first to sell, but he ended by giving up some guineas as well as his new pair at the faro table."

"I am so glad." Sarah sighed. "They could only belong to you. I worried they were lost."

"You should have more faith, Sarah," Davinoff drawled.

"I suppose I should," she said, as the coach clattered up the streets toward Lady Beldon's town house. "I was amazed that Lady Beldon should extend an invitation to so notorious a person as yourself, for instance. Yet you seem to have managed it."

"Lady Beldon has a weakness for the compliment. A predilection of your sex, I believe."

"I hardly consider Lady Beldon a representative example of our sex," Sarah protested.

"Then I will not turn your head when I note that you also are not representative of your sex tonight. You are quite more lovely than the average specimen," Davinoff murmured.

"You are teasing me!" she accused.

"Am I?" he asked.

Sarah sat back in the squabs. Why was she quarreling with the man when she had resolved to savor every moment of tonight, regardless of consequence? It would be their last.

Davinoff accentuated the consequences. "I understand Mrs. Nandalay will be present."

"Oh dear." It had not occurred to Sarah that Corina would be back in society yet.

"I have been wanting to speak with her." Davinoff's voice rose out of the darkness, his face illuminated only occasionally by a passing street lamp.

"Let us both stay as far away from her as possible." Sarah foresaw a dreadful evening.

"I think not," Davinoff mused. "Since you no doubt intend to continue in Bath, we should perhaps inform her that her silence will buy our own."

"Her silence?"

"She knew you took me away," he said gently. "She will make it her business to find that you were with me at the Dower House alone. She can cause you the discomfort of a scandal."

"You are her most likely target." She glanced away. "She is obsessed with you."

"Regardless of her target, we are agreed upon our course of action?"

"Yes." Leave it to Corina to cut up her peace on tonight of all nights.

The carriage drew into the line of coaches moving toward the huge columned portico of Lady Beldon's town house. A blockish building newly built in the classic style, it was a structure of little sympathy, grand without eloquence, the emotion of former ages diluted into mediocrity. A stream of revelers swirled and eddied through the great doors.

Davinoff descended and handed Sarah down. How many times had she felt the shock of touching him? The experience would not seem to dim. She placed her hand on his arm, and stepped from the coach, lost in his eyes. She found their power reassuring now. He enfolded her hand upon his arm. A ghost of a smile touched his lips. They turned and moved up the shallow stairs to the marble portico. As they came through the doors, several groups in the foyer stopped to stare at her and her dark companion. The looks were incredulous, but they held envy as well.

Chapter Fifteen

The butler called out their names as they stepped through the doorway of the first-floor ballroom and paused to survey all and be surveyed. Julien's name produced a wave of glances. A murmur of exclamation rolled across the hall. Several persons glanced up as their eyes moved about the room and then returned, transfixed, to the pair in the doorway. Soon everyone was staring and revelers poked their companions to turn and see. The orchestra skipped several beats as musicians looked up from their tablature to peruse the new arrivals, and two couples missed their turn to go down the line, and so fell out of the dance.

The room was ablaze with light and with curiosity. The younger women were straight pillars of pastel. Matrons indulged in the darker colors: dull gold, olive, browns, silver grays. No one was dressed remotely like Sarah in style or color, just as none of the men could match Julien's austere elegance. Two dozen couples danced, but most people stood in groups or sat at the small tables placed about the perimeter of the grand room.

Sarah knew her heart should have been sinking at all those

eyes. Many were obviously dismayed by her attire. They whispered coyly to those about them. But Sarah's hand on Julien's arm did not even quiver. As she surveyed the astonished room, she found herself smiling. Madame Gessande twinkled at her. Lady Beldon stood near the champagne fountain, looking marvelously shocked. Beside his mother, George was busy turning astonishment into anger.

"Shall we?" Julien whispered, looking down at her, the comma of his hair falling over his forehead with an artlessness Byron could never have mustered.

"We shall," Sarah said with relish. Julien took her dance program from the butler with a nod. They moved down the stairs into a sea of faces..The first to greet her was Lady Beldon.

"Sarah." She glowered, the topaz winking like yellow cat's eyes against her heaving bosom. Her dress was olive green. Sarah could hardly feel it was a wise choice, given her complexion. Lady Beldon turned to Julien and beamed.

"Mr. Davinoff, I am so glad you could attend our small soiree upon such short notice. And it was so kind of you to give an escort to Lady Clevancy, since George was needed here." Here Lady Beldon's eyes traveled to Sarah's attire and her mouth curved down in distaste.

"I am not known for my kindness, Lady Beldon," Julien remarked. "Lady Clevancy, on the other hand, was most kind to accept my invitation." Sarah could feel his eyes upon her. That almost compensated for the hard stare Lady Beldon sent her way.

"My dear, I am so sorry." George's mother smiled. "Did I not make it clear in the invitation that this was not to be a masquerade?"

Sarah suppressed a gasp of outrage. After all she had put up with from Lady Beldon, she deserved better treatment. Her embarrassment turned to cold contempt for the incivility.

"Lady Clevancy, I see Madame Gessande. Your servant, Lady Beldon." Julien moved off, with Sarah fuming by his side.

"That woman!" Sarah exclaimed between her teeth.

"She will eat her words within the week," Julien assured her. They moved toward the table where Vivienne Gessande waited, smiling, with Mrs. Piozzi.

"Sarah, you look divine," Madame Gessande greeted her, as Sarah bent to kiss her cheek.

"Just the opposite, if you ask Lady Beldon." Sarah managed to chuckle.

"You take me back to times when women knew how to dress!" Mrs. Piozzi declared.

"Monsieur Davinoff." Madame raised her hand, and Julien kissed it. "It is a pleasure to see you back in town. We thought you were lost to us."

"I very nearly was," Julien murmured, looking down at Sarah.

Madame's sharp eyes examined him.

"How were your holidays, Madame?" Sarah interrupted her line of thought.

"I cannot think. At my age, they all tend to run together. But where have you been, *ma petite?* You are certainly aglow."

"I took some time for myself at the Dower House," Sarah replied.

"All alone for Christmas?" Madame clucked.

"Well, nearly so." Sarah did not like to deceive, but she didn't want to answer questions.

Madame's eyes flicked to Julien. "Well, it is good to have both of you back in town."

"Have you seen that DuFond girl eyeing you?" Mrs. Piozzi quizzed. "Mark my words, she'll be at Courette's asking for waists on Monday and she will still get it wrong."

"Wherever did you find someone to make that lovely dress so quickly?" Madame Gessande asked. "It must be your own design, for no modiste I know has such imagination."

"I will tell you the story one day, if I survive the evening." Sarah laughed. The orchestra struck up a waltz. Sarah wondered that George allowed so scandalous a dance at Beldon House.

Julien bowed to the two venerable women. "You will excuse us, ladies. I lay claim to this dance." He took Sarah's elbow and turned her to the floor. Couples parted in front of them as he led her to the center. When she turned toward him, she looked up into those marvelous, powerful eyes, and wondered how she could ever have been afraid of them. She felt as much as saw his left hand stretch out, palm upward. Without taking her eyes from his face, her right hand found it. His other hand stole about her and came to rest upon her waist. Very deliberately, she placed the open palm of her glove upon his shoulder. A ghost of a smile flitted across his lips as the music swirled up and seemed to float them away on its tide. They glided about the room in sensuous circles of music and movement. His body, so close, was intoxicating. His arm around her made them a single leaf twirling on the mad music, rising and falling in the rhythm of the waltz. Sarah lost all sense of the crowd around her. She knew only the pressure of his hands on her body, the rustle of her dress as it belled out about her, the twinkle of the chandeliers overhead, and Julien's face above her. When at last the music stopped, Julien brushed her hand with his lips. She looked around, dazed. They were alone on the dance floor. Shocked silence seemed to roar in her ears. Sarah blushed and scanned the audience, for that was what the crowd had become. The older contingent whispered, disapproving. Some of the younger women looked speculative, others hostile. The men's eyes glowed.

Sarah wanted to hurry away from all those eyes. But she did not. She placed her hand on Julien's arm, mustering her dignity, and let him lead her from the floor.

Several of the unattached males pushed their way to meet her.

"I hate to gloat, Lady Clevancy, but I did predict this," Julien murmured as he dropped her hand. "Your dance card will be filled tonight."

"Thank you, Mr. Davinoff, for the dance," Sarah said, ignoring the room of people, the boys behind her clamoring for dances. How she longed for the privacy to call him Julien again.

"I will, by tomorrow, be accounted one of the fortunate few. I leave you now to your role as a lioness of fashion." He bowed crisply.

Sarah wondered if she dared ask him if he would take some air with her, or get her lemonade, or at least if she could place his name next to a country dance later.

Julien shook his head, as if guessing what she could not say. "You belong to the room now, Sarah." With eyes she could not read he bowed again and strode away.

Sarah turned toward her male admirers with some dismay.

For the next two hours, there was hardly a moment she wasn't dancing or telling some young buck she was promised. She barely had time to catch her breath and was forced, on several occasions, to cut short the dance in a search for refreshments or air. The waltzes were apparently especially prized, as each man imagined his own arm encircling that provocatively accentuated waist.

All the time, she watched for Julien. She saw him talking to Countess Delmont, then a moment later to Mr. Wilberforce. But he did not dance. When she could no longer pick him out, she thought he must have retreated to the card rooms for an evening of deep play.

George pointedly ignored her, and Corina was nowhere in sight. Sarah was relieved on both counts. At midnight the dancers moved to the windows to watch servants light fireworks in the garden. Ooohs and aaahs were replaced by cheers for 1819 and kisses shared among the lovers of the crowd. Sarah was acutely aware of Sir Kelston standing stiffly beside her, anxious in case she might require his services in this regard. She dared not hope that Julien would appear. He did not, and she went unkissed. Finally Lady Beldon announced supper in the grand dining room. Julien emerged from a drawing room where card tables had been set.

But it was George who appeared at her side. "Am I being presumptuous if I assume that you may deign to accompany your host to dinner?" he asked tightly.

"Yes, George," Sarah answered. "But I shall accommodate you just the same." He was fairly bursting with outrage. He put out his arm, and she laid her hand along it. She wondered how long it would be until his feelings found vent.

The party formed couples. To her surprise she saw Julien bowing in front of Madame Gessande, as the general escorted Mrs. Piozzi through the double doors. With everyone engaged, George was free to vent his spleen. "I cannot say I approve your choice of an escort. You knew I could not abandon my mother to escort you myself," he began in a lowered voice.

"I could come with Davinoff or come alone," Sarah noted. "Not much of a choice."

"I have not seen you lonely this evening at all," George remonstrated.

"No, your party has been quite delightful." Sarah knew she was annoying him.

"I thought you would have saved the first dance for me." George was a model of hurt pride, which put Sarah out of charity with him entirely.

"You were nowhere in evidence. Perhaps you weren't sure you should be seen with me."

"I vowed I would never bring it up, but since you have done so, I must say that I think it is too shabby of you to come to my mother's ball dressed like . . . like I don't know what."

"Some people seem to like my dress," Sarah returned.

"I'll wager I know just who likes it." They were forced to stand in line for the buffet.

"And who is that?"

"You know nothing about him, Sarah," George hissed. "He is more dangerous than a young person like you can know, and hardly suitable."

"George, I really don't think you know what is suitable for me," Sarah remarked, as she chose a filet of sole for the plate George held for her. The people around them were engaged in their own conversations, but still glanced furtively in their direction.

"I see the influence of Corina Nandalay." George's brow wrinkled in consternation.

Sarah looked up, startled. After a moment she said, "I think, George, that for the first time, you do *not* see Corina's influence upon me."

"Then this behavior is even more disturbing. I am only thinking of your reputation."

"Please don't, George. It isn't worth your effort."

"How can you say that, Sarah Ashton, when it is my reputation too?"

"Why would it be your reputation?" Sarah asked, her voice steady.

They were coming to the end of the long and bounteous table. "Well, everyone knows," George sputtered. "I mean one assumes . . ."

"Never assume." Sarah was shocked that she had said it. But it was inevitable.

"Lady Clevancy." Sir Kelston bowed. "I am sent by the table in the corner to ask you and Upcott to make up our party." He poked a thumb toward a table where Lady Varington and Paulette Cantonfield gestured, and Edgar Kerseymere, sitting next to his brother, John, waved a forkful of beef cheerily. Sarah was relieved to be spared further conversation with George.

When Sarah and George joined the table, John and Edgar Kerseymere made extravagant compliments on her dress. Paulette Cantonfield looked dubious. But Lady Varington greeted her shyly. "Lady Clevancy, I wonder if I could ever have the courage to dress so boldly."

John turned to her, obviously besotted, and patted her hand. "Of course you would, Lady Varington. Why, I think you would look famous in a dress with a waist."

Sarah saw a note of resolution come into Lady Varington's doelike eyes and felt for the first time that Julien might be right. She was beginning to enjoy herself, at least until Corina was announced by the footmen. People around the room looked up to see who came so late.

The woman who stood in the door was neither disheveled and incoherent, nor the old Corina, gay and devil-may-care. She was in total control, real or feigned. Her proud disdain floated over the room, daring anyone to remind her of past indiscretions. Her blue eyes glowed cold as she stepped down into the room. She wore cream-colored satin with golden ribbons down her back and run through the top of the tiers of the lace that graced her hem.

Corina shot like an arrow to Sarah's table. "You are back," she accused. "You must tell me about your journey." She grabbed Sarah's elbow and dragged her to an unoccupied corner behind the refreshment table, careless of her rudeness to those at the table. Glancing at Sarah's dress she said, "Why, Sarah, whatever are you wearing?"

"A new dress," Sarah responded, a little startled.

Corina frowned, then waved away the distraction. "Why did you not come straight to me upon your return?" she asked. "I have been on pins and needles. Did you have any trouble?"

Sarah bit her lip. How could she tell Corina the truth without risking a scene in the middle of Lady Beldon's ball? "It was a great deal of trouble."

"But were you successful?" the blonde whispered.

"Yes, Corina, but not in the way you might think."

"He is dead, then." Corina sighed, looking up to the lovely plaster ceiling. "I knew it."

As Corina turned her eyes toward Sarah's face, Sarah, who had her back toward the room, saw them grow big. Shock washed over Corina and then fear. She raised her hand to her mouth. Sarah glanced behind her, knowing whom she would find.

He came in from a balcony with Madame Gessande on his arm, all languid power, a devil in evening clothes. Sarah saw him as Corina must, obviously free of the drug, obviously a betrayal. "Corina, don't panic." She pulled her stunned friend into the passage from which a servant was emerging with a punch bowl.

"You bitch!" Her once-friend wailed. "You didn't take him away at all."

"How could I condemn him to death, Corina?"

"He isn't even drugged." She found enough control to resume her whisper. "He'll kill me, you fool! I trusted you!" Corina ran on, impervious to interruption.

"Stop!" Sarah cried. To her surprise, Corina subsided into frightened silence. Sarah began again in a whisper. "He will not take revenge, not even legal recourse. He promised that."

"Promises from such as him are worthless." Corina calmed. Her eyes narrowed. What was she thinking? The door to the ballroom opened and a servant came through with an empty punch bowl. He glanced at the two women, pressed against the wall in earnest conversation.

Sarah waited until he had passed. "He cannot tell the story, Corina. It does not redound to his credit that you drugged him and held him prisoner." Sarah strove to seem reasonable. "He stops only to clear his affairs and he will go. Hold your head, and you will clear this obstacle." Corina's calculating blue eyes gave her a nauseating distaste for her onetime friend.

"How did he get free of the drugs, Sarah?" Corina asked.

"He is strong, you know that."

"Did you take him to the hospital? Did George Upcott help you free him? Does everyone in Bath know what happened?" Sarah could feel the hysteria just beneath her friend's surface, and her own began to rise as well. If Corina couldn't master herself, everyone *would* know.

She took a breath. "No one knows. It is a secret among us three. I took him to the Dower House at Clershing. He went through withdrawal there."

Corina looked at Sarah, speculating. "Servants spread tales like this only too rapidly."

"No servants." Sarah knew what she had betrayed. It didn't matter. They both held loaded guns. Corina could not gossip about Sarah without betraying a crime far worse than indiscretion.

The woman blinked. Sarah knew she saw the problem clearly. "Help me, Sarah," Corina pleaded. "You must help me, as you always do. We must stop him. He will kill me, Sarah."

"You are mistaken, I swear," she vowed.

"No, Sarah. I know what he is. Do you?" Corina examined Sarah's face.

"Yes."

Corina paused, turning over that one word in her mind. "I believe you do," she murmured at last. "You are in league with the devil himself against me."

"Not against you, Corina, not against you," Sarah repeated in her most soothing voice.

The door to the passage opened again. Sarah prepared for another round of servants, but it was George who stood there. "Sarah, several young men are asking after you."

"I'll be there directly, George," Sarah said, grateful for an exit to this painful interview.

George could do naught but nod stiffly to this dismissal and back into the main room.

"I beg you not to get into a pelter over this, Corina. He will go. This will pass. No one will know." Sarah squeezed her former friend's arm briefly and pushed back into the hall, wanting only to escape the party. She searched the room, and saw Julien in one corner. He was talking with several men but he bowed out of the conversation with a murmured excuse and came to Sarah. "Is it time to take you home?" he queried lightly.

"Yes." She sighed. "If that is agreeable."

Downstairs, they met Madame Gessande waiting for her carriage. "Well, *mes petites*, that was quite the most exciting waltz I have seen danced this side of Vienna."

Sarah felt herself coloring. Julien nodded his agreement and smiled as he placed Sarah's cloak about her shoulders. "Are you ready?" he asked, and at her nod added, "You will excuse us, Madame. I believe Lady Clevancy is tired." He bowed and guided Sarah to the door. As she glanced back, Sarah could see conclusions forming in Madame's smiling eyes.

The carriage was a comforting retreat. Sarah settled herself gratefully as Julien stepped in behind her. She wanted to banish the cutting remarks, the admirers, Corina and George.

"How did Mrs. Nandalay accept the fact of my return?" Julien asked.

Sarah was only too aware that the ride to Laura Place would be only a few minutes at best. "Badly." She did not want to talk about Corina in the few moments she had left.

"She blames you?"

"I suppose. She is afraid of you."

Julien thought a moment in silence. "She will be better soon."

He meant when he was gone, Sarah thought bleakly. Gone. He seemed gone already. She felt like Cinderella at midnight, except she had not had the foresight to leave behind a slipper. The carriage pulled up in front of Laura Place. She was shrinking. She was too small, too small for a man like Julien. He leapt from the carriage and handed her down. His fingers burned her in the crisp air. Their breath smoked around them.

She watched helplessly as he leaned over her hand. "I return you to the world," he said. "I will allow there to be no consequences for your kindness to me." Her looked down at her with an unfamiliar expression she could not read. "You have restored my faith in humanity, Sarah. At least, in one human." He smiled. "I will never forget that."

Sarah felt her eyes filling. She would never have the courage to watch him turn and walk back to the coach. She turned herself and rushed up the steps to her door, pushing past Jasco as he opened it. Tears spilled down her cheeks as she headed for the stairs.

Julien waited in the shadows of the portico until Corina appeared. Servant boys sprang to get her coach. The woman looked distracted. Her features would sharpen with age, her beauty crumble. He had seen it a thousand times with women like her. He waited until the yellow landaulet was rolling to a stop before he called the darkness. When Corina settled herself in the seat, he was already there, in the shadows. "We must have words," he said and watched her start.

"What . . . what do you want?" she gasped, terror seeping into her eyes.

Let her be terrified. "I will be brief. You will not breathe a word against Lady Clevancy. You will take no actions against her. Do you understand me?"

"What right have you—" she started to reply.

"Rights you gave to me with your misdeeds," he barked. "You are not truly human."

"I? *I* am not human?" Corina cried, outraged. Then fear pulled her back into the cushions.

Julien leaned toward her. "Know this," he said through clenched teeth. "You deserve retribution. It is only that she does not want you harmed that saves you. You might be foolish enough to try to ruin her, in spite of the consequence to your own reputation. But if you so much as whisper her name, you will have me to deal with. Do you understand?"

Corina could only nod. She was immobilized. Just what was required. Let her remember what he might do to her each time she saw Sarah. He opened the door of the moving coach and prepared to step out. Corina sat forward, shaking. "I . . . I know how to stop you," she threatened, fear still disfiguring her face.

"I will drink no tea with you," he sneered, and melted out into the night.

Hysterical laughter echoed behind him.

Sarah sat in the study at Laura Place and watched the storm lash the darkening streets of Bath. She had toyed with a copy of *The New Monthly Magazine* all afternoon, wondering if Julien had gone to Thornbury Abbey to remove his treasures yet. It had been a difficult day. Amelia had ample time since her return to hear the gossip about Sarah and Julien and was most put out. When she saw Addie adapting dresses from the trunks upstairs, Amelia was scandalized. It was a pretty puzzle for her, really: She wanted to forbid Sarah to act in this hoydenish manner, but she was dependent upon her niece's good graces and generosity.

An insistent rapping at the front door interrupted Sarah's thoughts. Within seconds George was upon her in the study, bursting with excitement. "Sarah, dear, you are safe!" he said, his blond locks dripping from the weather.

Sarah looked up with an unfamiliar impatience. "Do sit down, George. Of course I am safe. Whatever do you mean?"

George did not take her advice, but paced the room. "I am sorry for this unseemly interruption, but I had to reassure myself of your well-being. I do not know how to tell you this, my dear." He paused for drama. "There has been another murder, clearly connected to those horrible murders in London, very close to Bath."

Sarah felt the blood drain from her face. She put a hand out to the arm of the chair to steady herself. "Near Bath?" she managed to query.

"Well, more properly out at Chambroke," George amended.

Sarah's throat closed around any words she might utter. In spite of his promises, Julien had taken his revenge. "Who?" she whispered, waiting for the name that echoed in her mind.

"Corina Nandalay's butler, Reece." George paused for shock value. "The blood was drained from his body."

It was not the name she expected. "Reece?" she echoed.

"He was killed some weeks ago and buried. Luckily, at this time of year much evidence was preserved. Mrs. Nandalay called on Snelling, that Bow Street runner, and me to gather the evidence. We dug up the body in the middle of that horrible storm this afternoon." George stopped pacing and examined her. "Are you all right, Sarah? I know this must be terrible for you, and I am afraid there is a greater shock yet."

"Reece." Sarah sighed, trying not to let her relief show. Of course it was Reece.

George sat in the companion chair to her own. His eyes gleamed, but his mouth was prim and solemn as he took her hands in his. "I know you will never credit the fact that I am sorry about what I am about to reveal. Yet I must put you on your guard."

"What do you mean, George?" Sarah asked, wary.

"Mrs. Nandalay and her maid say that Davinoff killed Reece. That links him clearly with the murders in London. Snelling thinks he is the perpetrator of those dreadful crimes as well."

Corina had revealed the one death for which Julien was actually responsible. It was not fair he should be blamed for trying to escape imprisonment and torture. He would be branded a monster and destroyed. She was about to jump to Julien's defense when discretion prevailed. What did George know—or more importantly, what did he believe—about Julien?

"What you say is most shocking, George." He looked like the proverbial cat who had swallowed the canary. "You must tell me the worst, for my own safety."

"Well . . ." George sounded dubious. "There is not much more to tell." Was he afraid of telling her that the newspapers had been more right than they knew when they called them "vampire" murders? She saw him speculate. "I think this Davinoff fellow is diabolically clever. He has some device even more efficient at extracting blood than my syringe."

"A scientific device?" Did he still not believe in vampires?

George rose and paced the room again. "I should like to know what it was precisely. Perhaps after he is behind bars, I will be allowed to question him."

"Behind bars?" Sarah gasped. "He is not even in Bath, as I hear." *As I hope*, she said to herself. "I am afraid they will never find him."

"We have a plan to capture him." George stopped to frown above her. "I hope you see where your imprudence has led you. You chose a murderer to escort you to my mother's ball."

Sarah swallowed. Not the time for willfulness. "Tell me how you will capture him."

Smug self-satisfaction was printed, perhaps indelibly, across George's smooth features. "Snelling has been watching him and knows his habits. He will be at Jackson's tonight, gaming until the wee hours. We shall take him there. Snelling gathers his forces even now. And he depends on me for assistance," George could not resist adding. "We will use a syringe of laudanum to ensure that he comes along quietly."

Sarah's heart skipped a beat. Corina had set them to this. It was the one way they could hold him. What could she do? She had to get rid of George first, whatever she did. It was not hard. George realized that discretion was the better part of valor. He took his leave with a final warning to lock her doors and not to answer the knocker again that evening.

Sarah heard the front door shut and paced to the window where the storm lashed at the trees outside. Its fury echoed her own tumult. Why was Julien not up at Thornbury Abbey where he was safe? He might escape, of course. But she could not imagine him invoking the darkness in the bright public rooms of Jackson's stylish gaming hell. He would not draw attention to his nature in that dramatic manner. He might let them arrest him, thinking to wait until he was alone in a darkened gaol cell to disappear. But by then it would be too late. They would give him laudanum, and his addiction would return. Then escape would be impossible.

No, she could not let that happen. Not when she could warn him. She glanced at the clock on the mantel. It was after eight, too late to intercept him at the Christopher. He would be at dinner somewhere before going to Jackson's. The only place she could be sure of finding him was the very place George and Snelling expected him. She had to get there first.

She walked calmly upstairs for a cape with a hood. It would be a foul walk in the rain.

Sarah turned north to Green Street, fighting against the storm for each step. It would be the end of her reputation to go into Jackson's. No female had ever crossed its threshold. That didn't matter. When she got there she stood across the street, checking the routine. It was an elegant three-story building with a wide front that faced the street and grand columns supporting the pediment of its portico. Pale brick and white trim gave it a cool, sophisticated feel. It might have housed a peer of the realm. That, of course, was just the feeling Mr. Jackson craved for his establishment. Smart rigs jostled each other at the entrance. None belonged to Julien. Two pairs of boys trotted the carriages round to the mews behind the house. Sarah steeled herself. A simple query, that was all. She fished in her reticule and pulled out a new pound coin. Extravagant, but perhaps a way to startle the ostler into acquiescing to an unthinkable breach of etiquette. She scurried across the street and leapt over the small river that ran in the gutter so as not to soak her half boots any further. The horrified look on the faces of the two ostlers as she scampered up the stairs was almost worth the price of her bribe in itself.

"My good man," she said, holding herself very straight. "I have a question."

"What is it?" the boy asked. He was easily stunned if the sight of a woman on Jackson's front steps could produce such incivility. "I mean, what question would that be, Your Ladyship?"

So they recognized her. Well, it could not be helped and might serve her purpose after all. "I wish to know if Mr. Davinoff's rig has pulled up here tonight." She placed the golden coin, flashing in the lamps set on either side of the door, into his hand.

"Lord, Yer Ladyship!" the boy cooed, her gender and its consequences apparently forgotten in the thrill of her largesse. " 'E's been here for 'alf an 'our." That such simple information should earn him so generous a payment was apparently amazing to him.

Sarah's spirits sank. She had hoped he wasn't here. She looked up at the great white double doors with their brass fixtures, so imposing, so impossible a barrier last month. How a month changed one. Once this Rubicon was crossed, there was no turning back.

Entering Jackson's was simpler than Sarah had imagined. All the male attendants, from the young ostlers and the footman to the butler hovering at the entrance, were so nonplussed by a lady of gentle birth boldly requiring entrance, she managed to sail past them with little resistance other than stuttered remonstrances. Sarah handed her cloak to the butler, saying firmly that she would be staying but a moment. She moved quickly toward the grand salon and hoped that Julien was not sequestered in some private parlor. She had vanquished only the pawns of the game thus far. Soon they would scuttle off to find reinforcements.

She pushed into the main salon, looking frantically about. The room was all dark wood and red brocade, beige and white cut carpets, and gleaming gilt. Men lounged about smoking cheroots quite openly or hovered over baize-covered tables heaped with stacks of money and scattered playing cards or dice. Gradually, as they became aware of her, all movement stopped.

The men of Bath looked up, aghast, to find Lady Clevancy in Jackson's principle gaming parlor. She noted that many men she knew were there tonight. She would not escape the consequences of her actions. Julien was nowhere to be seen. To her dismay, George Upcott entered from a back room. The shock on his face quickly turned to horrified disapproval. They were here already, waiting to spring their trap. She had little time.

George tore his eyes away and glanced toward the corner of the room. Julien straightened from rolling dice at the table where he apparently held the faro bank and towered over his fellows. A masculine tide of outrage and dismay swelled. The knots of men began to move again, as though released from an evil spell. One, probably Mr. Jackson, strode toward her.

She pushed toward Julien. Ned Snelling, looking most out of place in this exclusive group, shook his head and motioned her back to the door as if she had walked by mistake into the midst of his trap. *He will guess my purpose soon, and so will George*. She hurried on.

Julien glanced up from his bank. He did not look surprised or shocked. He only raised a single brow. Sarah wanted to shout with laughter or burst into tears at that familiar gesture. She did neither, but strode smack up to the table. The gentlemen on either side parted to let her pass as though she carried a plague. Her eyes were locked to his, all others quite forgotten.

"Lady Clevancy?" he rumbled.

"I must have a word with you, Mr. Davinoff," she breathed.

Mr. Jackson hurried up to her side. "Your Ladyship," he began.

Julien waved him away. "Jackson, you will bring Lady Clevancy a ratafia in the small salon." He gestured off to his left. "You do have ratafia, Jackson?" he drawled.

"I . . . I am sure we can procure some," the man stuttered.

"Good," Julien replied, dismissing him and taking Sarah's arm.

As Sarah turned she could feel the eyes of the room riveted upon their backs. George looked as if he would burst. It did not matter.

Three or four men sat in front of a fire in the comfortable room to which Julien led her. It required only a soft invitation of "Gentlemen?" and they closed their gaping mouths and made haste to the door. When they had gone, Sarah blurted, "Julien, you must leave immediately."

He motioned to one of the chairs by the fire and eased himself into the other. Sarah made no move to sit, but fidgeted with her reticule. "You don't understand. Corina showed George and Snelling Reece's body. They connect you to the murders in London." His eyes snapped to hers, and remained there. "They expect to take you here tonight."

"I see," he said. "And you have sacrificed propriety to warn me."

"Disappear, Julien," Sarah pleaded, "before their trap is sprung."

"They cannot hold me," he reassured her. "You need not have come."

He didn't understand. "Corina told them you are a crazed madman, capable of anything. George is prepared with laudanum." A smile touched his lips, not the reaction she expected.

"I should have told you." His smile grew rueful. "I did not want to frighten you. I have one more talent that will protect me from them." He gestured to a chair. "Sit down, Sarah."

She sat, still clutching her reticule. At that moment Jackson entered. She started, still expecting Snelling and his crew. The club's owner himself bore the silver tray with a single glass of ratafia, which he set on the table by their side.

"Thank you, Jackson," Julien murmured, dismissing the man with a wave of his hand. "Now, Sarah, please do me the honor of sipping your wine."

Sarah complied, hesitating. Whatever was he talking about?

"I have not liked to speak of the hypnotic power of my kind," Julien said at last. "I did not want to make you self-conscious, afraid I had bent you to my will somehow. I have not. At least, I tried only once, when the craving of the drug was on me. You will know the time."

Sarah knew. In the fearful dark of a cellar, red eyes had commanded her to come to him.

"They cannot give me the drug if I am on my guard."

Sarah sighed in relief. "I am glad of that. Is that another trait of your Companion?"

"Call it a heightened awareness on our side, a suggestibility in others." She saw a small crease between his brows as he looked intently at her. "Do you believe that I did not use my power of suggestion upon you?" he asked.

She smiled at his question. "Yes," she said simply.

The crease disappeared. "I am glad of that," he echoed.

She was about to plead with him to make his escape regardless when the door burst open behind her. She turned to see Ned Snelling, brandishing a pistol, leading a horde of four or five burly men all armed with pistols or stout sticks.

"Davinoff," the runner barked. "We're 'ere to take you to the round 'ouse."

The side door to the room crashed open and George pushed inside, ahead of three or four more men. He carried his doctor's case. He shot Sarah a look both grim and disapproving.

Julien rose calmly, causing a nervous shudder to run through the crowded room, as men fingered their weapons. They were afraid of him. Let them not be foolish and use those weapons.

"What, may I ask, is the charge?" His deep voice rolled over his accusers.

"Murder," Snelling hissed. "The murder of one Reece, butler at Chambroke, and maybe a dozen more in London Town."

George pulled a needle from his bag. Sarah saw the liquid of the drug gleam at its point.

"I see," Julien said, his eyes hooded.

"You come quiet like, or we'll 'ave to get violent," Snelling threatened. He glanced at George as if to make sure he was ready with the laudanum. Sarah could hardly breathe.

"I am at your disposal," Julien reassured them. Snelling lowered his pistol and took the shackles offered by one of his compatriots. Sarah cringed. Julien, however, offered up his wrists and Snelling snapped the irons shut around them with an awful, metallic clank.

"*If* you will," Snelling gestured toward the door with his pistol. Julien nodded, cast his eyes toward George, who looked suddenly blank and lowered his needle. Julien strode off toward the main salon. The crowd of burly men trailed after him.

Sarah was left to wander in their wake. Behind her, she could hear George scolding. "I cannot believe, Sarah Ashton, that you came to warn him. Did nothing I say get through to you?"

Sarah did not reply. George did not matter anymore. She followed the procession through the collectively stunned men of Bath and out through the main doors into the street.

The rain had abated its fury, curtaining the street in an evenly depressing downpour. A heavy square black coach pulled by two huge draft horses was drawn up to the curb. It had bars at the windows and a heavy lock upon its door. Its whole demeanor was squat and ominous. A prison wagon, Sarah thought numbly. Snelling unlocked the door with a huge ring of keys. Behind her, she could feel the portico overflow with men from the club, relishing this scandal.

Julien, standing almost a head taller than most of those around him, looked back at her with the ghost of a smile she knew was meant to reassure her. But at that moment, Pembly wheeled a familiar canary yellow landaulet up to the curb behind the prison wagon. Corina fairly leapt to the ground. She had on her blue pelisse trimmed in ermine. A blue parapluie protected her comely peacock hat, with its curling ostrich feathers, from the elements.

"Wait, Mr. Snelling!" Corina cried and pointed. "Do you intend to let his accomplice escape?" All eyes turned toward Sarah, some wondering, some accusing. "She lied to you and sent you off to Bristol. She knew where he was all the time."

Corina had found a way to destroy both her enemies with a single blow. But no gaol would hold Julien, so Sarah did not scream or cry. She did not protest. Her own fate did not matter. She merely looked to Snelling. She could see him considering his investigations, the evidence he had collected. Corina saw the process, too.

"Did she not fly to warn him tonight?" Corina almost shrieked.

Snelling nodded.

"Lady Clevancy is not involved." All eyes turned to Julien as his voice boomed over the crowd. "She is a girl, naive enough to warn a man she believed was innocent. Is that a crime?" His eyes swept the crowd. The crowd murmured in response, some understanding, some pitying.

Julien's words cut Sarah to the quick. She had always known how naive she must appear to him. He was defending her, but with a truth that judged her guilty of a crime she considered far greater than helping a suspected murderer.

Julien turned to Snelling. "A hard trial, perhaps, with sentiment on her side. A pretty prisoner in the dock is not easily convicted." Snelling rubbed his chin, not recently shaven, considering. "Why cloud the issue?" Julien almost whispered.

Snelling decided. "I 'ave no warrant for any but the London murderer. I 'ave no use for 'er." He motioned his prisoner into the murky interior of the coach. Sarah watched him duck his head and disappear. Part of her was elated that no shackles would ever hold him except by his own consent, and that he could defend himself against drugs. Yet there was no question that she had just seen the last of Julien Davinoff. He had touched her life with a brand of fire. Now he would move on. Snelling locked the iron door and beat on the side of the coach with his pistol.

"I'll meet you boys at the round 'ouse," he yelled, and heaved himself onto a horse held by one of the ostlers. The beadles and hired thugs piled into two carts pulled up behind Corina's landaulet. They clattered out into the street, as Corina stood, sputtering on the walkway.

"I am not done with you, Sarah Ashton," Corina shrieked at last. She spun on her heel and climbed into the carriage. The still impassive Pembly pulled out into the road.

Sarah stood on the step. The muttering men behind her dispersed into the club. She could not move. Her limbs had turned to mush.

"I hope you are satisfied." She heard George's voice behind her, so sure of itself. "This is the last straw, Sarah." The click of his boots on the wet stone receded down the street.

She was alone. The rain beat down, beading in her hair and dripping down her face like tears. She realized, after a while, that her hat and cloak were still at Jackson's. The walk home would be sodden and cold, like her soul. At last she managed to trudge off into the rain.

Chapter Sixteen

Sarah sat, curled in her bed, holding with nerveless fingers the tea Addie had provided. Her voluminous white linen nightdress, its bodice covered with spidery white embroidery, was warm and dry. Her skin was tight from the soap of her steaming bath, her hair still wet. All outward traces of her experience tonight had been removed. But nothing would ever erase tonight from her mind. The people of Bath would remind her of it, if she was received at all. That did not matter. Tonight would live forever as the last time she saw Julien and the night she saw herself so clearly, so painfully through his eyes.

The moment Julien called her naive she realized what dreams she secretly nourished in her breast. She wanted him to return her regard. *No, say it, Sarah.* Her love. She had recognized her love tonight in the very moment all desires were blighted. He would never love a girl like her. He was a different species. Homo Mordeus, George would say. Twenty-six. That had once seemed old to her. But it was a breath of age, hardly worth mentioning to one who had seen ages pass.

There was another pain. In one way, probably the one way that he desired naivete, she was not naive at all. He could not know that a girl of her station and demeanor had reveled in the feel of a man's body under her hands. She flushed in shame. Yes, she had enjoyed touching that boy on a humid evening in Sienna. Her mind flicked to the feel of Julien's thigh against her when she sat beside him in his curricle, to the times in the cellar when she had touched his flesh, to the feel of his shoulder beneath her hand as they waltzed. There was no mistaking those feelings and what they meant. Worse, she wanted more.

The words "only a naive girl" tolled like funeral bells in her mind, until the tears pushed up and overflowed into the wracking sobs she had suppressed ever since Julien disappeared into the prison wagon, vanishing from her life forever. She cried until she was dry inside and exhausted. Sometime in the night, sleep, that great betrayer of intense emotion, overtook her in spite of her commitment to her misery.

"You haven't drugged him?" Corina almost shouted. It was after midnight and the old stone gaol was quiet. She had thought it would take more to convince Snelling to prosecute Sarah too. He came cheaply. Now she was anxious to see Davinoff, and tell him what she'd done.

" 'E's locked up tighter 'n a drum," Snelling said. "Jes you don't be goin' near the bars, and you'll be fair and fine." Snelling unlocked the door to the ancient cell block.

Corina took a deep breath. What could he do, no matter what he was, if he was locked up? She rustled through the door. The lock mechanism clanked behind her as she turned into the dim stone corridor. A shiver of fear went down her spine. Locked up all right and tight, she told herself again and again. She wanted this last bit of victory, but it was bought at a price of fear. She could control that. Her footsteps echoed on the uneven floor.

She saw him at the end of the corridor, behind the bars of the last cell. His full white linen shirt made him look vulnerable. He seemed almost small, dwarfed by the weight of the stones and the bars. They had taken his cravat so couldn't hang himself. That would be left to the magistrates. "Well, monster," she said as she stopped in front of the cell. "You have been captured by the good people of Bath, and they are like to hang you."

"You must be relieved." The voice rumbled out to wash over her in the flickering light.

"Bath is relieved. And scandalized, of course, about you and Sarah Ashton." She was rewarded by a flash in those black eyes, felt more than seen in the dimness.

"Remember my warning," Davinoff said from between clenched teeth.

"What good is that warning now?" Corina let her voice drip sweetness. "I have already started upon her, and you can do nothing."

"What have you done?" His voice was like the thunder of glaciers cracking into the sea.

"I told everyone at the Cantonfields' rout tonight that she knew you were a murderer. I have hardly begun. There is yet the fact that you were alone together at Clershing."

"You will not succeed," Davinoff murmured. "Madame Gessande will counter you. Everyone knows you. The more vicious you are, the less you will be believed."

"I thought of that. I will be desolate at poor Sarah's sad fall from grace. And if you think an old fright like that Gessande woman can influence the younger set where it counts most, you are quite mistaken. I will have Sarah's reputation smirched beyond repair in a week." She watched him clench his teeth, his jaw working. "Your precious Sarah," she crowed. "I wonder if you would be so infatuated if you knew her as I do." The power of revelation rose in her.

"You have not the soul to truly know Sarah Ashton," Davinoff whispered.

"I know her better than you do, monster. Why, I wager you think she is a virgin." She saw Davinoff grow wary. "Romping with peasants in Sienna at eighteen. Quite a harlot, our Sarah."

"You are not fit to brush her boots." He thrust the words through the bars like daggers.

How could he defend Sarah when he knew the truth? "If you don't believe me, ask her."

"Only you could imagine it would make a difference."

"It will make a difference to her," Corina purred.

"If she would let me kill you," Davinoff muttered, his knuckles white upon the bars.

Corina laughed her tinkling laugh. "You can do nothing from a cell. You will soon be hanged, and she imprisoned."

"What do you mean?" he growled. "Snelling will not prosecute her."

Corina leaned against the stone wall, carefully out of his reach. "He thought it too much effort. *Some*one had to make it worth his while. I stepped gallantly into the breach."

He ran his hands through his black curls. "You bribe a corrupt runner to prosecute an innocent woman?" His voice rose. "You are the monster, madam."

"Innocent?" Corina fairly shouted. "She betrayed me. She took you for herself, instead of to the Continent to die. And I intend to make her pay. You will both pay!"

Corina expected him to beg for mercy for his light o'love. Instead she heard a low sound that sounded remarkably as if an animal had got into the cell with him. The passage had grown darker. She could not quite see what he was doing. Did his hands pull at the bars? She cringed against the wall and noted dumbly that he was enveloped in darkness. She remembered the time in the cellar, when he had seemed lost in darkness, and she shuddered. His eyes had a reddish cast, burning like coals in the blackness.

She could not move, could not rip her eyes from the two glowing embers growing brighter in the shadow. Seconds were stretched into minutes by terror. She pressed herself against the wall, panting. The blackness was a moving pool of dark water, swirling with currents. The eyes behind the bars drifted slowly toward her. Then the two glowing coals were not behind the bars. The darkness seeped into the corridor. The red eyes held her motionless. The darkness almost touched her. Her scream was stifled, turned in upon her mind instead of out into the world. *Come to me, Snelling. Come, someone*, her mind cried. *Save me from this evil*. The drifting darkness touched her. It was cold like death. It drifted up around her neck, its tendrils caressing her. Her stifled screams ate at her. The darkness grew denser. The flaming coals faded into black eyes. The midnight tendril caressing her neck became a strong white hand. Julien Davinoff stood in the hallway, bending over her, holding her with one hand and the power of those black eyes.

I should kill you. He did not speak, but she heard his words clearly just the same. His eyes drilled them into her mind. *Except I gave my word. But do not think you will escape.* He stepped back. "Call to your friend, Snelling," he commanded, his voice physical again.

Her mind gibbered with a thousand questions, a thousand horrific answers. What was he? No man as she knew men. He could tear her soul from her, kill her body. He could do unimagined things. He was an echo of Hell, a revenge of God upon her excesses, or the Devil come to claim her. Such a being should not exist. He was not real. He was too real. Her mind gasped and trembled before him.

"Call to your friend." But she could only shiver, wide-eyed, against the wall. He raised his white hand once again to caress her cheek. *Call,* he echoed in her mind.

The dam that held back her screams burst and she was screaming, screaming.

Julien listened for the sound of Ned Snelling running down the corridor behind the shrieks of the Nandalay woman. He hoped the runner came alone. His plan depended upon that. He needed only a moment. After what seemed like an hour, he heard footsteps and the clink of metal as a key jittered in the lock. Snelling heaved the door open, pistol drawn.

Snelling stopped dead, taking in the situation. Corina was collapsed in a heap upon the floor, sobbing. Julien leaned against the stone wall across the corridor. He could practically hear the tumblers in Snelling's mind turning. The prisoner was outside his cell, the cell door shut, its heavy lock securely fastened. Someone must have let him out, but Snelling had the only key. "A pretty problem," Julien observed.

" 'ow did you get out?" Snelling squeaked.

"I am sure Mrs. Nandalay will tell you when she recovers." Snelling glanced at the hysterical woman, and fingered the pistol. "Do not bother with your pistol," Julien drawled. "I require only your keys." He forced Snelling to move along the passageway, his pistol forgotten, holding out his keys. The man's mind was not strong. Feet clattered against the stone as his cronies came down the stairs. They would be here in a moment.

Julien whirled to unlock the cell. Then he placed the keys back in Snelling's still-outstretched hand. "I believe these are yours," he said politely. "Don't say what you see. Asylums are far worse than prison cells, or so I am told." Julien stepped back and drew the darkness.

Snelling called to the gaolers, galloping up behind him, "Did ye see 'im disappear?"

In the corner, Corina moaned and then began to laugh. "He disappeared," she choked. "With his two red eyes. Red eyes, he had. Red eyes."

The field winked out, the giggling still echoing after him. Julien left Snelling to explain whether he was crazy, as Corina no doubt was, or criminally negligent. They deserved what they got, both of them. At least now, neither could harm Sarah. And he had not broken his promise.

Now he had a far more dangerous mission. He melted into the shadows of his room at the Christopher. He owed Sarah a last visit. He owed her everything, actually. She had not simply freed him from Corina's hateful bondage, but more. He had told her once that vampires were not the undead, but had he not been dead to the world for centuries? She had brought him back to living, to feeling, once again. He loved her. He knew that. He was more sure than he had been in all his long, dreadful life. But it gave him no joy. No, there could be only pain ahead, and all the protection of not caring had been stripped from him. What was next? St. Petersburg? Pei-king? A weight descended on him. What matter? Only one place held any interest for him now, and it was the one place he could not stay, for her sake. He could not deny he had hoped for a little more time with her. And only see what his greed for time had wrought.

He pulled the rolled parchment from one of his boots at the bottom of his trunk. The future chilled him down to the core of whatever soul was left to him. But there was no choice. Making her a vampire was a crime against his kind. His failure with Magda still haunted him. True, Sarah was a good and generous person, without a shred of Magda's cold selfishness. But would he condemn her to the life he had been born to? He could not curse Sarah with his disease. Nor could he ruin her life with constant reminders of her mortality, as she aged and he did not.

She would forget him soon. Only he would not forget. He should not go to her tonight. But he could not resist one last moment together with the woman who had changed him forever. He gathered the darkness of his Companion and prayed for strength to any god who would listen.

Sarah was not sure when she wakened. The moon peeked through the heavy draperies. The pain of Julien's loss seemed distant, a compartment closed by the violence of her tears.

She felt more than saw a stirring in the corner by the wardrobe. All numbness vanished in the certainty that something was in the room with her. She could feel movement, though there was no sound. Someone was being careful not to wake her. She dared not move. She must lie quiet and control her trembling. She must wait until the form moved away from the door. A last, mad, dash was all that was left to her. She clutched the bedclothes, ready to fling them back.

The strong hand that covered her mouth took her completely by surprise. She gasped in preparation for a scream, but she could get no air. "Sarah, it is I." His sweet scent, male yet not male, told her it was Julien as surely as his dear voice. She went limp with relief.

He took his hand away. "Julien," she breathed.

His weight bent the mattress as he sat on the edge of the bed. The pressure of his hip against her thigh made her feel faint. His skin glowed white in the moonlight. His black hair gleamed. "I came to give you a gift and say good-bye." In the darkness she could not read his eyes, but she felt them burning with all the intensity that made him more than man.

Sarah pushed herself up. He was too close. The moonlight made him too much like a dream. "Are they looking for you? Are you in danger coming here?"

"It will take them a while to sort out my trail. There is time."

Time? There was no time. All was lost after tonight. There was only this moment, here where the world was black and white and shadowy. Julien held a rolled paper tied with a ribbon that might be black or might be red or might be royal blue. He saw her glance at it.

"My excuse for coming." He handed it over almost tentatively.

She laid it unopened on the night table. Why had he come? Why did he bother with such a naive girl? "You have no need of an excuse." Her nightdress was open at the throat, loose against her breasts. His hip burned her through the quilts. All the feelings suppressed so ruthlessly since Sienna were back, throbbing inside her, fighting to be released. "I can hardly repay you for what you brought into my life," she whispered. She should try to get control, even now, but her nature was betraying her. She didn't want control.

He seemed to be struggling, too. He shook his head, convulsively. Suddenly, his hand brushed through her hair to cradle her neck, a shock of flesh on flesh. "You have no reason to thank me," he said fiercely, turning her head up toward him. "But *my* debt will never be repaid."

In the dim light, she recognized the need in his eyes, echoed by the need she felt in her own body. Her mind raced. Everything was changed and not changed. He wanted her, but that did not mean forever. She was still a naive girl who could not hold the interest of a man like Julien for long. The chasm between mortal and immortal was too wide. Tomorrow he would be gone. In a way, that freed her, demanded that she take what she could tonight. The sunlight of Sienna washed through her in the moonlit room, and she welcomed it. She remembered all the sensations of body on body, and she wanted that with Julien. He wanted it too, if only for tonight. *Shout yes to the moment*, she told herself. *Sienna taught you how.*

Julien pulled himself away and jerked his eyes from hers. She could hear his rasping breath.

Don't struggle against it, she wanted to tell him. *Give yourself up to it, before it's too late.* Instead, trembling, she ran her fingers along the line of his jaw as she had in the cellar so many eons ago. She moved her hand round the nape of his neck, under his curls. So soft, so vulnerable were men's napes. His eyes questioned hers as she pulled him toward her. She smiled, and she knew the smile was sure.

How did vampires make love? Would she need to purchase a scarf in the morning to hide the place where he had quenched his need? It did not matter. She tilted her head and touched his lips with hers, lightly, softly. How long she had wanted to do that! The feel of his lips on hers, tentatively returning her caresses, made her want to scream and cry, even as a tingling jolt of sensation erupted between her legs. His hand tensed on her neck as he gave himself to the kiss and pressed his lips to hers. She opened her mouth. The wondrous intimacy of his moist tongue made her shudder as he gathered her into his arms in a crushing embrace. This was where she belonged, if just for this night. He wrenched his lips away, but he did not let her go. Instead he pressed her head to his shoulder.

"Damn me for a weakling!" he whispered, stroking her hair. She nestled into his shoulder and breathed in the scent of him. "Weak," he said again, louder this time. He took her shoulders and tried to move her from him.

She looked up and said softly, "Then let me be strong." She drew his head down out of the moonlight and into the shadows for another kiss. This time it was her tongue that searched his mouth. She pulled the soft linen of his shirt out from his breeches and ran her hands over the bunching muscles of his back as they clenched her to his body. The physical dimension of their bodies required exploration as though it were an undiscovered continent, vast and mysterious, stretching out before them as they stood upon the slender ribbon of the beach. She unbuttoned his shirt, and moved her kisses to his chest, lightly covered with dark curling hair. She could feel his groan of desire in her lips, as well as hear it. Julien pulled her up to kiss her once again, deeply, searching her mouth with his tongue, then lowered her gently to the pillows. Now she would know another thing about vampires. If it was a matter of blood, he might never need to know that she was not as naive as he expected.

That thought stiffened her. Was it right not to tell him, even if his kind did not make love as she knew it?

He felt her tense and raised his mouth from hers. "Do you want me to go?"

"No," she moaned, not knowing how she could possibly say what she must. But she could allow nothing between her and Julien as lowly as a lie, even a lie of omission. She took a breath. "I am not what you may think me."

His face, hanging over her in the night, creased with worry. But an instant later his brow smoothed as he bent to kiss her cheek, his forelock brushing her face, a smile in his eyes. "Such things do not matter in the slightest," he whispered in her ear.

"No, you do not understand," she whispered, pushing his shoulders away. She screwed her courage to the sticking point. It would be the first time she ever said it and perhaps the last. "I am not a virgin." The words were stiff and cold.

His lips softened into a ghost of the smile in his eyes. "Neither am I. Should I confess it? Will it make a difference to you?" He bent to kiss her tenderly. Her last remaining reservations melted; she gave herself up to his kisses with the sweet abandonment of desire, untainted by the future or the past. It was she who helped him remove his shirt. It was she who took her gown over her head while he unbuttoned his breeches. They wanted nakedness. She wanted to feel the hair of his chest against her breasts, teasing her nipples into wakefulness. Her hands moved over his body, seeking new silky skin to touch as his hands caressed her breasts, now swollen with longing. His manhood was hard against her thigh. His hands moved to her buttocks and then around to her secret parts. He was no inexperienced boy from Sienna. He had centuries of pleasing women. Her hips circled with the waxing pleasure. About to burst, she gripped his arm. Her breath came in shuddering sobs. Even when she thought she could stand no more, he was merciless, sucking at her nipples, rubbing her. He finally pushed her over some cliff of feeling, and she jerked against his hand as her senses flooded.

As her senses returned he kissed her more insistently. The glow of man-made warmth met the cold light of the moon slicing across their bed. How did one give a vampire the most pleasure possible? That was what she wanted to give Julien. She moved the hair away from her neck and bared it to him. He leaned down into her. But instead of feeling the two piercing needles of his canines, he only nibbled at her ear.

"I am afraid it is not nearly that exotic, my love," he breathed. He stroked the skin over her ribs and down her hips as he kissed her throat and ears and so came round to her mouth again. His strong hands kneaded her buttocks as his kisses grew stronger, more demanding. She knew what she wanted now. His caresses were a delightfully torturous denial of their mutual need. Finally, his right hand touched her knee. As though a special catch had been released, she spread her legs to him. He pushed his erection into her gently, opening her bit by bit. Her hands moved over the undulating muscles of his back and loins to his buttocks as they thrust him fully inside her. She kissed his chest, his throat, his shoulders, as he slid in and out, slowly filling her again and again. When he groaned and bent his lips to her uplifted mouth, he began to move more urgently inside her. The inevitable crescendo ended in a trembling tightness of his body. He arched above her for a long moment as she throbbed around his jerking member, hardly able to get enough breath. He melted against her at last and they gasped together in the moonlight.

They lay entwined. The luxury of skin on skin was all the body comprehended. He murmured endearments as he brushed her hair with kisses. She had pleased him. And what she experienced was so much beyond mere pleasure she didn't know how to describe it. What she had done with the Italian boy was but a pale shadow of what she and Julien had done tonight.

Sarah did not know when sleepy fulfillment turned to actual sleep. But when she wakened, the beam of moonlight had moved across the coverlet. An ineffable sadness came over her. She looked up to where the fringe of lashes brushed his cheeks. At her movement, his eyes opened. A wall of distance rose up between them as each realized what must happen next.

She touched his face. The smile came naturally. "Time to go, before they find you, love," she said. Was her strength from accepting love, dark side, and blinding light together? Sienna seemed a faint, distorted reflection on the water, erased by the ripples of her love for Julien. Lust was exorcised by lovemaking. She would never be ashamed of what had happened here.

Julien clutched her tightly to his chest and buried his lips in her hair. She could hardly breathe, whether from his crushing embrace or from the pain emanating from him, she could not tell. She heard him groan her name and was startled by the passion in his voice. He held her face into his shoulder so she could not look up into his eyes.

"I came to say good-bye," he whispered. "But I can't do it, Sarah. I can't leave you."

He was in danger, with everyone looking for him. "You mustn't stay, my love."

Abruptly, he held her out from him. The pain and conflict that stirred in his eyes were palpable, even in the dim light. "Come with me." The words were torn from him.

Sarah felt the bottom drop out of her stomach. He couldn't do this. She was not that strong. He wanted her. He might even think it was love, though he had not said it. But she was still naive, still mortal, still not of his kind. She felt it as keenly as he must. She would grow old and he would not. He would grow tired of her, naive mortal that she was. And her decrepit body would make her repulsive to him. How would she bear the distance that would creep into his eyes, the excuses, the absences? "We are not alike," she choked. "It could not last."

"I know I should not offer. It is the one true crime. But I am weak, Sarah. I am weak." His rumbling voice was anguished. He took her shoulders and stared into her face. "We could be alike. I can make you vampire." Then he lost his nerve and clutched her to him, because he could not look at her. "It is not a gift, but a curse I offer you. Immortality, and a need for human blood."

Sarah was stunned. Then the numbness turned to fear. Immortal was too long a time. She had seen what a trial it was to Julien, drifting without direction through a world that changed but stayed the same. She had not the stuff of immortality. She was just a girl, one who could be petty, and vain—not worth immortality. And what about vampire? The immortality, in itself a doubtful gift, came with a price that stunned the senses. To be the stuff of nightmares, cut off from all humanity! To need human blood? An image rose of her caressing the muscular neck of some young buck, aching to suckle at his carotid artery. How could she do something like that? Was such a deed not just like using that boy in Sienna? She had not embraced true darkness after all. It might drive her mad, as it had driven Julien's redhead mad, Magda, who killed so many in London. Her mind fluttered. She would instantly be cut off from all she knew. She did not know what to say. How could he spring this upon her? Not fair, she cried inside, not fair! And not possible.

She stared wildly into his eyes, until finally words were wrenched from her. "I am afraid."

He must have felt her stiffen, drawing away from the future he offered. He searched her face, and she saw him realize the truth of what she said. He slumped against the pillows.

"I don't know why I said it," he murmured, releasing her. In his turn he drew away.

Now she found herself with more words than she could manage. "It wouldn't last. Too many years. We would drift apart, slowly or quickly, I don't know. I don't think that . . ."

He pressed two fingers against her lips. "You are perfectly right." He rose abruptly and began to dress. His silhouette against the moonlight was stark. The bed felt cold as well as empty. She wanted to take back her words. But to what purpose? "My parting gift is too small, Sarah," he said, breaking the silence. But I want you to have Thornbury Abbey. You deserve to know all passages to your villa belong to you." As she roused herself to protest, he smiled down at her, with a ghost of a smile that broke her heart. "I will not take no for an answer."

The villa and the abbey were all she would have left of him. She stared at the scroll on her night table as though it were some talisman, and felt the world grow alien around her.

"You must promise to visit my storeroom before you begin to excavate," he continued. "I will leave one or two things I would like you to have."

"I will not take your most prized possessions, Julien. You cannot ask it."

"Then hold them in trust for me, my love, and enjoy their beauty for your lifetime."

Sarah's heart contracted. For her lifetime. "A mere moment in the passing scheme of things, isn't it?" she asked, in a small voice.

"You will fill it with living," he said, as he dressed. "You will excavate my home and save it for posterity. You will rebuild Clershing and leave the land better than you found it." His voice rolled out of the darkness and surrounded her, almost harsh. "You will marry and have children. Someday I will find a dynasty of strong sons and daughters who have inherited your intelligence, your generosity, your belief that things change for the better."

"You see my future so clearly." He laid her life out from a distance given him by time. Time she would never have with him.

"Yes," he breathed. "And I envy you."

"All but my mortality," she said bitterly.

"That most of all." The words were stark. "The one time it was possible, I was too weak to end it. And you and Corina refused to oblige me. Now, I go on."

Sarah felt herself drifting out away from him, their conversation a tenuous line that held them together. What had she done? I have no choice, she wanted to scream.

When he was dressed, he came to stand over her. "Sarah . . ."

Her gaze roved over him, drinking in his silhouette for the last time. He paused, his eyes boring into her with more intensity than she had ever seen in him. He reached out and with one finger, touched her cheek. A deeper darkness whirled quickly up around him, its inky blackness still touching her cheek. Then he was gone.

Sarah stared out of her bedroom window into one of those crisp winter mornings where mist burning off the streets evaporates into a day so white, so pale that the light seems to shine right through everybody and everything. The beadle had questioned her regarding the whereabouts of Julien. Jasco told him firmly that the doors were locked all night, and no one could come in without his knowing. The beadle stationed two of his minions to watch her house. She could see them at the corner. She received the intelligence from Amelia that Corina was mad and Snelling in his own gaol with little interest. Julien was probably already in Bristol shipping his treasures to some safer hideaway. They could not touch him. Neither could she. That was all that mattered.

She turned from the window and surveyed the room wildly with something quite like horror growing in her bosom. Her gaze only steadied as it came to rest upon the old and slightly tattered parchment tied, it turned out, with a bloodred ribbon. She touched it softly and gathered it in to her lap as she sat on the bed. It was the last she had of him. She pulled the bow of the ribbon until the roll rustled and relaxed. As she unfurled it, a slip of paper drifted onto her lap. She recognized the hand immediately and her heart clenched.

Dearest Sarah:

Lestrom has the letter that cedes all rights to the abbey lands to you. This deed proves my own entitlement, in case you should need to demonstrate my right to leave the land as I choose. I hope the abbey gives joy to you and all your progeny. Please know I want you to have the best life can offer.

With my heart,
Julien.

Sarah was on dangerous ground as she unrolled the parchment itself. The note was so final. She hardly saw the carefully painted Gothic letters interspersed with tiny colorful paintings instead of capitals. The signature was familiar: *Henry VIII, R,* in flourishes. Henry had given this to a Julien who looked just as he looked last night, just as he would look for how long? She rolled the parchment carefully and retied its ribbon. As for her, gray would soon frost her hair. Each birthday would etch its mark upon her until, in a mere breath of time to one as old as Julien, she would be an ancient hag. But it didn't have to be so. Julien had offered to wipe away death for her, but at a price she was not big enough to pay.

The dike she had built in her mind burst. She had sent him away! She turned her head toward the ceiling. Tears rolled down her cheeks. He had offered her a choice, a bridge for the gulf between them, and she had refused. She was afraid of immortality, afraid of being vampire, of needing blood. She was afraid she might enjoy how she got it. Sienna! She had worried for years that her willing embrace of the sex act made her evil. Now she realized there were darker acts yet, just as the crypts below the abbey had stairways to lower levels still. She was too small to change from a lowly mortal caterpillar into an immortal butterfly with bloodred wings.

She threw herself into her pillow. This time there were no

numbing sobs to keep her soul from tearing at itself. She did not know if she cried or not; she simply clenched the pillows to her face as her mind battered against reality like a moth at the window, trying to get to the light.

If there had been a knife to hand, she might have acted upon her despair, her hatred of herself and the of life she saw before her in the only way that would quiet the storm of her emotion for certain. But she did not have the means. More than that, somewhere inside, she knew she deserved despair. It was her fault.

She threw herself to the window and grabbed the heavy drapes to close them against the sunlight. She paced furiously from one side of the room to another. Tears coursed down her face. She did not notice when her fingers began picking at the lace covering the bodice of her new waisted dress. When Addie scratched at the door, Sarah shouted at her to go away, and the shout spiraled up into a wail of pain, until she clapped her hand over her mouth to stop it.

Sarah heard Madame Gessande in the hall shush Amelia's tears. "Go downstairs, my friends. I will handle our *jeunne fille*." Madame would find the door unlocked. Sarah had opened it this morning. Was it the third day, or the fourth, since . . . since it happened?

As the door opened, she saw Amelia, wringing her hands, alternating between admonishments and entreaties to Madame to make Sarah come out. Addie hovered behind them. Sarah turned back to the window. This morning, when she had glimpsed her tattered lace bodice, her hair down in places from its knot, the glazed and sunken eyes surrounded by dark circles, she had been surprised how like Corina she looked. She hung on the heavy velvet drapes and leaned against the window, peering out through the crack. That was when she had unlocked the door.

"Sarah," Madame called softly, stepping into the room and closing the door on the others.

"I know," she murmured. She couldn't manage to put her life in her voice. She turned with effort to Madame, who tried not to register her shock.

"What do you know, *cherie*?" Madame whispered.

"You are come to tell me I must get on with things." She took a wavering step toward Madame and sank to the floor.

Madame rushed to kneel beside her, clutching her to her breast. She brushed Sarah's forehead with a kiss. "At the very least, it is time to eat."

Chapter Seventeen

Sarah entered the drawing room of Madame Gessande's cozy house on Queen Street feeling remote. She knew why the woman had invited her here. The room was warm and inviting, the windows fogged against the cold drizzle outside; the red Persian rugs and the faintly exotic air created by the many artifacts Gessande had collected in her travels made it feel as lively as the animated conversations filling it. It was filled with her friends drinking tea and brandy and ratafia. In the corner, a group was talking to Dr. Parry. They hadn't noticed Sarah.

"My diagnosis?" the doctor was saying. "Hysteria, plain and simple."

"Do you think the condition permanent?" Mrs. Piozzi asked.

"No, no," Dr. Parry blustered. "She became aware of herself enough to stop talking about the monster with red eyes, though I could tell she still believed in it. But the nightmares continue, and she always stuffs a shawl under her door at night."

"What is your prognosis, Doctor?"

"What she needs is quiet. We bundled her off to a convent in Lyon yesterday."

"Corina Nandalay in a convent," Mr. Wilberforce mused. "I did not think to see that day."

Madame pushed forward, seeing Sarah, eagerly followed by George Upcott. Madame had invited George? He was the only one her age in the room. He had called earlier in the week to walk with her in the Grand Parade. Each time she saw him, he seemed flushed and excited.

"Welcome, my dear," Madame said, holding out her hands. "Come sit by the fire."

"Thank you, Madame," Sarah murmured. Madame was drawing her back into society.

George bowed, and looked self-satisfied. "May I procure you a glass of ratafia?"

"That would be nice, George," Sarah agreed. Madame bundled Sarah off to sit with Mrs. Piozzi and Madame d'Arblay. Mr. Wilberforce and Mayor Palmer hovered in the background. Sarah took the ratafia from George with a distant smile, but did not join the conversation.

Madame d'Arblay finally addressed Sarah directly. "I must recommend Mrs. Stanhope to you, Lady Clevancy. I know you enjoy novels."

"I'm sorry, Madame d'Arblay," Sarah murmured. "But I have given them up."

"Given up novels?" Mrs. Piozzi peered at her.

Mayor Palmer changed the subject. "The last time I talked to you, Madame d'Arblay, you were all afire over the new story by that fellow Byron. The one about the vampire." Sarah blanched. Did they mean to torture her? "It was his secretary, Polidori, who wrote it after all."

"That makes me so angry." Madame d'Arblay shuddered. "They publish it under Byron's name to ensure a healthy sale. Then after everyone is talking about it, they admit it was the secretary who wrote it."

"What do you think, Lady Clevancy? You are our resident expert on Mr. Byron." Mr. Wilberforce passed her a plate of cakes he took from Madame Gessande's man Melton.

"I do not read Mr. Byron anymore, or Mr. Shelley either." She passed the tray on without taking a cake. "They do not live in the real world, either of them."

"The countess thinks it prerequisite for the job that poets *not* live in the real world," Mayor Palmer observed.

"I am more at home among Mr. Wordsworth's comforting daffodils. I am growing fonder of Mr. Southey, too," Sarah said resolutely.

"Our pedestrian poet laureate?" Mrs. Piozzi gasped.

"He has some very good qualities," Sarah defended. After a little silence, the conversation jerked on to the latest moves of the prince's parliamentary adversaries.

George invited Sarah to refresh her glass, though it did not need refreshing. With dread tickling her throat Sarah went with him to the sideboard. "It is time we had a conversation, Sarah." He spoke with great determination. "I ask for your hand in marriage."

Sarah looked up, almost bewildered. Had Madame Gessande arranged this, just as she was arranging today for Sarah's acceptance into society again? "Why now, after all this time?"

George was bursting with anticipation. "Because . . . because you would be the perfect wife for me. You would further my career immensely." Sarah stared at him. "And . . . and because a refusal would devastate me."

A wife with a smirched reputation was not an ideal match. She'd thought George would certainly drop their association. But what did it matter now? She nodded. George grasped her hand and raised it to his lips. A satisfied smile played over his face. Sarah felt only resigned.

George turned to the room and raised his voice. "I say, everyone. Lady Clevancy and I have an announcement to make." What, did he mean to make it public right now?

Silence fell over the room. Mrs. Piozzi and Madame Gessande exchanged startled glances. Sarah realized that they had not expected George to propose. Everyone turned toward the couple. Sarah looked up at her affianced husband. There was a triumphant gleam in his eyes. Did marrying her mean so much to him? There was no love in that look, no tenderness.

"I wanted you all to be the first to know that Lady Clevancy has done me the honor of accepting my offer of marriage."

There was a moment of stunned silence. Then Dr. Parry moved forward to shake George's hand. "Good show, old man." Soon everyone crowded around, offering congratulations to George or mock condolences to Sarah. Cups of tea and glasses of claret and ratafia were raised in salute to the couple. When they were done, George raised his own glass.

"To my betrothed," he toasted. "May I make her happy for years to come." Sarah looked up to see a secret smile play across his face. "Now, I am due at my laboratory."

There were cries of "No" and "You can't leave your betrothed at a moment like this."

But George shook his head, smiling, and captured Sarah's hand in his. "This is the life of a doctor's wife, my dear. Many doctors hardly ever see their wives except over the dinner table. You will have to get used to it, for I must go when duty calls."

Sarah smiled bleakly as he kissed her hand and made his way to the door.

Madame started forward. "Come back to the fire, *cherie*. All this excitement," she murmured as she drew Sarah to a seat in front of the crackling logs, away from the crowd.

Sarah hardly moved during the rest of the afternoon. She spoke only to murmur thanks for parting congratulations as guests took their leave. It had grown entirely dark outside. Melton came in with more wood for the fire. Finally, there was only Sarah staring into the fire, and Hester Piozzi and Madame Gessande. Sarah glanced up to see the two old women looking at each other decisively. She had seen Madame look that way before. What were they about?

"Ah, the announcement of a betrothal always takes me back to the great romance of my own life." Mr. Piozzi sighed, peering at Sarah. Sarah turned back to the flames. "Everyone thought that I ought to marry Samuel Johnson when my Mr. Thrale died."

"You had been friends for years," Madame pointed out. "It was natural to think so."

"But he was not my soul mate," Mrs. Piozzi said with decision. "Yes, I know." She waved her glass of sherry to ward off interruptions. "He was a great man. His intellect was fascinating. He will be remembered far longer than I will be, or my poor Gabriel. And I liked him very well. But none of that mattered in the end. I am sure I scandalized everyone in Bath by marrying Gabriel instead of Mr. Johnson. Gabriel was my daughter's Italian singing teacher, you know, younger than I was and poor," she said as an aside to Sarah.

Sarah sipped her sherry. Her attention shifted to Mrs. Piozzi's animated old face, lit from without by the fire and from within by a passion for living. "Bath did not matter in the least to Gabriel and me." Mrs. Piozzi fairly glowed. "We were in love. We left for the Continent, and lived in Venice for a time. It was so exciting."

"You left Bath altogether?" Sarah asked in a small voice.

"It is a large world, my dear, much larger than Bath. You should know that. You have been to the Continent. Where we were did not matter so much as the fact that we were together."

"May I ask a question, Mrs. Piozzi, if I am not impertinent?" Sarah searched her face.

"Nothing is impertinent to one as old as I am." Mrs. Piozzi smiled.

"Did the difference in your ages bother you?"

"What you mean is, was I afraid that he would get tired of an older woman?" Sarah nodded slowly. "Well, child, that was always a possibility. I like to think I would have had the courage to break it off if it had come to that. But it didn't. We had fourteen wonderful years together. He died, you know, of consumption." She said it wistfully. "That was hard."

Mrs. Piozzi sipped her sherry. "Vivienne, you have had passion in your life and tragedy."

"I lost a family to the guillotine." Pain still drenched Madame's voice, though it must have been fifty years since her loss. "It was a horrible time. I loved them very much."

"Did you never love again?" Mrs. Piozzi asked.

"I did, twice."

"Any regrets?"

"Only one. The first came too soon after my family's death. He was the younger son of an Austrian baron. But I was still grieving. It seemed disloyal to my family to marry again." It was Madame's turn to stare into the fire. "I rejected his suit. But in spite of my grief, I know I loved him." Madame took a shuddering breath. "He shipped off to Brazil with the consul general."

"So you regret that he was lost to you," Sarah mused.

"He *wasn't* lost. That was my mistake. When I finally woke

to the fact that there is a difference between grief and penance, and that I loved him, my regret is that I did not chase off to Brazil," Madame replied tartly. "Of course, much later Jacques Gessande found me and my young diplomat faded. I loved Jacques, too, in a way. But it was not the same."

"You must forgive old women their reminiscences, Lady Clevancy. But passions light one's life, and deserve to be remembered."

Sarah glanced from one to the other, stricken. Mrs. Piozzi leaned forward and patted her knee. "Oh, you were a little uncomfortable today with all the congratulations, but that will pass. Don't think of the formalities, my dear, they mean nothing. Think of the passion."

"It was a very public commitment," Sarah said slowly. Her gaze drifted back to the fire.

"It is the private commitment that counts," Mrs. Piozzi said, rising. "Without it, all else is nothing. Call my carriage, Vivienne, before I sink irretrievably into sentiment."

Madame accompanied her to the hall, leaving Sarah by the fire. What were they saying? That difficulties didn't matter? It was all very well to say that passion was everything. They couldn't understand her situation. Sarah wandered into the hall, dazed.

"One cannot but make a push to avert disaster. That goose Amelia will never do so," Mrs. Piozzi was saying briskly as she pulled on her gloves. What did she mean? Sarah searched Madame Gessande's face, but she saw only kindness and a trace of self-satisfaction.

"It is time I was going too, Madame. I have imposed upon you long enough."

"Very well, child. Perhaps Hester can save you a walk." Madame kissed Sarah on the cheek. She talked to Mrs. Piozzi about small inconsequential things until the carriage came; then she shushed them both out into the night.

By the time she got into bed that night, Sarah's nerves were frayed and raw. The numbness she had cultivated for the past fortnight deserted her. *Curse those two old women*, she thought, as she tossed and turned. Before their stories of passion, she had reconciled herself to the fact that Julien was gone from her life. She'd thought her life over, too. It had been a matter only of walking through the rest of the years. That was why she'd accepted George, knowing full well he would despise her when he found she was "tarnished goods." What did it matter, when there was no love between them?

But now possibilities clattered about in her brain like a child's game of marbles. What should she believe? That Julien was gone for good? That she could never be immortal? That having to drink another's blood would kill her or drive her mad? That she should marry George? She had committed herself to George publicly tonight. But even here, Hester Piozzi seemed to say that conventions did not matter. She and Madame Gessande had as much as told her that she should follow her passion, regardless of the cost. Hester Piozzi had nursed her lover through the terrible sickness of consumption. Was Julien's disease really so much worse? Had she really shouted "yes" to opportunity, merely by taking one night with Julien?

Her resolve had been shaken further upon her arrival in Laura Place. Somehow, Amelia had already heard the happy news. She was so effusive, so obviously grateful that Sarah was to be safely wed that her congratulations were only oppressive.

"I could hardly believe my ears!" she kept exclaiming. "Now we have the happy end in sight. Why I could not help imagining just how it would be, with both of us ensconced at Beldon House with Lady Beldon, taking the waters every day, and you the young doctor's wife."

Sarah could imagine it, too.

Now as the night lengthened, she found herself a trembling mass of doubts and fears. Everything was in chaos. She just couldn't go back to quiet and predictable. But did she love Julien enough to sacrifice her mortality, to become a hateful thing herself? Handy stores of fresh blood were wishful thinking. She would have to face the drinking of blood. No, she wouldn't. He couldn't want her after she had rejected him. If he accepted her, he would tire of her, immortal or not, she was still sure. Were a few years together enough to justify sacrificing everything?

She felt herself sinking once again into that state of distraction that had consumed her a fortnight ago. Sarah shook herself, mentally. She couldn't follow Corina's path to madness. She had to take some hold on herself, however tenuous. But *how* to decide what she wanted?

It was five in the morning when she sat straight up in her bed and knew the place she must be, the place that would help her decide. It was the only thing she knew for certain.

The horse slowed to a walk up the steep hill. The wind tore at Sarah's hair under her black felt bonnet. The afternoon sky was alive with clouds and wind. When finally she reached the top, she sprang out of the hired gig and led the horse inside the ruined abbey walls to graze.

Glancing up at the broken walls, she hurried to the corner tower that held the stairway. The hole gaped and the great flat stone lay to one side. Julien's invitation to her. She stood on the edge of darkness and looked down. The stone stairs were wet from recent rains. She resolved not to think about what she might be starting here, but plunged into the crypt. At the bottom of the stairs, a torch was laid carefully upon a low stone bench cut into the wall, clearly visible in the weak light leaking from above. A striker lay next to it. She lit the torch and held it high. She had never been here alone. Fear crept up her spine.

Fear of what? Sarah chided herself. How could she fear death? Was it not what she had chosen instead of immortality? The dead must surely be lucky in her eyes for her to want to join them so badly. She started off across the dusty floor, under the Romanesque arches. She spared not a glance for the gaping coffins, but pressed on to the next staircase.

Julien was all around her. His spirit still inhabited this abbey—his for so many centuries. Now it was hers. The ruined stone walls, the crypts and coffins, the winding stairs, all belonged to her. In some small way, she was joined to him through the land. She came to the second stairwell, twisting into the darkness below. She closed her eyes. Was she capable of descending to the next level? That was really the question. She blinked and took the first step.

She could not go wrong, for the tunnel led only to one place. The door to the storeroom was unlocked, as he had meant her to find it. She pushed it open and lifted her flaming brand to light a companion torch set in a wall socket. The storehouse was empty, except for dust and a small lumpy stack under a canvas in the center.

She lit another torch and another. The room danced in light and shadow. She threw back the canvas. The melancholy companion to Mona Lisa stared up at her. I understand unhappiness, it said. Sarah put her hand up to her mouth to stop the tears that threatened her. The painting seemed an accusation. I brought it on myself. All choices might have led to unhappiness, but I chose the one way sure to devastate my life.

She knelt and touched the book beside the painting. *Paradise Lost*, of course, the book that painted Julien as Satan. And, carefully wrapped in paper, the iridescent goblet of Roman glass she had first seen in the stone coffin with Corina. A small chest filled with mint-new coins of many nations winked gold. To anyone else they would have meant a secure future. Once, they would have achieved her dreams. Pressed into the mound of coins was a note in Julien's distinctive hand. A single scribbled line leapt out at her. *For the upkeep of the abbey, Love. Adieu.* She breathed in melancholy with the dust.

Finally, behind the chest, she saw the little model of the flying machine. As though man could fly! Why had Julien left a reminiscence of a man who believed in the impossible? She clutched the book to her breast, tears streaming down her cheeks. He had left her a fortune in coins that no longer had value for her, a book that was a symbol of his outcast state, a painting of melancholia incarnate, and a little flying machine that spoke of hope against all odds. And then there was the chalice. A vessel intended for ceremonial drinking, surely. What did it mean?

All her emotions, all doubt and fear came together in an explosion inside her mind. She knelt in the flickering torchlight, small and mortal, shaking and streaming tears. But as she raised her head, her thinking was blasted clear. She knew what he meant. She had been right. Here, in this place, she could decide.

One had to try. That was all there was. That sentiment defined who she was, as it turned out. Had always defined her. One had to try. Fear didn't matter. It didn't matter if one's chance of success was infinitesimal. It didn't matter that one was not worthy, or what the cost would be. It did not matter if what one sought was ephemeral, and lasted but a single moment.

She gasped for breath. She knew, finally, who she was. She was a woman who took risks, who cherished life, whose body knew how to love, and whose soul was made to be made whole by loving. It wasn't sin. It was destiny, a larger destiny than the small souls of Bath could comprehend. Madame knew this truth, and Mrs. Piozzi. Sarah knew it now, too. And she would act on it. Julien still offered it, or he would not have left the marvelous glass chalice, an invitation, surely, to the drinking of blood. There were new experiences ahead, not necessarily sins, and she would descend the staircase Julien had built for her. Had there not been a treasure at its end?

Tears rose to her eyes. This clarity of vision would fade. She drank in the feeling of it, the sureness, as deeply as she could, so it might last her through all the disappointments, all the fear ahead. From some core of strength, a laugh rose up through her throat into a shout that echoed about the ancient storeroom and laughed back at her. She filled the room, she and Julien. She whirled about the dusty stones in a crazy waltz; the book waved above her head in triumph. She might not find him. He might reject her. It might not work between them for more than a moment, even if all else succeeded. If he gave her immortality it would be bought by sharing his disease. She would drink the blood of the living from the chalice he had left her, and they would give it willingly, a sexual revelation for them as well as her. She could not understand the life that loomed ahead, not yet. It did not matter. Nothing would take this moment from her.

As she drove the gig home, she laid feverish plans for detaching herself from her society. She might be gone for a long while. Who knew where Julien had gone? He had been to China and to India, to Mother Russia. Perhaps he had gone to the Americas. And she was far behind him. It had been more than a fortnight since he had departed. He knew where he was going and she did not, so he would gain ground on her at every turn. But as she sat in the freezing carriage, the euphoria of her dervish waltz in the villa storeroom stood her in good stead. It did not matter if it seemed impossible. And she just might know a way to focus her search.

She was still euphoric when she arrived home and stunned Amelia by telling her she was going abroad. Amelia wailed, Amelia moaned. But Sarah was impervious. Amelia would have all her creature comforts. Julien's cache of coins would see to that. A predictable round of small social engagements would suit Amelia much better than playing chaperone to a headstrong young niece likely to drag her reputation through the mud at any moment.

Finally, with a night behind her filled more with packing than with sleep and a household in uproar, she strode along Upper Borough Walls coming away from Monmouth Street and Mr. Lestrom's office. Last night sleet had coated the town with wet in time for the freezing temperatures just before dawn. Now, though it was nearly nine o'clock, everything was coated in a translucent ice that made the town shine in the sun peeking through the clouds. She felt she could melt the ice herself, just by her passage, she burned so with energy. *Don't put on your best face for me this morning,* Sarah told the city sternly. *I see just what you are behind your shining surface. You are comfort. You are George and Amelia and Lady Beldon. And I am not for you.*

Mr. Lestrom was stunned by the king's ransom in strange coins. She told him they were from her villa and arranged to have him sell them slowly and to manage Amelia's allowance. He would send Sarah funds when he received direction from her.

She walked to Beldon House. George was in the breakfast room, finishing his coffee.

"Sarah," he exclaimed, rising as the footman showed her in. "Where have you been? I called twice in Laura Place only to have your odious butler tell me you were not at home."

"He was right, George. I was not at home." Sarah sat in the chair George pulled out for her, and waved away coffee. "I was up at Clershing."

"I should think you would tell me, love, when you going out of town." George appeared uneasy as he sat back again to his breakfast. "After all, we are betrothed."

"Actually, George"—Sarah mustered her resolve—"I wanted to discuss that with you."

"My mother has delightful plans for the wedding. The announcement will appear today in the papers. We have not been idle while you have been gallivanting about," he teased.

Sarah's heart sank. Things had gone so far already!

"We both think we should wait for the ceremony until the weather is assured of being fine," George continued. "I proposed May to Mother, and she thought that would do nicely." He talked around a mouthful of toast.

Wasn't it strange? The fact that George talked about their wedding with his mouth full stiffened her resolve. One couldn't acquiesce to life with such a man, simply because there was some embarrassment involved. "George, I cannot marry you," she said, not trying to dress it up.

His coffee cup stopped in midpassage from saucer to lip. "What?" he asked.

"I can't marry you," Sarah repeated.

"But it's all arranged. You cannot cry off now." George gathered himself for anger.

"You may be angry all you like, George. I deserve that."

His eyes flicked about the room. He looked desperate. That was odd. "You must marry me. I said I would make you happy. What more do you want?"

"George, you and I would never suit."

He became stern. "You will never be received in Bath if you call off this marriage."

"I intend to leave England, George." She hoped her tone of voice conveyed that she did not care whether Bath received her. She rose to go. "I am truly sorry."

"But what about my career?" George practically shouted. Suddenly, his eyes narrowed in an ugly look she had not seen before. "You're going to *him*, aren't you?"

Sarah felt her flush betray her. How could he have guessed?

"You're going to ruin everything." George's voice was low and venomous. "His bargain with me means nothing if you call off our betrothal."

"What are you saying?"

"I get nothing from him if I do not marry you," George spat.

"Oh, I look a rare fool! You go to him, leaving me mortified, my career in shreds. He need tell me nothing more about the blood. Blundell will discover everything before me. He's probably already on to using citrates to prevent clotting. And you!" George's chuckle was hardly amused. "Were you in it all along?"

"He struck a bargain with you to marry me?" Sarah asked in a small voice.

"He came to me after he escaped. He wanted me to gallant you about, acknowledge you. I was forced to tell him that would never do the trick, not with what you had done. I would have to marry you to save some shred of your reputation—and for my sacrifice, I wanted his knowledge. You should have seen the look on his face!" George's own face flushed with his triumph. "I might have hit him with a mallet to less effect."

"He, he only wanted you to take me to parties," Sarah said slowly.

George caught himself and paused, looking down at the ruins of his breakfast. When he lifted his head to Sarah, he said coldly, "Oh, he wanted me to marry you, all right. Probably foisting damaged goods on me to tie up his loose ends. It would have been worth it to know what he knows about blood. But he never meant to honor the bargain."

Sarah knew he was punishing her for calling off the engagement. She wouldn't care if he admitted that his devotion was a sham. But he was trying to use Julien to hurt her, too.

"You barter with my life to forward your career and you call *Julien* dishonorable? You are the blackest pot calling names at the kettle I have ever seen, George Upcott." Sarah felt the tears of anger begin. "You deserve to be the laughingstock of the entire town." She ran from the room, not caring that the footman saw her tears as she collected her coat and her gloves. Out in the street, she hurried toward Madame Gessande's house in Queen's Parade, as to a refuge.

It was several blocks before her pace slowed. If George's soul was small enough to marry to further his career, then his punishment was to live with a small soul. She cursed herself for not realizing his deceit. If he wanted to marry her, why had he not proposed these last three years? George's rage had done her a good turn. He had blurted out the truth. Julien might not want her still. But for one moment he had been dismayed when George told him the price of her reentry into society. She turned into Queen's Parade. She must hurry if she was to leave tomorrow.

Madame Gessande received Sarah in her drawing room, now lit with cold winter sunlight.

"You look much improved this morning, my dear," Madame observed.

"I feel much improved, Madame." Sarah wanted to tell her friend what she had learned from the story of the lover who went to Brazil.

"I think you look decisive." Madame's eyes crinkled slyly.

"I am going abroad for a while." Sarah smiled. "I think you know why."

"Ah." Madame sighed and motioned Melton to put the tea tray on the table next to her chair. She began to pour out two cups as he disappeared. "I am glad to hear that, Sarah." They made no pretense between them. "Do you know where to start?"

"I have an idea about how to trace him. I hope I do not have to go as far as Brazil."

"Brazil is not so very far after all," Madame observed. "Whom do you take with you?"

"Jasco and Addie agreed to go." Sarah frowned. "Amelia was out of the question. Still, dragging them all over who-knows-where does not seem a kindness. I wish I could go alone."

"I should like to offer my services as duenna." Madame raised her brows.

"Oh, Madame, whatever are you thinking?"

"I am thinking I have stayed rather too long in Bath."

It was such a perfect solution to her distress about taking Jasco and Addie that she had to protest. "But I don't even know where I am going!"

"I shall see my banker while Juliette packs. Shall we take Melton? He travels with me."

Sarah put her teacup aside, kissed Madame's old cheek. "We shall," she whispered.

"I should be nothing loath if our way led to Vienna. I have not been to Vienna in years."

Chapter Eighteen

Sarah and Madame Gessande took the road out of Amsterdam in a hired carriage southeast toward the place where the Ij River joins the Rhine. Julien was only four days ahead of them, bound for Vienna on the *Schwaerte Schaep* according to Mijanheer Leiden, head of the Dutch East India Company. Mijanheer Leiden had been so anxious to send a message to his most important investor that he had sent it even with a girl from Bath. Sarah had found Mijanheer Leiden by tracing a load of twenty-seven boxes, labeled as tools for export, shipped from Bristol to Amsterdam. The boxes had started from Littleton-on-Severn, a small town near Thornbury Abbey. Entirely plausible, except that there were no manufacturing establishments there, and the order had been written in Julien's hand.

Sarah peered out impatiently over the wide Ruhr Valley and a huge river that looked lazy and cold as it moved inexorably toward the sea behind them. Her eyes roved constantly among the vessels on the river, barges large and small, boats pressed upstream by oarsmen standing on the decks, pushing and pulling at their oars. The *Schwaerte Schaep* must be long gone. She could not expect to see Julien striding along her decks. But she looked just the same.

It had been a shock to see Julien's face peering out from the small dark portraits of the original directors of the East India Company in Mijanheer Leiden's office. It had been labeled with the name of Alexander Trenescu, but she would know him anywhere. He had shaped the world for hundreds of years. Now, he was pulling out of the Dutch East India Company and gathering his treasures along the way, withdrawing his interests in society. What could it mean?

The great river was lined with plowed fields, vinyards, and towns engulfed by factories. She didn't see much of the towns as they raced through them. The names melted into one another, Amersfoort, Utrect, Arnheim. Sarah had plenty of time to think about Julien, where he was, whether he would welcome her intrusion into his life. She knew full well she had taken an incredible risk, that she could not turn back. She had cut herself off from George, from Corina, from Jasco and Addie, from Bath society. Madame Gessande was now her only link with who she had once been. She found herself reaching out to hold Madame's hand at odd moments in this frenzied journey.

They passed into the Kingdom of Prussia and thus into the German Federation in the afternoon. They traveled almost eighty miles that day, changing horses often. Sarah would have gone on through the night in spite of the jolting and the cold. But as they approached Koln she saw, in the icy darkness of the coach, that Madame looked exhausted. She chided herself for her inattention and called to the driver to pull up for the night in Koln. Sarah escorted Madame to a room, watched her order bread and a steaming bowl of broth, and then retreated to her own room to take the greenish glass goblet from her trunk and touch it, as she did each night. He left it for you for a reason, she told herself. At that moment, he had wanted her to change her mind, had he not? He could have changed his own since then. That was another risk. She would never know if she never caught up with him. She could not think of that.

Julien stood at the window of the drawing room in the house at number five Domgasse, his small residence for those rare times he stayed briefly in Vienna. He had acquired it as a reminder of his lapse of responsibility. Mozart had died in penury here while he had been in Spain. Julien should have left provision for him. He had counted on the Hapsburgs—always a mistake after Maria Teresa died. Sometimes Julien could hear the strains of "Figaro" wafting through the rooms where it had been composed. Sometimes the house was just filled with a sense of loss, loss of a musical genius, a life cut too short contrasted with life too long. Tonight, loss won out.

The butler, Mallnitz, and his wife were never happy to see the arrival of their master. But he paid them well, just as he did those who had kept his houses in St. Petersburg, and Madrid, and rarely troubled them with his presence. He had closed up all his other houses through the auspices of local agents. This one would soon follow.

Mallnitz brought in the brandy tray. Julien stood with his hands in his pockets and looked out over the street. Crystal clinked behind him. Outside, carriages and link chairs negotiated the narrow streets. Tiny flakes of dry snow disappeared on the wet cobblestones. *Hardly worth the effort of snowing*, he thought, as his own dry regret snowed inside him. His anger, so close to the surface in Amsterdam, had drained away, leaving an emptiness even less tolerable. Absently he fingered the smooth porcelain and gold filigree of the miniature painting of her he had taken from George Upcott the night he bargained away his future in return for the lore of blood. He kept it always in his pocket. He no longer needed to look at it. He had memorized each line until the likeness itself became unreal. He need only touch it and the portrait came alive. Perhaps he would be able to discard it when he reached the monastery. But not yet. Not yet.

He turned into the room and poured out a brandy. Khalenberg had summoned him tonight. That was odd. They were not on good terms. Julien did not ordinarily obey a summons. He had contemplated ignoring it. But like called to like and Vienna belonged to Khalenberg, who was a stickler for the Rules. And the Rules demanded that he who owned a city be obeyed as long as one was passing through. Julien downed the last of his brandy and turned to dress.

It was midnight when he met Khalenberg in a private smoking room above the gaming tables of a very exclusive club. It was small and rococo and dimly lighted by two sconces. Davinoff closed the door after them. Khalenberg folded his long frame into a wing chair by the fireplace and motioned Julien to its mate. He leaned over, opened a carved wood box, and offered a cheroot. Julien took the cigar and settled himself for an unpleasant conversation. Using the lighter provided, he studied Khalenberg's hawk face and ruthless gray eyes. There was a subtle sag about the thin lips Julien thought was new in the years since he last had seen him. The man's dark hair was still shot through with a gray that those who did not know what he was would call premature. He looked to be in his prime, just as they all did.

The man seemed lost in thought. Julien raised a brow. "What do you want with me, Khalenberg? You have long been immune to the need for my company."

"What are you going to do about *her*, Davinoff?" Khalenberg began his conversation as though he swung a battle-ax against an enemy, an act he had performed in truth many times over during the centuries. He and Julien's differences had pitted them against each other in more than one war, in more than one battle of intrigue. Julien was taken aback. Khalenberg couldn't know of his near lapse with Sarah. Her name washed over him, and with it came the pain, all over again. "With whom?" he managed.

"An error of yours, I believe. Flaming hair. Goes by the name of Magda Ravel."

Magda? Here in Vienna? Damn! She should be immured in Mirso Monastery by now—she and her rat-faced companion. Julien studied the glowing tip of his cigar, not willing to let his old enemy see his discomfiture. Then he turned it and brought it to his lips, drew in a long breath, and let the smoke pour slowly from his nostrils. He was for Mirso himself. The last thing he wanted was to stop and take care of Magda. "I sent her home to Dacia."

"It has been called Transylvania for a hundred years, Davinoff."

Julien nodded. "My lapse. I take it she is misbehaving?"

"There are only three murders so far," Khalenberg grunted. "But there will be more."

Julien sighed. Magda was his responsibility. Khalenberg was right. He said, "She must be stopped. I am sorry to inconvenience you." But he gazed at Khalenberg with some curiosity. There had been no scorn yet, no disdain for his Crime. "As the Master of Vienna, you will be able to give me her direction."

The man's eyes lost their razor's edge. He sighed and pressed his lips together as he watched the smoke from his cheroot curl upward. There was a long silence, Julien did not press him. One did not press Khalenberg. He rose and went to a small escritoire. "She lives with one Johann Villach just off the Stephanplatz." He scribbled the address on a scrap of paper and handed it to Julien, who glanced at the paper and put it in the inside pocket of his coat. There was something more here.

"You wonder why I do not take this opportunity to remind you of the strict Rules governing the spread of the Companion," Khalenberg said stiffly. His eyes turned inward. "I always believed that our kind must not be made willy-nilly by exchanging blood."

"You were not wont to be generous when it came to my faults," Julien agreed.

"Ah, but that was before I shared them." Khalenberg pushed the smoke from his lips in a pillar toward the ceiling and watched it rise. He glanced at Julien. "When you go to the Stephanplatz, you will meet my own mistake, no doubt. He is beautiful, I will give him that." Khalenberg stood, straight as a ramrod. "And ruthless. Hoisted on my own petard."

"Villach?" Julien asked.

Khalenberg nodded. There was another long silence. Finally, he continued reflectively. "It always changes them, doesn't it? Giving the Companion, I mean. It finds the smallness in their souls and magnifies it. You would think I would know better, given my sentiments about tradition." He chuckled bitterly. "We're two old war horses looking for new vigor in our lives, companionship to share the triumph and the tragedy of immortality. Pitiful, are we not? We cannot accept the destiny of solitude that is our heritage."

Julien did not answer. It was too painful. He addressed Kahlenberg's first question instead. "I don't think the Companion changes them. Has it changed us? We have had it for millennia.

Magda was always selfish, wanton, a sexual predator, though I did not always know it. I think we just chose badly." He owed Khalenberg more. "It is a great temptation, when you think you have found a soul mate and mortality is in the way." He bared his wound in kind. "I was tempted most sorely in Bath of late, in spite of experience. She was not like Magda. She is blessed with a large soul. If it is any consolation, I despise myself for my weakness."

Khalenberg searched his face. "It cannot work—for them or for us. We are not meant for companionship. Remember what happened at the court of Charlemagne?"

Julien stared into the fire and clenched the arm of the chair. That one had committed suicide when she realized in full what he had made of her. Suicide for their kind must needs be horrific. "I shall remove my indiscretion from Vienna," he said after a moment.

"I hoped mine would come round." Khalenberg tapped his cigar ash on the grate. "But he prefers your redhead's company to mine. Out of curiosity, what will you do with her?"

"I will take her with me when I go to Mirso." Julien let the name hang in the air.

Khalenberg let his razor eyes search Julien's face. "You would not guess it, but I am sorry to hear that is your destination. You are young to take the Vow. It is a kind of death, you know."

Julien didn't acknowledge the sympathy. "I thought of suicide." He made certain his tone was nonchalant. "I cannot do it. Perhaps that means I have not given up all hope. And if I take the Vow, if I practice faithfully under the Old Ones, perhaps I can find peace. Who knows? I may even find meaning. Under their teaching, I can certainly reduce my need for blood."

"Taking the Vow is admitting defeat." Khalenberg was frightened. Julien could see it.

"Don't think we have everything in common," he said wryly. "If I have come to the last resort, it does not mean that you are right behind me. I am resigned."

"You didn't seem resigned in Amsterdam according to Beatrix." Khalenberg took another tack. "Aren't monks supposed to leave rage and sullenness behind?"

Julien didn't rise to the bait. "I do what I can, old friend. And what I will do now is rid you of Magda Ravel. I hate to foist her upon Rubius. But the Elders are better equipped than I to decide her fate. I can no longer serve as judge and jury."

Khalenberg stubbed out his cigar and tossed the remains into the grate. "If you remove your indiscretion, I shall deal with mine. Upon that you have my word." His hawk face hardened further. "But he is not destined for Mirso. He is not worth that." With one more searching glance, Khalenberg turned and strode from the room. He left Julien to finish his cheroot in the dim light, feeling very much like an old war horse.

"Well," Madame greeted a wet and tired Sarah as she returned just after luncheon to their private parlor in the Hotel Lofer, one of the most correct addresses in Vienna. "I dare say my news is better than yours, from the look of you."

"Oh, I hope so." Sarah sighed as she removed her gloves, her hat and cloak, all dusted with melting flakes. "I could not find the cartage firm at all." Her remarkable run of luck seemed to have ended. She could find no trace of Julien's cargo, which had grown as she followed it until it was a huge load of boxes and barrels, enough to fill a dozen wagons. There had been hints in Strasbourg that he had been Guttenberg's partner, Johann Faust, who built the first printing press in the early seventeenth century. Of course Julien would have named himself Faust. He had removed a fabulous collection of first editions from Strasbourg. He had also been the patron of Vermeer and now removed a treasure of art from Germany. He had come as far as Vienna, she was sure. But now where?

"Never mind, *cherie*," Madame adjured her. "I have connections here."

Sarah could see there was something else that Madame wanted to tell her. The woman was blushing. She could not say she had ever seen her blush before. "I wager we shall have a visitor soon ourselves." Madame pulled over some needlework lying discarded on a side table.

"And whom are we likely to receive?" Sarah asked.

Madame harrumphed self-consciously. "One never knows. It could be almost anybody."

Though Sarah could pry no further commitment from her,

she was alert to Madame's mood. When, at almost two, a note was delivered by one of the hotel staff, Sarah raced to the door and took it from the boy. It was addressed in a precise male hand to *Madame Ravelyn.*

"Boy," she called in English. "There is no Madame Ravelyn in this room."

Before the boy could turn back, Madame snatched the note from her. "My first husband's name," she threw over her shoulder. She took the paper to the fireside and sat poring over it.

Sarah apologized to the boy with a douceur she pressed into his hand. Madame did not look up until she had read the sheet through twice. "Well?" Sarah asked.

Madame cleared her throat. "The note is from Baron Arlberg, at least he is a baron since he has succeeded to his brother's title, though not when I knew him, of course. At any rate, he is in Vienna, attached to Metternich's diplomatic corps. He . . . he wished to escort us to tea in the hotel dining room." Madame's old eyes, usually so wily and wise, now filled with tears. "Would you mind, my dear? I should like to see him."

"It sounds as if you don't need me, Madame," Sarah said with a smile. "I wish you a delightful tea and a joyful reunion."

"He expressly invited both of us," Madame answered with a note of urgency in her voice.

"Much to his credit, Madame, not to leave what he must believe to be your charge, alone," Sarah agreed. "But as we know, I am not your charge."

"True," Madame agreed. "But I would like your company."

"Never tell me you need a chaperone!" Sarah laughed. "This is a twist."

"Well, sometimes reunions are easier in company. He knew that." Madame folded the note carefully. "What if we turn out to be strangers, after all these years?"

Sarah began to think herself very stupid. Tears over a man who was in the diplomatic corps, a younger son? "Madame, this man is never your young consul who shipped to Brazil?"

Madame nodded. "But I have changed since then." She blinked away her tears and looked up into Sarah's eyes with steady gray ones. "I am old Madame Gessande now, not young Madame Ravelyn."

"What a delightful surprise your baron has in store for him," Sarah said and bent to kiss her friend's cheek. "I shall send our acceptance. I would not miss this tea for the world."

Sarah climbed the stairs to her room after tea, feeling wistful. She was a good chaperone, it turned out. She had drawn the two old lovers into talking about the first time they met and so had gotten over the awkwardness they both felt. The baron then led the way. He was, after all, a diplomat. Just what she would have wanted for Madame, come to think of it. He was handsome, with iron-gray mustaches and a faintly military demeanor, softened by laughing eyes. And Madame . . . who would have thought to see her smiling like a glowing girl? Madame had always wanted their journey to include Vienna. Had she known her baron might be here? Sarah might not be the only one who had chased across the continent in the name of love.

Sarah wished her own quest progressed as well. The baron did not know Julien. But he had promised to make inquiries. A man like the baron would move in the highest circles. Certainly he would be able to find Julien for her, if anyone could.

It was just coming on to dusk when Julien was ushered into Khalenberg's elegant residence in the Graben. The impassive butler was a thin stalk of a man much like his master. He took Julien's coat, hat, his cane and gloves, and left him to kick his heels in a first-floor salon done in somber grays and browns. Soon Khalenberg strode into the room where Davinoff stood with his back to the crackling fire.

"Good," Khalenberg barked. "You got my note."

"I wanted to see you urgently myself."

"Eh?" Khalenberg grunted. "What's to do?"

"I went to the Stephanplatz today," Julien drawled. "Magda was not there. But I saw your Villach. Our job is more pressing than I thought. Our indiscretions are themselves planning to be indiscreet, if they have not already. Even now our job may be expanding."

Khalenberg's eyes narrowed. "Fools! I should have thought

they wouldn't want to share the power. Why not keep it to themselves?"

"They envision a salon of their own kind replacing the likes of you and me." Julien rocked back and forth on his heels in front of the fire while Khalenberg paced the room. "They think us reticent about using our powers, needlessly solitary. They would be bolder, as Villach says."

"Then we must act tonight." The words were torn from Khalenberg's entrails.

Julien nodded. "Magda will be at a concert. I wager Villach will be with her. I had planned to take Magda away immediately after the last curtain."

"Join me in the Stephanplatz during the concert. We finish any who remain afterward." Khalenberg looked out at the street. March snow covered the city like a sodden blanket.

"Agreed," Julien said shortly and made as if to go.

"One more thing," Khalenberg said without taking his eyes from the street. "You are like to meet an old acquaintance if you attend the concert tonight."

Julien looked up sharply. There was an edge in Khalenberg's voice that demanded attention. "Who?"

"Baron Arlberg asked me today if you were in Vienna. It seems a dark beauty from some backwater . . . Bath, I believe, has been asking after you. You mentioned Bath, I think?"

Julien felt the room recede. Dimly he heard Khalenberg continue. "I took the liberty of making certain inquiries. I even saw her dining at the Krenplad. She is not just in the usual style. I expect she will take Vienna by storm. Do you wish to be found?"

For a long moment, he could not gather himself for a reply. His heart had begun to leap in an old way, yet it leapt now into his mouth in fear. Sarah was in Vienna. She'd asked after him. He should never have been weak enough to leave the mementos. She should never have been resourceful enough to find him. He focused again on the room to find Khalenberg staring at him.

"I know you will be wiser than I have been, and stronger," the other man said in a rough voice. "For her sake, for the sake of us all."

Julien searched the face of his old adversary-turned-ally as if he might find answers there. Sarah was in Vienna. She had asked after him. He could not think what it meant. He needed to go away. He had to think. Khalenberg wanted an answer, and then he could go. "Of course," he finally croaked and pushed his way into the hall.

His steps slowed when he reached the wall at the Danube Canal. His mind began to think again, enough to let in pain. Why now, when he had rubbed the filigree frame of the tiny portrait shiny, when the picture had begun to transform itself into an icon rather than reality? Why, when he was just about to make his escape into Mirso Monastery?

The bright outline of a future filled with love and engagement with the world pushed through his dark thoughts. Sarah looked at the world like that. He shook his head convulsively and leaned over the stone wall. Not real. Reality was Khalenberg, Magda, and Villach, his own sordid past. She was in Vienna to accept the offer he had made so rashly in Bath because she did not know the risks. She did not know about the solitary destiny of a vampire, the weight of years, the dreadful experience of human inhumanity. And he was vulnerable to her offer. He had proven that. Some childish part of him wanted a soul mate, no matter how impossible that was for one of his kind. That vulnerability frightened him. There was no other word for it. Even the fact that he could be frightened after all these years betrayed his belief about who he was.

Julien studied the black water below him swallowing bright snowflakes as it swept on, a thousand miles to the sea. He closed his eyes for a moment. Vulnerable or not, he must refuse her offer, for her own good as well as his. Perhaps he could just avoid her in Vienna. He would do his duty by Magda and escape into the Carpathians and the sanctity of the Vow, where she could never enter. The prospect of his escape did not excite him. Fighting a bone weariness, he pushed himself upright and walked down the snowy street toward number five Domgasse.

The boxes of the Burgetheater brimmed with the cream of Vienna tonight. The boards of the stage had been cleared to make room for the orchestra. Feathers nodded, jewels winked, silk and satin shone. As the baron led them to their box, Sarah scanned the crowd. Madame thought Julien certain to be here.

So many faces, so much movement. She didn't see him.

A diminutive woman with creamy skin and sparkling blue eyes approached. The baron introduced her as the Marquise de Foucault. Sarah barely had opportunity to nod in acknowledgment as the baron murmured their names. "Oh, but Lady Clevancy, you are *Anglais, bien sur*. I knew by your dress! *Tres ravissant!* My dressmaker in Paris—I go to Fanchon, of course—Fanchon was saying only the week before I left that we would have waists again. She had been to England to visit her *cousine*, and waists were all the rage. *Tres curieuse* that England should set the style for France! But here you are, English, and I quite see how Fanchon would feel that such a thing would be. I say again, *ravissant*."

In the face of this onslaught, Sarah only smiled absently as she searched boxes behind the marquise. She had almost forgotten her dress might be scandalous. Addie had remade many of her mother's dresses. Tonight she wore white rouched satin trimmed with black Austrian fringe. When finally the marquise wound down, Sarah murmured, "Thank you for your kindness."

"Oh, I am never kind about matters of fashion, Lady Clevancy, not kind at all." The marquise twinkled. After pointed questioning, she concluded that her Fanchon was actually the cousin of Sarah's reliable Courette. Sarah confided that she had been the one to wear the first waisted dress in Bath. This was enough to win the marquise's good graces.

A very young man in a military uniform approached for an introduction. Sarah did not quite catch his long name. When he asked her to share his family's box, she politely declined.

"My dear," Madame whispered frantically. "You just dismissed the young crown prince."

"I have no time for crown princes," Sarah said as they took their seats.

The baron directed their attention to a wild-haired man of about fifty making his way to the conductor's podium. He was disheveled, even in his evening clothes, and his broad face with its beetling brows scowled out over the room. A spontaneous ovation rippled across the huge room. "Beethoven," Madame whispered.

"Why does he not play the piano?" Sarah asked as the soloist also took his seat. "I understand he is a virtuoso."

"He has been deaf for twenty years," the baron said, leaning forward. "He still composes and conducts, but he can no longer play."

To be cut off from the sustaining passion of one's life! Tragedy was carved in the face of the man taking the podium, as well as passion. Sarah thought suddenly that she should study those lines. They might disfigure her own face some day.

Boys raised the great chandeliers, snuffed the candles, turned down the lamps. The room dimmed. She couldn't see to find Julien. Had he seen her? If so, would he be making his way to her side, or calling for his carriage? *Remember the chalice*, she thought, to bolster her courage.

The orchestra emitted soft, cacophonous tuning sounds. A woman with flaming red hair on the arm of a blond and dapper young man with a small mustache engaged Sarah's attention as they made their way to a box to the right of the stage. Sarah's mind darted back to a London night in the autumn. She could not be mistaken. There could not be two heads of hair just that shade. She peered into the gloom and saw the woman's face turn from profile to full-on as she arranged her gaudy skirts of cerise. Sarah recognized the hard lips and eyes, the sharp features. It was the woman she had seen in the glow of a streetlight where passersby gawked at a murder. Julien had said she was vampire, and that she had done those dreadful murders.

Shock shivered through her system. How could she be here, at a concert in Vienna, when Julien said he sent her back to wherever vampires came from?

The music of "The Pastoral" wafted peaceful notes over the hushed crowd. Sarah's soul was hardly in harmony with those sweet strains. A thousand thoughts skipped through her head. Was this woman the reason Julien had chosen Vienna? Had she drawn him across a continent through love? How much easier for Julien to love one of his kind than a silly girl of six and twenty!

Could she sit until the interval? Perhaps it was the music that calmed her. She waited, drenched in music and darkness, her eyes straying often toward the box where the red-haired woman and her companion sat. In the dim light from the stage, she could make out a boy delivering a note to their box. The blond man excused himself. The woman wanted to go with him but he pushed her back into her seat. Sarah's curiosity deepened.

When the lamps were turned up for the interval, the red-haired woman looked nervously about her. Sarah saw her rise and make her way out of her box. Impulsively, Sarah rose as well. "I see an old acquaintance," she murmured: The woman might be a link to Julien.

Madame searched the crowd. "It can't be . . ."

"It isn't." Sarah smiled. "I do not need an escort, Baron," she added as that gentleman rose.

He looked stubborn until Madame patted his hand and pulled him down. She knew very well that the last thing Sarah needed tonight was an escort.

Sarah glanced over to see cerise skirts disappear among the swishing velvet curtains of a side entrance. She hastened after them. Her way was blocked by a very large woman in voluminous skirts of dull gold, trundling slowly toward the exit curtains, complaining all the while of the draft. The woman's escort towed his graceless barge up the aisle. When finally they reached the corridor Sarah managed to squeeze around them. But when she reached the exit, there was no sign of red hair or cerise dresses. The grand lobby, gilt and ornate, was a crush of people. The crowd talked and sipped champagne as it folded and refolded itself without revealing anything. Sarah found an alcove out of the way and surveyed the room. There she was! The redhead, off to her right, searched the lobby, too. They scanned the throng together.

Sarah stood stock-still as the crowd parted. It always parted in that manner for him. He towered over the Viennese men and cut his black swath smoothly through the glitter, in a diagonal across the lobby toward the redhead. Sarah jerked her gaze toward his destination. The redhead was white-faced and startled. Was meeting Julien unexpected? Sarah's gaze raced back to Julien. She hardly recognized the hardness there. What did he want with this woman? Was he come to claim her as his own? *I am yours!* Sarah wanted to shout. She put her hand to her mouth. She must watch this meeting play out. She had to know how things stood before she declared herself.

Julien took the redhead by the arm and turned toward the door. They stood not five feet from Sarah. He called to a footman for Mademoiselle Ravel's cloak. Sarah drew back into the shadows. He must not see her. She need not have worried. He had eyes only for the redhead.

"You cannot be surprised, Magda." His deep voice washed over Sarah for the first time in a month, almost brought tears to her eyes. "Villach must have told you I called."

"Where is he? What have you done with him?" the woman hissed.

"That is up to Khalenberg, not to me," Julien snapped. "You are my only concern." He stopped short, as though a new thought had occurred to him. "Where is Keely?"

The woman tried to sound casual. "I can't remember where I left him. Was it Paris?"

Julien's mouth grew ever more grim. "Don't defy me, Magda. You can't protect him."

Sarah was confused. Julien did not sound like a lover.

"Oh, very well, he's at Villach's house." The redhead pouted. Then she practically hissed, "I won't go with you. We have friends now, more of our kind."

"You state the problem clearly." Julien claimed her cloak. "We are for Mirso Monastery."

The redhead started to struggle in his steely grip, and the pair began to attract attention. A man with dark hair shot through with iron gray and a hawk nose came through the doors to the theater and headed straight for them. His eyes sliced like daggers around him. All color had drained from his face and his mouth was bleak. At his approach, the redhead went still. Julien grunted a greeting to the thin man. "Is it done, Khalenberg?"

The man opened his mouth, but nothing came out. Finally he nodded.

"What have you done to Johann?" The redhead accosted the newcomer Julien had called Khalenberg. Then, as she looked into the man's cold eyes, she began to whimper. "Oh my God!"

Julien locked his gaze to the redhead; both men did. Sarah knew they were bending her to their will. But to what purpose? Julien had said, "We are for Mirso Monastery." They were not words of love. What were they about?

Sarah had no chance to solve the puzzle. The crowd melted away from the strange threesome and wandered back to their boxes for the next movement. Julien jerked Magda toward the doors. Should she call to him? Unconsciously, Sarah moved out of the alcove, racked with uncertainty. Khalenberg looked up and passed his eyes over her, revealed now by the dissipating crowd. His eyes went on, then came back. They sharpened into focus, strong eyes, gray and piercing. He reached out one hand and touched Julien's arm.

Julien glanced briefly back at the man who signaled him, then followed his gaze until he saw Sarah. Everything stopped. This was the moment, the moment she would know whether all her longing, all her journey had been in vain or no. She stood silently. Their eyes locked together. Her own filled with tears. His face contorted in an instant of pain and longing. A turbulent current of emotion seared her as it rolled over her. *Yes*, she thought somewhere deep inside. She found herself moving forward into the power of his gaze. She embraced the darkness willingly. She wanted to touch him, his face, his hand. She wanted to feel the flesh of him.

Then she saw his mouth set into a thin line. His eyes, so fierce with those emotions she had seen in the darkness of her room one night in January, dulled. His face slowly hardened. He handed Khalenberg Magda's wrap. "Take care of this one for me," he said. "I will meet you shortly in the Stephanplatz." He turned then to Sarah.

"Be careful, Davinoff," the other man warned roughly. "She will be your Waterloo."

Julien did not answer but waited as Khalenberg guided the now-docile redhead into the night. "I'll get your cloak," he said to Sarah, and moved away. Liveried vassals scurried in all directions.

Sarah stood, abandoned for the moment, torn with doubt. She had seen how he felt. And she had seen it disappear. She trembled in the aftershock of her own emotion.

When Julien returned carrying her cloak, he had mastered himself. "You must be here with friends," he said brusquely. "What box?"

"Sixty-two," she heard herself say in a voice she did not recognize.

"Boy," he called. "Box sixty-two. Tell them the lady has the headache. Davinoff took her home."

Sarah thought she might faint at the pressure of his hands placing her cloak about her shoulders. It was the touch she had longed for, but now it chilled her with the threat of loss. Julien spun his cape about his shoulders and placed his hat carelessly upon his head. Then he took her arm in that old electric grip and drew her out of the theater and into his waiting carriage.

She sat in the cold dark and watched him climb in across from her.

"What is your direction?" he asked, no emotion in his voice now.

She gave the address of her hotel, and he called it to the driver. She shivered and pulled her cloak about her. What would she say to him? She had imagined this moment many times, but not like this. The horses clattered off over the snowy cobblestones and the well-sprung carriage glided after them. The silence grew taut between them. She tried to think of the glass chalice and what he had once let it promise, but her talisman did not ward off the grim set of his lips.

"What brings you to Vienna, Sarah?" he finally asked.

"You know that." She could allow no games between them. "You bring me to Vienna."

"How did you find me?" he asked. It was more a weary lamentation than curiosity.

"Oh, bills of lading, cartage companies. I met Mr. Leiden in Amsterdam, who wants you back as an investor." She took an absurd pride in her ingenuity.

There was another silence. "I am sorry it was all for naught."

Sarah took her heart in her hands. She tried to focus not on what he had just said, but on the look in his eyes in the lobby of the concert hall, before the grim resolve had entered them. Why else had she come all this way if not to make a push for what she wanted? "My courage failed me, back in Bath. I am so very sorry. The differences between us seemed too great to be bridged. But I have found my courage now, Julien. I know what I want."

"It is a false courage, my love," he whispered. "You do not know the obstacles."

Sarah heard him call her "my love" and drew strength from that as well. She leaned forward and touched his knee. "Then tell me," she said, and let all her love pour out toward his dark shape in the corner. "I will face eternity with you, Julien. I accept the need for blood, and how I will have to get it. I will risk all." She felt light-headed now that the words were said.

She could see his chest heaving in the darkness while he struggled with himself. "You don't understand!" he finally said through gritted teeth. She sat back as though she had been slapped. "I should never have offered the Companion. It is strictly forbidden. And only evil comes of it. Khalenberg is right about that, though not the way he thinks. It is a terrible burden, a curse." He jerked his face to the window, then turned back deliberately. He seemed to consider before he spoke. "It finds the smallness in one, magnifies it. Look what it did to Magda." He had some hold upon himself that strained the muscles in his shoulders.

"Curse or blessing, it does not matter," Sarah said simply. She saw him shake his head, but she pressed on. "It is who you are. Can you not accept that, and share it with another?"

"You are an innocent," he returned, his voice harsh. "You only see the sunshine."

He called her naive once more. The pain shot through her, but she persisted. "It was I who thought it wouldn't last, that you would grow bored."

"You appear to have changed your mind," he said, almost bitterly.

"I'll take what time you will give me," she whispered. "Let us be together until you tire of me." She heard his sharp intake of breath. He ran his fingers roughly through his hair.

"You deserve better," he growled. In the illumination of a passing street lamp, she saw his mouth was grim again though his tone was light. "I hear you will be the toast of the town, if you aren't already. Bath was too small to hold you."

He could not distract her that way. "I have never cared for such things and you know it."

"You will find someone you need not have courage to love."

"I will love only you." She said the words. They too were final. She hoped he could hear that in her voice. "Tell me you do not care for me in return," she challenged.

"Not the point. Many can love, but . . . things stand in the way." He sagged into the squabs.

"Don't give the gift, if that is the barrier. I will take any years you offer until I grow too old to be attractive to you." Did he know that would be the hardest sacrifice of all?

His eyes grew tender for a moment, as though he would say that age didn't matter. Then he took a breath. "That would tear us both apart. No, our story may be the stuff of tragedy to us, but it is unimportant in the grander sweep of time, believe me."

"You can throw away what we have together?" she whispered.

His jaw clenched. "You will feel this way again with someone more suitable."

Sarah froze. He *would* throw it all away. The carriage began to slow. They were nearing the hotel. In another moment, he would hand her out of the carriage and out of his life. "I so wish I had taken your gift when you offered it that night," she blurted. "Don't leave me with a lifetime of regret for my cowardice."

"If you had taken what I so rashly offered, you would be wishing me at the devil. I know you don't believe that. And you think your regret will always be as sharp as it is now. But all things fade, dear Sarah, even in a single lifetime." Sadness crept into his harsh tone.

The carriage stopped. Sarah's eyes filled with tears. He refused to be convinced. Then he opened the door and stepped down. He took her arm and led her up to the bright doorway of the hotel where the doormen waited. They swung the doors wide. She stopped and turned to him. As she looked up into his face, her tears spilled over in frustration. She could feel despair lurking just beyond the edges of her mind. She must think of some last word to change his mind.

"Good-bye, lovely Sarah," he whispered. One hand touched her chin. He bent and brushed his lips across her forehead. She imagined a fiery brand would still be visible there when she looked into a mirror. Her breast began to convulse in sobs, as he jerked away and stepped into the coach. He pulled the door after him and disappeared into the darkness without a backward look.

Sarah stared after the carriage long after it had rounded the corner. Tears streamed openly down her face. Her breath came in halting gasps.

"Fraulein? Are you all right?" one of the doormen called in halting English. With a start she realized what a sight she was. Shaking her head, she stumbled past their curiosity and through the lobby, up the stairs to the refuge of her rooms.

Chapter Nineteen

Sarah ran up to her room and bolted the door behind her. Panting more than her mad dash warranted, she tore off her fine white dress to get into her nightclothes. He had rejected her, just as she had so foolishly rejected him so long ago in Bath. She had told him all, stripped bare her heart. She had done everything she could, and still it wasn't enough. A sob crept into her throat. Now she would never see him again. He would make sure of that. Already she felt empty. She had no home. Bath meant nothing to her. Madame Gessande was her only friend.

Pulling her nightdress over her head, she turned down the lamp and dove under the quilts. The only light in the room was the flicker of the fire in the grate. She trembled as she clutched the covers about her, but not from cold. She barely heard the scratching at the door.

Madame Gessande called softly, "Are you asleep, *cherie?* Did Davinoff bring you home?"

She could not answer, but something in her reached for human connection. A sob escaped her almost against her will.

"What has happened?" Madame fussed, coming in to sit upon the bed.

"He doesn't want me," Sarah sobbed.

"Oh dear." Madame rocked Sarah and patted her shoulders through the racking sobs. After a while Sarah subsided into tortured gasps, and Madame held her away to look into her eyes. "I could have sworn he loved you, *petite*. I have seen men in love before and this one had the look if ever I have seen it. He wouldn't get over something like that in a few weeks."

Sarah hiccuped and Madame provided a handkerchief from her reticule. "Oh, he loves me, underneath it all." she said then blew her nose resoundingly.

"So, what can the problem be?" Madame asked with some incredulity.

"He . . . he thinks we are too different." Sarah knew it would sound inconsequential.

"Oh Lord, never tell me he's being noble! Foolish boy! You'll not make me believe he's low-born, or that it would make a difference to either of you if he were."

"It's not that kind of difference, Madame," Sarah said in a small voice.

"Then what?" the woman asked, holding Sarah's shoulders. Sarah owed her more of the truth. "He . . . he has a disease, Madame," she stuttered. "It would be . . . distasteful to some."

"And you once expressed distaste?"

Sarah nodded. "I recoiled from him in Bath." But Madame still misunderstood.

"He should know that where one partner has syphilis, you simply make adjustments."

"It isn't anything like that." Sarah sighed. "It is a disease of the blood."

"So that's how he knew so much about George Upcott's specialty," Madame mused. She examined Sarah. "You have decided you can live with it?"

"I could even share it."

"You have told him so, I take it."

Sarah nodded once more, and closed her eyes. They felt sore and swollen, like her heart.

"This heroism is misplaced. I shall talk with him. I found out tonight where he lives."

Sarah sighed. Madame would find Julien gone. Neither of them would see him again.

"You get some sleep, *petite*," Madame whispered, and kissed her cheek. "All is not lost." She rose and tiptoed out of the room, leaving Sarah, sleepless, to her thoughts.

They told her she would have to learn to live without Julien.

In the wee hours of the morning, as the fire burned its last gasping coals in the grate, Sarah began to grow angry. He *did* love her! She was sure of it. As each word tonight, each expression replayed in her memory, she grew more certain of what she had told Madame instinctively. Didn't the gift of the little flying machine from Leonardo whisper to her that they must, together, try the impossible? She could not believe his choice of that most symbolic gift was accidental. Hadn't he, at one point, believed enough in a life together to leave her the Roman chalice? It was a chalice made for ceremonial drinking. What *could* it mean to Julien but drinking blood? That chalice was a promise and a challenge. It had drawn her across a continent. He might have lost his courage, but she had not.

He could not doubt *she* loved him when she had trekked halfway across the world to find him. No, he did not doubt her love. What could it be? He said the Companion found out the smallness in one and magnified it. Ahhh. Like the mushroom in Sienna. That gave her pause. Did he think she would become like that dreadful red-haired woman, killing wantonly? She sat up in her bed and purposely let the light-filled memories of Sienna wash over her, and acceptance. She had enjoyed it. She had enjoyed what human bodies could do together. And while the mushroom had robbed her of the will to stop those visions of Corina's sick torture—they had seemed unreal—Julien had taught her that she did not enjoy another's pain. Everyone had darkness inside, but making love wasn't that darkness. It was something she had never understood until she'd made love to Julien. Humans were created to make love to one another, to embrace abandon as well as control, the physical as well as the spiritual. It was their complexity, their destiny, maybe even the way that they were most like God. Julien was wrong. Sarah wasn't Magda, or Corina. She was just finding out that she was Sarah, and Sarah alone.

Julien thought power corrupted. But *he* lived with that power. Why couldn't she learn to do so? His doubt made her angry all over again. Why had she not brought him to book for his misgivings? She'd sat in that carriage like a dumb beast being led to slaughter.

It was forbidden to make a vampire, he'd said. But he had made the redhead. And he was not a man to let anything stand in his way. She would not accept that excuse.

What *was* standing in his way? Why had he rejected her? She lay there in the faintly graying light, her tears gone. He knew she was not like Magda. In the end, Julien was afraid, as she had been, that there were too many obstacles. Was he protecting her from the consequence of their love? Or was he trying to protect himself? She was the strong one now. She looked inside and marveled for a moment. She knew she must say to him what she had not said in the carriage. He must hear what she thought of his cowardice. She must have courage for them both.

She reviewed again every detail of that evening. She knew where he was going. He was going to Mirso Monastery, wherever that was. That gave her heart. But there were too many things she didn't know. Who forbade the giving of blood? Why did the Companion change one? There were dozens of questions. Almost the only thing she did know was how to start defining what was yet unclear. Julien said Khalenberg had sinned as well. That meant there was one at least in Vienna who knew more about Julien's kind than she did, including, no doubt, the precise location of Mirso Monastery.

The next morning Sarah ordered one trunk repacked and taken downstairs. She took only traveling clothes and the treasures Julien had left her. As she approached the concierge desk, the entire staff buzzed with excitement. "I should like to ask a direction," she announced to the impeccably dressed man obviously in charge.

"How may we help you?" He made a shushing motion to the two young men behind him.

"I wish to send a note to a Mr. Khalenberg." The man's stricken look took her up sharply.

"Fraulein doesn't know?" he gasped. "There were terrible

murders last night in the Stephanplatz. Terrible."

"Torn limb from limb, all of them," a young man behind him announced with relish.

Sarah felt faint. Hadn't Julien said that was one way to kill a vampire? The concierge glared at his assistant. "Who was killed?" she whispered. Julien? Khalenberg? The one was unthinkable, the other might derail her quest.

"Johann Villach, and several less respectable characters," the concierge confided.

Sarah sighed. Not Julien. Not Khalenberg. "What has this to do with Mr. Khalenberg?"

"Villach is one of Khalenberg's 'familiars.' They form a triangle with Magda Ravel," the young man behind the concierge blurted.

"Back to your work with you," the concierge ordered. The two others retreated reluctantly.

Villach must be the blond man who had left Magda. A familiar. Sarah knew what that meant. She remembered Khalenberg's ashen face in the lobby of the concert hall. Was Villach Khalenberg's sin? And who had killed him? "Was Miss Ravel injured?" she asked.

"*Nein*," the concierge answered. "But she is nowhere to be found."

Sarah sighed in relief. "Is Mr. Khalenberg implicated?" she asked. She could not see the hawk-faced man in a gaol cell.

"Of course not, Fraulein! He was at the theater. The murders were at the Stephanplatz."

Sarah did not enlighten him as to how someone like Khalenberg could seem to be in two places at once. "I should send my condolences," she said. She was going to see a man who might well tear people limb from limb. Sarah knew she must go to the address the concierge printed on a card immediately, before her knees or her courage failed her. She hoped Khalenberg would see her. Julien would be her calling card. But what then? How did one press a creature such as this and come out whole?

Sarah sat stiffly in a brocaded chair next to a window that looked out upon the Graben and waited. All doubt was gone now, if not all fear. Her way lay through Khalenberg's drawing room. Whatever trials might be presented, she must pass them before she could go on. Danger pressed palpably on two fronts. He might refuse to see her. If he did, she would have to coerce information from him.

Khalenberg entered at last, all angular disapproval. She thought he still looked ravaged. His face was parchment white, his eyes deep-set in hollows, whether because he had lost a lover or rid himself of a problem at great personal cost, she could not tell. In either case he was a man who had himself rigidly under control. "He is gone, you know," he said without preamble.

"Yes," she returned, mustering her courage. It would never do to show fear.

"Then why are you here?"

"I want to know things that only one of his kind can tell me," she answered. Her knowledge was the first salvo in this siege. She had the satisfaction of seeing him start.

"So he told you what he is," he returned harshly. "This had gone further than I thought."

"He did not have to tell me." She saw curiosity flick through Khalenberg's gray eyes and rushed on, her words tumbling over themselves. "He was too ill to control the manifestations. I saw everything, and guessed what he must be."

Khalenberg looked at her strangely. "You interest me." He sat in a wing chair opposite her and deliberately crossed his long legs.

Sarah took a breath and plunged ahead. No threats and no orders to leave yet. "You know he loves me. I love him. You advised him against sharing his Companion with me. Why?"

"I reminded him of his obligation." Khalenberg's mouth twisted.

She pressed on. "What is his obligation?" Only if she pushed him beyond what he was willing to tell her would she find what she needed.

"He is not allowed to spread the Companion."

"And not allowed to share the power," Sarah observed, then silently cursed herself.

Khalenberg grunted. "Davinoff was mistaken. You are all alike. You want the power."

"No, that is *not* it," she returned fiercely. "*I* was the one who first refused his blood. You think everyone wants immortality? What is this power you speak of, anyway?" she sputtered. "You pop in and out of places and make people do as you wish. But look what it has done to you and Julien! Bored wanderers, cynical, belonging to no one. I cannot believe you are happy."

Sarah was shocked at her outburst. She waited for Khalenberg to order her to leave or to advance upon her with glowing eyes. Instead, cultivating boredom with apparent difficulty, he said, "There are periodic liaisons, some more intense than others."

So intense you sinned by sharing blood, Sarah thought. "You are bitter because it did not work between you and Villach," she observed, finding the strength to speak.

"It never works," he rasped. His anguish was so palpable, Sarah was suddenly sure he had been the one to dispatch his once-lover. Khalenberg rose, as if to end the interview. "But all this is neither here nor there. You will never find Davinoff now." She could see he felt he had said too much already.

Now was the time for her trump card. "I know he has gone to Mirso Monastery," she announced with seeming assurance. "And I intend to follow him."

Khalenberg spun on his heel and glowered at her. "Foolish chit!" he exclaimed. "You have no idea what you do. What you want would only bring disaster."

"Tell me why," Sarah pleaded. "Tell me why or kill me. For my mind is quite made up."

Khalenberg glared at her. She lifted her chin and returned the vampire's stare. A silence stretched between them until his lips twisted in a grimace that might have been a smile. "Davinoff would not look favorably upon the easiest solution. As well you know."

Sarah realized she had been holding her breath. Now he would try to frighten her with all the most chilling details of vampirism. His straight back and uncompromising gray eyes said that at least he would not lie. "Tell me why Magda murders people," she asked.

Khalenberg laughed. "She likes the taste of the last drop. With the ebbing of life there comes a feeling of ultimate power. You draw strength for your Companion, then from your Companion. The life passes from a victim's body to yours. It is a very seductive feeling."

"Very well. She is addicted to an experience that is immoral. Did the Companion make her that way, or was it always there in her?"

"Whatever is there is magnified by the use of power."

"Julien says sharing blood is forbidden. Who forbids it?" This she must know.

"The Elders, those at the Source. They are Powers to be reckoned with, far beyond anything you have known in your small world."

Sarah got her imagination under control with difficulty and stopped constructing nightmares. "How were you and Julien made if no one shared their blood?"

"We got the Companion from our mothers."

"Was it always so? Who were the first?" Khalenberg had a mother?

"You have too many questions, Fraulein." Khalenberg frowned. "The Companion came from the Source, a fountain sprung from rock. The Elders built the monastery around it."

"If the fountain contains the parasite," she mused, rising, "Why do you bother to share blood with those you make? Would it not be easier to drink the water from the fountain?"

"Do not think of stealing immortality, young woman," Khalenberg warned. "If you take the Companion, you die unless you also have the blood of a vampire."

"Why?" she asked. "And why do you survive it?"

"You want to know more than is good for you." Khalenberg sighed, but he continued. "When the Companion enters the body, it wars with the blood there. Only a few of the First Ones to drink the water survived. They became immune, and our kind was born. We share that immunity, as well as the Companion itself, when we share the blood. The blood is the life." He said it as though it were a benediction. "In the soft modern world no one survives the Companion without infusions of a vampire's blood to follow. The death that ensues is really quite terrible."

Sarah swallowed hard, and turned her thoughts back to the startling fact that Khalenberg had a mother. "It is hard to imagine a child vampire." She saw chubby cheeks stained with blood.

"There are no more children now," he said stiffly.

"None of your people had any more children?" she asked, stunned.

"What need of children when you live forever? And who would condemn a child to this life? No, they stopped condemning children right after Davinoff and Beatrix Lisse," he grated. "At first we chose to prevent it. But as more of us joined the Old Ones and the pool of eligible mates contracted, it seemed it was no longer possible." His voice was matter-of-fact.

"No renewal," she murmured. "No one from outside, no children. How empty."

"And what if there were thousands made as we are?" Khalenberg barked. "If everyone had a Companion to satisfy, there would be no satisfying any of them. That is why there is only one of us allowed in a city. We must be discreet."

She sighed. "Is there no way around the drinking of blood?"

"Julien hoped to make the blood someday," Khalenberg sneered. "He was dreaming. The Old Ones meditate to cut down what they need. But there is no dispensation from our curse."

She thought she would have to prod him, but he seemed to want to tell her more now.

"Finding blood constantly becomes a strain. Some like their victims to struggle. Personally, I go to them at night. They think it is a fever dream of passion. No struggle at all. It is a passionate act, the taking of blood. There is a bond between the giver and the taker, however brief. Then we move on, looking for the next new face to satisfy the need. It dulls the senses, after a while, to their humanity. There is only the need, and the act of slaking it, the momentary passion." His eyes seemed to see through to her soul. "Does this frighten you?"

"Yes," she said, in a voice she wished were more sure. "But I haven't changed my mind."

He looked at her narrowly. "You know all this, yet you persist?"

"I will be with him, at any cost," she whispered.

A shadow of pain passed over his face. He stared at her for a long moment. "I think you believe what you say, at any rate," he said shortly. Then after a moment, "You are not what I imagined you would be. It is perhaps lucky Davinoff is out of your reach."

"I will find him, Herr Khalenberg. I expect that Mirso Monastery is somewhere in the Carpathian Mountains. You may save me time if you tell me where, but with you or without you, I will find him." She let her resolve seep through her and overcome her dread of his anger.

"Do you know, young woman, *why* he has gone to Mirso Monastery?" Khalenberg stared down at her under his fierce brows.

"He wants to take the redheaded woman there."

"A side benefit only. He wants to take the Vow and lock himself away from the world. He is lost to you now. Once he takes the Vow, he can never set foot outside the gates again."

Sarah suppressed her shock. "Surely he can renounce his oath!"

"You do not know the Old Ones. The Vow is permanent. You will only torment him if you find him. He cannot return your regard from inside a monastic cell."

"Why did you not tell me?" she cried, her fear of the man forgotten. "He is only hours ahead of me. Save me time, Herr Khalenberg. Tell me where I may find Mirso Monastery!"

"Have you not heard all I have been telling you?" Khalenberg asked, his patience evaporated. "It is forbidden to give you the Companion. You have said yourself it would be onerous to you. In any case, when you arrive it will be too late and your presence can only cause him pain. Can you not leave well enough alone?"

He was right, of course. What could she say? But she mustn't give in to dumb submission as she had in the coach with Julien. She looked up at Khalenberg, depending upon intuition now for guidance. "You saw me today hoping to find I was a despicable creature," she said slowly. "You tried to frighten me so I would give up my search, though you say Julien is beyond my reach. Do you wish to tell me why, Herr Khalenberg, or shall I guess?"

"I want you to go home willingly to your backwater in Bath." Khalenberg let his gaze play fiercely over her face. "I want to give you a dose of reality."

"You want proof there are no choices, Herr Khalenberg," Sarah corrected, wondering at her burst of courage. "You want confirmation that I am either a self-serving power seeker or a frightened child. You want Julien to be wrong about love, and you to be right."

"What do you know of the feelings of our kind?" Khalenberg almost wailed. "You should leave this house, Fraulein, before I tire of your impudence."

Sarah did not mistake this final sally for strength. "You have loved, Herr Khalenberg," she said on impulse. He turned to the window. His knuckles whitened as he gripped the brocade of the draperies. "I know it did not end well. But some piece of your heart still yearns to find love. You sacrificed all rules, all doubts once on the chance of happiness. I know it. And some part of you you would deny, would do it all again." She took a breath. "Well, I am at that point, Herr Khalenberg. I know all is ranged against us. To protect me, he has thrown away both our futures. But it is too late for protection. I have already risked my entire life's happiness. My only chance of winning back is to face all the other obstacles." She sighed. "I am neither an adventuress nor a frightened child. Do not deny the possibility of love, for us, or for yourself. Tell me," she pleaded, and let her heart flutter upon her sleeve. It was the only argument that remained. "I may yet intercept him."

She watched his silent back until it sagged out of its accustomed stiffness.

"Outside the village of Tirgu Korva, between Sibiu and Horazu." The harsh, clipped words, torn from his throat, were music to her. "Take the Danube as far as the Iron Gate."

She wanted to cry. The first test was passed. But Julien was just the kind of man who would let a monastic vow stand in the way of love. "You won't regret this, Herr Khalenberg," she said, as she let herself out of the double doors

"We will all regret this," drifted from the form leaning against the window.

Chapter Twenty

Sarah was amazed to arrive alive at a little inn that evening. The long boat ride up the Danube had ended in Moldova Veche, where she had managed, with her Romanian phrase book, to engage two brothers, young Stefan, who spoke a little Latin, and his fearsome brother Mihai, to take her as far as Horazu. Her coin had bought her passage, but did it not also proclaim that she was worth robbing? She had dressed as a peasant boy, hoping that would insulate her from the danger of traveling alone. Still, as their cart wound its way past the frothing narrows of the Iron Gate she expected the brothers to stop and do their worst at every turn. The gruesome Mihai, of scarred face and stoic mien, had not said a word and Stefan found Latin laborious so their journey was silent as they made their way into a forest reminiscent of wolves dressed like your grandmother and witches who killed children. She had cradled the little pistol she had bought in Vienna in the pocket of her coat, and tried to remember Mihai's gruff promise to deliver her to Horazu. But all she could recall was his appraising look. Her nerves frayed raw.

That night at the inn Sarah went down to supper with mixed

feelings. A spotted mirror told her that her disguise was still in place, but still she felt transparent. Only a gold coin had stilled the landlady's questions. She wore her coat over her shirt and vest to be certain her breasts would not reveal her and smoothed her hair up into her round cap. She had to go down to dinner. If Julien had passed this way, she might get word of him. She prompted Stefan to ask the other guests about her quarry and sat at the common table between the two brothers.

There were perhaps eight other guests at the inn. Sarah could feel their eyes upon her. She tried to concentrate on the sorrel soup served with a dollop of soured cream, the calf's brains with rosemary and mushrooms, and a meat and vegetable dish called *kachen*, all washed down with stout ale. She kept her head down and her cap on. But soon the party grew raucous. One of the men called her "boy" in a loud voice, his guffaws revealing rotted teeth. His tone said he knew the truth. Taunting tones around the table urged him to action. Sarah didn't know whether to run from the table and trust he wouldn't follow, or stand her ground.

Then, next to her, the silent Mihai took out his long knife, curved just at the end. It gleamed along the edge where it had been sharpened. Mihai's eyes never left his plate as he skewered a piece of pork with his fork and sliced it with the great knife. Eyes around the table followed the knife back and forth until Mihai laid it down next to his plate. The man with the broken teeth sat down abruptly amid a smattering of nervous laughter.

Sarah snatched a glance at Mihai's frightening countenance. It revealed no more than it had all day. In some ways, by his action, he had claimed her. But for what?

Sarah stared at the backs of the two brothers as the cart jolted along the track the next morning. They lurched along the frozen ruts as the track rose through a steep gorge. The world she knew seemed far away now. Julien must be long before her, but she had no trace, no word of him. Perhaps he was already lost to her. She was suspended between the life she had known and the unknown ahead, able to reach neither.

As the cart came round a blind curve, Sarah was startled into awareness. The huge lout with the blackened teeth from the inn last night blocked their way. He stood in the snowy road brandishing an old fowling piece that had seen better days. The grin that revealed his chipped and rotting teeth was not a smile of welcome.

"Stop," he yelled in Romanian. Sarah understood only that he was threatening, but she could guess what he wanted. The cart lurched to a stop. She fingered the heavy little gun in her right pocket for comfort and glanced at her companions. Mihai seemed hardly to register their situation except by a certain narrowing of his eyes. Young Stefan, however, was shocked. The man with the blackened teeth strode up to the wagon. Mihai peered into the thick forest on the right and down the steep slope of the gorge to the left. There was no escape for the cart.

Mihai jumped down and came to the back of the cart. He held up a callused hand and motioned her to get down. She shook her head violently. They were going to give her to this villain, just like that! Was she worth so little to them, even for the value of her purse? She glanced back at Stefan, but he seemed frozen. Mihai motioned once again and grunted. Well, she wouldn't go without a fight, she thought furiously. Then her brain cleared. But not with Mihai. That would do no good. She only had two bullets in the double chamber of the little gun before she would have to reload. No, she would wait until Mihai and Stefan left them and she was alone with the other man. She willed herself to be capable of shooting someone. Even if she killed him, she would be alone in the middle of a snowy forest, easy prey to the next villain she met.

Shaking, she jumped to the snowy, rutted road, disdaining Mihai's proffered hand. Glaring at Mihai, she turned to face the robber. Mihai took her arm, in spite of her efforts to shake him off, and marched her toward the grinning man, who still waived his ancient gun. When they were about three feet away, he let her go and pushed her toward the robber. The man reached out and grabbed her right arm as she stumbled in the snow. She could feel the rancid breath of his rotting teeth as he drew her close.

All thought of waiting vanished when she felt him grip her arm and smelled his body. From that moment, she could not plan. She could not think. She just rebelled. Frenzied, she struggled to break his grasp. He grunted in surprise and tried to draw her close, but she kicked out to keep him at bay. He held her right arm. She could not get her gun. Her panic almost engulfed her. She tried to reach around with her left hand, but the pocket faced the wrong way. They turned and slipped in the snow like awkward dancers. Sarah shrieked and growled, all reason gone. She had only the urge to freedom and the need to get her gun. She lurched to her knees in the wet snow. The robber raised his own gun to bring the butt down upon her head. She watched it descend in slow motion. This would be the end of her small insurrection.

She jerked to one side. It would not be enough. Her fingers fumbled their way to her gun at last. She raised it, left-handed, to her attacker's midsection. The blow reached her, but the power had gone. His face above her slackened. The butt of the gun glanced off her shoulder. Her grunt of pain sounded distant. She almost collapsed to the snow in his loosening grip. She watched her finger pull the trigger. An explosion erased all other sound. Her body jerked back as the tiny gun slammed against her. Her persecutor slumped slowly to his knees, to reveal Mihai, standing impassively behind him. Blood ran out between the robber's broken teeth as she stared into his glazing eyes not six inches from her face. To her horror, he slowly sagged against her. She made a small sound of terror and wriggled away. The bone handle of Mihai's wondrous knife stood at attention in the robber's back.

Without a word, without even looking at her, Mihai grabbed the handle of his knife and pulled it out of the man's back. The gleaming silver now was streaked in red. It dripped into the trampled snow, leaving pink dots about, like a sprig muslin dress Corina once had. Mihai rolled the man onto his back with one toe, then bent to wipe his knife on the rough fabric of the man's coat. His fingers strayed to a small black hole with the torn edges. He raised his eyes to Sarah.

Sarah slowly put her hand to her mouth. Her stomach rebelled at what she had done, at what Mihai had done. She clutched the pistol to her breast for comfort and leaned over, gasping for air. From a distance, she heard someone calling out "*Doamna, doamna,*" over and over again, the Romanian word for addressing a married woman. Then Stefan was by her side. He

said something in Latin. She couldn't understand him. *Lea*
He wanted to leave this place. He tried gently to take her g
from her, but she shook her head and clutched it tightly as
lifted her up.

She could not take her eyes from the body as Mihai drag
it to the side of the road. She had killed someone, someone w
had been alive just a moment ago.

By the time they got her back in the cart she was crying.
sobs, just tears. "You were brave," Stefan said in Latin. Mi
wrapped a blanket around her, gun and all. Stefan handed
her hat. She realized her hair cascaded down her shoulders.
secret was gone, if secret it had ever been. Then the cart v
jolting over the rutted, snowy road as fast as it could go.

They made good time that day, in spite of the narrow mou
tain roads, as they raced away from that place of death. Sa
came to herself slowly. The strange lassitude receded and v
replaced by a throbbing in her shoulder. She could hardly
her arms to wind her hair back into her hat. She put her g
back in her pocket. Mihai still clucked to the horse with
turning round. Stefan looked anxiously at her from time to tir

They had saved her. For themselves? Then why not rob
and take whatever else they wanted while they might blame
body on the other man? She couldn't think. She hardly ev
cared anymore who was an enemy and who a friend. Her jo
ney continued. She had survived to take the next step. She
not know whether she had killed the thief, or if it was Mih
knife. And really it didn't matter. She could have killed hi
would have killed him. Therefore it was just the same as if s
did. She wondered if that had always been there in her, t
possibility. She thought a lot that afternoon about Sienna a
Corina.

Julien stood at the one uncovered window of the round tov
room looking out at the stars, a goblet filled with wine in
hand. The window overlooked the valley a thousand feet belc
Heavy velvet hangings at the other windows were drawn sh
against the cold. The room was furnished with a great b
whose posts were carved with twining grape leaves and che
bim, a large chest and wardrobe in rough, dark wood, an

table with two chairs in the corner. A fire burned in the grate. Besides the one candle sitting on the table, it was the only light. He listened to footsteps trudge up the worn, winding stairs into the tower. They were carrying weight. It must be the Eldest One. Father Rubius didn't wait for an answer to his knock before he opened it.

"Not meditating on your Vow, boy?" Rubius asked to announce his presence.

Julien did not even turn his head. "The Vow will come soon enough, Father," he grunted and tossed back the rest of his wine.

"Magda has calmed somewhat. Brother Flavio thinks introspection will profit her."

Julien's laugh was ugly. "She pays for my sin as well as I."

"Your deed was a sin. But it is a lesson to us on the evils of giving the Companion. And she may yet come through it. May I sit down?"

Julien came to the table, poured a glass of wine, and gestured magnanimously to one of the chairs. "But don't lecture me upon my drinking. Soon I begin the ascetic life." He sauntered over to the chest to put the empty bottle with its many fellows. "Eat, drink, and be merry, for tomorrow we die." His voice was harsh. "Well, not exactly."

Father Rubius pursed his lips and tapped his finger upon the table. He seemed to be thinking. "You . . . do not seem to be quiet in your mind, boy."

"Is it not enough that I am willing?" Quiet might never be his again.

"I have seen many come to take the Vow. I am the Eldest. Never forget that."

Julien glanced at the countenance some would call jolly, the round belly, and saw the iron below the surface. He sat at the table. "Forgive me, Father," he muttered.

Father Rubius smiled and shook his head. "Aspirants have already renounced the world by the time they reach us. They are ready to accept our discipline."

"I accept the discipline, Father." Julien forced his voice to calm.

Father Rubius stared at him with old, keen eyes. "You are not a shining example of acceptance. You want to burn out the passion in your soul, and we are a conveniently hot poker."

"Perhaps, like Magda, I may yet come through." He swirled the wine in his glass.

"I have been struggling with myself since you returned. I am not certain you are ready."

Julien glanced up. "Do not deny me, Father," he whispered. "It is all I have left."

"I am not so sure." Father Rubius pushed his bulk up out of the chair. He paced the stone floor. For perhaps a minute, maybe more, his footsteps made the only sound in the room. At last, he stopped and turned to face the younger man. "Tell me the true reason you seek us out, Davinoff. You are one of the youngest. I did not think to see you for a thousand years."

"I have never been good at confessions," Julien demurred. "You have heard the sordid details from many others, in any case." He tossed off most of the wine he had just poured.

Father Rubius did not disagree with him. Nor did he change his requirement. He wanted a confession. Julien lifted his eyes to the Old One's. He could feel the ancient blue eyes start, slowly, lightly, to demand. This was to be a demonstration of the humility required of an aspirant, no doubt. Julien had always responded poorly to demands. Hie eyes sparked and snapped with resistance before he could prevent them. Father Rubius demanded again, in a crescendo of seesawing wills. Julien jerked away. What purpose did it serve to challenge the Elder?

"Now, what has brought you here?" Rubius asked calmly. But his breath was coming fast.

Confession was now set as the price of entrance into their society. There was a long period of silence, as Julien leaned against the window embrasure to look out across the valley. Father Rubius waited. Why not? He had all the time in the world. "There was a woman," Julien said finally. "God, but that sounds trite."

"It wasn't?" Father Rubius prompted, sighing. He had apparently heard it all before.

"I wonder how many women I have known?" Davinoff asked of no one in particular. "A thousand, five? But none like her."

"A beauty?" Father Rubius asked. He seemed bored.

"No, not a beauty in the usual sense."

"It was her intellect took your fancy, then."

Julien chuckled. "She would hate to be thought a bluestocking." After a moment he continued, "I don't know precisely why there are none like her."

When nothing else seemed to be forthcoming, Father Rubius said, "Not good enough, Davinoff. This does not convince me you are ready. She found you out? She was horrified?"

It was Julien's turn to stride about the room. "It is an old story," he blurted finally. "Long after all had grown dull, I wandered the world, expecting nothing but the worst. In my time I have been angry at my fate and I quenched my anger in the blood of war. I played the artist until I found art meaningless. I became a bored collector of things that could not satisfy me. Then I reveled in the fact that there was no value. I thought complete freedom might be a substitute. I sank to bestial enjoyments. I tried everything, and nothing sufficed. When I thought I needed someone who could understand my trials, I made a woman in my own image, twice in fact, in all the years. The first committed suicide, the second was Magda. After that, there was nothing left."

"Now you sound like an Aspirant. Why else did I found the monastery except to help poor creatures who were brought to such a pass? Was this girl the first you made?"

Julien stopped pacing. He went back to the window and gazed out at the moon, small and distant in the night sky. "No. She found me weak and helpless, and helped me. She was tender, giving, even to a creature such as I. She accepted me, knowing everything, though I must surely be a monster in her eyes. She became a friend. She even grew to love me. But more than that"—he searched for words—"she gave me new eyes with which to see the world." He put his hands over his face. Drawing a ragged breath, he said, "I caught a glimpse of a life I had never known. It only occurred to me later it could never be mine."

Father Rubius was appalled. "You are still attached to the world! You must resolve this, Davinoff. You must go back to wherever it was you left her and resolve your feelings about living before you take the Vow. You have unfinished business."

Julien turned on him. "You don't understand, Father. I offered to share the Companion with her. I was weak. Thank the gods she refused it and by the time I saw her in Vienna, I had come to my senses. I know it is wrong, and wrong for her. Look at the results of my last disobedience! I will not repeat my indiscretion. But I cannot trust myself to 'finish' this business." He turned back to the window. "The Vow is all that is left to me."

Father Rubius sat in stunned silence. Finally he said, "I did not know you had committed the Crime twice, and nearly a third time. We forgave your sin with Magda because you brought her here and you were contrite. Any new lapse would bring down our wrath." Father Rubius let his voice fill with command. "You would be a double outcast, reviled by the world who doesn't understand you and exiled from the solace of the only ones who share your nature. It is the most terrible of fates, one known by only a few of us, in all my years."

"I understand," Julien said softly. "I will be fine, once I have taken the Vow."

Father Rubius rose. "The sooner the better," he said shortly. "We will find a way to cleanse you of the desire for this girl." He strode from the room.

Julien poured another glass of wine, and turned once again to the window.

The way to Tirgu Korva wound always upward. It was reached by roads still barely passable in April and so narrow they could hardly accommodate a cart. A dozen times Sarah almost slipped over some precipice into oblivion. She had left the brothers in Horazu. They were so fearful of Tirgu Korva, she couldn't ask them to take her there. Stefan helped her buy a horse, even as he tried to talk her out of going on. She only won acceptance when she told them she needed someone trustworthy to look after her trunks. She took only the chalice, bound into her coat, and abandoned the rest with instructions that the brothers could have them if she didn't return in four days. They stuffed her pockets with garlic and put a fragrant herb Mihai bought from an old hag in her cap. It was wolfsbane. That was daunting.

But she would not lose courage now. She gave Stefan a hug, and kissed Mihai's scarred cheek. With only her horse and the wolfsbane for company, she toiled up the pass to Tirgu Korva.

For the first time in the course of her journey, she met no one, either coming or going, though some carts had surely been through there, for there were ruts to guide her own progress. Now there was only the silence of the snow, and the wind soughing through the trees. She scanned the road and the woods, for what she could not tell.

Sarah began to be affected by the palpable dread in the air. The anger that had sustained her through all of her journey slowly drained away. All the dark hints Julien had dropped about the nature of his homeland, of his kind, all the information she had gleaned from Khalenberg, rolled around in her mind until it seemed she might be riding into hell itself. And for what? Even if he was not yet initiated into the monastery, what chance did she have with Julien? He was the stuff of myths, and she had never felt smaller.

It was coming on to darkness as she rounded a final bend. Wet and cold, dispirited, she still could not help but gasp. Across a little valley at the base of a breathtaking mountain of sheer stone, lights winked in the little village that must be Tirgu Korva. And looming above it was a wondrously carved and turreted structure, growing out of the stone of the mountain. Its complicated spires reached sinuously for the sky, its massive base rooted in the mountain. Mirso Monastery. Sarah was mesmerized. She had never seen anything remotely like it.

The horse, forgotten, edged nervously to a stop. Sarah suppressed a shudder. She was sorely tempted to turn right around and go back. But that would have made her fearful journey all for naught. If she went forward she might face death, or something worse. At the least there might be rejection, final this time and irrevocable. But could she do less than everything there was to do in search of her future? If she had done everything, perhaps even if her reward was not to be a life with Julien, she would have left some shred of herself. It would be a shred she had not had before she met him, before she opened the door on Sienna, before she took him from Corina, before she walked down into the darkness of the cellar at the Dower House.

She gave the horse his office to start and, after some sidling reluctance, he trotted down into the hollow in which the village lay, snorting nervously. Sarah grew calmer. Her thoughts returned again to Corina. Did Corina, in the silence of her convent in Lyon, have the courage to journey inside and find the balance she needed? Sarah was amazed to think she had once been in awe of Corina. No longer. But, for better or for worse, she saw clearly now what she shared with her friend. She too would do anything to get what she wanted. She thought she could drink blood. She knew she could kill a man. Poor Corina. She sent a silent thought out over the still air toward Lyon. *I understand you, finally. And I wish for you that you will make yourself whole.*

Sharp air filled Sarah's lungs with cutting life as she came to the first rude buildings. She found a public house. Sore to the bone, she climbed down from the horse. The noise of people drinking wafted out into the cold. Behind the building the mountain and the monastery towered into the night. The moon had risen. In its light the fortresslike structure looked almost soft. The very stone seemed translucent in the moon's glow. As she watched, the effect was intensified by a light that flickered on in some cell, and then in another. The stone around the windows glowed. The two lights, in fair proximity, took on the aspect of eyes, shining into the dark to search out her soul. They were joined by another light, and still another, in differing parts of the fortress. The monastery seemed sentient as no building she had ever seen. The hair on the back of her neck prickled against her jacket.

Sarah jumped as the valley filled with an echoing howl, then clutched herself, wide-eyed, as one became three and then a dozen or a hundred. *Wolves*, she thought, *wolves on the hunt*.

She turned her eyes with effort to the coarse inn in front of her. The prospect of finding out just who lived in Tirgu Korva was not alluring. But the prospect of setting out for Mirso Monastery alone on foot in the dark and the freezing cold was less so. It was the villagers or the wolves. She took the great iron handle of the door and heaved it open.

Chapter Twenty-one

Inside the inn perhaps a half dozen men sat around a roaring fire, talking and laughing loudly. Their peasant garb still bore the grime of work. The atmosphere was thick with the smell of old sweat and paprika. A buxom woman carried spirits reeking of malt and barley to the fireside on a tray held at shoulder level, above the danger of wildly gesticulating arms. Upon Sarah's entry into the room, talk ceased as everyone turned startled faces toward her. Sarah stood just inside the door, out of place and feeling incredibly vulnerable. Her disguise as a boy seemed transparent; her carefully loaded gun, farcical. The men were of a piece, she saw, as she stared around the room. Black eyes, black hair, long straight noses, and rather thin lips. She wondered, with a queasy feeling, just how long the village had been isolated by its terrible reputation. The eyes turned hostile. Several men got up and started forward.

"I want to go to Mirso Monastery," she said in broken Romanian. She pointed up to where the translucent monolith must hover, unseen, behind the public house.

The landlord paused and turned back toward what must be his spouse as if he expected her to handle this strange intrusion.

The woman shook her head. "You don't want to go to Mirso Monastery," Sarah managed to make out of their colloquial Romanian.

She nodded. "Tonight," she managed to remember from her phrase book. She pulled a handful of coins from her pocket. The landlord and his wife threw dubious looks back to the crowd of men. The matter was discussed ardently, with the room apparently evenly divided between those who wanted to rob her and cut her throat, and those who were curious about why someone wanted to go to Mirso.

Only a man with a graying beard and swollen knuckles, quietly nursing his brew in the corner, seemed to be paying any attention to Sarah at all. Finally he stood up, and without a word, took a heavy coat down from an irregularly hewn peg in the wall. He walked forward, grunted to Sarah and motioned her to follow him. The room's cacophony subsided.

Sarah stood for a moment, irresolute. The man shrugged on his coat. As he grabbed the handle of the door, he looked back and barked an inquiry. She saw fierce black eyes and an ageless face. He might have been forty or seventy. His lip curled disdainfully as he waited for her decision. She roused herself from uncertainty. He was her way to the monastery. There were far worse choices in the room. She nodded briskly and stepped out into the cold behind him.

As he harnessed a shaggy horse to a cart with two giant wooden wheels, she examined her rough companion. His cap was pulled down low to protect him from the cold, his scarf was drawn across his mouth. But she could see his eyes. He seemed stoic about a journey to the monastery, almost unconcerned. In fact, none of the villagers had seemed afraid. There had been no gestures designed to ward off evil when she spoke its name.

What kind of men were they, who lived to serve the needs of such a monastery? What did they do? Grow food perhaps, raise livestock, and act as the workmen for the monks. She wondered why they didn't leave. But then where would they go? They were from Tirgu Korva and in the eyes of the world they were tainted, outcast. They were not vampires themselves. There was no aura of power about this man. He looked like a peasant—one who had seen much, but just a peasant all the same. And he did not guide her out of kindness. How did he serve his masters at Mirso Monastery by taking this intruder to their fortress?

As they wound up the mountain behind the nodding draft horse, she lost sight of the heavy stone structure made magic by the moon. But she could feel it there, hanging above them. Julien was there. Perhaps he had already taken his vow. Her heart shrank within her. Perhaps she would be turned away at the gates. Perhaps if she saw him, her words would shrivel within her. Whatever words she had once wished to say. She could not think what they were. Go back, she almost shouted to herself. You are not ready. But it was too late for that. They made the final hairpin turn and drew up to a small flat area before the monastery gates. The huge structure stretched above her into the dark, blotting out the stars. At close range, she could see the stone was of a kind of quartz or onyx. The light of the moon seemed to penetrate its surface and illuminate the floating flecks within. In the sunshine, it would positively sparkle. Massive doors, plaid with iron straps and dotted with huge studs, broke the stone. They looked as though they meant to lock out the world forever, or to lock something in.

Her impassive escort jumped down and made his way to the right of the huge doors. He seemed undaunted by the place. She scrambled down and trailed after him. In a niche, he found a bell pull and hoisted resolutely upon it. Into the silence a deep and resonant tolling rang out, a frightening breach of the sanctity of the night. At least no one could ignore their presence. The bell was no doubt heard even in the village, just visible far below.

As the echoes from those bells drained away, Sarah and her guide stood in silence in front of the doors that stretched above them. The world held no motion, no sound, only the remembrance of sound. Just when she had despaired of entering, she heard scratching sounds.

Suddenly, one of the great doors swung outward with surprising ease. Sarah leapt back to avoid its arc. A gray-robed and hooded figure, tiny against the scale of the doors, stood silently in the opening. Its face was shrouded in shadows, but Sarah could imagine piercing eyes, perhaps glowing red, if she could only make them out. Her escort stepped aside and motioned her in. She was now beyond his help, if he was ever wont to help her.

Slowly, she approached the robed figure. Lord, she felt as though she were walking through that dreadful novel by Mr. Walpole. Somehow that thought gave her courage to go on. Too bad Mr. Walpole had never had the opportunity to stand in the gateway of Mirso Monastery. It would have helped the power of his prose.

"I want to see Julien Davinoff," she said. Her words bounced back off the stone walls.

There was no answer. The figure simply turned and moved off into the darkness of a huge courtyard, silent and empty. She could not quite be sure it did not float, so quietly did it move. *My God*, she thought as it retreated. *Is this the moment when I must choose?* She stood, frozen, as the monk diminished in the darkness. She had to choose. . . . *Sarah*, she thought severely, *did you not choose to leave Bath? You chose in Vienna and at the tavern just moments ago. The day you stop choosing is the day you die*. With a feeling of casting herself over a precipice, she entered through the great portal. The monk had stopped to see whether she would follow or not. He did not beckon. He did not speak. He just stood, a sentinel or a beacon, waiting for her.

As she hurried into the darkened courtyard, she felt she was melting into the unreality of her setting, disappearing into some timeless nightmare that took no notice of the centuries passing in the valley below. The sudden sonorous bang of the giant doors behind her made her gasp and turn, hand held to her mouth as the echoes died around her. There was no escape now. She could see no one who might have shut the doors. She had thought that teeth chattering in fear was something made up in books. Evidently not. The figure turned and moved across the immense courtyard. Sarah followed.

In the middle of the courtyard a stone pool shimmered in the starlight. There were no ornate carvings, as there were at cathedral fonts. There were no ceremonial goblets, or altars, or podiums for preaching, just a stone circle and a pile of rough-hewn onyx rocks like the monastery itself, out of which water burbled up from somewhere below in a steady stream. Yet Sarah realized with dreadful certainty that this was the Source that Khalenberg had spoken of, the fountain of water that contained the parasite that made all vampires.

There was no evidence of the Companion who gave eternal life or terrible death, just the trickle of water. What would happen if she stooped to trail her fingers in it? When you were confronted with the ultimate in taboos, you were always tempted to disobey. But there was no point to disobedience. The waters could not grant her Julien's love.

The sound of a heavy wooden door opening at the far side of the courtyard made her realize she had fallen behind her escort. She was grateful for her breeches as she hurried ahead.

The monk disappeared inside the monastery itself. Sarah tiptoed into the darkness after him. He ascended some stone steps angled up the curved face of a wall that stretched above her into the gloom. As he lighted a torch that flickered and smoked at the landing, Sarah closed the door against the cold. She could not bear the thought of it closing by itself.

The mysterious monk lit a torch at each landing. Sarah climbed after him until they reached a landing with a door. The monk opened this and led Sarah down a long hall, lined with what might be monks' cells. She thought it strange they met no one as they wended their way through the corridors. Were all the residents at prayers somewhere? And to whom did they pray?

At last, the monk turned into a small, Spartan room with no windows. It held two carved wooden chairs, medieval in design and most uncomfortable looking, along with a small square table. A single candle burned on it. Hardly a welcoming place, but it seemed less drafty than the corridors. The monk motioned for her to sit. He shut the door firmly as he left.

She waited for nearly half an hour. In spite of the fact that the room was warm, her hands were shaking. If only Julien knew she was here he would not let anyone hurt her, even if he decided he could give her nothing more than his protection. He must be here. He had started before her and probably made better time as well. God, let him be here.

When the monk finally returned, he guided Sarah to an amazing room. Its stone walls were masked with tapestries. A rich Turkish carpet covered its stone floor. A fire roared in a huge grate, spewing warmth over burnished leather chairs and a dining table set with two places. Her eyes lit on oil paintings and pieces of sculpture and shelves filled with very old books. Everything was of the first water. This sumptuous room hardly fit with the rest of the cloister. Rising to greet her was another monk, his cowl thrown back to reveal a startling countenance. His face was merry and old, with ruddy cheeks and crinkled blue eyes. His white hair spread out below a balding pate. He carried an intricately carved staff of gleaming wood. But for the fact that he was clean-shaven, he might have been a model of St. Nick. Sarah was shaken. Could this jolly-looking old man be a vampire?

"Leave us," he said in Latin to her shadowy escort, sweeping him out the door with a motion of his plump hand. When he turned she saw that his blue eyes were not merry, as his countenance promised, but so old they were distant with age. "I shock you," he said in English.

Sarah recovered her wits and closed her mouth. "I did not mean to be discourteous," she stammered. "You were not what I expected."

The old man looked down at the belly that protruded under his habit. "Alas, I am less disciplined than I should be," he said ruefully. "But you must be tired. Come sit by the fire."

Sarah had no intention of sitting by the fire with this strange creature. He might well be coveting her blood. She stood her ground. "I have come with a purpose, sir," she announced with hardly more than a faint tremor in her voice. She did not know how to address him. Was he a priest? Was he religious at all in the way she knew religion? "I want to see Julien Davinoff."

"So I have been told. Now do sit down. All your energy makes an old man tired."

Sarah had no intention of complying, yet she found herself sitting abruptly in one of the leather chairs without ever having precisely decided to do so. The old man bustled about and poured her a glass of ratafia, without asking whether she wanted any. "I find you rather shocking yourself," he called over his shoulder. "I knew you existed. But I hardly dreamed you would appear on our doorstep. In some ways that simplifies our task."

Sarah's fear rose into her throat. What did he mean? What was their task?

"This will warm your insides." He brought her ratafia and stood over her, his old eyes inscrutable. "And do take off your cap. It must be uncomfortable with all your hair tucked up."

Sarah stared at him, frozen in shock.

"Well, you can't imagine we would think a *boy* was at the bottom of any affair involving Davinoff," he said reasonably. "Even if you look like one at the moment."

Slowly, Sarah pulled her cap from her head. Her hair tumbled around her shoulders.

"Your coat? The fire is quite warm."

She shook her head. Giving up her coat meant giving up the gun in its pocket. It occurred to her that her gun was useless in this keep of vampires. But she shook her head again.

"As you wish." He moved about getting his own brandy with a grace surprising for his bulk. As Sarah sniffed her ratafia warily, he said, "Don't worry. We have no need of drugs."

He could will compliance, Sarah thought, and shivered. In which case, she was already lost. Resolutely she sipped. It was a way of defying her fear, however small the gesture. "Has Mr. Davinoff taken his vows, sir?" she asked. She must know whether she was in time.

"We do not get visitors here," he observed as though he hadn't heard her. He eased his bulk into the other armchair. "I may rightly claim the indulgence of a pretty guest for dinner, since I saw you before he did. Will you join me? There is plenty of time to talk about Davinoff."

He was here! "Let me see him," she demanded. "I have come a very long way."

The old man shook his head thoughtfully. "I am curious about you, my dear. After you have satisfied my curiosity, we shall see what to do with you."

Sarah's stomach sank. Some test lurked here that she could not divine. She mustered her courage. "If those are your terms, I will join you, sir, and answer whatever questions you like."

He nodded as though he had not threatened her. "One almost forgets the social graces." He sipped his brandy in a leisurely fashion Sarah found vexing. "What is your name, my dear?"

"Sarah Ashton," she answered, wondering what she would say to convince him he should tell Julien she was here. She did not use her title. It seemed quite irrelevant.

"I am Father Rubius. Are your traveling companions in the village?"

His blue eyes were guileless, but Sarah knew he had a purpose for wanting to know if she was alone. She lifted her chin. "I traveled with a friend as far as Vienna. I came on with only two guides from there and they have gone back down the mountain."

"How very determined you are," Father Rubius marveled. "Where do you go from here?"

"I don't know," she answered in a small voice. "Perhaps just back to Vienna."

"Perhaps," he agreed. "We shall see. First you will have dinner, and you will tell me all about yourself." He rose and started toward the table. "You are the first to come here, you know."

Sarah got up slowly. This vampire, no matter how unlikely looking, stood squarely between her and her goal. She pushed her fear down. Khalenberg had stood in her way, too.

Father Rubius gestured toward her seat and rapped sharply on the floor with his stick. As she sat, the other door to the room burst open and spewed forth a stream of monks carrying dishes piled high with steaming food. Their cowls were thrown back to reveal eyes sharing a calm certainty Sarah found disconcerting. At least none of them glowed red.

The old monk sat to his meal with obvious relish. Monks or no, they laid a sumptuous table. Sarah had not eaten since breakfast. She felt positively light-headed, either from the altitude or from anxiety. But she couldn't say she was hungry. She took a bit of the cabbage soup, then toyed with a shred of venison, and concentrated upon what the old man could want of her. She resolved to be courteous, even forthcoming, if that was what it took to satisfy his curiosity.

The monk's first questions hardly seemed to the purpose. "What did your friend in Vienna think of your journeying on without her?" he began, as he piled his plate with delicacies.

"I did not test her opinion," Sarah admitted, watching him warily.

"So, no one knows your destination?" He must not care that she knew his purpose, his ploy was so obvious. Sarah found that anger battled with her fear.

"You might at least try to conceal your motive in asking such a question," she replied, and noted with satisfaction that the monk's eyes snapped up to hers. "But I believe I can relieve your mind. No one knows my destination. At least no one who is like to come looking for me." She faced his eyes for a moment and felt the power in them, subtler than Julien's, more wily. To her surprise, the monk chuckled.

"How did you find our humble cloister?" he asked, waving a fork. "We are a long way from Bath."

Had she told him she was from Bath? She refused to consider the possibilities nipping at the edges of her mind and pushed on. "At first I followed Mr. Davinoff's trail."

"I wonder he is so careless these days as to leave a trail," the monk remarked.

"Oh, he used different names. He was not careless." Sarah felt obliged to defend him. "I traced him mostly through the goods he was shipping."

"He has not received any shipments of goods here," Father Rubius noted pointedly.

"I am sure they will arrive shortly. I lost their trail. But I overheard Mr. Davinoff say he would take a woman named Magda to Mirso Monastery and I cajoled a Mr. Khalenberg into telling me where it was."

"You must tell me sometime how you did that." The pudgy lips curled wryly as he poured himself another glass of wine. "I find Herr Khalenberg difficult, myself."

Sarah nodded. "He was quite difficult."

"You must be persuasive." He made it seem a fault. Was she failing the unknown test?

"I am, as you say, determined upon my course."

"Sometimes determination outweighs good sense," the monk remarked. "What do you think of all of this?" Again he waved his fork, his gesture encompassing the entire monastery.

"I find it frightening, if that is the admission you wished to elicit," Sarah replied.

The monk nodded. "You should." His eyes glanced to the beautiful objects scattered about the room. "We, however, find it comforting. We love being surrounded by our history, something outsiders could never appreciate."

Sarah was stung. He implied she was too different to love Julien. "I can appreciate the first-century Roman glass that holds your candles," she said, gesturing to the table. "I have never seen Roman glass not spoiled by being buried. And that Greek vase is one of the finest red-figured amphoras I ever encountered." She saw the ancient, distant eyes come back from touring the room to rest upon her. "If I have not lived your history, I can still appreciate it." *Silly*, she thought. How small he must think her. On top of all else, she had probably offended him.

He seemed oblivious to her small barbs. "And where did you learn about Greek and Roman artifacts?" he asked her. "Such things are not in the repertoire of English governesses."

"No. But I never had a governess. My father taught me," Sarah explained. "There was a Roman villa on the land at Clershing. It belonged once to Mr. Davinoff, as it turns out. My father and I would have liked nothing better than to have restored it."

"Why did you not?"

"Money, primarily." Her growing impatience made her blunt.

"Then you require money." The monk nodded in satisfaction.

Sarah was outraged. "I do not," she stammered. "My father may have left me lands encumbered, but I have come to the right about, and I shall do very nicely now, all on my own."

"My apologies." The monk retreated. "How did you, er, come to the right about?"

"I sold what I could and managed the rest within an inch of its life. One may love history, but one must have the courage to let go one's own past."

The old monk pushed his plate away and fixed her once more with that evaluating look. "Thank you for dining with me, Miss Ashton." He tapped his strange staff upon the floor again. The serving monks came in and took all the plates.

"Thank you for your hospitality," Sarah said as they were retreating. "Have you satisfied your curiosity?"

Father Rubius looked her over with some spark in his distant eyes that had not been there before. "In one way, yes, Miss Ashton, and in another way, not at all." He rose and poured his brandy glass full again. This time he held up the ratafia bottle in inquiry and she shook her head. He darkened several of the lamps and motioned her back to the chairs by the fire.

"Now, tell me why you have come all this way to see Davinoff." He sat and waited.

What to say? This was the test. "Sometimes people can be confused about what will make them happy," she began carefully. "They close off that part of themselves which would most give them joy. I know all about that. Oh dear. This is a stupid way to explain why I am here."

"I quite follow you," he said softly. "Do continue."

"Even recently . . ." Here she cleared her throat uncomfortably. "I did not want to take the final risk, to reach beyond what I knew and what I was." She looked down at her lap. "I think because it always seems that there is a dark side to the light. In order to be happy, to be as much as you can be, you have to find the darkness in yourself, as well as the light." She got up suddenly and went to stand looking into the fire, now a tentative flicker. "You have to admit that you need the darkness, that you want it, that without it you cannot be whole. And that anarchy, abandon, even chaos, are part of the rhythm of your life, too."

"Have you done that?" the monk prompted, his voice a mellifluous goad.

"Yes," she said clearly, raising her head. "So I am come to find Julien Davinoff."

"What do you want of him?"

Now she must skirt the difference between what Father Rubius was like to sanction, and what she would offer Julien.

"Whatever time he will give me," she said steadily. "I know it is forbidden to give me his blood. I don't expect you to condone that." She turned abruptly to face him. "Khalenberg thinks I want the power." She found the courage for a bitter laugh. "I would so much rather Davinoff was the squire down the road, with no power at all except as justice of the peace. But he is not. And I accept him, darkness and light together." She came and stood in front of the monk, who sipped his brandy meditatively. "I want to share whatever years I have with him."

The monk raised his eyes slowly to her face. "If Davinoff t
you what he was, what we are, I am surprised you came to
us."

"He did not tell me. I am sure that is forbidden, too." S
sighed and sat once more. "I discovered it for myself. I kn
this will sound far-fetched. But a woman I knew wanted h
so much to admire her that she went mad when he did n
She gave him laudanum in large doses."

The monk leaned forward, his snow-white brows drawn
gether, his voice tinged with horror. "The one way to suppr
the Companion."

Sarah nodded. "I hid him in my cellar while he threw off
effects of the drug. He had not had blood in a long time, thou
I did not know that." Her eyes grew big, remembering.

"He . . . threatened you?"

"On the contrary, I realized later he was trying to cont
himself. But the craving for the drug was on him. He show
me all. He could not help it. I realized what he was."

The monk breathed his question in the fading light of
fire. "What did you do?"

"He was dying. So I gave him the one thing I thought wo
give a vampire strength."

"Your blood. The blood is the life," he whispered.

"Yes. He couldn't take it himself. So I drained it out of
arm and fed it to him."

The monk sighed and sat back. "You make my life diffic
young woman." She could not read his expression, but his e
were distant, as though he looked at something long ago.

"I know he loves me. I want to tell him he should take w
happiness we can find. If not forever, then for today. That's
that's why I came."

"I see." The monk seemed to be contemplating the fing
just touching across his belly. At last he sighed. "Davinoff to
the Vow at sunset, child. He is lost to you now."

For one long, horrific moment, Sarah could not speak.
her future blighted! It couldn't be true! She lifted her head a
stared at the ceiling. Her eyes were blind to her surroundi
as despair welled within her. "You knew this all along," s

finally accused, focusing again on Father Rubius. Tears flooded her eyes. This monk was lying, lying to her, she decided. He had to be lying. "I want to see him, vow or no," she demanded.

"Not possible." Father Rubius shook his head. "He is preparing for his new life."

"I have come too far to take no for an answer," she insisted fiercely, her tears spilling down her cheeks. "You may do what you like with me. But I want to see him." Almost to her surprise, the monk sighed and stood as well. "Perhaps you are right. He should see you. I shall tell him so. But I guarantee nothing."

"I know he will see me, once he knows that I am here," she sputtered.

The monk examined her once more but she no longer found his intensity frightening. She wanted Julien. That was all that mattered now. He would tell her it wasn't true. Even if it was true, when he saw her, he would renounce his crazy vow. The monk seemed frozen for a long moment. Then he abruptly turned and left by the side door.

Julien raised his eyes from his folded hands to see Father Rubius open the door to the meditation room. The fat old man slid into the silence and came to stand over him. His eyes were serious, speculating. Julien raised himself from his knees.

"I must interrupt your meditation, Brother Davinoff," Rubius said, as Julien lifted his brow in inquiry. Something was bothering the wily old devil. He saw the old man chewing the inside of his lip in thought before he spoke again.

"She is here," he said simply.

For a split second, Julien could not think what Rubius meant. Then the realization washed over him and with it the astonishing longing. Desperately, he tried to master himself and close his features over the pain. "Here?" he heard himself ask, his voice breaking.

"I had dinner with her tonight."

Julien's glance flickered about the bare room in desperation. "How did she find me?"

"I will spare you the details." Father Rubius puckered his lips in disapproval. "Suffice it to say you must have been careless, and she is a remarkable woman."

Julien paced off the narrow confines of the room. "Has she gone? I hope you sent her away." He could feel her spirit infusing the sterile stone around him. The monastery was changed forever by the fact that she had walked here, talked here. It was no longer a sanctuary. Suddenly, he stopped pacing and stared narrowly at Father Rubius. In his distress, he had forgotten the implications of her presence here. "What have you done with her?" he asked quietly.

"Nothing, yet. She is in my chambers, demanding to see you." Rubius examined him.

"You will not harm her, Rubius," he warned, wondering if he could protect her from the consequences of her folly.

"Your challenge is unnecessary and unseemly in an Aspirant," Father Rubius snapped. "She shall leave freely with an escort as far as the Danube." He fingered the knots in the cord at his waist in abstraction and seemed to change the subject. "Her appearance here is fortuitous. You have an opportunity to purge your passion. You must go down and tell her that your devotion to your new life makes further contact impossible."

"I cannot," Julien found himself whispering. "I have told you that."

"Not even now that you have the security of your Vow?" Father Rubius asked pointedly.

Julien merely lowered his head. The weight of his future seemed to drag it down until he could not lift it. Sarah. The name he could not speak filled his mind until there was no space left for any other thought. He saw himself telling her. He saw her hurt, her disbelief, as he had seen it in Vienna, only magnified by the incredible journey she had undertaken to reach him. She must be very sure of her love to trace him to his hiding place. He imagined the effort that would be required to hold himself hard and aloof as she cried. "I cannot do it," he finally gasped. "Is it not enough that I send you to say I will not come to her? That will break her spirit. And mine. Is that not enough?" He raised his eyes to Father Rubius's face. "You cannot *ask* more," he almost shouted. His strength flooded the room with the force of his emotion, his demand.

The eyes of the Elder were still opaque. He sighed. "Write it, then. At least then you will not have abrogated your responsibility entirely." He produced a paper and a quill from a crude desk in the corner of the room, meant for recording devotions, not love letters.

Julien snatched up the pen. But for a long moment, he stood immobile over it. How to say the unspeakable? His insides churned. He could not think of anything except her name. Finally he let that name drive the pen toward the paper. He scrawled her name. With a shaking hand he jerked the pen through other words—totally inadequate, senseless words—and scratched his name at the bottom. What did the words matter, when he could not avoid their result? He took the hateful paper and held it out to Rubius, a symbol of his complicity in her demise, the price of her salvation. The monk nodded silently and twisted the paper into a screw.

Julien pressed his eyes shut. The input of his senses was too much. The only thing he could grasp was the pain he felt, the pain he would cause. What had he done? He had just turned her away without even seeing her! He opened his eyes, ready to tell Rubius he would see her after all, but the room was empty. The Old One had let himself out as silently as he had come. For a brief, tortured moment, Julien considered running after him.

But it was better this way. It was better not to see her. His head sank again with the weight that pressed on his spirit. He could not think clearly. Not when his brain echoed so with the sound of her name. *Sarah*.

She paced the chamber in front of the dying fire. Each moment stretched into an eternity as Sarah waited for Julien. What would she say? What could she say? He must renounce this Vow. Of course he would renounce it once he saw her. The alternative was unthinkable.

The door opened as Sarah spun and held her breath. But it was only Father Rubius. "Where is he?" she cried.

"He will not see you, child," the monk said quietly.

"You lie," she hissed. "You did not tell him I was here."

The old monk's face grew stern. His eyes fixed her, as though she were a butterfly in one of George's display cases. He thrust the truth upon her, whether she would or no. Julien had refused her. She felt her spine give way and her knees. She simply sank upon the floor, the sobs sounding as if they came from some other poor abandoned creature. Father Rubius bent over her, saying something she could not understand as he pressed a screw of paper into her hand. She stared at it, uncomprehending. It must be from Julien. That was what he was saying. She ripped at it with fumbling fingers. Someone's tears were soaking the paper so she could hardly read the terse scrawl.

Beloved Sarah,
It is not meant to be. Let go of it, for your own good.
Julien

She clutched the paper to the rough shirt at her breast and rocked herself back and forth. "He won't even see me," she heard a detached voice in her mind say. "There is nothing more tc do." She heard sobbing. Were those her tears soaking the paper? "It's down the mountain for you, girl," the voice said again. "Down the mountain, down the mountain to nothingness. Nothing more to do. Nothing more to do. Nothing." It was a little chant that rolled over her in the rhythm of the rocking.

She felt the monk's staff tapping on the floor, rather than heard it. She couldn't hear anything except the calm voice spewing out its rocking, rhythmic theme of nothingness. Then hands lifted her up, led her to the door. "Taking you away," the voice observed. "Down the mountain, down to the village, down to Vienna, down the Danube, down to the sea. Lost in the sea until you are nothing. Nothing more to do." She felt herself walking between two monks down into the maze of the monastery, through the bowels of the place, past the torches, down the stairs into the darkness where no light could penetrate, and out, out into the courtyard under the stars. Cold stars, so distant, so far away, just like the voice, singsonging about nothingness.

It was a comforting voice. She wanted it to go on forever. "Down the mountain, down to the village." That's where she would go. Perhaps they would kill her. She felt a smile make its way up to her lips from deep inside her. Nothingness. Nothing to do.

But what if they didn't?

Sarah came to herself with a start. The voice receded. *No*, she thought. *Come back*. She found herself by the fountain in the middle of the courtyard, hugging her elbows and rocking silently. Slowly she stopped as the rhythm of the distant voice, so calm, so satisfying, faded. Pain washed over her. She realized she was crying uncontrollably, all by herself. A monk, perhaps fifty feet away, called to another to hitch up a cart. Another monk led a horse to be hitched.

What if they didn't kill her? Where was the comforting nothingness then? Nothing left to do, she said resolutely to herself. But the voice had faded beyond hearing. What if she woke in the inn tomorrow, without hope, without Julien, without the possibility of love? What if she came back to Vienna, broken and hollow? What if she went back to Bath? She wanted the numbing voice to beat back the pain eating at her as the fox ate at the Spartan boy.

With a groan, she fell to her knees and collapsed against the stone rim of the fountain. The rock was cool against her cheek. She heard the monks in the background, readying the horse to take her somewhere she had no desire to go. Would they hitch up a horse if they were going to kill her? It was to be the village and Vienna and Bath. Julien had no doubt refused to let them kill her. A giggle rose to her lips. He probably thought he was sparing her.

She wouldn't do it. She would run away. She would make them kill her. She pushed herself up with effort and stared into the clear water of the fountain. What if they didn't kill her? The panic rose until it threatened to shut off her mind entirely. At the moment she thought she would descend into an incoherent scream of pain, the distant voice said calmly. "Can't trust them. They won't do it. Can't trust them. Do it. Do it." It seemed to come from the gurgling water, trickling over the rocks into the stone pool. *The fountain,* she thought clearly, over the voice singsonging in the background. *The parasite without the blood to follow*. No one would give her blood here. She wanted to crow her victory. "Don't need them," the voice sang. "No pain. Don't need them. They won't do it. Do it. Do it." Sarah closed her eyes. Yes. One sure way. "Do it. Do it." She opened her eyes and watched her hands cup themselves to dip the water. It was ice-cold, numbing. "No pain. Do it." She raised the water to her lips and drank it down greedily, as the voice crescendoed its victory. "Nothing more to do. Nothing. Nothing more."

Julien dragged himself to the window. Meditation was impossible. No salvation existed for so vile thing as he was. His nature left him no way forward. He could only wound Sarah, no matter what he did. Life stretched ahead with no remorse for the pain it would inflict.

Down in the courtyard Julien could see Brother Flavio struggling with an unruly horse, trying to back it into the traces of a cart. Where could he be going so late at night? Sarah. They were taking her away. His glance darted around the courtyard. She must be here somewhere. Could he bear to see her? Could he bear to turn away? But where was she?

His eyes came to rest on the figure of a boy cast limply over the rim of the Source, hand trailing in the water, the picture of defeat and despair. God no, that was hair, dark hair cascading into the water. Sarah!

She cupped her hand and drank. A guttural cry escaped him and echoed across the courtyard. *Sarah, no!* Eyes turned up toward him, but not Sarah's. She was locked inside her despair. She understood what she had done. He had broken her. She took the last escape.

There was no time to lose. Rubius would be here at any moment. Julien gathered the whirling darkness around him and transported himself down into the courtyard.

"What have I done?" he sobbed brokenly as he knelt to gather Sarah into his arms.

Brother Flavio scurried up, panting, his horse forgotten. "Brother Davinoff, she was entrusted to me," he gasped. "Return to your meditations."

Julien turned on him, all his rage washing over the little monk, who reeled backward as though he had been shoved. He was overpowered and dismissed in one fluid spray of will. Rubius would not be so easily removed. Other monks spilled out from the inner sanctum in response to the commotion. Rubius would not be far behind.

Julien stood in the gloom of the courtyard, cradling Sarah's limp form. She was in shock from ingesting the Companion. The condition was temporary. She would seem to recover. But soon the sickness would come on and she would die in excruciating pain unless she got immunity. He saw the horror in the monks' eyes as they realized what he meant to do. He glanced down at Sarah, blinking into consciousness. Doubt seemed irrelevant, suddenly. Calmly, he turned and strode toward the gates.

"Give her over, Davinoff." The reverberation of power in the Eldest's voice made all other motion cease in the courtyard—all motion except for Julien, who spun around. It took all the strength he had. Rubius stood in the center of a whorl of monks, frozen in their pursuit.

"I won't let the Companion eat her alive," he shouted. "Not when I can stop it."

Father Rubius walked slowly toward them. "She forces your hand," he accused.

"You know as well as I she is a suicide, damn you!" Julien gasped for breath in the face of Rubius's silent command. Sparks of will seemed to shower off the Old One, all his concentration upon his rebellious Aspirant.

"I won't let you share the Companion in our own Sanctuary, in front of all our Order."

Julien looked down at Sarah, so light in his arms. It was not her weight that made him tremble, but the effort to resist the Eldest. To his knowledge, none of his kind had ever been able to do so. Slowly Julien shook his head, as if gathering himself for a dash to the gate. Instead, he mustered his waning strength. *Companion mine, hear me and ready yourself*. He saw Rubius hold out a hand in command as though he moved through water. He was surprised to see that hand shaking. *Now, Companion*, he commanded, and felt the tingling engulf them all at once. "As you wish, Rubius," he shouted as he brought blackness whirling up around him. Only dimly did he see the monks pouring forward, murmuring their shock. The last thing he heard was Father Rubius shouting orders that faded into nothingness.

Chapter Twenty-two

Sarah felt far away from herself and all the shouting. A warmth glowed in her body. Her head rested on rough dark cloth. Once, she opened her eyes. But when she did, the stars were so far away, so cold and uncaring, that she shut them again against the immensity of the universe. Whatever they were shouting about could not touch her here. She had already done the final thing. There was nothing more to do.

A rushing sound made her tingle. Then a burst of sensation flooded her as though she had been popped inside out. It made her gasp and open her eyes again. The stars had disappeared. The voices were far away. The tingling and wind receded into comforting blackness and she settled into half awareness again. There were sounds below her. A hand moved across her mouth, as though she would ever make the effort to utter any sound again. She felt prickling sensations, and smelled a scent she couldn't name. She drifted.

Sometime later, her eyes opened again. It was dark. Horses, she thought lazily. She smelled horses and hay. Julien lay beside her. He was wearing something strange. A black robe. He put his hand over her mouth.

"Be still, my love," he breathed over her. She could hear people shouting somewhere.

"Of course," she might have told him. "I will always be still now." But she just stared at him from far away. He was like a dream, like the boy in Sienna. This dream would pass. All dreams would pass. They could not touch her now. She was safe. There was nothing left to do.

Sarah stared at nothing in the darkness. Finally, when there were no more sounds from outside, Julien began to talk to her again. He shouldn't do that. She wanted to be still now, always. She tried to recede to a place where she couldn't hear his voice, couldn't feel his hand on her hair. He shouldn't touch her. She turned her head away, and a little crease came and sat on her forehead. Somehow the action of turning her head made his words clearer.

"My fault," he was saying. "You are the one with the courage. I was running away."

Running away from what? What was he talking about? She turned her head toward him. She could hear him distinctly now. "Come back to me, Sarah. Give me another chance."

He should leave her to be still, she thought with annoyance. After all, there was nothing more to do. "I couldn't face the odds against us," Julien said. "I didn't trust us to come through."

His cheeks were wet. Moonlight streaked in from somewhere. It glazed his face with silver. "We didn't," she said slowly.

"Sarah. My God, Sarah." He took her in his arms and pressed her to him.

Sarah felt an indescribable sadness as the dreamlike distance faded and pain seeped under the flaps of her carefully sealed mind.

"Forgive me for my cowardice, love." His voice cracked as he held her to him, stroking her hair. "It's not too late, Sarah. You'll have my blood. We'll be together. I'll find some way to take care of Rubius."

He dragged her back into the maelstrom. "Leave me alone," she muttered.

"I will not force you. But there is not much time to decide. You'll become sick, and soon they will be here to stop me. They are searching even now." He rocked her back and forth. Now she did not find the motion soothing. With each passing moment, the peace receded further. She could hear animals moving about under them. They were in some kind of loft. And Julien wanted her to do something, when there should be nothing left to do.

The voice above her was prodding as he rocked her. "Our time is out of joint. When I was sure, you were not ready. When you were certain, I faltered. Now there is no time."

"Like a dance," she murmured.

"Yes," his voice insisted. "We have been dancing. But we are not in step, my love." His hand stroked her forehead, her ear, her neck. The pain flowed into her, and the desire, the anger, and the need. Into this vortex, Julien's voice floated. "We can fall in step, Sarah. You thought so too, right here at Mirso Monastery tonight." The hand around her shoulders stroked her hair, the other encircled her waist. "We must have courage at the same moment." His voice grew more insistent. Its urgency called to the whirling emotions inside her. He turned her face. His eyes overflowed with feeling. "You have shown the way. Now you must decide whether you will take this step with me."

"I will disappoint you," she said, quite clearly now. And though she might regret it, she knew that there was no way back to the peace and the distance.

"We are both afraid," he whispered, moving his lips over her ears and neck. She turned her face up and he kissed her, softly at first, and then with such intensity she thought her soul would be drawn out through her lips. She clung to his neck and felt her breasts pressed to his chest through the rough wool of his robe. Let him do what he would. Let him decide. When at last he drew his mouth away, he looked down, a question in his eyes. He wanted more than acquiescence. He wanted her to do something, long after she thought there was nothing left to do.

Tears coursed down her cheeks. She closed her eyes. There was no peaceful place in which to think what she should do. She had such a little shred of will left in her. She wasn't sure it was enough. She opened her eyes. Had she come across a continent to find him? She could not think why. It had to do with the stones at Avebury, somehow, and a room with mosaics on the floor, and George Upcott in some way, too, and Corina and the boy in Sienna and Madame Gessande and a cellar in the Dower House and a deed from Henry, Rex, and a night in her room in Laura Place. Suddenly all the whirling memories took her and made her shiver and sob. She clenched her eyes tight, but when she opened them his face was still there. He looked at her steadfastly and asked her to be strong. She did not think. Suddenly, she did not need to think.

She took a deep breath. "Dance with me," she demanded, though her voice trembled through her tears. He closed his eyes, and turned his face up in thanks as he gathered her in to him. He kissed her again, tentatively. She clung to him and felt him hard against her, as she had once before. She moved her hands over the muscles and sinew beneath the coarse robe and felt her own flame flicker up, signaling she was alive again, brought back from the smoldering coals she had sought to extinguish. She burned against the night.

Julien pushed Sarah back into the hay of the loft and fell beside her, chewing gently on her ear as he unbuttoned her shirt and slid his hand across the warm flesh of her breasts. He felt the wonder of her decision coursing through him, giving him strength and a welling desire he had not known in all his long life. But now he must go carefully, even though the wolves were at the door. What he would ask of her tonight would be distasteful, frightening to a woman. He could not risk asking too much, now that he asked everything. He could not risk getting out of step again. So he restrained his urge to rush. He wanted this to be a wonderful moment, a rite of passage, not an act of desperation, painful to remember. So he pushed his worry that they would be found out of his mind. He pushed away his fear of Rubius's wrath after the deed was done. He let his mind be filled by the silkiness of her skin, the way her nipples hardened at his touch and drove her mouth to seek his and demand kissing. The rhythm to this dance must be obeyed. He gave himself up to the whirling steps dictated by the time and by the ceremony at hand.

As Julien's fingers slid over her nipples, Sarah awoke to his touch with a snap of longing and lifted her mouth to his. This time she made no pretense of innocence. There was no fear of judgment from him. He would guide her into a new world. No more questions, no more doubts.

She pushed herself to her knees in the moonlight. Julien looked surprised. But she was not falling out of step. She began to unbuckle the belt at her waist. He knelt in front of her and did the same with his own knotted cord. Slowly, deliberately, they shed their clothes in a moonlit loft, made warm by the beasts below, and musty with the smell of the stable.

When they were naked, they stopped and simply looked at each other, incandescent flesh in the moonlight. Their world scaled itself down to two bodies and the feel of hay and the low noises of the animals moving about.

Below them, suddenly, they heard shouts, and the rush of many feet. Julien pulled Sarah to him, and put a finger to his lips. They knelt, cleaving together, as their sanctuary was invaded. The lanterns below chased away the magic of the moonlight and gave everything a hellish glow. Sarah and Julien could hear the monks make their way through every stall, banging the doors and knocking staffs against the mangers to make certain there were no hiding places left unexplored. The horses neighed in protest. Sarah shuddered. What would happen if they were discovered now? She grew stiff with holding herself motionless and still the noise went on. At last she heard a shouted conclusion that the miscreants were not in the stable and an order to proceed to the creamery. The monks filed out toward their next goal.

Sarah had been holding her breath. "We must get out of here," she whispered.

He shook his head. "We are safe for a while. They were an interruption, no more. You will have need of what I give you tonight." He stroked her back and the warmth of their flesh and the silvering moonlight began to exert their pull once more. Her breasts brushed his chest, the hardening throb against her belly brought an answering roar in her loins. She gave herself up to the demands of the moment, more urgent than any threat from outside. Julien's hands kneaded her buttocks with mounting urgency. His lips brushed her hair. He was silent. They were past words now. She clutched at his back and pressed her breasts against his ribs.

He pulled her backward into the hay and let his tongue open her mouth, caressing her inside and out. Her hands found his erection and stroked it softly, lovingly. She heard him groan under his breath. He rolled onto his back and she rolled with him, not wanting to part from his sweet flesh. He pulled her knee until she was astride him and she sat up, unable to keep from moving a little, rubbing her moist flesh against him. His eyes closed in ecstasy, she was sure, as he lifted her buttocks slightly to ease her down upon him. Sarah took in a long breath of delight. It was so right to feel him inside her. She raised her arms from his chest to stretch them into the air, fingers spread, reveling in the feel of being full of him. His hands on her buttocks showed her how to move with him, slow stroking in the rhythm of a dance everyone discovered one step at a time each time they danced it. She turned her head up to the rough boards of the stable roof and felt her hair cascade down her bare back, swaying to the rhythm of their moving bodies.

Then she couldn't bear not to feel his chest against her breasts and she descended upon him to smother him in kisses, pressing herself into his chest. He held her close and rolled her over until he was on top of her. She could feel his mounting urgency, held in check to match the figures of the dance. She knew what she wanted next. She wanted to give everything to him. When she had nothing she had not given, she would have everything. She pushed her hair from her neck and turned her head away from his kisses. She had offered once before. But this was different. Tonight, she would not take without giving in return.

He raised himself a little. She stared in invitation with all the emotion that churned inside her. His eyes held that mix of passion and gratitude and surprised reverence that result in love. Then he clasped her to him with such ferocity it took her breath away. He murmured her name as he brushed his lips across her ear, her cheek, and moved inside her. She knew what would come next. It was a sharper kiss that signaled her gift was accepted, a sear of pain that made her gasp. His hips moved more urgently now as he sucked at her throat. The peaceful feeling came over her, as it had at the Dower House. She held him to her and arched her back, offering up her neck as he matched the ardor of his kisses to the mounting demand of his passion. He sucked convulsively as the shudder of his release took him.

Finally, she felt his body relax over her. He kissed her neck one final time, gently, and raised himself upon his elbow to look into her eyes. A faint smile touched a single corner of her lips and was answered by his own.

Julien's eyes never left her, as he moved his wrist to his mouth. The prickle of the hay was the only thing that told her this was not a dream. It was his turn to give, hers to receive. This dance required balance. She saw him draw the power, just a vagueness in his outline and a glow in his eyes. His canines flashed. He did not cry out as she had done when the teeth pierced his flesh. His outline merely sharpened once again, and when he bent to kiss her gently, her tongue found no trace of sharper teeth. He moved his wrist to her lips. A gash there seeped blood against the pale skin. She kissed his wounds and licked the blood slowly from her lips as she looked into his eyes. A softness was there, an indescribable tenderness. He moved off of her, and caressed her with his other hand, first her breasts, then down to her belly, as she licked his wound. The blood welled quickly now. She felt the beat of his heart push it into her mouth, warm and salty tasting. He began to rub her gently there in the moistness between her legs. She thought she might faint. She was locked within her body, conscious only of the urgency in her loins and the warm blood seeping over her lips and tongue.

"Drink, my love," he whispered as he brought her inevitably toward ecstasy. "The blood is the life. Life everlasting. We share the Sacrament of Blood tonight." She sucked at his bleeding wrist, the blood spurting into her mouth as the wracking moans of pleasure took her.

When the dance was done, they lay together in the ghostly light of the moon coming through a dusty window in the loft. Somewhere wolves howled, but they did not bother her. She was beyond their reach in a place from which there was no retreat. Julien pulled his robe over her like a blanket and cradled her against his shoulder. "We will have to leave this place in a moment, love," he murmured. "We are not safe here. Later, I can deal with Rubius."

Sarah thought she heard a doubt in his voice. "Is it done?" She felt no different, though she felt sure of herself, perhaps for the first time ever. She had made her decision.

"Not quite. You will grow sick soon, Sarah. You will need more of my blood until you have your own immunity," he whispered.

"Where will we go?" she asked, without real curiosity. Their adventure was not to be a journey of where.

"I will take care of everything." But his eyes snapped away from her face, all tenderness gone, as they heard the rustle of feet below them. She grabbed for his robe and scrambled to her knees as Julien gathered her into his arms.

A familiar voice in the corner of the loft behind them said, "Well, Davinoff, your fall from grace is now complete."

Julien tried to blink out once again. He drew the power from the loft. It gathered about him slowly, a whirling darkness. Too slowly. Then the power and the darkness drained away. Julien was shaken. Rubius had not been able to stop him before, but now the damn monks below were creating a wall of will at Rubius's command, sucking all the power out of the immediate vicinity, to prevent Julien from drawing off enough to escape.

"Effective, Rubius," he drawled with mock calm, as he clutched Sarah to his naked body. He could feel her trembling.

Rubius smiled grimly. "I regret I find the need for such a ploy, but better safe than sorry. Now, young lady, why don't you give that robe to Davinoff, and get back into your clothes? We have some matters of mutual interest to discuss."

Sarah started as Rubius slammed the door. She and Julien were alone with him now in the chambers where she had dined with him last night. It seemed eons ago. The fire had died out, the lamps had guttered, and the room was chill. Rubius left the monks outside in the corridor with specific instructions to contain Julien in shifts so their circle of will was never broken, even for an instant. Sarah's heart sank. Apparently, Julien would not be able to thwart them if they worked together, no matter how strong he was.

The moment the echo of the slamming door died, the old monk turned his wrath on Julien, who stood ramrod straight by her side.

"You fool, Davinoff! The blood is the life! You disobey the most primal of our Rules for the third time, and within the Sanctuary of Mirso itself! Have you no shame?" He did not wait for an answer, but stormed on. "You are a threat to the very order of our lives here. If you had your way, the regularity, the simplicity that comfort us would all be torn to shreds. There would be nothing left to protect us against the ravages of our nature."

He stopped to breathe.

"What would you have had me do?" Julien asked quietly.

"The girl made her choice, Davinoff. You should have honored it."

"She made that choice as a result of my cowardice, Rubius." Sarah heard Julien's voice grow hard above her. "I could not let both our lives be lost when I could make it right."

"You of all of us should know the results of this particular sin." Rubius began to pace.

Julien spread his hands over the ancient wood of dining table. "Have you been an hour in Sarah's company without knowing she is more worthy of the Companion than either of us are?"

That stopped Rubius in his tracks. "I do not deny you chose well, but such talk is sacrilege. Exactly the sort of behavior that makes you dangerous."

"One more of our kind will not break the bank." Julien pressed on. "You know that."

"It is the principle," Rubius insisted. "I cannot even appear to sanction such a violation."

"But the deed is done. She is infected. I have given her my blood. By morning she will need more. What then?" Sarah moved close enough to touch her shoulder to Julien's arm.

"There will be no more blood." Rubius closed his face against them. "We can perhaps make her passing more merciful."

Sarah looked up to see Julien casting about for some solution to their dilemma. She felt helpless. Her head seemed muddied.

A burning in her veins tingled along her extremities.

"You will have to rend me limb from limb to keep me from giving her the protection of my blood," Julien warned. "I'll take lives and the peace of the Sanctuary with me."

Rubius looked thoughtful. But he said, "So be it."

Sarah was outraged. "You want to murder us? Is that what your beliefs dictate? Safety over kindness? Violence used to combat love?"

"You left me no choice, young woman," Rubius barked. "You stole the Companion, and your prince consort here disobeys me in front of the entire population of the monastery! We will have a hundred more mistakes like you if I do not stop it here."

"This is not a mistake and you know it, Rubius!" Julien insisted.

Sarah saw a struggle take place in the monk's face between duty and inclination. He did not want violence and death. He wanted to be well out of the whole matter and rid of them both. But neither could he condone their sin. What would sway him? She must fan his inclination. She lifted a hand to her forehead, trying to think. Her face was clammy with sweat. There was a key here somewhere. It was the final question on the test that Rubius had set for her.

She blurted a question into the tense silence. "Why are you old, Father Rubius?"

"I am the Eldest," he said stiffly.

Julien looked at her strangely. She knew it seemed irrelevant. But Rubius *was* different than the others. Perhaps that was why he was secretly in sympathy with her and Julien. "You are, all of you, old," she pressed on. "But everyone else here looks as if they are in the prime of their lives." She looked at Julien. "Would you ever grow to look like Father Rubius?"

Realization dawned in Julien's face. He snapped his gaze to Rubius, who suddenly looked very uncomfortable. "You were old already when you became one of us, Rubius," he speculated. "I cannot think why I did not see the significance before. Perhaps you did drink the Companion at the Source, but that doesn't matter. An old man would never have survived the ravages of the sickness without blood from one of us." Julien straightened, and looked down at the wizened monk accusingly. "You were made, weren't you, Rubius?"

Sarah could see the Eldest consider. Was he thinking to lie? Or was he considering what would happen if they should spread their knowledge about? What prohibition could there be against making vampires, if their own leader had been made? His carefully constructed sanctuary might be at risk. Would that make him more inclined to let them go, or less? She couldn't think.

"Come, Rubius," Julien said slowly. "It is your turn for a confession."

Sarah could feel the tension growing in the room. Rubius's eyes had gone stony. She glanced up at Julien, and saw that they were locked in a channel of will, struggling for supremacy. Here was the moment that would tell their fate. All was up to Julien. She shuddered, as chills began to rack her, though her veins burned. With effort, she focused her eyes on Rubius, as though her small share of will could help Julien against a creature such as he.

All at once, Rubius turned away. Had he given up the battle? Had Julien won?

"I choose to tell you," he said roughly. "Since you know, in some sense, already." He fingered a small statue of Diana on the sideboard. "The Hunter tribe had drunk from the Source on one of their expeditions into the mountains. Some survived ingesting the Companion. They raided and ravaged for their blood our tribe of Gatherers below." Sarah heard the words through a haze of pain, her own, and his. They jerked out of the old man as though they were spoken at great cost. "Then once, in a struggle, one of our tribe inflicted a wound. The attacker's blood mingled with her own. We watched her fall terribly ill. But then she recovered." There was a long silence. Was that all? "We knew then it was a secret of the blood that made our tormentors strong. The night her eyes grew clear, some of us took her blood that we might help her fight our enemies on their own terms. I needed more blood than the others, but I too survived. We began the Great War against the Hunters. The outcome was inevitable. They didn't know about making reinforcements. We did."

That was his secret then. He was made. But there was more.

Why else would he be in sympathy with their cause? "Were you made for love?" Sarah asked softly.

He turned back toward them and examined Sarah. He made a decision. "I was too old. I would never have been chosen to protect the tribe. But it was my daughter who was made by the Hunters. She insisted I be given the strength she had found. She gave her blood afterward to give me her immunity."

"Are they all gone, the original ones?" Julien asked abruptly.

"Over the years, yes. Accidental dismemberment, murder. I am the Eldest now." He looked up at them steadily. "And in my countless years, I have learned that obedience is a thin defense against our nature, against insanity. I cannot sacrifice the order we have constructed here, no matter that you find the prohibition hypocritical. The Sanctuary is everything."

No, Sarah thought frantically. He couldn't intend to kill them anyway. Not when he himself was made for love. "Killing us now is far worse than the violence of your primitive Hunters. They killed for blood. Your action is premeditated murder!" she cried.

"I will tell your secret," Julien warned.

"We will close our minds against you. The others will follow my lead. I have given them the only peace they have known in long, painful lives." Rubius's voice had grown hard with all his years. What could move a man who had seen the rise of the whole human race?

"Rubius," Julien almost pleaded. "We are the hope for the future. I know you believe that we are doomed to a solitary existence." Julien leaned over him. "Do you also think life in Mirso Monastery is inevitable? I don't believe either anymore. Sarah and I will prove it."

"I would it were true," Rubius whispered. "But I know the odds better than you do. We are not meant for the solace of love. And sooner or later, you will want to take the Vow more than anything else in the world."

"For God's sake let us try!" Julien cried. "Banish us, forbid us for eternity the Sanctuary. But don't keep us from a life together!" A look of astonished horror crossed Rubius's face. The key, Sarah thought with rising certainty. Julien had found the key!

"You do not know what you are saying," Rubius stammered. "You would be better dead than prevented from joining our Sanctuary. How could you live knowing you were cut off forever from the only source of peace our kind has known?"

Julien looked at Sarah. Victory shone in his eyes. "The monks will think we have been punished more severely for our sin than merely killing us, Rubius. And you will be rid of us, without any more trouble."

The fever in her blood rose up around her. She was lightheaded with risk. She, who wanted peace so badly a few hours ago, now put peace aside. "Banish us," she said clearly.

Julien embraced her and stroked her hair as he turned back to Rubius. Sarah's knees threatened to abandon her, but Julien's arm about her was strong. She could see astonishment in Rubius's eyes, glowing with all his years. Banish us, she shrieked silently. Banish us to living.

"What is your word, Rubius?" Julien's voice rumbled in the ear she pressed to his chest.

"You have made your choice. You are both forbidden for eternity from taking the Vow to join our order. The Sanctuary of Mirso Monastery is lost to you," the old man intoned. Just like St. Nick giving gifts at Christmastide, Sarah thought, through the haze of fever. He gave her the gift of life with Julien. The room began to spin as Julien picked her up in his arms and her world turned bloodred then black.

Julien roused himself from the chair he had drawn up next to the great bed with a start. Pounding. Someone was pounding on the door. As his head cleared, his gaze jerked to Sarah, her form so small amid the red velvet hangings, the carved pilasters of the bed. She no longer tossed with fever, but lay dreadfully still, her eyes hollow, her skin translucent. The sheets were twisted and disheveled. He pushed himself out of the chair, ignoring the calls from the corridor, and pulled the covers over her, smoothed them gently. Both his wrists were crisscrossed with blue-black lacerations, but they were swollen closed for the moment, healing, if slowly. He placed the chalice she had brought, his memento to her from long ago, upon the table. He had never been more glad that he was weak enough to leave it for her. Now it was stained with his blood. She had not been able to drink from the cup for some time, but suckled directly from his wrist. He glanced in the mirror as he pulled away to answer the door. He looked as ill as she did. The thumping on the door, the muffled cries of "Davinoff," made his head ache.

He shoved the heavy latch back and swung the door open. Sarah might be past eating, but he dared not refuse food. He had to make more blood for her. One monk held the tray, the other's fist was frozen in midair, prepared to pound the door again. "Good evening." A whisper seemed all he could muster. He took the offered tray. "Thank you." He moved to close the door.

"Uh . . . Davinoff." The monk stayed the door with one hand. It might be Brother Flavio.

"What is it?" he whispered. He had no wish to spend strength on these two.

"Well, some among us think your punishment too harsh. No one has been refused sanctuary in a thousand years." The monk looked down. "We wanted you to know."

Julien nodded, then nudged the door closed. He didn't bother to throw the latch. He had to get back to Sarah. It took longer with the strong ones. They struggled too hard against the Companion. She would need more of his blood to stop the warring in her body. His blood was her life, literally. He set the tray down on the table and uncovered a steaming bowl of venison stew. All the while he ate, his gaze flitted to Sarah. *Grow strong*, he urged himself. Was his immunity too weak to help her? But he was all she had. No other would give her blood. He didn't know how much more he had to give. He only knew that she must come out of it soon, or she might not come out of it at all. That was unthinkable. Not when he had just begun to believe that a lifetime of love was possible, even a lifetime such as his kind was cursed with.

Was it really a curse? A trial, perhaps, a test of courage that most failed? But if one could survive experience and win through to acceptance, was that not a prize worth all? Hardly won, but valued more. He had begun to believe in that damned William Blake's second innocence, the ability to find love and joy even though you knew the truth about the world. Gods, he must be hallucinating. Had he not always thought Blake a lunatic?

Julien barely tasted the thick broth laced with paprika, the musky meat, the root vegetables in the stew he gulped. The moment he saw Sarah commit suicide at the fountain, he had made the leap to faith. He knew that by saving her, at whatever cost, he might save himself and perhaps all of his kind. Now, he could just be on the verge of accepting what he was and who that made him, after nearly two thousand years of struggling against it. Sarah accepted him. It was she who had pressed him to embrace his nature. But he must take the final step himself.

He pushed the bowl aside and rose, knocking over the chair. His realization was worth nothing without her to share it. He leaned against the table, staring at her wraithlike countenance. Without even looking at his wrist, he drew the darkness and opened a vein.

Sarah slept fitfully and tossed with fever. Waking and sleeping merged into an awful concatenation of wracking chills and burning veins and periods when she could not think where she was. She dreamed she had turned into a monster with dreadfully long canines, howling like the wolves at Tirgu Korva, bestial and supernatural at once. She dreamed of Sienna, and Julien's naked body bathed in Tuscan light. At times she knew she was dying, and she was afraid that vampires really were undead things. Her reflection in the mirror hanging on the wall opposite the bed looked as though she were long dead, with glazed eyes and putrefying flesh. When she cried out at these visions, Julien would come and rock her like a child.

Through it all there was the blood. She drank his blood again and again, from the chalice, sucking at his wrist, his neck. And she wanted it. She wanted the warm red fountain to flow over her lips and tongue and down her throat, the red of life, the red of death, the red of vampires.

Finally, she became aware of herself once again. All she could see was red. A red blanket of pulsing life covered everything. She took a sharp breath and realized her eyes were closed. She snapped them open to morning light leaking through the velvet window hangings. Above her, Julien's head drooped as he held her in his arms. He was asleep. Numbly she noted the dark circles, the drawn lines about his mouth. He had weakened himself to give her new life.

She *did* have new life. Wondrously, her eyes coursed over the room, noting every detail, every mote of dust in the light. She could feel the blood coursing through her, full with the presence of something new. She felt strong, stronger than she had ever been. No, that was wrong. She was whole, for the first time in her life. Did the Companion bring this sureness, this feeling of being more together than any one being could be alone? She looked across the room at the mirror that hung over the washbasin. Her reflection would not change, perhaps forever.

She raised her eyes to Julien's face and saw the dark fringe of his lashes flutter. His eyes came open. She smiled at him, ever so slightly. His eyes swept over her face.

"Sarah?" he asked tentatively. Then he held her so tightly she could hardly breath. "Welcome, my love. You are reborn."

"Shall we dance?" she whispered.

He nodded, eyes brimming with emotion. "The world is ours. I will show you things . . ." He stopped. A crease appeared between his brows. "Are you afraid?"

"Yes." She managed to chuckle, though her eyes brimmed. She reached up to smooth the crease away. "There is no life without a little fear. We must take risks to know we are alive."

"I may be cynical, still." He shook his head in apology.

"You gave me the blood of life. Doesn't that mean you hope as well?"

His eyes said yes, no matter how tentatively. The dark lock of hair dropped over his forehead. But it was her turn to doubt. "You loved me for my naivete," she whispered. "What will happen if I lose it?"

"Nothing is certain." He warned himself as much as her.

"We can but try," she said softly, feeling the new power course within her. Then she lifted her lips to his as though for the first time.

Author's Note

I must admit that I have bent historical accuracy to serve the needs of my story. The historians among you know that medical texts do not credit the discovery of blood types until the first decade of the twentieth century. I can't think why George would not have published his work, but so it must be. And if waists in dresses did not come in until 1820, one can only assume that Sarah's innovation was slower to penetrate the world of fashion than the marquise surmised. For these and any other small inaccuracies, my apologies.

BLOOD MOON

✠ ✠ ✠

DAWN THOMPSON

Jon Hyde-White is changed. Soon he will cease to be an earl's second son and become a ravening monster. Already lust grows, begging him to drink blood—and the blood of his fiancée Cassandra Thorpe will be sweetest of all. Is that not why the blasphemous creature Sebastian bursts upon them from the London shadows? But Sebastian's evil task remains incomplete, and neither Jon nor Cassandra is beyond hope. One chance remains—in faraway Moldavia, in a secret brotherhood, in an ancient ritual and in the power of love.

- -